Praise for Michelle Shocklee

"A riveting historical romance. . . .
mystery and romance in this spell
xenophobia and the bravery of th
timely and expertly crafted tale."

PUBLISHERS WEEKLY on *Count the Nights by Stars*

"Captivating. . . . Rich in history and mystery, *Count the Nights by Stars* is a novel that will teach and inspire."

HISTORICAL NOVEL SOCIETY

"'That is our mission, dear. To see people for who they are beneath the pain. Beneath the sin. To see them as God sees them: a beautiful creation, with plans and purposes only he knows.' This is my favorite quote from *Count the Nights by Stars*, a moving historical fiction that explores darkness as well as the beauty that can emerge from it when the right person takes on the purpose of seeing people for who they are beneath the pain."

T. I. LOWE, author of *Under the Magnolias*

"In her latest compelling novel, Michelle Shocklee brings to light the long history and hidden forces of human trafficking as well as our country's treatment of immigrants, the poor, and those we view as different from ourselves. *Count the Nights by Stars* is a timely reminder that caring for our neighbor is a privilege that requires our time, patience, and resources, as well as the courage to step outside our comfort zones, freeing our hearts to leap in faith."

CATHY GOHLKE, Christy Award–winning author of *Night Bird Calling*

"Shocklee's masterful descriptions thoroughly transport the reader to this unique time and place while bringing to light an issue both historically troubling and heartbreakingly current. *Count the Nights by Stars* is a beautifully written reminder of our need to see—and be seen—by both God and others."

"Experience Tennessee's Centennial Exposition, presented by Michelle Shocklee as a sensuous feast in *Count the Nights by Stars*, then look deeper as two women, one in the late nineteenth century, the other in the 1960s, uncover the lavish celebration's dark, disturbing secret. The story's main setting, the Maxwell House Hotel, is a vivid character itself in its splendid heyday and decline, but it's the heroines who call it home, Audrey and Priscilla, who give this story its true shine, as each seeks to forge a life of purpose, integrity, and love, despite the obstacles she faces. With a mystery that unfolds with irresistible suspense, I predict late nights of page turning for fans of Michelle Shocklee's books and new readers alike."

"Shocklee beautifully unveils Frankie's past while developing Lorena's awareness of inequality. Though set years ago, this title resonates today, and many struggle with the same issues and questions of racial reconciliation. With its haunting message of forgiveness, this is a must-buy for any Christian or historical fiction collection."

"Shocklee elevates the redemptive power of remorse and the grace of forgiveness in this moving saga."

"*Under the Tulip Tree* . . . is an inspiring story of incredible courage in horrific circumstances, of faith, forgiveness, redemption, love, and friendship."

"Get ready to fall in love with characters who step from the pages of history straight into your heart. With exceptional skill, Michelle Shocklee weaves a tale of betrayal and redemption that will long reside in the reader's memory. I cannot recommend [*Under the Tulip Tree*] highly enough!"

TAMERA ALEXANDER, *USA Today* bestselling author of *With This Pledge* and *A Note Yet Unsung*

"*Under the Tulip Tree* takes readers into the heartache of the broken Leland family during and after the Great Depression. The story of Rena Leland captured me from the first page, and I loved reading about her journey as one of the writers for Roosevelt's Federal Writers' Project. *Under the Tulip Tree* moves seamlessly between two time periods, beautifully capturing the relationship between Rena and a former slave woman whose powerful story begins to heal the entire Leland family."

MELANIE DOBSON, award-winning author of *The Curator's Daughter* and *The Winter Rose*

"As a fictional account of one of FDR's slave narratives, *Under the Tulip Tree* gives testimony to not only the social injustices of a country fueled by slavery, but the wounds that would last well beyond the field hospitals of war. In some ways, Rena and Frankie's conversation is one that America should have with itself: one that faces the pain head-on and brings a true spirit of repentance. Then, and only then, will we see healing begin."

ALLISON PITTMAN, author of *The Seamstress*

"*Under the Tulip Tree* is a brilliant and authentic look at the power of story to break through the complicated entanglement of racial tension. Brave, authentic, and moving—Michelle Shocklee takes readers on an adventure of historical significance that is sure to leave them with hope. A grace-filled and beautiful reminder that every story—and every person—matters."

HEIDI CHIAVAROLI, Carol Award–winning author of *Freedom's Ring* and *The Tea Chest*

"*Under the Tulip Tree* left an indelible stamp on my heart. A story of pain, forgiveness, and restoration—Frankie and Rena's story will forever remain a testament to the power of love . . . and God's peace in the midst of heartache."

TARA JOHNSON, author of *All Through the Night* and *Where Dandelions Bloom*

Appalachian Song

A Novel

Appalachian Song

Michelle Shocklee

Tyndale House Publishers
Carol Stream, Illinois

Visit Tyndale online at tyndale.com.

Visit Michelle Shocklee's website at michelleshocklee.com.

Tyndale and Tyndale's quill logo are registered trademarks of Tyndale House Ministries.

Appalachian Song

Cover designed by Sarah Susan Richardson

Edited by Erin E. Smith

Published in association with the literary agency of The Steve Laube Agency.

For information about special discounts for bulk purchases, please contact Tyndale House Publishers at csresponse@tyndale.com, or call 1-855-277-9400.

Library of Congress Cataloging-in-Publication Data

A catalog record for this book is available from the Library of Congress.

ISBN 978-1-4964-7243-4 (HC)

ISBN 978-1-4964-7244-1 (SC)

Printed in the United States of America

29	28	27	26	25	24	23
7	6	5	4	3	2	1

For JRS

And in loving memory of John Warren

For all who are led by the Spirit of God are children of God. . . .
You received God's Spirit when he adopted you as his own
children. Now we call him, "Abba, Father." For his Spirit
joins with our spirit to affirm that we are God's children.

ROMANS 8:14-16

Prologue

APPALACHIAN MOUNTAINS
NORTH CAROLINA
FEBRUARY 1, 1943

My heart thumped hard beneath Mama's thin coat while I waited for Amos at our secret place. Holes in the chinking of the old trapper's cabin let in frigid mountain air, with another storm brewing by the looks of heavy gray clouds in the sky, but I couldn't leave for Tennessee tomorrow without seeing Amos one last time.

Tears blurred my vision.

I didn't want to go. I didn't want to leave North Carolina, but mostly I didn't want to leave Amos. Pa said Amos was a good-for-nothin' kid, but I loved him. He was the first boy I'd ever kissed. Last week after Pa announced we were movin' to Tennessee, I begged Amos to marry me.

"We can wed soon as you turn sixteen," he said, holding me while I cried in his arms right here in this cabin.

"But that's almost two years," I sobbed. "I wanna be your wife now."

He'd gently lifted my chin with his thumb until I looked up at him. "I'm right anxious for you to be mine, too, but I'm only seventeen. In two more years, I'll be a man and can take care of you proper-like. 'Sides, if the war don't end and I gotta join the Army after my birthday, you'd be all alone till I got back. It's best to wait."

He was right, of course. Still, I couldn't leave without him knowing how much I loved him.

Peering out the frost-covered window of the cabin, I waited. Icicles hung from the eaves, and the forest beyond wore a fresh blanket of white, lovely yet dangerous should someone get turned round and head deeper into the mountains. I used to wish I could get lost in those woods and disappear, but all that changed when I met Amos Cole last summer. His laughter and steadiness filled in the holes Mama's death and Pa's neglect had left in my heart. I knew I'd love Amos forever.

It wasn't long before I saw him, his red plaid jacket a bright spot in the snowy world. Tall and handsome, the sight of him always took my breath.

I hurried to the door. I'd taken care with my hair and worn Mama's best dress. I didn't want Amos to think of me as a fourteen-year-old girl today.

His face was red from the cold wind, but he smiled when he saw me. "You look real pretty." He stomped snow off his boots before entering.

"You do too."

He chuckled, then looked around. "It's cold in here."

The cabin had been abandoned for ages and only held a table, one rickety chair, and a narrow log bed frame with a stained straw tick.

"We can make a fire," I said, indicating the stone fireplace.

"I can't stay long. Pa needs me to chop wood before the storm gets here."

His words reminded me our time together was short. My own pa was expecting me to help with the packing.

I swallowed hard. "Amos," I began, more nervous than I'd ever been. "I . . . I love you."

He reached for my hands and squeezed my icy fingers. "I love you too."

I gathered my courage. "I want to be with you. Now. Here, in our secret place."

The widening of his eyes told me he understood my meaning.

"I don't think we should." He cast an uneasy glance to the bed. "It ain't right."

I put my fingers to his mouth to shush him. "I'm leavin' tomorrow and don't know when I'll see you again." Tears slipped down my cheeks. "Please, Amos. Make me yours. For always."

We stared at one another, the magnitude of what I was asking between us.

Just when I began to fear he might turn and leave, Amos pulled me against his chest, where his heart thundered.

"I love you more than anything," he whispered before his lips met mine. Not in the chaste, gentle way we'd always kissed before, but with a passion I hadn't even known existed.

When he led me over to the bed and loved me, I knew I'd never be the same.

I became a woman that day.

One

DEEP IN THE GREAT SMOKY MOUNTAINS
TENNESSEE
JUNE 15, 1943

A gunshot pierced the morning stillness of the holler. Ol' Clem commenced to barking up at the house, sending a flock of sparrows fluttering to the safety of a stand of blooming tulip poplars.

Bertie straightened from where she'd been stooped over a row of young tomato plants and turned in the direction of the sound. The same green hills and tree-covered mountains she'd seen the entirety of her fifty-two years of life filled the view, offering no answers as to which neighbor had fired the weapon. While it wasn't uncommon to hear gunshots in their part of the Appalachians, the time of day—nearly noon—made it so.

Another shot sounded, followed by a third.

"Someone huntin' this late in the mornin'?" Sister Rubie, who'd been working at the opposite end of the garden since sunrise, came toward Bertie where she stood with her ear tuned to the echoing report. Sound carried for miles in the hills, ricocheting off damp earth and ancient oaks, until one couldn't be certain from whence it first came or where it might find a resting place.

"I s'pose." Bertie, who'd misplaced her hat at some point that morning, noted her sister's face was amply shaded from the bright morning sunshine by the wide brim of her bonnet, thus avoiding the redness Bertie was certain her face sported. It wasn't the first time she'd suffered her own neglect and it wouldn't be the last. "Most critters are tucked in the shade of the brush by now. Seems foolhardy to be out huntin' in the heat of the day."

"Sounded like it came from Mooney Point. Aren't there new folks livin' over thataway?" Rubie looked to the north, but their own land was all that was visible from the garden, not far from the two-room cabin Papa'd built for Mam after they married in 1870.

Bertie nodded. "I haven't become acquainted with them yet but heard tell a family with a passel of young'uns moved into the Tucker place some months back."

They listened a while longer, but no more shots were fired.

"We best get indoors, Sister." Rubie's keen gaze studied Bertie's face. "You're beginnin' to look like one of Papa's McIntosh apples."

Bertie huffed. "One would think after all the years of workin' the garden I'd have sense enough to keep up with my head covering."

"'Tisn't that you aren't sensible, dear. You simply have too much on your mind. I know you're worried 'bout the Alister babe, even if you won't admit it."

Her empathetic words unlocked a load of frustration.

"Ramsey Alister is actin' foolish, and I don't mind sayin' it." Bertie punctuated her opinion with a firm nod. "There's no cause for him to take that sweet young bride of his to Knoxville. I've delivered half a dozen breech babies, all of 'em healthy. You mark my words. Them city doctors will cut Sharalyn open without so much as a by-your-leave, with Alister parked out in the waitin' room, banned from being by her side. Wouldn't it be better for me to work with God and nature and bring that child into the world without maiming its mother?"

The stiff, starched bill of Rubie's home-sewn bonnet lifted until sparkling blue eyes, the hallmark of the Jenkins family, were visible. "Certainly it would be best for you to attend the birth, Sister, but Ramsey is as strongheaded as his pa. There's naught else to be done but pray the wee one arrives safe and sound with no harm to Sharalyn."

The statement held simple truth. There was naught else to be done. Ramsey Alister was the babe's father and had made his decision.

Still, Bertie's hackles wouldn't settle. "What gets my goat is the man tellin' me I'm too old to midwife for our mountain folk anymore. Why, I was there when he himself came into the world, blue-faced and silent. I don't take credit for breathin' life into him, as that's God's job, but the Lord and I have been workin' together for nigh on forty years. I'll stop deliverin' babies when he tells me to and not a moment sooner."

With a gentleness none of the other Jenkins siblings possessed, Rubie laid her hand on Bertie's cheek. "It is still God's job, Sister, even when you aren't there to assist him."

The mild rebuke hit its mark.

Bertie's rigid shoulders dropped. "Papa always said you were wise beyond your years, even as a young girl."

"Papa also used to take a switch to my legs when I expressed my *wisdom* a bit too loudly."

Their shared laughter worked to soothe Bertie's ire. "We best get to the house and help with the noon meal. Otherwise—" she winked—"Jennie might take a switch to us both."

Bertie led the way down a narrow path, around mounds of cucumber and squash plants, past the peas and onions, before she came to a rusted metal gate. The paling fence Papa had built decades ago kept out deer, wild hogs, and other critters large enough to destroy the life-sustaining garden, but there wasn't much they could do about rabbits and other varmints small enough to squeeze beneath the gray, weathered slats.

As they made their way to the house, Bertie did a mental inventory of everything she and Rubie had accomplished that morning, as well as work that awaited them on the morrow. Not nearly as big as it had once been when Papa and Mam's large family lived at home, the garden and everything it produced provided life and liberty to Bertie and her four sisters. Only the corn and wheat fields held greater importance, and that because a good portion was cash crop. Although the sisters' farm produced nearly everything they required to live, a few necessities like sugar, soda, coffee, and salt must be purchased at the general store in Cosby Run, an hour from the homestead by mule or half that if they went on foot through the woods.

Bertie chuckled to herself, hearing Papa's booming voice in her mind. *"Life and liberty, you say?"*

Yes, sir, she gave silent answer.

Five aging spinsters living alone in the mountains of Tennessee fought for life and liberty every single day. Papa'd been gone for twenty years now. His sons were good to see to their sisters on occasions of great need, but Bertie, Rubie, Jennie, Amelie, and Bonnie couldn't rely on their brothers for the day-to-day needs of their farm. Thomas and Chad had farms and families of their own, as did Catie—or Catherine, as she liked to be called now—the only Jenkins sister who'd married and moved away from Brier Creek. The five sisters who remained on the family land worked hard to preserve the independent yet solitary life they'd chosen.

Bertie paused and surveyed her surroundings with gratitude.

The two-room cabin where Mam and Papa raised eleven children. The barn, corncrib, smokehouse, gristmill, and spring-house filled with crocks of butter, cream, and milk. She and her siblings used to hide in the small building on hot summer days long ages ago, dipping their bare toes in the cold mountain water. Hogs lazed in their pens while chickens clucked about on a never-ending search for bugs and lizards. Bees happily buzzed among wildflowers, garden plants, and even Papa's apple orchard, where several varieties were just beginning to bloom due to a late freeze. The tiny pollinators eventually made their way to the half-dozen hives Rubie tended with unhurried care each day. Bertie's mouth fairly watered at the thought of the fresh honey they'd enjoy now that the mountains were once again alive with glorious blooms.

Theirs was a good life, indeed, if unconventional in the eyes of outsiders.

When she and Rubie reached the house, the usual daily activities of their sisters greeted them. Bonnie stood near the spring-house with hands deep in a washtub set over a low fire despite her recent flare-up of arthritis—Bertie made a mental note to make her sister some chamomile tea to ease the joint pain—while Amelie pinned damp handmade skirts, blouses, and underthings on a line to dry. With eleven children, Mam had Papa fix a sturdy clothes-line as close to their water source as possible. Though just the five sisters occupied the homestead now, laundry was still done outdoors unless frigid winter days kept them inside.

Jennie, the eldest at sixty years, looked up from where she sat on a bench on the porch churning butter. "You hear the shots?"

Bertie and Rubie mounted rock steps and joined Jennie in the shade of the covered outdoor area where the sisters often took their work, sewing, or even meals during the warmer months.

"Rubie thinks it came from Mooney Point." Bertie sat in a wooden rocker, crafted by their father years ago, and fanned herself with her apron. "Odd time to be huntin', we figure."

Jennie glanced her way and frowned. "Alberta Mae, where is your bonnet? Your face is as red as—"

"One of Papa's McIntosh apples. I know."

"You'll be sorry come mornin'." Jennie's thin lips pinched. "Rub some aloe on it so it won't blister."

Bertie clamped her mouth shut. She wasn't a child in need of Jennie's mothering. She was, after all, the family member who did most of the doctoring.

Jennie served a noon meal of cold mutton, applesauce from last season's apples, and biscuits. Later, while Bertie slathered an aloe salve on her sunburned skin—not because her bossy sister said to but because everyone knew aloe soothes sunburns—her mind drifted to the cause of her distractedness that morning.

Concern for the Alisters had occupied her mind since Ramsey knocked on the cabin door the previous day to inform Bertie they no longer required her services as midwife for the impending birth of their first child.

At the last checkup, Bertie found that Sharalyn's baby hadn't turned as it should. She'd massaged the mother's huge belly to no avail and proceeded to explain the process of a breech birth to the frightened couple. Yes, it came with risk, she'd told them, but every birth did. A bottom-first baby could still enter the world naturally; they'd just need to be especially vigilant in monitoring its progression and heartbeat. The young parents, anxious but willing to trust Bertie, agreed. Bertie went home to prepare a special birthing kit with items she'd need for a breech delivery that was sure to commence in the next week and had it waiting by the door.

Then Ramsey'd shown up without a hint of apology and said he was taking his wife to the city for the delivery.

"How many babies has Ramsey Alister birthed?" she muttered as she settled in a chair on the porch with a lapful of knit stockings in need of mending. "None. How many babies have I helped bring into the world? Too many to count. But nooo, Bertie don't know what she's talkin' about when it comes to *his* baby. Them city doctors know better than Bertie."

Her one-sided conversation would have continued had Clem's ears not perked up just then. He lifted his head and emitted a low growl from his place at her feet.

"What's ailin' you, boy?"

Bertie followed his intense gaze, fixed on the wooded area past the corncrib. Something moved in the brush, but her eyesight wasn't as good as the big yellow dog's was, even at ten years of age.

"It's probably just a deer. Cats and bears ain't gonna come callin' this time of day."

Despite her droll declaration, Clem raced off the porch, barking as he passed the corncrib and disappeared into thick foliage. Bertie hoped there wasn't a polecat waiting for him. That dog had been sprayed more times than she cared to deal with.

His barking quieted a moment later, yet whatever was in the brush hadn't run away.

The figure moved again. Was that a person?

"Hello? Is someone there?" Bertie set her mending on the plank floor and stood. "Come on out. No need to be unneighborly."

Jennie appeared in the open doorway to the kitchen, hands covered in bread flour. "Who are you talkin' to?"

"There's someone in the bushes over yonder." She indicated the spot with her chin.

Jennie squinted in that direction. "I don't see anyone." She gave Bertie a look, as though she thought sun sickness might be the culprit.

A thud sounded. Like something hitting the ground.

Clem commenced barking again, but this time he came out and stood with eyes fixed on Bertie for several beats before he returned to whatever hid in the bushes.

"We best find out what's got that dog worked up fore he barks himself hoarse."

Bertie and Jennie left the shade of the porch and made their way past the log corncrib, empty and ready for a new crop come harvest. When they poked through the foliage, both women drew up short at the sight before them.

Clem stood over a girl, not more than thirteen or fourteen years old, collapsed on the ground.

"What on earth?" Jennie exclaimed.

Bertie knelt beside the girl and smoothed long honey-colored hair from a pretty but pale face. "She's fainted."

With experienced eyes, Bertie took note of several clues. Swollen breasts. A slight bulge beneath the homespun dress. Although the stranger didn't appear to be more than a child herself, Bertie was certain a babe grew within her womb.

"We best get her to the cabin, out of this heat," Bertie said.

When she slid her arm beneath the girl's shoulder, a warm, sticky substance met her hand. She pulled it away to see bright red staining her skin.

"Good gracious," Bertie breathed. "She's bleeding."

Jennie knelt on the opposite side of the unconscious girl and together they carefully rolled her over so Bertie could examine her.

She tugged the loose neck of the blood-soaked dress and eased it down until an ugly, oozing, perfectly round wound was revealed in the flesh of the girl's thin shoulder.

Bertie gasped, but she knew her eyes didn't deceive her.

"What is it?" Jennie asked.

"She's been shot, Sister," Bertie hissed. "This wound is fresh." Her gaze darted to the woods behind them. Normally so familiar and peaceful, they suddenly seemed dark and sinister.

Who could have done such a ghastly thing? One of their neighbors? An outsider?

She met her sister's bewildered gaze.

"Whoever did this," she said, her voice low and alive with fear, "could still be out there."

Two

THE EVERYDAY QUIETUDE of the Jenkins cabin shattered in a rush of activity.

"Boil some water!"

"Put her on the sofa."

"The blood'll leave a stain. Use the cot there in the corner."

"What happened? Who is she?"

Bertie's sisters' anxious voices filled the gathering room, each attempting to speak over the others, as she and Jennie carried in the unconscious girl. Though the stranger was slight in size, it had taken every bit of strength she and Jennie possessed to carefully lift the child from the forest floor and make their way to the cabin. It was a relief to settle her on the cot near the cold fireplace. The narrow bed was used only when they had a visitor or when a sister couldn't sleep and didn't wish to disturb the others in the sleeping loft above the kitchen.

The excited chatter frayed Bertie's already-taut nerves.

"She's been shot." Her voice rose above the din, returning the room to welcome silence.

Eyes wide, her siblings stared at her, shock and confusion on their sun-wrinkled faces.

"We've no answers to your questions and no time to waste. That bullet's gotta come out and the wound cleaned. Amelie, bring my bag. Bonnie, we'll need bandages. Rubie, get Papa's rifle and set it by the door. We don't know if the varmint who shot her is nearby, but we can take no chances. Get to it, Sisters."

The women sprang into action, darting about the cabin on their missions.

"Do you reckon the one who done this will come searchin' for her?"

Jennie's low-spoken, ominous words drew Bertie's attention. The worry she saw in her sister's eyes reflected the rising dread in her own heart. "I don't know what to think." She glanced down at the girl. "But if we don't get that bullet out and the wound closed, it won't matter. She's lost a lot of blood already."

"You've never taken a bullet out of someone before."

Bertie thought of the many cuts, gashes, bruises, animal bites, and broken bones she'd tended over the years. "I reckon there's a first for everythin'."

After a long moment, Jennie nodded, touched Bertie's arm in an uncharacteristic show of affection, and headed to the kitchen. "I'll boil water. You'll need a poultice, too."

With each of her sisters busy at their assigned tasks, Bertie returned her attention to the girl on the cot. Before they'd lifted her from the forest floor, Bertie'd used her apron as a bandage, hoping to stanch the flow of blood. Now she carefully undid the knotted material.

The many questions her sisters asked echoed through her mind as she worked.

Who was this girl? Who'd shot her and why? The father of her child? Had it been a terrible accident or was this the result of something far more sinister?

The realization that Bertie might have endangered her family by bringing the girl into the cabin was a sobering thought, yet she'd had no other choice. The Bible's Good Samaritan hadn't considered his own safety when he helped the man who'd been beaten and robbed. Bertie and her sisters could do no less, could they?

With gentle care, she lifted the girl's arm to peek at the wound. A moan parted the patient's lips. "Don't . . . don't hurt me. Don't hurt . . . my baby."

Bertie stilled.

Although the girl's eyes remained shut, the weak, frightened words told Bertie this was no accidental shooting. She placed her hand on a warm cheek. "Rest easy, dear one. You and your babe are safe."

After a moment, the girl's body relaxed, and she slipped back into unconsciousness. Bertie prayed she would remain so, at least until the bullet was removed from her body.

For the next hour, with her sisters' help and encouragement, Bertie painstakingly sought to locate the bullet embedded deep in the torn flesh. Her simple medical instruments, useful at birthings, weren't designed for surgery of this kind, but somehow Bertie managed to extract the hateful metal, bringing with it a fresh flow of dark blood.

"I need to sew the wound closed," she said to no one in particular, her focus on quelling the river of red that ran down pale skin onto the sheet.

Amelie handed her a threaded needle. "It's been sterilized," she volunteered.

Bertie nodded her thanks and set to work. With careful, even stitches, she closed the wound, mindful not to pucker the skin. Next, she took the poultice Jennie had prepared—the odor telling her it was a mixture of garlic, mustard, and yarrow—and placed it over the clean, stitched-up bullet hole. The warmth and herbal mixture would draw out infection that tried to settle in the wound as well as help with swelling.

After wrapping the entire shoulder with clean bandages, Bertie sat back on her haunches, rotating her neck to ease the tension in her muscles. "Well, that's all we can do. It's up to the Lord now."

The five women bowed their heads as Jennie said a brief-but-to-the-point prayer over their patient, asking God for quick healing and safety for them all. Late-afternoon sunshine out the window reminded them chores awaited.

"I'll milk the cow, Bertie." Rubie's words were directed to her sister, but her soft gaze stayed on the girl. "The poor child may need you."

"Let's hope she sleeps. I fear she'll be in much pain when she awakens."

Rubie reached to smooth a strand of honey-colored hair. "So young. Why would anyone wish to harm her?"

Until they learned more about the girl, the circumstances of her arrival at their cabin would remain shrouded in dark mystery.

Bertie circled her arm around Rubie's thick waist. Together they studied the lovely face, pleased to see a bit of color had come to their patient's cheeks. Bertie hoped it was brought on by a return to normal blood flow to the girl's heart rather than fever.

"Take Amelie with you when you go to the barn, Sister. I think it best if no one goes out alone until we know how this happened."

Rubie nodded and left for her chore. From the next room, the aroma of roasted pork drifted to her, along with hushed voices and the clink of cutlery being set out on the worktable.

Bertie sank onto one of Papa's handcrafted ladder-back chairs someone had placed next to the sickbed, exhaustion washing over her as her bones settled against the hard wood. She closed her eyes and checked off a mental list of what needed to be done in the coming hours.

Change bandages. Make a new poultice. Spoon fluids. Pray.

It had been some time since she'd doctored a seriously ill patient. Most mountain folks didn't bother with hospitals and school-educated doctors. With Knoxville nearly two hours away by automobile, it was too far for illness or injury that wasn't life-threatening. Many mountain families tended their own sick, with the Jenkins family as no exception. Bertie'd learned about herbs, medicines, and midwifery from Mam, who'd learned it from her mama. She'd attended her first birthing at the age of eleven, awed by the miracle she'd witnessed. Afterward, Bertie told Mam she wanted to learn to be a healer. Papa'd been pleased to hear such and allowed her to spend time with Mam mixing teas and medicinal concoctions rather than weeding the garden or cleaning out the chicken coop.

"Sister?"

Bertie's eyes sprang open. Darkness filled the world out the window above the cot, and the glow of kerosene lamps illuminated the cabin. She stretched and wondered how long she'd been asleep.

"You should eat something." Jennie stood next to the bed, her hand on the forehead of the unconscious girl. "I'll sit with her."

With a groan, Bertie stood, her neck and limbs stiff. "I suggest we find a more comfortable chair if we're to keep watch through the night." Her glance went to the stars sparkling in the inky sky. "Best we draw the curtains, should anyone come lookin' for her."

So saying, she moved to tug the faded fabric, so lovingly sewn by Amelie as a surprise for Mam many years ago, across the windows on either side of the stone fireplace.

"I'm thinkin' the one who done this won't be stopped by a drawn curtain if they come for her." Jennie carried over a rocking chair with a cushion and set it near the cot.

Bertie hoped her elder sister was wrong, but after she pulled the curtains on the kitchen windows, she slid heavy bars in place across the outside doors in each of the two rooms. They only barred the doors when a curious bear or a strong wind threatened to push them open. Tonight, something worse than a hungry bear lurked in the darkness. Papa's rifle stood in the corner, loaded and ready.

Low voices came from the sleeping loft above the kitchen while Bertie sat at the table and ate the supper Jennie had left warming for her on the back of the wood-burning cookstove. The soft chatter of her sisters preparing for bed, nourishing food in her belly, Papa's well-built cabin offering time-tested protection. It all served to remind her God had always seen to their needs and safety, and he would do so again and again.

Now he'd brought a wounded lamb for them to care for. Bertie hoped answers about who she was and what happened would come with the morning sun, but first they had to make certain the girl survived the night.

They took turns sitting with their patient, with each sister waking up the next every two hours. Bertie couldn't settle in her bed and instead stretched out on the sofa. Sometime around midnight, she and Bonnie changed the bandages and poultice. Bertie was pleased to see only a small amount of blood escaped the tight stitches, but infection was still possible.

By sunrise, the five sisters were up and dressed and preparing for the day. The injured girl still hadn't awakened, but Bertie wasn't overly concerned just yet. The body and mind often required a break from reality when trauma occurred. She'd keep close watch over the child and pray God's healing hand would mend and restore while their patient slept.

"I figure to take Kit to Cosby Run and see if there's talk about a missin' girl," Jennie said later when she approached the sickbed, where Bertie bathed the girl's face with a damp cloth. "Do you need anythin' from the general store while I'm there?"

Bertie noted her sister was already wearing her Sunday go-to-meetin' hat and gloves, so there was no use arguing against the plan. "I can't think of a thing." She clamped her mouth closed, mindful that Jennie didn't take kindly to being told what to do any more than she did.

"I see you have something to say."

Bertie never could hide her feelings from Jennie. She kept her attention on the girl but said, "I figure it best to wait till she wakes up and we hear her story before we go askin' questions of folks. Wouldn't want anyone gettin' suspicious."

Jennie huffed. "I ain't addlebrained, Alberta Mae. We need sugar and soda. Figure it can't hurt to put an ear to the day's gossip and see if there be any talk. I'll take Bonnie with me."

Bertie nodded and watched her sisters leave the house. Kit, the family mule, wouldn't be too happy about them riding double to town and back. Bertie wouldn't be surprised if Jennie ended up walking most of the way to give Bonnie's arthritic feet a break.

"They won't mention our sweet visitor to anyone."

Rubie approached and handed Bertie a cup of steaming coffee. She settled in the rocking chair while Bertie remained seated on the edge of the cot.

"I hope not. You know how Minnie Abrams down at the mercantile can sniff out a scandal like a hound on a rabbit." Bertie sipped the bitter liquid and let the warmth settle her. "I reckon I'm just anxious, is all. God brought this child to us, and we need to keep her safe till her people can come fetch her."

"She's expecting a wee one, isn't she?" Rubie asked softly.

Bertie shot a look at her sister, surprised. The signs of pregnancy were barely noticeable. "She is."

Rubie sighed. "Even after all these years, I sometimes wonder what it would've been like to carry Caleb's babe in my womb. To feel it kick and squirm. You would have come to deliver him when it was time, and Caleb would've beamed with pride when you handed him our son."

Bertie had heard the words of longing many times over the last twenty-five or so years, but they never ceased to break her heart anew. "I'm sorry you lost your Caleb before you could marry him, dear one. You would've been a fine wife and mother."

A tear trailed Rubie's cheek unchecked, and a sad smile lifted the corners of her lips. "Thank you for sayin' so, Sister." She glanced toward the kitchen, where Amelie peeled a mound of potatoes for soup. "I best not let Amelie hear me goin' on. It would only make her sad to think on it."

Bertie nodded. Amelie's William had died in the same terrible logging accident as Caleb. Their sister suffered such terrible grief, she'd never been the same.

Rubie rose from the chair. "I'll clean Kit's stall while Jennie has him out."

Bertie suspected her younger sister would find a lonely place and remember her fiancé in private. Papa always declared it wasn't beneficial to dwell on the past, but Bertie couldn't help but wonder why God didn't stop the load of heavy logs from coming loose from the railcar or move her sisters' fiancés, as well as three other young men, out of the way. Neither of her grief-stricken sisters courted again; they joined Jennie, Bonnie, and herself as spinsters.

Alone with the patient, Bertie gently placed her hand on the bulge beneath the sheet. If she had to guess, she'd say the girl was four, maybe five months along. She wasn't wearing a wedding band, although that didn't always mean anything. Jewelry wasn't a priority to mountain folks. Perhaps Jennie was right to go to the general store to find out if anyone was indeed searching for the girl. If the shooting had been accidental, someone was sure to be frantic about the whereabouts of the mother-to-be.

Jennie and Bonnie returned with sugar and soda but no news.

"Nary a peep was said about a missing girl." Jennie carefully removed long pins that held her worn hat in place and lifted it without disturbing her gray hair, wound in a bun on top of her head. "Lots of talk 'bout the war though. Two more families in town lost boys fightin' them Germans. I wish the Allies would put Hitler in his place and be done with it."

Bertie knew Jennie's gruff words masked the sadness they all felt when heartbreaking news reached them in their isolated part of the world. Two of their nephews were fighting the war—one on a ship in the Pacific Ocean and one flying over Europe in a big airplane, serving as something called a turret gunner—and the sisters prayed their names would never be on the lists nailed to the door of the post office each day.

But it wasn't just soldiers in harm's way. Just last week Bertie read an article in the paper about a British passenger airplane that had been shot down by the Germans, killing all seventeen people aboard. One of them, an actor by the name of Leslie Howard, was among the dead, grieving Sister Catie. She'd seen him in the movie *Gone with the Wind* when it played in Knoxville. They'd all read the novel by Margaret Mitchell, and the character of Ashley Wilkes was a favorite among the Jenkins sisters.

Bonnie hung her hat on a peg while Rubie and Amelie joined them in the gathering room, eager to hear any news.

"Minnie Abrams was there, of course," Jennie continued, "chattin' up anyone who'd give her an ear, but she mostly wanted to talk about war rations and the price of beef. We figure if that woman knew anythin' about a missin' girl or a criminal in the area, we'd've heard it for certain."

Bertie sagged as the breath she'd been holding poured from her lungs. "Thank the Lord."

"Yes," Jennie said matter-of-factly, "but we still have no answers as to who the girl is or how she ended up with a bullet in her. We don't know if we're harborin' a fugitive or a victim. I can't help but wonder if we shouldn't get word to the sheriff and let him handle the matter."

Bertie stood to protest. "Let's not be too hasty, Sister."

The five women began to talk at once, posing questions and offering opinions on what they should or shouldn't do and how best to proceed. Their voices grew louder, with each trying to be heard above the others, like a coop full of cackling hens.

A cry from the sickbed, however, brought the racket to an abrupt end.

When Bertie turned, she found the pale girl staring at the sisters, large hazel eyes full of fear.

Three

Reese Chandler smiled down at the tiny babe in her arms, his face red and swollen from his recent journey through his mother's birth canal. "Welcome to the world, little one," she said as she gently rubbed him with a warm towel to stimulate his breathing. "What do you think of it so far?"

He answered with a lusty cry.

Joel, his father, laughed. "It sounds like the little dude is upset he had to leave his warm cocoon."

Reese clamped the umbilical cord; then Joel used sharp scissors to cut it. When the baby was wrapped in a soft blanket, she handed him to the new father. "Here's your son. Linda still has some work to do before she can rest."

A short time later, with the family settled in their converted school bus home, Reese packed her midwifery bag and prepared to leave. The hippie commune was a good thirty-minute drive from her clinic in Piney Ridge, close to the North Carolina border, so she wanted to visit another expectant mother on the one-hundred-plus-acre property before heading home.

"I'll be back to look in on you, but if you experience heavy bleeding or cramping or have any worries about the baby, use your neighbor's telephone and call me right away."

The radiant new mother wore a tired but happy smile as she cradled her son. "We can't thank you enough, Reese. Since Peggy moved back to California and left our community without a midwife of our own, we're grateful you're willing to come out and deliver our babies."

"It's my honor. After I attended my first birth during nursing school, I knew this was what I wanted to do." She reached down to touch the sleeping baby's silky cheek. "Every birth is a miracle."

"It was the most psychedelic experience we've ever had, for sure," Linda said as she gazed at her son.

"I guess you'll get even more business now that you're famous," Joel said, his long beard unable to hide his teasing smile.

Reese laughed and shook her head. "An article in a Nashville newspaper about an obscure midwife in the hills of East Tennessee doesn't exactly scream fame and fortune."

"It was a nice write-up though," Linda said, her eyes beginning to droop with exhaustion. "You gave a good argument for the practice of midwifery. I hope more women will choose to have their babies at home rather than the hospital after reading it. I'm proud you were our midwife."

Reese thanked her, bid the family goodbye, and headed for her red Volkswagen Beetle. She'd call Mom as soon as she got home and tell her about the birth. Ever since Reese decided to leave her position as a labor and delivery nurse at the hospital in Knoxville and start her own midwifery clinic in Piney Ridge, Mom had been her biggest supporter. The journey hadn't been an easy one, what with state regulations, licensing issues, and a plethora of bureaucratic red tape to overcome. When she'd finally been given the green light to practice midwifery in the hills of East

Tennessee three years ago, she'd hung a wooden signpost in the front yard of her small cottage and began seeing to the needs of women who might not otherwise seek professional medical advice for their pregnancies. Superstition, lack of money, or lack of trust often kept mountain women, as well as the women of the nearby hippie community, from visiting a doctor when they became pregnant. Since Reese first opened her door, she'd delivered over thirty babies, with more to come.

The Beetle scraped bottom as she carefully maneuvered the small car over rain-washed ruts in the dirt road of the commune, heading to a house that was little more than a shack. Despite the primitive conditions of the compound—no running water and no electricity—Reese admired the hippies' tenacity to create their own unique environment far away from the hustle and bustle of the world. It wasn't a perfect place, since too many of the residents dabbled in drugs, free love, and strange religious beliefs, but Reese had gotten to know many of the women and found there was more to them than the unconventional persona most people saw.

She thought back to the day Mom came out here with her. Reese had grown accustomed to the makeshift housing of the hippies, as well as their colorful clothing and odd language, but Mom's eyes remained wide throughout the visit. Afterward, however, she expressed how proud she was of Reese. "I may not understand why those people choose to live like they do, but every expectant mother should know she and her baby are in capable hands when it comes time for the birth. You're giving that gift to them."

Those words were particularly special to hear from her mother, since she herself had not had the opportunity to give birth to a child. Instead, as Mom liked to tell the story to anyone who would listen, God had something different in mind: the perfect plan of adoption.

After Reese visited with Inez, who'd delivered her first child in a California hospital and wanted her second baby born at home, she pointed her car down the mountain toward Piney Ridge. She'd barely walked in the front door of her cozy home when the telephone rang. Expecting Mom's voice on the line, Reese laughed when she answered it.

"I was just getting ready to call you."

Silence filled the next moment before a man cleared his throat.

"Um, is this Reese Chandler?"

Heat filled her cheeks. "Oh, my, I'm sorry. I was expecting someone else. Yes, this is Reese Chandler."

"My name is Ray Nelson, from Nashville. I saw the article in the newspaper last week about your work, and I hope you can help me."

Reese sat in the chair next to the telephone table and grabbed a pen and notepad. "Of course. Is your wife expecting a baby?"

An odd sound came through the line, almost as if the man had choked on something. "No, no. That's not why I'm calling. Jeepers, I'm not even married." He cleared his throat again. "I'm calling because I have a client who recently learned he was adopted back in 1943. He was born somewhere in East Tennessee, but we have very little information to go on. I thought you might be able to help. Maybe point us in the right direction."

Reese put down the pen, confused. "Mr. Nelson, I'm a midwife. I deliver babies and help women during and after the birth of their child."

"But the article said you were also an adoption advocate."

"Yes," Reese responded, trying to recall exactly what the reporter had included in the write-up. With midwifery an anomaly rather than the norm it used to be in childbirth, the newspaper lady was quite interested in Reese's decision to practice it. "If a mother decides to put her child up for adoption, I help navigate the choices and decisions she must make, as well as the often-confusing legal information she's given. If I understand your client's situation correctly, he needs the help of an attorney to track down his birth information, not an adoption advocate. But . . ." She paused. She didn't want to squash the man's or his client's hopes, yet honesty was always best. "You should know that adoption records in Tennessee are sealed. Even with legal assistance, your client most likely won't be able to find out anything beyond what he already knows."

"That definitely isn't news I want to pass on to my client. You're sure there isn't anything you can do to help us?"

"I'm sorry, Mr. Nelson, but no, there isn't. I have a friend who's an attorney in Knoxville—Bill McClain. I've known him most of my life and worked with him on several adoption cases. He'll be able to give you more detailed information on how to proceed."

Reese gave him Bill's office telephone number, apologized one last time for not being able to help, and ended the call. She felt bad she couldn't offer more encouragement, especially if the man's client truly hadn't known anything about his adoption until recently, yet there wasn't anything she could do about it.

As she'd done throughout most of her life, she whispered a prayer of thanks for Mom and Dad. They'd never hidden the fact that she was adopted. When Reese was thirteen years old, Mom told her about her birth mother—a young woman who'd fallen in love with an older, married man. She was the daughter of a family friend, so Reese's parents had more information than most adoptive families. Still, it had been difficult for Reese to process the circumstances of her birth. She'd gone through a dark period of anger and rebellion, trying to cope with the fact that her birth father was a jerk. She could well imagine how confused and angry Mr. Nelson's client felt right about now, learning about his adoption after all these years.

She was on her way down the hall to her bedroom when the front door squealed on its hinges and loud barking ensued.

"Hey, Reese," Kathy, her next-door neighbor, called over the din. "Oreo saw you pull into the driveway and couldn't wait to come see his mama."

Laughing, Reese returned to the living room to find her petite neighbor struggling to hold on to the leash attached to a medium-size black-and-white dog. His whole body wagged when he spotted her.

"Hi, boy." Reese came forward but stopped just short of the dog. She held up her hand and Oreo instantly grew quiet and plunked his backside down.

Kathy shook her head. "I wish he would obey me like that." She unsnapped the leash, but Oreo didn't move. "Of course, my own kid doesn't, so why should I expect obedience from a dog?"

Reese sent her friend a sympathetic look. "Ryan just turned two, Kath. He doesn't obey anyone."

"True." Kathy stood in the open doorway, watching her son. "He saw a worm in your driveway and refused to keep walking. Ah, he's on the move, worm and all. Come over here, Ryan. Come see Auntie Reese." Her shoulders sagged a moment later. "Nope. He stopped again."

Reese hid a smile when she heard Ryan babble something unintelligible and turned her attention back to her dog. "Oreo, come."

The dog bounded over and licked Reese's hand to let her know he'd missed her.

"How's the new hippie?" Kathy shot a quick glance at Reese. "Everything go okay with the delivery?"

Reese sank onto the sofa and Oreo leaped up beside her. "It did. Joel and Linda have a healthy new son." She scratched the dog behind his ears and Oreo's eyes drifted closed.

Kathy's gaze shifted from her son to Reese. "Then what's wrong? You seem troubled about something."

Reese grinned. "Am I that easy to read?"

"Yes." Kathy winked.

Reese shrugged. "I got a phone call from a guy who needs help with his client's adoption from back in 1943. He read the article about me in the paper and thought I could . . . I don't know . . . track down his client's birth parents, I guess."

"Wow. That's heavy."

"Yeah." She sighed. "I feel bad for the guy, you know. I can't imagine being thirty years old and just finding out."

Kathy gave a slow nod. "What did you tell him?"

"I gave him Bill's number."

Her friend sent her a sly look. "Is Bill still trying to get you to go on a date with him?"

Reese rolled her eyes. "Bill and I are friends. He has no interest in dating me."

"Uh-huh. That's why he sends you flowers on your birthday every year."

"Friends send flowers to friends, Kath. I've sent you flowers."

Kathy let out a belly laugh. "That isn't the same at all, but I won't argue with you. I better get going. Mike's shift at the firehouse ends at five, so he'll be home for dinner. I want to make his favorite—lasagna and garlic bread." She glanced outside and horror filled her face. "Ryan, do not put that worm in your mouth!" She flew out the door and down the steps.

Reese lifted the curtain on the window behind the sofa and watched her friend dig something from the little boy's mouth. Ryan pointed at the ground while he babbled, but Kathy shook her head, picked him up, and carried him into their small house next door.

"Oreo," she said as she let the curtain fall back in place and looked down at the dog, his alert attention on her after hearing his name. "You need to give Kathy a break and obey her better, okay? She's got her hands full with that little guy and doesn't need my rambunctious dog giving her grief. Got it?"

Oreo peered at her with adoring brown eyes, his head tilted as though saying, *"Me? Rambunctious?"*

She scratched his ears one last time, walked over to the telephone, and dialed Mom and Dad's number. Since she'd moved away from Knoxville, her long-distance telephone bill had increased, but it was worth every penny to stay connected to the two most important people in her life.

"Hi, honey. How'd it go?" Mom said, eagerness in her voice.

"Great. Linda and Joel have a healthy little boy."

"I'm so glad to hear it. Dad and I have been praying."

"Thanks, Mom." She sighed.

"What's wrong?"

Reese chuckled. "How does everyone know me so well? Kathy knew something was troubling me and now you do too." She told Mom about Mr. Nelson's client. "I feel bad that I couldn't offer any help. He's just a couple years older than me."

"How sad for the young man." Mom's sympathy came through the line. "I hope Bill is able to help him, although with adoption laws the way they are, I'm not sure how much he'll be able to find about the birth parents."

"That's what I told Mr. Nelson, but it's at least worth a shot." A lump formed in Reese's throat. "Thanks, Mom, for always being honest with me."

"You're welcome, honey." She paused. "It wasn't an easy decision though. Your father and I seriously considered keeping the adoption a secret. In some ways, it would have been easier to let you and the world believe you were our biological child. But a handful of people knew the truth and we were afraid someone would reveal our secret before we could. In the end, even though our reasons weren't quite as honorable as they seem now, we're glad you've always known you were adopted."

They enjoyed several more minutes of conversation before

Reese hung up the telephone and headed for the pink-tiled bathroom down the hall. After a day that started well before sunrise, a hot soak in a bubble bath sounded divine.

But despite the relaxing, sudsy water soothing her tired muscles, Reese's mind wouldn't settle. She couldn't stop thinking about the man who'd recently learned he was adopted. The stranger was no doubt confused and angry, emotions she remembered experiencing herself. He needed far more than she or Bill could offer.

"Help him, Father," she whispered, knowing there was only One who could bring healing to this hurting soul. "Make your purposes known and help him find the answers he's searching for."

Four

FIVE OLDER WOMEN STARED AT ME with as much shock on their wrinkled faces as I must have worn on my own.

"Where am I? Who are you?"

The woman closest to where I lay on a narrow cot offered a warm smile, although neither she nor the others moved toward me.

"You're safe, dear. We're the Jenkins sisters and you're in our cabin."

After several tense moments, my body relaxed against the small bed. "How long . . . ?"

The woman slowly eased closer. "We found you yesterday afternoon, just past our yard, in the woods." She paused, then indicated my shoulder. "You've been injured, dear. Do you recall what happened?"

I touched the large bandage, confused to find it there. How had I hurt myself and ended up in a stranger's cabin?

Suddenly my mind flooded with images.

Pa's angry face. Arguing. Gunshots. Blinding pain.

Fear rose in my throat. "Pa. He did this to me. I gotta get outta here. If he finds me, he'll finish the job."

I pushed myself up. The movement caused me to cry out as fire raced through my body.

The woman hurried forward and gently pressed me back onto the cot. "Lie still, dear. Your wound is quite deep. You'll tear the stitches."

Tears filled my eyes, and my lips trembled. "You don't understand. Pa was liquored up, but he knew what he was doin'. Said he won't take care of some no-good fella's brat and tried to make me drink a nasty potion his witch of a wife made." My hands protectively went to the small bump on my belly. "I wouldn't let them kill my baby. Said he'd have to kill me first. That's when Pa got his gun and started shootin'."

Compassion filled the woman's face. "You're safe here. No one knows you're here but us."

"If Pa learns my where'bouts, you'll all be in danger."

"Let us worry about that. You concentrate on gettin' stronger and takin' care of that babe of yours."

It took a moment for the kind words to hit their mark. When I understood she and the others were willing to help me despite the risk, tears slipped down my cheeks. "Thank ya," I whispered. "I don't know what woulda happened if . . ." I didn't finish the thought.

The woman smiled. "I'm Bertie. These are my sisters—Jennie, Amelie, Bonnie, and Rubie."

I didn't tell them my name, even though I knew it was rude. But the less these women knew about me, the better for them, I figured.

"You get some rest now." Bertie shooed her sisters from the room. "I'll bring some broth in a bit."

I watched her follow the others into the adjoining room. Low voices reached me, but I couldn't make out their words. No doubt they were horrified by the tale I'd told, but it was the truth.

Something evil lurked in Pa. Always had. Mama'd been afraid of him, and I'd seen the bruises on her face and arms. Some might think he meant only to scare me into obedience with the gunshots, but I knew his real intention.

He'd tried to kill me and the babe I carried.

My eyelids felt heavy, and I let them close. My mind, however, kept whirling.

I couldn't remember how far I'd run after Pa shot me, but I hoped this cabin was miles from him. I needed a few days to lay low and let my shoulder mend; then I'd be on my way. Where I'd go, I didn't know, but I couldn't stay here. My presence put these kindly women in danger.

A flutter in my belly reminded me I wasn't just responsible for myself anymore.

"I'll keep you safe, little one," I whispered and placed my hand where my body hid Amos's child. "I promise."

Sometime later I woke to find Bertie sitting next to the cot. "I've some broth for you, dear." With care, she eased a second pillow beneath my head, then spooned thin liquid into my mouth.

We both remained quiet until the bowl was empty.

"If you feel up to it, I'll help you use the chamber pot," Bertie said. At my surprised reaction, she chuckled. "With five sisters and many years of being a midwife, I'm long past the point of embarrassment over normal bodily functions."

Once I was settled beneath the covers again, I cast a curious glance around the room. "Your cabin is bigger than ours. Got lots more things in it, too."

Hewn log walls were covered with newspaper, pages from magazines, letters, calendars, family pictures, and greeting cards, creating a colorful and homey hodgepodge. In addition to the pasted-on wall decor, hooks and nails held framed pictures, dried herbs, yarn, thread, baskets, coats, hats, and even a pair of men's overalls.

"Our papa built the cabin and just about everything inside, too," Bertie said, her pride in her father's craftsmanship obvious.

Handmade chairs, two spinning wheels, chests, a faded sofa, bookshelves loaded with worn volumes, and a large stone fireplace that surely kept things toasty during cold weather made up the room. It was a fine and comfortable home. The kind I dreamed Amos and me would share one day.

My gaze landed on Bertie again, curiosity getting the better of me. "How come you and your sisters live together? Ain't you got husbands and children?"

"This has always been our home," Bertie said. "We five sisters chose to remain here, together, although one of our sisters did marry and move away, as did our brothers. They have homes and farms nearby, and our nieces and nephews visit and keep us company."

"Your family sounds real nice. I got lots of brothers too." Sadness crept into my heart, and I looked away. "After Mama passed on, Pa married up with a gal and had more young'uns. She never took to me and my brothers though. The boys eventually run off and left me all alone."

Bertie's face bore her sympathy. "What do they call you, child?" she asked softly.

I considered my answer for a long moment. "Mama liked to call me her little songbird 'cause I was always singin'. Reckon I don't got much to sing about these days."

Bertie reached out and laid a gentle hand on my arm. "Songbird. I think that's lovely. Perhaps sometime you'll bless us with a song. We do enjoy hymns."

A tiny spark came to life inside me. "Mama liked 'em too."

Bertie smiled, seemingly pleased at the small connection we'd made. "You rest now, dear. I'll be near if you need anything."

With a full belly and a safe place to rest, I drifted to sleep on a cloud of contentment, the likes of which I hadn't known in years.

⚞

For long minutes, Bertie studied the pale features, wondering how a father could be so cruel as to want to hurt his child and grand-child. She'd delivered plenty of mountain babies to unmarried girls, so Bertie doubted it was a matter of shame on the father's part. From the brief story the girl shared, it sounded as though her pa had darker issues that drove him to commit such a ghastly deed.

Low voices met her when she entered the kitchen and found her sisters gathered around the worn worktable.

Jennie waved Bertie to an empty seat. "We need to alert the sheriff, Sister. If what the girl says is true, her pa should be in jail."

The other women nodded in agreement, but Bertie frowned. "I understand what you're sayin', but think of what'll happen to the girl. She'll be taken back to her family, who may or may not welcome her. Then she'll have to appear in court in the city and testify against her own pa, not to mention the disgrace of everyone knowin' her indiscretion."

Bertie glanced toward the other room, although the cot was not in her line of vision. "We know nothin' about her or who the father of her babe is. There's more to the story, I 'spect." She faced her sisters again. "But I believe the Lord brought her here for protection, Sisters. If we alert the sheriff, we may be puttin' her in even greater danger."

Jennie scowled but, after a bit of thought, gave a slow nod. "You might be right. Till we learn who she is and more about her family situation, it may be best if she stays here."

Bertie glanced around the table at her other sisters. "I s'pose we should vote on it, being that we could be puttin' ourselves in danger by allowin' her to stay." Their habit of voting on important decisions had saved them from many arguments over the years.

"All for keepin' the girl here, at least until we find out more about her, raise your hand."

Five hands went up.

"But," Jennie said, a grave look on her face, "if her kin come lookin' for her, there's naught else to do but let 'em take her away. It may sound selfish, but I won't sacrifice our safety for hers."

Bertie didn't like it, but she kept her thoughts to herself and returned to the sickroom.

The girl slept peacefully. If all went well and they staved off infection, it wouldn't be long before she was up and about.

Bertie's gaze drifted to the rounded bump.

The young mother would need a good midwife to help bring her child safely into the world.

Ramsey Alister's thoughtless words about Bertie being too old to midwife resurfaced.

Am I?

The silent question sprang from nowhere, taking her by surprise. It was the first time uncertainty crept in, crowding out the confidence she'd had since Mam allowed her to witness the miracle of birth. From that day forward, Bertie'd never experienced a moment of doubt that being a midwife was her God-given gift.

Until now.

Frustrated, she bowed her head. "Lord," she whispered, "I don't know why you brought this wounded lamb to us, but I 'spect it'll take more than a simple bandage and broth to help her heal. Give us wisdom, Father. Help us—help me—know what to do."

Whether the Almighty whispered the thought into her heart, or she came up with it on her own, Bertie suddenly knew what they needed to do. With a last look at the sleeping girl, she marched into the kitchen with determined steps. Jennie and Rubie sat at the table peeling turnips and carrots for stew. Both looked up at Bertie's bold entrance.

"You've got that look in your eyes, Alberta Mae." Jennie laid her paring knife and a half-peeled turnip aside. "I'm not going to like what you're fixin' to say, am I?"

"No, you're not, but I know I'm right to say it."

The two sisters seated at the table waited.

Bertie took a deep breath. "I believe Songbird should stay with us as long as she needs a home." Her chin rose. "And *I* intend to deliver her child."

Five

A COLD RAIN PELTED THE WINDSHIELD of Reese's VW Beetle as she neared home after a long day. She'd been to the hippie commune to check on Linda and the baby, who were both doing well, then drove an hour, deep into the mountains, to call on Hettie, a mother expecting her ninth child. The woman declared she could give birth in her sleep, but Reese was concerned. The baby appeared larger than it should with two months remaining, if her calculations were correct. She'd ruled out twins, and although Hettie had no history of gestational diabetes, it often affected older pregnant women. Reese would need to keep a careful eye on things. If the baby grew too large, it could require surgical delivery in a hospital, not in a primitive cabin deep in the Appalachians.

A long, black limousine sat in the street in front of Reese's cottage when she arrived home. No patients were scheduled that afternoon, nor could she imagine who would arrive in such an extravagant vehicle. Pulling her Beetle into the gravel driveway that separated her small house from Kathy's, Reese cut the engine and made a mad dash for the covered porch, chastising herself for forgetting her umbrella.

Oreo barked from the opposite side of the front door, eager to be let outside. He'd be a muddy mess if she didn't snag him before he ran out into the rain.

She'd just slid the key into the lock when the rear passenger door to the limo opened. A black umbrella popped open, followed by a man with a short beard, wearing casual business attire. A second man remained inside the car. When Reese briefly made eye contact with him, he slammed the door closed. Oddly, he looked familiar.

"Miss Chandler?" The bearded man dodged a puddle on the uneven sidewalk that led to her porch.

"Yes?"

Oreo's barking grew louder at the sound of a stranger's voice.

"I'm Ray Nelson. We spoke on the telephone last Friday about my client's adoption back in the forties."

Confusion spun through Reese's mind. "Mr. Nelson, I don't understand. Did you contact Bill McClain?"

"Yes, we did. And as you predicted, he didn't offer much hope of finding more information about my client's birth than what we already know."

Reese kept her hand on the doorknob, ready to release Oreo should she feel the least bit threatened. Although the man seemed harmless, the fact that he'd come to Piney Ridge—a five-hour drive from Nashville—despite her insistence that she couldn't help him made her cautious. "May I ask why you're here? If Bill doesn't believe he can help you, I'm sure I can't."

Mr. Nelson glanced back to the limo. When he faced her again, his expression took on a look of desperation. "Miss Chandler, I know it's a shot in the dark, but my client's had a hard time of it since he learned about his adoption. It's like he doesn't know who he is anymore. Couldn't you at least meet with him? Hear his story or at least what we know of it?"

His words dislodged a memory from long ago.

The meanest girl in junior high somehow discovered Reese was adopted and confronted her in the cafeteria as the entire student body looked on.

"I heard those old people you live with aren't your real parents. I heard you don't even know who your mom is and that your dad is probably some horrible criminal, locked up in prison." She sneered and looked at Reese as though she were something the girl had scraped off the bottom of her shoe. "No wonder you're so ugly and weird." Laughter from the other children followed Reese as she fled to the bathroom and cried her heart out.

Although she wasn't the biological child of Wilburn and Ethel Chandler, Reese had always been their daughter. Yet the cruel words of a thoughtless girl plunged Reese into a tailspin of depression and self-doubt. Only time and the steadfast love of God and her parents set her feet on solid ground again.

She stole a peek at the limo and remembered her prayer for the man inside. Whoever he was, he deserved the same kind of support Reese had received from her family and friends. She didn't know anything about his situation, and she had serious doubts about being helpful, but she could lend a listening ear and maybe offer some words of encouragement.

"All right, Mr. Nelson. I'll meet with your client. I still don't believe I can help him find information about his adoption, but I can listen to his story."

Mr. Nelson blew out a breath. "Man, that's a relief. I didn't want to have to get back in that car with bad news."

"May I ask what type of business you're in?"

He hesitated. "I . . . manage things for people."

The vague answer annoyed Reese, but she didn't pursue the subject. "You and your client are welcome to come inside."

"Thank you, Miss Chandler. We both appreciate it." Mr. Nelson jogged back to the car through the steady rain that seemed in no hurry to let up.

When he reached the vehicle, the tinted rear window opened just enough for Mr. Nelson to speak to the occupant. Reese couldn't hear the conversation as he gestured toward her. After a long moment, the mysterious client emerged from the car wearing bell-bottom jeans, a wrinkled T-shirt, and an Atlanta Braves ball cap pulled low on his forehead, hiding his eyes. Although the client had at least two inches on him, Mr. Nelson held the umbrella over the man as they came toward her.

She turned and opened her front door. In the next second, Oreo bounded out, greeting the visitors with a ferocious bark and bared teeth. Before she could issue a command, the dog flew down the steps toward the men, who'd stopped halfway to the house.

"Oreo, heel," she called.

He didn't.

Instead, he danced around the rain-soaked yard, barking, growling, and barking some more.

"Oreo, heel."

The dog glanced her way.

"Come here, *now*." She snapped her fingers and pointed to her side.

With one last bark at the men, the dog ran to Reese. His tongue lolled and tail wagged as if nothing out of the ordinary had just occurred.

"Sit. Stay," she said once he settled next to her. She glanced back to the men. "I'm sorry. He's very friendly, I promise."

The mysterious client muttered something to his manager before they continued up the walkway and mounted the steps. Yet before Reese could invite them inside, Oreo darted over to the stranger, stood on his hind legs, and plunked his muddy, soaked paws right in the middle of the man's chest.

"Oreo, down!" Reese shouted, mortified.

When Oreo was once again beside her, she grabbed hold of his collar through wet fur and faced the man. Two perfect paw prints adorned his chest, with a trail of smudged mud beneath.

"I'm so sorry. He's usually much better behaved."

The bill of the ball cap lifted as the man's gaze went from his muddy shirt to Reese. It took only a moment for her mouth to gape in stunned recognition.

"Miss Chandler, may I introduce Walker Wylie?" Mr. Nelson appeared amused at her starstruck silence. "Walker, this is Reese Chandler."

Mr. Wylie held out his hand. When Reese didn't move to shake it, his left eyebrow quirked.

"Oh . . . sorry," she stuttered. She gave his hand a quick, awkward shake. "I . . . it's . . . a pleasure to meet you."

She tried to pull her gaze away, aware that staring was incredibly rude and immature, but—

Walker Wylie was standing on her porch, for crying out loud!

The famous singer was taller than pictures in the Hollywood gossip magazines led one to believe. Of course, everything she knew about the man came from paid rumormongers. After his song "Moonlight in Tennessee" hit number one on the country music charts several years ago, he shot to stardom. According to the weeklies Kathy bought at the grocery store, the singer had been romantically linked to several starlets, including Vanessa Gibson, the leading lady in the blockbuster movie *Love on the Cumberland*. The two had been photographed around Nashville while the movie was being filmed.

Oreo whined and tried to work himself free of her grasp, forcing her to come out of her ridiculous daze.

"Please, come in."

She led the way inside but didn't stop in her tiny living room.

"Make yourselves comfortable," she said over her shoulder. "I'll put Oreo in the bathroom and be right back."

Once the dog was settled on the bath mat, she washed her hands and tried to compose herself. Finding the handsome bachelor on her porch rattled her. Even though the men weren't clients of her clinic, she needed to act like the professional woman she was, not a starry-eyed teenager.

She returned to the front room to find the men standing in the middle of the small space, their size making it appear even teenier. She didn't look at Walker. "Can I get either of you something to drink? Coffee? Coca-Cola?"

Mr. Nelson glanced at Walker, who shook his head. "No thank you, Miss Chandler," he answered for them both. "If it's okay with you, we'd like to get down to business."

"Of course."

Reese settled in an overstuffed chair that had once belonged to her grandmother. She motioned the men to the sofa, where they sat on the edge, looking out of place on the floral-printed fabric. She'd unapologetically decorated the room with pregnant women in mind, with soft pastel colors and feminine touches throughout.

An uncomfortable silence fell over them. Neither man seemed inclined to initiate the sensitive conversation, leaving Reese to rack her brain for how to begin.

"So, Mr. Wylie." She met his guarded eyes. It was quite surreal to find the singer, whom she'd seen on the cover of several magazines, in her living room in tiny Piney Ridge, Tennessee. Kathy would flip out when Reese told her about it later. "Mr. Nelson tells me you've recently learned you were adopted."

The man's jaw, darkened with several days' worth of stubble, clenched. "Yes."

The single word told Reese two things: Mr. Wylie hadn't yet

come to terms with the circumstances surrounding his birth, and he wasn't happy about sharing the personal details with a stranger.

"I'm sure Bill McClain explained that adoption records in Tennessee are sealed," she said, keeping to the nonemotional facts of the case.

"He did. What I want to know is, what can you do to help me?"

"Mr. Wylie, as I told Mr. Nelson, I'm not convinced I *can* help you. Without the court's permission to view the adoption records, it's not possible to obtain the information you're looking for. And unfortunately, gaining permission from the court is incredibly difficult. There must be extenuating circumstances that go beyond mere curiosity to convince a judge to open them."

Walker shook his head, his frustration evident. "That's nuts. All I want is information about my own birth. The article said you were an adoption advocate. I need an advocate, Miss Chandler."

Reese met his intense gaze, seeing not the famous singer but a fellow adoptee. "I wish there was something I could do to help you, but the laws make it difficult. Maybe your parents could—"

He didn't wait for her to finish. "I see we made a mistake coming here." He stood and moved toward the door.

Reese and Mr. Nelson rose simultaneously.

"Walker, wait," Mr. Nelson said. "It isn't Miss Chandler's fault the law doesn't allow adoptees to search their adoption records. Let's not give up just yet."

The manager glanced back to Reese. His eyes implored her to say something, anything.

Reese understood the helplessness Walker surely must feel. Even though locating his birth records was beyond her power, there *was* something she could offer.

"This may come as a surprise, Mr. Wylie, but I know how you feel."

His eyes met hers across the small room. "I doubt that."

"I'm adopted too."

A look of surprise flashed across his face before he schooled it.

"I know what it is to stare into the mirror and wonder who I look like. To question why this happened to me. To feel unwanted."

She needed him to know he wasn't alone, even if it felt that way.

"I do understand the meaning of the word *advocate*," she said, "but being an advocate doesn't mean solving every problem or situation that's presented. It means standing in your corner with you, cheering for you or crying with you. It means offering every bit of compassion and wisdom I possess to help you along your adoption journey." She gave a small shrug. "I can't make any promises, but if you'd like to tell me your story, I'm willing to listen."

Oreo barked from down the hallway, the only sound in the house. Reese waited for Walker's answer, refusing to break eye contact despite the feeling of being in over her head.

Finally his stiff shoulders dropped, and he nodded. "All right."

Reese retook her seat while the men returned to the sofa. A dozen questions came to mind, yet most of them were too personal to begin with.

How did he learn of his adoption?

Who were his adoptive parents?

Why had they kept the secret from him?

She doubted the singer was ready to share those details. "May I ask what information you have regarding your adoption?"

He and Mr. Nelson exchanged a look before he nodded to his manager, who produced a piece of paper from his pocket and handed it to Reese.

"The man who arranged my adoption gave this to my mother."

Reese glanced at the brief handwritten note, yellowed by the years.

Baby Boy was born October 27, 1943, in Sevier County, Tennessee. He's healthy, eats well, and isn't fussy. Take good care of him.

God bless you.
Bertie Jenkins, midwife

Reese looked up. "This is all you have?"

Walker shrugged. "My mom has some baby clothes and a blanket that looks handmade, but that's it. The thing is, my birthday is in February, not October. That makes me think this note isn't legitimate."

"Your adoption wasn't handled by an agency?" Reese asked.

He scoffed. "A preacher from East Tennessee handed me off to my parents. That's the entirety of my pathetic tale. Who knows if anything they were told about me is true."

Reese heard bitterness in his voice. He had a right to feel confused and even angry, but didn't he understand there was much more to the story?

A woman carried him in her womb for nine months, went through the birthing process, then gave him up for reasons unknown. She'd chosen life for her child, and that was a gift, whether he saw it as such or not.

Yes, there was far more to the story than what a simple, handwritten note could tell.

"Did your adoptive parents know the preacher?"

Walker studied her for a long moment before answering. "No. He was the cousin of our longtime pastor, but he died several years ago. There's no way to get answers from him unless you're willing to host a séance."

She let the sarcastic comment slide and looked back to the note. "Bertie Jenkins, midwife." She drummed her fingers on the arm of the chair, sorting through the scarce information revealed in the brief missive. "Most midwives back then weren't medical professionals. Many of them learned the skill from their mothers and grandmothers. But . . ." She paused as an idea began to form.

"But what?" Walker leaned forward, genuine interest in his eyes for the first time since their conversation began.

"But even mountain people need birth certificates for their children, whether they were born at home or in a hospital."

"You read the note. It says *Baby Boy*. I didn't even have a name until my parents gave me one. Which means I don't have a birth certificate." He shook his head with frustration. "Another dead end."

"Not necessarily." Reese hoped he'd find her next words encouraging. "You may not have a birth certificate, but other mountain children do. It's highly likely Bertie Jenkins attended the births of other babies, which means her name will be listed as midwife."

She waited for a spark of hope to appear in his eyes, but it didn't come.

"And how many births have taken place in Sevier County over the past thirty years? Hundreds? Thousands?" He looked at Reese as though she'd grown a second nose. "Are you suggesting I search thousands of birth records, looking for the name of some mystery midwife? Do you know how long that would take?"

Reese shrugged. "It won't be easy, but if we find the midwife, it could lead us to the information you seek. Besides, it's the only option we have at this point."

"We?"

His eyes narrowed. She hoped he didn't think she was trying to create an opportunity to be with him because of his stardom.

"It's the only option *you* have at this point."

Mr. Nelson, who'd remained silent while listening to the exchange, gave a slow nod. "It's worth a shot, Walker." He turned to Reese. "Will you help us?"

Before she could respond, Walker scowled. "Wait just a minute. I'm not digging through endless files looking for something
we aren't even certain is there. It's a waste of time."

Reese waited for the manager to remind Walker this was *his*
life and *his* adoption they were discussing. Didn't that warrant a
little elbow grease and some of his precious time? There weren't
any guarantees they'd find information about the midwife, but
wouldn't he want to exhaust every avenue, every lead?

Mr. Nelson took out a small pocket calendar and perused it.
"I've got a couple meetings I can't miss tomorrow, but I could
probably free up the rest of the week." He returned his attention
to Reese and offered a charming smile. "How about it? You and I
can drive down to the courthouse day after tomorrow and see what
we can find." He glanced at Walker, who briefly inclined his head;
then Mr. Nelson returned his attention to her. "We're prepared to
offer you a generous fee for your assistance."

Unbelievable.

Did he really think money solved everything?

Reese crossed her arms, her gaze going from Mr. Nelson to
Walker. "Let me understand this. You're too busy to search for
information about *your* adoption? I thought it was important to
you since you showed up on my doorstep. I see I was wrong. It's
you who's wasted *my* time, Mr. Wylie."

Mr. Nelson started to speak, but Walker waved him silent,
his eyes on Reese again. "You know nothing about my life, Miss
Chandler, so don't presume to judge me based on a few minutes of
conversation. Why does it matter who sorts through the mounds
of information? The results will still be the same."

He asked a good question.

Reese thought back to the day the girl in junior high school
ridiculed her, and the shame and helplessness that engulfed her
afterward. She'd gone to Mom and demanded to know everything

about her birth and adoption. While the information wasn't what she'd expected, knowing it had given her a sense of control she hadn't had before. Never again would she allow anyone to use her adoption to make her feel unwanted or unloved.

"It does matter, Mr. Wylie." Reese let her arms and her irritation drop, convinced Walker needed to come to the same conclusion she had all those years ago. "Up until this moment, you've had no say in how the details of your birth and adoption were handled. Your birth parents. Your adoptive parents. Even a mountain preacher and midwife. Each of them made decisions about what information you were given and what information was withheld." She handed the yellowed note back to him. "Now you're the one in the driver's seat. Searching through the records may seem like a trivial task, but I see it as you finally being able to *do* something yourself. Whether you find what you're looking for or not, the important thing is you'd be the one in charge."

Walker continued to stare at her, his hard expression unchanged. Just when Reese began to regret her impassioned speech, his tense muscles eased.

"I see your point." He blew out a breath. "And you're right. Everyone involved had information about my birth, but no one bothered to share it with me."

"I don't know your family, Mr. Wylie," Reese said, "but most adoptive parents withhold information with the best of intentions. They think an adopted child won't feel accepted and loved if the truth is revealed. Or they worry about how others will treat the child. I've found, though, that honesty is best in the long run."

Walker nodded. "So how's this going to work? Are you willing to help me? I won't hold it against you if you aren't interested."

Reese weighed her decision in the silent moment that followed his request. Although he'd acted like a jerk during their brief meeting, she believed it had more to do with his circumstances than his normal personality. She also felt a sense of responsibility, being that it was her idea to search through the vital records.

Decision made, she stuck out her hand. "All right, Mr. Wylie. None of my expectant mothers are due for several weeks, so I'm free the next couple days. We can take my car over to Sevier County tomorrow if that works for you."

Walker reached to shake Reese's hand, but Mr. Nelson waved his calendar in the air between them.

"Nope, that won't work. I've got a meeting in Nashville tomorrow I can't miss. Then we're getting close to the weekend and the courthouse will be closed. How about next week? Say, Tuesday? We'll pick you up in the limo and ride down in comfort."

Reese stole a look at Walker, who seemed to have no objection to his manager's plan. She, on the other hand, did.

"I don't mean to be rude, Mr. Nelson, but you aren't invited. Mr. Wylie must do this himself."

Both men seemed taken aback by her statement.

"Now wait just a minute—" Mr. Nelson began, only to be stopped by Walker.

"She's right, Ray. I need to do this." He put his hand on his manager's shoulder. "Besides, you've got to get back to the city. I threw my overnight bag in the car, just in case."

Mr. Nelson's frown remained in place. "I'm not sure I like this idea. I wouldn't want the press to get wind of anything. What if someone recognizes you and figures out what's going on? It'll be in all the headlines by Sunday: 'Walker Wylie and Mysterious Female Friend Uncover Truth about Wylie's Secret Adoption.'"

Reese nearly laughed at Mr. Nelson's melodrama. "I don't think you need to worry. No offense, but it's doubtful anyone will know who he is. Mountain people listen to country music, but they don't pay a lot of attention to Nashville gossip."

"You recognized me," Walker said, his gaze intense.

Heat filled Reese's face, but she didn't look away. "My neighbor likes to read that type of stuff. She gives me her old magazines for the waiting room. I admit I've seen some stories about you, but I don't believe everything I read."

Walker eyed her as though judging to see if she was sincere or not.

"Good to know," he finally said.

It seemed she'd passed the test.

Six

I GAINED STRENGTH WITH EACH NEW DAY.

Bertie smiled when she found me sitting in the rocking chair beside the cot four days after bringing me into the Jenkins cabin.

She handed me a bowl of warm porridge. "Maybe you'd like to spend some time on the porch today. It's already gettin' warm outside, but it's nice in the shade."

"Thank y'all for bein' so kind, Miss Bertie. I 'spect me and my baby woulda died out yonder if you hadn't helped me. It reminds me of a story Mama used to tell us. Somethin' 'bout a Good Samaritan."

Bertie sat on the edge of the cot. "I've always liked that story too. Jesus told it to his disciples. A Jewish man went on a trip, walking from Jerusalem to Jericho, but robbers attacked him and left him half-dead on the side of the road."

I shuddered, thinking of how close to death I'd come. Only it wasn't robbers who'd hurt me. It was my own pa.

"Several people passed by, but none stopped to offer help. Finally a Samaritan—that is, a man from Samaria—saw the injured fella and had compassion for him."

"Why didn't the others stop?"

Bertie shrugged. "Maybe they were scared. Maybe they thought

53

they were too important, or they just didn't care about helping a stranger. But Jesus surprised his listeners when he said a Samaritan stopped to help."

"Why's that?"

"Because folks from Samaria were the enemies of folks who were Jewish. Jesus told his followers this tale to remind them we're to love all people, even those we consider our enemies."

I pondered the story while Bertie changed the sheets on the cot.

I never thought I'd consider my own pa the enemy, but the fact that he'd shot me, his flesh-and-blood daughter, revealed a truth about him I'd ignored for far too long.

Mama hadn't been gone much more than a month when he married Vera, a widow with three young'uns. Her dislike for Mama's children seemed to fuel Pa's indifference and meanness toward us. My brothers were old enough to hightail it out of there, but I was only ten years old. I'd felt scared and abandoned when they wouldn't take me with them. Pa made me cook and clean and take care of Vera's kids while she practiced her spells and made potions for folks who came to the house. When she was unhappy with my efforts, I'd feel Pa's wrath. I blamed myself at first and would try harder to please Vera, but it never worked.

After I finished the porridge, Bertie helped me to the outhouse, then settled me on the porch in a rocker. She sat on the bench against the wall and told me stories about growing up on the homestead. Some were so funny I couldn't help but laugh.

Jennie came through the open kitchen doorway a little later, a scowl on her face. Her glance went from me to Bertie. "I'll feed the chickens and fetch the eggs while you sit here in the shade and enjoy yourselves."

She snatched up the egg basket, stomped down the rock steps, and headed toward the chicken coop near the barn.

I looked at Bertie, feeling responsible for her sister's anger. "I'm sorry to cause ya trouble. I'll be fine if there's things you need to tend."

Bertie, however, didn't seem bothered. "Don't concern yourself with Jennie's bluster. Amelie volunteered to take over my share of chores while I saw to your wound. Now that you're feelin' better, I 'spect I don't need to stay as close to the house."

She appeared sincere in her declaration, yet I couldn't help but worry my presence caused a disruption to the sisters' lives. Just yesterday they'd been in a panic when their brother Tom arrived unannounced, bringing several pounds of fresh venison to be made into sausage. Jennie, Bonnie, and Rubie kept him on the porch while Bertie and Amelie hid me beneath a quilt and pillows. Thankfully, he didn't linger and soon left, but I was drenched with sweat when they uncovered me.

"Y'all have been so kind," I said, sadness creeping over me at what I knew had to be done. "But I best be on my way tomorrow. I don't wanna overstay my welcome."

Bertie frowned. "Your wound isn't healed yet, dear, and we don't want to take any chances with infection. Besides," she said, glancing around as though to make sure we were alone, "I believe the Lord brought you here. I believe you're meant to stay with us till the baby comes. Maybe even after."

Her words took me by surprise. "You really think the Lord brung me here, Miss Bertie?" I looked toward the chicken coop. "I ain't too sure Miss Jennie would like it much if I was to stay. She ain't never got a smile when she looks at me."

Bertie chuckled. "My eldest sister ain't never got a smile when she looks at me either."

After a shared laugh, Bertie sobered. "Jennie's scared your kin'll come lookin' for you. She's the oldest, so she feels responsible for us, even though we're well in our years." Her eyes softened as she met my gaze. "Can you tell me what happened, child? If I knew more about your situation, I might be able to convince my sister to let you and your babe remain here as long as you need a home."

The last few days were the first time since Mama's passing that I'd felt loved and cared for. I didn't want to leave. Would telling them the truth, like Bertie said, change Jennie's mind?

"We lived over in North Carolina mostly," I began, ashamed of the things I'd have to confess. "Pa, he's a moonshiner. Them revenuers been after him a long time, but he al'ays manages to stay one step ahead of 'em. Come winter, he says we got to move to Tennessee, where the revenuers don't know him. I didn't wanna go, 'cuz I had me a beau, Amos. Pa never cared much for Amos. Said he was good-for-nothin', but that ain't true." I shrugged and looked away. "I wanted Amos to know I loved him before I left, so we coupled. Didn't never think we'd make a baby, but sure 'nough, we did."

I ran a hand over my belly. "After I missed my monthly two times in a row, I figured I's in the family way. I wrote a letter to Amos tellin' him he's gonna be a pa and that he should come get me. His ma wrote back and said Amos joined the Army and got sent to Europe. She said he wasn't my baby's pa anyhow and that I shouldn't write to him anymore." My lips trembled when I met Bertie's gaze. "Pa's wife found the letter and told him I's in the family way. Said if I'd drink a potion she fixed, wouldn't be no more baby. Pa says do it or he'd make me sorry." Tears slid down my cheeks. "But I wouldn't drink it. I couldn't kill mine and Amos's baby."

Bertie clutched at her heart, as if it hurt after hearing the sad tale. She took a hankie from her pocket and handed it to me. "You done a good thing, child. God formed that babe in your womb. I've seen enough young'uns come into this world to know that every one of 'em is a miracle."

I used the hankie to wipe my nose. "Pa said if I didn't get rid of the baby, he'd do it himself. I almost made it to the woods when I heard the shots, but I just kept runnin'. Didn't know I'd been hit till I stopped to catch my breath. Figured I'd just keep goin' till I dropped dead."

"Our place isn't easy to find," Bertie said. "I'm more convinced than ever God brought you to us. It sounds as if you were led here."

"Why would God help me, Miss Bertie?" I asked, wishing her words were true, but the guilt inside told me they weren't. "Me 'n' Amos sinned when we made this baby. Seems to me God's angry with me, like Pa."

Bertie took my hand. "Dear one, God isn't anything like your pa. He loves us, even when we do wrong. Instead of punishin' us, he forgives us. All we have to do is ask."

Our conversation came to an end when Jennie and Bonnie walked toward the house. Bertie followed them into the kitchen, leaving me on the porch alone. Her words, however, circled my mind like a hawk hunting prey, honing in on an astonishing thought.

Did God really care about me enough to bring me to the Jenkins cabin?

It seemed impossible and yet . . .

With everything inside me, I hoped Bertie would be able to convince her sisters to let me stay.

❧

Songbird volunteered to help sort beans using her good arm, hoping to prove herself useful. When Jennie found her there a short time later, Bertie noticed her sister's narrowed gaze on Songbird. No doubt Jennie viewed the bit of progress as one day closer to the girl's exodus from their home.

Sure enough, early the next morning, Jennie called the sisters down to the springhouse while Songbird slept inside the cabin.

"Sisters, I believe it's time to send Songbird on." She gave a firm nod. When Bertie opened her mouth to argue, Jennie raised a hand. "Hear me out, Alberta Mae. Brother Tom can take her to Sevierville in his car, where she can buy a train ticket to Knoxville. We'll give her money for a boardin'house till she can find work. We've done our Christian duty by takin' her in and mendin' her, but it'd be foolhardy to 'llow her to stay any longer."

Bertie glanced around the circle of women to see if her other sisters agreed with the woefully inadequate plan. When no one spoke up, she took that as a good sign.

"Sister, I understand you want to keep us safe," she said, gaining nods of agreement from the others, "but what kind of work do you reckon a pregnant teenager can find? Songbird is a child herself. She needs lookin' after, especially as the babe grows. Who'd be there to help when she goes into labor? How will she work and care for a baby?"

Jennie scowled. "I don't see how that's our problem. We've done our duty. It's time she moved on."

Bertie pressed her lips tight, lest she say something she'd regret about Jennie's *Christian* duty.

Rubie bowed her head. Amelie and Bonnie cast cautious glances between their older sister and Bertie, neither giving indication of which argument they agreed with.

After a handful of tense seconds, Jennie crossed her arms. "Well, Sisters?" she said in the authoritative tone Bertie had heard her whole life. The tone that brooked no arguments. "Are we settled? Do we ask Tom to come get the girl tomorrow?"

"I believe we should vote on it."

Rubie's sweet, soft voice surprised them all. Their youngest sister seldom spoke up when disagreements arose between the siblings, but when she did, it was always with thoughtfulness and wisdom.

"I agree," Bertie said. "I'll abide by whatever we decide, even though I'm convinced God brought Songbird to us."

Jennie's lips disappeared, revealing her ire. "That girl ain't a stray critter who needs lookin' after. She's got kin. Maybe has folks who'd help with the babe. We don't even know her real name. 'Sides, she got herself into this predicament by fornicatin' with a man. It ain't right to bring that kind of woman into Papa's home."

Her sister's judgmental attitude rankled Bertie. "Sister, if I recall, when the Pharisees and teachers of the law brought a woman who'd been caught in adultery to Jesus, he said, 'He that is without sin among you, let him first cast a stone at her.'"

Bonnie's eyes widened, and she gave Bertie a look of warning. Jennie prided herself on being the family member who read aloud from the Bible each morning, often sharing her thoughts on the passage as Papa'd done throughout their lives. If any of them knew the Scriptures, it was Jennie. But readin' 'em and livin' 'em out was the crux of the issue at hand, wasn't it?

"Let us vote, Sisters," Rubie interjected before things escalated. "May the Lord direct each of our hearts."

"Very well." Jennie's jaw clenched. "All in favor of sendin' the girl on . . ." Her hand shot up.

Bertie held her breath and glanced about the circle to see which of her sisters agreed. No other hands were raised. "All for lettin' Songbird stay."

She squelched the urge to gloat when three hands joined hers in the air, albeit the others were raised rather hesitantly.

Jennie's face turned red. Their older sister never took kindly to being outvoted. "We'll be sorry, mark my words. If that pa o' hers hears she's hidin' here, there ain't no tellin' what trouble he might bring to our home. It'll be on your heads if we end up shot." With that, she stormed back to the house.

Bertie watched until Jennie was out of hearing, then turned to her sisters. "Many thanks for voting with me."

"She's right, Bertie." Bonnie made eye contact with each sister. As second oldest, she often acted as bossy as Jennie. "I voted to let Songbird stay on 'cause we can't turn the poor child out. But we don't know nothin' 'bout that girl or her kin. Best we stay cautious."

The sisters agreed.

Bonnie and Amelie made their way back to the house, although their slow gait indicated they were in no hurry to get there. They knew as well as Bertie that Jennie's displeasure would be on full display for days. As Papa used to say when Mam was in a dither: "The coop ain't no place to be when the hen's got her feathers up." He'd hightail it to the hills with his gun until things calmed down. Bertie wished she could do the same.

"I'm glad Songbird's stayin'. She's a sweet thing."

Rubie's voice drew Bertie back to the present. "She told me some 'bout her people and how she ended up here. It's a sad tale, Sister. She's got no place to go. No one to care for her and the babe."

A soft smile lifted Rubie's mouth. "'Twill be nice to have a baby in the house again. Catie's girl Hannah was the last babe born into the family, and she's nigh on twelve years old. I hope it's a boy, though. Caleb always talked 'bout havin' a son."

A faint alarm sounded in Bertie's head as she watched Rubie follow their sisters' footsteps to the cabin.

Had she acted too hastily insisting that Songbird stay on?

She'd only been thinking of the girl's well-being.

Yet, if she was honest, her desire to tend the birth and prove Ramsey Alister wrong played a role in it too. A selfish role, at that.

It hadn't occurred to her until this very moment that dangers that had nothing to do with the girl's angry pa came with allowing Songbird to stay. Bertie and her sisters, Rubie especially, could become emotionally attached to the baby once it arrived. What would happen if the young mother decided to leave or found someone to marry?

The Jenkins sisters would be heartbroken, that's what.

But hadn't God orchestrated this whole thing? Hadn't he sent Songbird to them? Not just to mend her body but possibly her soul?

"Lord," Bertie whispered. Some of the satisfaction of being victorious over Jennie seeped from her as she too began a slow trek to the house. "I can't see into the future and how this is gonna work out, but I trust you. Give me grace to trust you more."

Seven

WALKER AWAKENED WITH A JOLT. Remnants of the all-too-familiar nightmare lingered as he opened his eyes to a bright but strange room.

Where was he? Hollywood? New York City?

One glance at the outdated furnishings in the tiny space convinced him neither guess was correct.

He blinked once, twice, three times before his brain kicked in.

He wasn't crisscrossing the country promoting his new album. He was in a run-down motel room that reeked of mildew in backwoods Piney Ridge, Tennessee, about to embark on a crazy search for the woman who'd given birth to him.

The recollection didn't bring relief.

Walker closed his eyes.

He'd lain awake until the wee hours of the morning while questions swirled like a hurricane.

Was this whole thing a huge mistake? Did he really want to dredge up long-forgotten details about his birth? Obviously his biological parents hadn't wanted him. Why then did he have this deep-seated need to unearth information about them?

He blew out a breath.

He wished he could talk to Mom about all of this. They'd always had a special bond, even during his teenage years. But she seemed like a stranger to him right now. She'd blindsided him with her revelation the day after Pop's funeral.

Memories from that awful conversation came alive in his mind.

"We need to talk, Son," Mom had said from her place at the breakfast table, her face ashen. "I need to tell you something that will come as a great shock. Your father's attorney thinks it's best you know before the will is read."

She'd looked haggard, and Walker was concerned. "This can wait, Mom. You're exhausted. There's nothing you can tell me that changes the most important thing: we're a family. Even with Pop gone, I'll always be here for you. I'll always be Annie and Warren Wylie's son."

Red-rimmed eyes met his then, full of such torment that instinctively Walker had known this wasn't about Pop's death. "But that's just it, Walker. You're not. You're not our son."

Her words had been so unexpected, so ludicrous, Walker could only stare at her. "What are you talking about?" Was she in her right mind? They'd just buried her husband, after all. Had the stress of tending Pop while he was sick and the grief of losing him finally taken its toll? Walker had wondered if he should call Dr. Bergson. Maybe get some sedatives.

"Your dad—your pop—had the mumps as a teenager," she'd said, further confusing Walker by the odd turn in conversation.

"I know, Mom. He was deaf in one ear because of it. That's why he was declared 4-F and couldn't join the military after Pearl Harbor was bombed."

She'd nodded. "Yes, that's true. But deafness wasn't the only complication he suffered." Moisture filled her eyes again. "He couldn't father children."

Walker's mind had tried to process the implications—scandalous implications—of her confession, but nothing made sense. "Are . . . are you saying Pop isn't my father?"

"I'm saying we both wanted children, but we couldn't have them."

In that terrible, silent moment, the world Walker had known for thirty years slipped off its axis. He couldn't speak, couldn't breathe.

"You aren't our biological son," she'd whispered as tears trailed down her face. "We adopted you when you were a baby."

Those words left him reeling. Four months later, he still hadn't come to terms with it all. Grief, anger, and confusion filled his days, and he'd sunk into a dark depression. No one understood what he was going through. Ray tried to be a friend instead of a manager and let Walker work things out in his own time, even if it did wreak havoc on his career. Vanessa was finishing a movie shoot and couldn't attend the funeral, but she'd come to Nashville as soon as she could. She'd been as shocked as he was with the news, but when he didn't bounce back and feel up to their normal social schedule while she was in town, she grew frustrated.

"Really, Walker," she'd said, ruby-red lips in a pretty pout. "What's the big deal? You're still the same person you were before you found out you were adopted."

While her statement was factually correct, her lack of compassion didn't sit well. They'd had a major fight that ended with her leaving town and refusing his calls once she was back in LA.

The sound of a car engine outside the motel window reminded Walker that Reese Chandler would pick him up at nine o'clock. He'd offered to hire a car and driver to take them to Sevier County, but she'd insisted on driving them herself. They'd have more freedom if she took her VW Beetle, she'd said, in case they found information on the mystery midwife and needed to head into the hills.

Walker rubbed his face with both hands and swung his legs

over the edge of the lumpy mattress. If he was going to do this, then he needed to get moving.

The stained carpet felt tacky beneath his bare feet as he made his way to the bathroom. After a lukewarm shower, Walker brushed his teeth and attempted to make himself presentable, although he found he hadn't brought a razor or a comb. It didn't matter. He wasn't out to impress Miss Chandler and, quite honestly, didn't think he could even if he tried. She'd made it clear she wasn't interested in his famous persona. She simply wanted to help a fellow adoptee.

Which, he realized with surprise, made her the one person who did indeed understand how he felt.

With his overnight bag packed and ready, Walker sat on the bed and leaned against the pillows to wait. Unbidden flashes of the nightmare he'd had last night floated across his mind. The same images that had haunted his sleep for weeks. Fragments of scenes, like a movie reel cut into pieces. The only thing he clearly remembered each time was a woman setting a baby down in the middle of the forest and walking away.

Beep, beep.

A glance out the dingy curtain revealed Reese's red Volkswagen idling in the motel parking lot. Walker didn't relish a two-hour drive in the cramped vehicle but, with little choice, grabbed his bag and sunglasses and exited the room.

"Morning," she said when he opened the passenger door.

"Morning," he returned and tossed his bag into the back seat. It only took a second to assess the lack of legroom in the small car. With a sigh, Walker folded up his six-foot-four-inch frame and climbed in.

Reese's eyes widened, with her expression landing somewhere between horror and humor. "I'm sorry," she said, fingers pressed to her lips. "I didn't realize . . . well, you're taller than I remembered."

Walker tugged the door closed, his knees level with his chest.

"And your car is smaller than the insect it's named after." When Reese worried her lip, Walker chuckled. "That was a joke. It's fine. I've been in sports cars that have less legroom than this."

Indecision hovered on her face. "Are you sure? If you still want to hire a car, we can."

Walker declined. "I'm fine, really."

With that settled, they headed for the edge of the small town and were soon enveloped by the Cherokee National Forest. Reese took back roads he'd never been on, seeming to know where she was going. Walker decided to sit back and enjoy the exquisite scenery out his window.

After several miles, he felt more relaxed than he'd been in weeks. "I'd forgotten how beautiful the mountains are in the fall."

"I'd venture to say the mountains hold a unique beauty unto themselves in every season."

He grinned at her reply. "You sound like a poet, Miss Chandler."

She chuckled but kept her attention on the road.

Walker did a surreptitious study of her from the corner of his eye.

Although shapely blondes like Vanessa were more his type, he had to admit the waves of chestnut curls falling past Reese's shoulders looked soft and attractive. Her profile revealed a pert nose and lightly freckled skin surprisingly free of makeup. In the years since his songs topped the music charts and thrust him into the spotlight, Walker had come to understand that Nashville's and Hollywood's glamour girls never allowed themselves to be seen in public without a layer of creams, powders, and whatever else was deemed vital to their appearance. His mom wore makeup, as did most women he knew, but not to the extent that Vanessa and her friends caked on the beauty products. Reese, however, appeared perfectly comfortable—and quite pretty—without any additional help whatsoever.

His observation next went to her wardrobe. Faded bell-bottom jeans, a simple cream-colored turtleneck, and if he wasn't mistaken, hiking boots. Certainly not the outfit Vanessa, or his mother, for that matter, would have chosen for an outing.

"I meant to ask you—" She glanced his way and found his attention focused on her. Surprise widened her eyes, and she quickly looked back to the road.

Walker felt like a junior high boy caught gawking at the high school cheerleaders. Nothing he could do about it now. "Yes?" he said nonchalantly, hoping his sunglasses had concealed his intense gaze.

She didn't turn his way. "I wondered if it would be okay if we made a quick stop. I have a client out this way, and I'd like to check on her before I leave town. It won't take long."

"That's cool with me. I'm in no hurry."

Reese nodded, although Walker sensed her discomfort lingered. He returned to studying the forest out the window. He certainly didn't want her to get the wrong impression. Even though his and Vanessa's relationship wasn't back on track yet, he hoped they could work things out.

Minutes later, Reese slowed the VW and steered off the paved two-lane highway onto a dirt road. They followed it for several miles, a cloud of dust behind them. Farmland and pastures with goats or cattle peeked out from the hollers and valleys they passed, but Walker wasn't prepared when they whizzed by a black buggy pulled by a horse. He swiveled in his seat to get a better look as Reese tapped the horn to give a friendly *beep-beep* along with a wave. The buggy driver—a white-bearded man dressed in black, including a rounded hat—waved in return.

"What was that?" Walker faced forward in his seat again and grimaced when his knees banged into the dash.

Reese grinned. "There's an Amish community not far from

here. I've been called out a couple times to deliver a baby when their own midwife wasn't available. They're nice people."

"Wow." Walker took one last glance behind them, although he could no longer see the buggy out the small rear window. "I had no idea. They're the ones that don't like modern stuff, right? No cars or electricity?"

"It isn't so much that they don't like them." She gave a slight shrug. "If I understand correctly, they feel those things distract from what's most important, which is their faith in God. They can serve him better, in their opinion, by abstaining from worldly inventions like television, radio, and telephones."

Walker pondered the statement. He'd gone to church with his parents as a kid, but after he left home, it wasn't a priority. Life got too busy. He still believed the things he'd been taught about God, but he couldn't remember the last time he'd picked up his Bible or even prayed.

"That makes sense," he said, "but why not automobiles? Driving a buggy seems a bit much, don't you think?"

"Cars carry them away from their loved ones, and family is extremely important to Amish folks. They remove the temptation to travel great distances by using horse-drawn buggies."

Guilt pricked Walker's conscience at her reference to the importance of family.

His relationship with Mom was strained these days. He couldn't get past the feelings of betrayal. On his last visit, she had given him the handwritten note from the midwife and tried to explain why they'd kept his adoption a secret, but Walker hadn't wanted to hear it. Both his parents had deceived him by withholding the truth of his birth from him, and it was going to take time for him to work through his feelings.

Would this trip into the past help or hinder? he wondered.

Reese slowed the car and turned onto a rutted private drive that disappeared into thick vegetation. They passed two small shacks tucked into the trees, both with children playing in the yard. Reese beeped and waved but didn't stop. Instead, their journey ended at an old school bus painted with large, colorful flowers and a big blue peace symbol in the center of it all.

Walker didn't bother to hide his surprise. "This is where your client lives?"

She smiled. "There are twenty or so families sharing this piece of land. Most live in converted buses, although some built small cabins like the ones we passed."

Walker's jaw dropped. "Are you saying this is a *hippie commune*?" He'd seen pictures of communes that existed in California and New York, but to find one here in Tennessee? Crazy!

"It's a community." She paused, her gaze on him. He wasn't certain what he saw, but after a long moment she said, "If you'd rather wait here, I shouldn't be more than ten or fifteen minutes."

She didn't stick around for his response. Reese opened the door, exited the car, and walked to the front of it. There, she opened a compartment where the engine would've been located on any other vehicle. Although Walker would never purchase a Volkswagen Beetle, he did admire the unique design, which included an air-cooled engine in the rear of the car, leaving room in front for storage. The fact that Hitler and his Nazi regime had been instrumental in the design of the "people's car" hadn't prevented thousands of the economical vehicles from being sold in the US.

When Reese emerged from behind the hood, she carried a large pink-and-blue knit shoulder bag. Without a glance at him, she headed for the bus.

Walker drummed his fingers on his knee. He could wait in the car as she suggested, or he could see for himself if the wild stories he'd heard about hippies, communes, and free love were true.

She'd almost made it to the makeshift home when he reached for the door handle.

"Wait up," he called as his stiff legs unfolded.

Reese turned. He couldn't discern the look she gave him, but he continued forward until he stood next to her.

"This is the home of Jean and Patrick. Jean is expecting their third child. She's shown signs of vitamin deficiency, so I've brought her some prenatal vitamins."

As Reese moved to knock on the door, Walker thought of his mom and how she enjoyed volunteering at the Family House. She and Pop opened the halfway house a number of years ago when they heard about people like Jean and Patrick arriving in Nashville with no place to stay. Pop used his real estate connections and got a good deal on a large, aging Victorian mansion not far from downtown. He worked with local businesses and area churches to create a space where families could stay until they found more permanent housing. Food was donated by restaurants and grocery stores, and many of the residents themselves offered to cook, clean, or do yard work to help pay their way. Walker had always called them homeless hippies and hadn't given much thought to the people that arrived there.

The door to the bus opened. A woman far younger than Walker anticipated, considering she was pregnant with her third child, greeted them with a happy smile. Her long, straight hair, tie-dyed bohemian-style dress, and bare feet, however, fulfilled the image he had of what a hippie looked like.

"Reese, what a surprise. And you've brought a friend. Welcome."

After Reese introduced him with little fanfare—"This is Walker"—Walker followed her into the bus.

He wasn't sure what he'd expected to find, but the cozy, eclectic space was not it.

The bus had been completely gutted of the normal, uncomfortable benches that carried children to and from school. In their place was furniture. Real furniture. A sofa with dozens of hand-made pillows was shoved against the back wall, and bright, multi-colored curtains stretched across the rows of windows where plants hung in macramé holders. A small table and two wooden chairs sat opposite a blackened wood-burning stove with a smoke pipe disappearing out a window. Funky, abstract wallpaper covered the ceiling, and a swath of bright-yellow shag carpet covered the floor, completing the homey, hippie vibe.

It was a warm and inviting place.

"You just missed Patrick," Jean said. She motioned them to the sofa while she lowered herself onto a chair. "He and some of the other guys are building a barn. We're hoping to buy sheep in the spring and sell the wool."

"How long have you been out here?" Walker asked, surprising himself with his curiosity. It apparently surprised Reese as well, considering her raised eyebrows.

"Nearly a hundred of us drove our buses out from San Francisco last year. Our leader, Stefan, searched for a place where we could enjoy clean air, grow our families, and live in peace." She smiled with obvious contentment. "This place is a haven. We're eager to clear the land and begin farming."

Walker had a dozen more questions he wanted to ask, but he wasn't here to interview the woman. He listened as Reese explained why they'd come, leaving out the part about driving to Sevier County to locate information about the midwife who'd attended his birth.

"The babies are down for a nap," Jean said, indicating a curtained-off portion at the back of the bus when Reese asked about the children. "But I couldn't sleep." She cradled her pregnant belly with both hands. "This little fellow has really started kicking lately. Patrick is convinced it's another boy." Joy radiated from her face at the prospect of a son.

While Reese put her hands on the woman's belly, asking the mother how she'd been feeling, a troubling awareness crashed through Walker.

His birth mother, whoever she was, had looked just like Jean at one time. She'd carried *him* inside her. Felt *him* kick her.

But unlike Jean, she hadn't wanted her baby. Hadn't wanted to be pregnant.

Hadn't wanted a son.

Dark thoughts swirled through Walker's mind. His breath came heavy.

Had she considered aborting him? Of ridding herself of the unwelcome life growing inside her womb? Abortion had been in the news a lot lately, with the Supreme Court issuing its ruling in January in favor of a woman's right to privacy according to the Fourteenth Amendment. Legal abortion, the justices felt, fell into this category. For the most part, the arguments for or against abortion had been abstract and distant to Walker. They didn't involve him.

Until now.

Until it was the value of *his* life they were discussing.

"Walker?"

Reese's voice startled him. He looked up to find both women watching him, yet it was Reese's look of compassionate concern that undid him.

"I'll wait for you outside."

He practically ran for the door and stumbled down the steps. Walker didn't glance at the little red car nearby and instead headed for the woods.

Woods that looked just like those from his nightmare.

Eight

IT SOON FELT AS IF SONGBIRD was a member of the Jenkins family.

Despite her shoulder remaining sore, requiring her to move with care and not overdo, she happily pitched in with chores without being asked. Cooking, cleaning, helping with critters, and—her favorite—working in the garden with Bertie and Rubie. There wasn't anything she wasn't willing to do, and even Jennie's perpetual frown eased some when the girl sang hymns for them in the evenings.

On a bright morning, Bertie and Songbird knelt on opposite sides of a large wooden garden box, grayed over time, working among all manner of herbs. Some for cooking, some for healing, some for both. From the moment they'd begun their chore, Bertie'd patiently answered dozens of questions about the plants, explaining how God created each with a purpose.

Feverfew reduced fevers and helped ease headaches.

Chickweed aided the kidneys or, if used as a salve, cured skin rashes.

Thyme helped fight off colds and sore throats.

"What'd you use on me?" Songbird wanted to know, showing real curiosity about the healing properties of the different plants.

On and on, as the hot sun moved higher in the clear blue sky, the questions kept coming. Bertie didn't mind. It was nice to have someone new to chat with.

"Miss Bertie," Songbird began again after a quiet spell, "how'd you come to know so much 'bout plants and how to use 'em to heal folks?"

Bertie lifted her head so she could see the girl from beneath the wide brim of her bonnet. Thanks to both Rubie and Jennie, she hadn't misplaced her head covering since the day Songbird came to them.

The girl continued to pick small green weeds from the dark soil, her own bonnet hiding her face from the sun. She wore one of Rubie's dresses that Amelie altered to fit her, and it gave her the appearance of one of the sisters rather than a young visitor.

"Mam taught me when I was younger than you, and her mama taught her." Bertie smiled when Songbird's gaze met hers. "I 'spect if I'd had a daughter, I'd've passed it on down too."

That comment seemed to trouble Songbird. Her brow tugged into a frown. "Did you never have a beau or want to get married?"

Bertie kept turning soil with her gardening trowel, comfortable now with the question that used to bring dread when she was a younger woman. "There weren't any boys round here that caught my fancy. Jennie'd decided to be an old maid, and I figured I'd keep her company. After Catie married, Bonnie, Amelie, and Rubie determined they'd find husbands too." She paused, remembering the heartache her sisters endured. "Bonnie gave up the search soon after it began, but Amelie and Rubie met some fellas who worked for a logging company over in Hartford."

A glance at Songbird revealed her rapt attention. "What happened?"

Bertie sat back on her haunches and heaved a sigh. "They were both killed when a load of logs broke loose from a railroad car."

She shook her head, the sound of her sisters' mourning echoing in the painful memory. "Amelie wasn't ever the same. Papa said the grief affected her mind. And Rubie," Bertie said with a glance to the far end of the garden where her younger sister worked, "she still pines for her Caleb these many years later."

Songbird's gaze also sought Rubie. "That's sad. I don't know what I'd do if somethin' happened to Amos while he's fightin' the war in Europe."

"I didn't think you had a way of communicatin' with him."

"I don't." The girl shrugged. Her hands cradled her growing belly. "I'm hopin' that when he does finally come home, he'll come lookin' for me. For us."

Bertie's heart ached for the young mother-to-be. From what Songbird had said, Amos's ma had no intention of telling her son about his child. Declared it wasn't his, in fact. How could a woman deny her own kin? Her own grandchild?

They worked in silence for some time before Songbird stood, stretched, and came to Bertie's side of the box.

"Miss Bertie, I've been thinkin'." Her voice held a note of excitement, and Bertie looked up, curious what had gained her youthful attention this time. "I wanna learn to be a healer woman, like you. Learn 'bout them herbs and helpin' folks. Would you teach me?"

If Bertie hadn't already been seated on the ground, astonishment would've landed her there. She gazed up, gauging whether the girl was sincere or not.

"Come now, do you really want to learn 'bout all this?" She waved her hand to indicate the tangle of growing plants in the box. "It's a great responsibility, you know, tendin' folks who's ailin'. Tell me, why do you want to learn 'bout healing?"

Songbird pressed her lips, then took a deep breath. "Pa's wife, she claims to be a healer, but I know she ain't. She ain't kind and carin' like you. She puts spells on folks she don't like. I wanna learn 'bout doin' good with them herbs." She gave a slight shrug and dipped her chin shyly. "You ain't got a girl of your own, and I ain't got a ma, so . . ." She didn't finish the sentence.

Her meaning, however, was perfectly clear. "Oh, child." Bertie stood as moisture filled her eyes. Ignoring the dirt on her hands, she held them out to Songbird. The girl grabbed hold with her own soil-covered hands. "I'd be honored to teach you what I know 'bout herbs and doctorin', if you really want to learn."

"I do." A smile stretched across Songbird's face.

Warmth spread through Bertie, and she wrapped her arms around the slight girl.

For the first time in her life, she knew what it felt like to be a mother.

☙

The weeks went by.

Bertie and Songbird spent many pleasant hours discussing countless plants—their roots, leaves, stems, seeds—marveling how God made each one to benefit the human body in different ways. Jennie disapproved, declaring the time wasted when more important tasks could be tended to, but Bertie paid her older sister no mind and enjoyed every minute she spent with the sweet girl.

And she wasn't alone.

Bonnie gave Songbird cooking lessons, with them giggling and chattering over pies, biscuits, and stews. When Songbird lamented her lack of knitting skills, Amelie's eyes took on a shine. The two quickly set to work with colorful skeins of yarn, the makings of a soft blanket for the baby well underway. In the evenings after the supper dishes were washed, Rubie spent time with Songbird on the porch reading in the fading daylight. Songbird confessed she'd never attended school, but her ma had taught her the basics of reading and writing. Rubie, who'd taught at their one-room mountain school some years ago, made it her mission to further the girl's education with poetry, history, and mathematics.

Jennie, however, remained cold and distant from their guest. She made her displeasure at being overruled known to all, and they tiptoed around their elder sister, never knowing what might set her off. The situation was fast becoming wearisome.

On the morning Bertie announced she'd invited Songbird to join them in their Bible reading after breakfast, Jennie's fiery glare from across the kitchen practically scorched Bertie's skin. A short time later, she followed Bertie to the chicken yard on the pretense of helping gather eggs, a chore Bertie usually did alone.

"There's no reason the girl needs to join us for mornin' readin'," Jennie stated the moment they entered the henhouse. "She can hear just fine from the gatherin' room, like she's been doin' since she arrived."

Bertie reached beneath a red hen sitting in one of the nesting boxes. A warm egg was her reward. "Come now, Sister. Songbird didn't feel comfortable enough to join us in the beginnin'. Now she does. Nothin' but good can come from teachin' her the truths found in the pages of Papa's Bible." She moved on to the next hen.

"That girl is a sinner," Jennie hissed, her face mottled and hands in fists. "Evidence of her sin is there for everyone to see. I heard her say she ain't never stepped a foot in church. I won't have her joinin' us at the table, tainting memories of Papa readin' from the Word. It's bad 'nough she's sleepin' in his home and eatin' his food. You've forced this wanton girl upon us, Alberta Mae, but I'll be hanged if I let you ruin our time with the Lord."

The vehemence in her sister's speech stunned Bertie. "How can you say such things, Sister? You know Papa welcomed friend and foe alike to his table. And I daresay there were sinners among them. Why, don't you remember the down-on-his-luck fellow

Papa hired to help around the farm? He stole Mam's pearl brooch. We never saw him again, but both Papa and Mam forgave him."

Jennie huffed. "It ain't the same thing. That man hightailed it outta here, knowin' he done wrong. He didn't keep showin' up at Papa's table for Bible readin'."

"Maybe he should have. He might not've chosen a path of sin if he'd heard the truth about God's love and forgiveness."

"I won't have you preachin' at me, Bertie." Jennie crossed her arms over her chest. "I'm of a mind to have Brother Tom come get that gal and be done with this."

Bertie stiffened. "You may be the eldest, Eugenia Jenkins, but that don't make you king. We voted on it. Songbird stays. And while she's with us, she needs to hear the Word. Jesus said it's the sick that need doctorin' and the sinner who's in need of repentance. I 'spect he's talkin' 'bout little lost sheep like our Songbird, don't you?"

Jennie's nostrils flared like a bull ready to charge. "I don't know what kind of spell that girl has cast over you, but I want no part of it."

She turned and stalked out of the chicken yard, heading away from the house despite it nearly being time to break the fast.

Bertie watched her go, regretful over the friction between her and her sister, yet at a loss how to rectify it. "Lord, I'm certain you brought Songbird to us, but this trouble stirrin' among us can't be good."

She left the prayer open-ended, gathered a dozen eggs, and made her way back to the house. Bonnie and Songbird were busy in the kitchen cooking a breakfast of bacon, grits, and biscuits.

"Is Jennie with you?" Bonnie asked from her place in front of the big, blackened stove. "It's not like her to disappear fore settin' the meal on the table."

Bertie cast a look at Songbird, who was occupied laying out

forks and knives on the table, then returned her attention to Bonnie. "She's ponderin' some things."

Bonnie frowned. When Bertie indicated Songbird with her eyes, her sister gave a nod of understanding.

Amelie and Rubie came in from the barn a short time later, and the five of them sat down to the meal, Jennie's place at the head noticeably vacant.

"I'll ask the blessing," Bonnie said, her somber tone evidence that their eldest sister's absence troubled her as well.

Neither Amelie nor Rubie asked after Jennie, making Bertie wonder if they'd seen her after she left the henhouse. If they had, they'd no doubt gotten an earful.

Songbird surely must have been aware of the tension because she quietly ate without her usual chatter.

When the meal came to an end, they cleared the table in silence. The dishes washed and leftover food covered, the only thing that remained before their work could commence was opening Papa's Bible. Something their eldest sister had overseen since Papa's passing.

Clearly, however, Jennie had no plans to participate today. And although Bertie knew her sister to be wrong, she felt responsible for the unrest around them. Determined to see this thing through, she took the worn, black book off the shelf and turned to face the others.

"Since Jennie isn't here to continue our readin' of the Psalms, I've a mind to hear from the apostle Paul." So saying, she returned to the table and opened the book to Romans, one of Papa's favorites.

Bonnie, Amelie, and Rubie exchanged worried looks, and even Songbird seemed hesitant.

"Miss Bertie, I don't have ta join y'all if . . . well, if it's gonna cause trouble."

"Nonsense." Bertie motioned her to an empty chair. "No trouble can come from hearin' the Word of the Lord."

When the women were seated once again, Bertie cleared her throat the way Papa had always done.

"Romans, chapter 8. 'There is therefore now no condemnation to them which are in Christ Jesus, who walk not after the flesh, but after the Spirit. For the law of the Spirit of life in Christ Jesus hath made me free from the law of sin and death.'"

Bertie glanced up to find Songbird's rapt attention on her. Pleased, she continued to read until she came to verse 15.

Now she knew why the Lord led her to this passage.

"'For ye have not received the spirit of bondage again to fear; but ye have received the Spirit of adoption, whereby we cry, Abba, Father. The Spirit itself beareth witness with our spirit, that we are the children of God.'"

Bertie stopped reading and closed the book, her heart full of the truth in those words.

"That was one of Papa's favorite Scriptures," she said. "He knew he was a sinner, just like everyone else. But he also knew the savin' grace found in Christ Jesus that makes us clean and free from sin and death." She took out a hankie and wiped her nose. "When we're made clean—" she smiled at Songbird—"we become the adopted children of God. And oh, what a good, good Papa he is."

"Amen, Sister," Rubie said.

After Bonnie prayed over their day, the kitchen emptied, with each sister going about her daily chores.

Bertie and Songbird made their way into the gathering room to retrieve their bonnets from the hooks by the door.

"Best we get to the garden afore the sun sends us inside again." Bertie headed for the porch only to be stopped by Songbird's voice.

"Miss Bertie, what'd you mean by *adopted*?"

Bertie turned, taken aback by the question. "Child, haven't you heard of someone being adopted?"

The girl shook her head.

The earnest expression on Songbird's face revealed she wasn't fooling with Bertie. "Well, adoption means that a pa and ma who made a baby—" she indicated Songbird's protruding belly—"give the child to someone else to look after."

"For always?"

Bertie nodded. "Yes, for always. The new folks become the baby's pa and ma."

The girl seemed to process the information. After a long moment, she asked, "What's that got to do with God?"

Belatedly, Bertie realized she should have explained the passage—so familiar to the Jenkins sisters yet unknown to Songbird—in a way the girl could understand.

She took Songbird's hand and led her to the cot, where they sat on the edge. "Your ma, she told you 'bout Jesus and him dyin' on the cross, didn't she?"

Songbird nodded, so Bertie continued. "When Jesus went to the cross, he took our sins—yours, mine, ever'body's—upon himself, offerin' us freedom from the punishment we deserve. All we got to do is confess those very same sins to Jesus and he'll forgive every last one. It's like gettin' scrubbed clean, from the inside out. And once we're clean, God the Father calls us his children, adoptin' us into his family."

Songbird's face revealed that she was working out the explanation in her mind. They'd sit here all morning, if need be, to make sure the girl understood about the gift of grace.

The clock on the mantel ticked away a full minute before Songbird looked at Bertie. "I know me an' Amos done wrong makin' this here baby. But if what you're sayin' is true and God can forgive me," she said, lips trembling, "I want him to be my Papa."

"Oh, dear one, he wants nothing more than to be your Papa."

Songbird's voice quavered as Bertie led her in a simple prayer, asking Jesus to wash away her sins and adopt her into the family of God.

At the end of the brief petition, Bertie heard Songbird whisper, "And be Papa to my baby, too."

The women hugged, then laughed with the joy that comes when a lost sheep is found. Jesus will always leave the ninety-nine and go looking for the one who's gone astray. And oh, the celebration in heaven when the wandering soul is found and brought safely into the fold.

As they pulled away from each other, a noise from the porch drew their attention.

Jennie stood in the open doorway, her gaze fixed on Songbird.

Twin trails of wetness streamed down her weathered cheeks.

Nine

LAUGHTER FILLED THE JENKINS CABIN one sweltering August morning.

The sisters and I sat around the breakfast table after the dishes were washed and the Word read. No one was eager to get to chores now that the weather had turned hot and disagreeable. The heat wouldn't stay long, Bertie said. Two or three weeks at most, but it made life for us and the critters miserable in the meantime. Lingering at the table, telling tales, was far more pleasant.

"If Papa could be accused of anything, it would've been pride in his long white beard. Why, it nearly touched his belt buckle when he stood," Jennie said, her face its usual mask of seriousness. A hint of humor, however, sparked the edges of her blue eyes as she continued. "I'll never forget the day Mam threatened to cut it off. He'd been to town and came home with a rascally grin. When Mam asked why he was so jolly, he proceeded to impart how ol' Cordelia Howerton oohed and aahed over his handsome beard when he'd seen her at the mercantile. Said Cordelia sure wished her man had such a fine set of whiskers. She'd wash and comb it for him ever' mornin'."

The faintest smile touched Jennie's mouth.

"The thing is, Cordelia Howerton and Mam didn't get on. Mam always said that gal enjoyed flirtin' far too much for a married woman. 'Well,' says Mam, just as serious as a preacher, 'if Cordelia's so fond of your whiskers, let's just give 'em to her. I can weave 'em into a hankie or somethin' she can keep with her.' So sayin', she took up a pair of scissors and came for Papa."

I gasped, wide-eyed. Had Mam Jenkins really done it?

"'Now, wait just a doggone minute,' Papa says, backin' away from Mam, his face gone nearly as white as his beard. 'I'm right fond of my whiskers.'" Jennie folded her arms as her ma must have done that long-ago day, face in a deep scowl. "Mam stood on her tiptoes and looked Papa right in the eye, sayin', 'Then I 'spect you best keep that foolish grin from your face next time you see Cordelia Howerton and mind whose scissors can remedy your pride.'"

I couldn't help but giggle when the women around the table crowed.

"Mam wasn't a very big woman, but she ruled the roost," Bonnie said.

"But she also followed the Bible's instruction to respect her husband," Bertie added, then winked at me. "It just didn't apply when he was actin' foolish."

"We best get on with the day." Jennie stood. "Them chores won't get done on their own."

The sound of an automobile coming up the mountain, however, stilled them all.

"We aren't expectin' Brother Tom, are we?" Jennie moved to the window, with Bertie on her tail.

I hoped it wasn't Tom. It was too hot for me to hide beneath my bedcovers again.

I stood on tiptoe and peeked over their shoulders. A dark sedan emerged from the road cut through thick forest. Clem commenced to barking and ran off the porch.

"That ain't Tom." Bertie squinted to make out the visitor. "Looks like Earl Dunn." She turned so quickly, she nearly bumped into me. "Rhoda's babe isn't due for three more weeks, but if Earl's here in his automobile, I 'spect he's come to fetch me."

Without waiting to see if her guess was correct, Bertie hurried to gather the things she'd need to attend a birth. Her sisters flew into action too, while Jennie went to greet the visitor.

"I'll take an overnight bag in case labor don't progress as quickly as we hope. Even though this is Rhoda's fourth pregnancy, you can't rush a babe when he's got a mind to stay where he is."

I wondered what Bertie meant about babies wantin' to stay where they were. Lately I'd been thinking ahead to my own baby's entrance into the world, mostly because I had no idea what was involved with giving birth to a child.

I ducked into the kitchen just as Jennie entered the cabin, followed by Earl.

"Earl, how's Rhoda?" Bertie asked. "Has her labor started?"

"She ain't painin' too bad yet, Miss Bertie," he said, "but she's a-wantin' ya to come."

"I've got my bag just 'bout ready. I'll be out directly."

The man exited the house.

When I came around the corner, Bertie glanced at me, then looked at her sisters. "Best start a-prayin' for the wee one."

"Miss Bertie," I said, set on the plan that had sprung to mind as I'd listened to the exchange, "I wanna come with you."

Five pairs of eyes full of surprise landed on me.

"I don't think that's a good idea, Songbird," Bertie began. "I don't know how long I'll be away. 'Sides," she said with a wink, "you'd miss Jennie's tales about Papa and the farm."

I didn't smile. "Just the same, I'd like to come." I looked down to where my baby grew. "I . . . I ain't never seen a baby born. I'm Mama's last child afore she passed. Pa's wit . . . wife—" I corrected myself, knowing I shouldn't disrespect Vera, even if I didn't like her—"she didn't want me in the house when she had her babies."

Bertie stared at me, her mouth agape. "Child, I had no idea you didn't know what to expect when your time comes." She paused. "Rhoda's given birth to three strapping boys with no problem, but every pregnancy is different."

"I'll stay outta the way," I said, my voice pleading. "I promise."

After several beats, Bertie gave in. "All right. You can come. I 'spect Rhoda'll appreciate help with her young'uns while she's laborin'."

I hurried to tuck a hand-me-down dress Amelie had altered to fit me into Bertie's already-bulging bag and followed her outside.

Earl simply nodded in agreement when Bertie informed him that I was a family friend and would accompany her at the birthing. We waved goodbye to the sisters and set off. Bertie confessed she didn't often ride in automobiles. Brothers Tom and Chad owned vehicles, as did Catie's husband, she said, but the sisters had no need for such extravagance. Ol' Kit was all they required to get to the store and perform farm chores.

The drive through the mountains to the Dunn place took twenty or so minutes. Bertie didn't seem to enjoy the scenery around them, with her mind fixed on the birth ahead, but I let my long hair blow in the hot wind coming through the open window. I was excited to witness new life enter the world. I hadn't told Bertie yet, but I hoped to be a midwife like her someday.

Soon, a small cabin came into view. Tall weeds filled the yard and several dogs lazed near the open door. Unlike the Jenkins home, no porch offered shade from summer sunshine or a place to get out of the rain on stormy days.

Earl parked the car, and we climbed from it. A stark-naked boy of not more than three years ran out the door to his pa, babbling something I couldn't quite make out.

Earl lifted the child, who bore dirt smudges everywhere. "I'll bring in your bags, Miss Bertie."

Bertie nodded her thanks and made her way into the house, with me on her heels. Natural light from the doorway and two small windows wasn't enough to truly illuminate the room, but when my eyes adjusted, I saw Rhoda sitting on the edge of the bed in the corner to the right of the door, clothed in a nightgown pulled up to reveal her bare legs.

"Thank ya for comin', Bertie." She grasped her enormous belly. "The pains . . . they ain't comin' like they should. Just crampin' mostly."

Bertie knelt in front of the woman, lifted the gown, and placed her own hands on the babe's hiding place. "Let's take a look-see."

She let her palms rest on Rhoda's skin and waited for the next contraction.

I watched with wide eyes, finding it impossible to imagine my own belly growing so large.

Bertie turned to me. "Please bring my bag, dear."

I hurried to obey.

Rhoda offered me a tired smile when I returned. "I see it'll be your turn soon."

I gave a shy nod. "Yes'm."

After Bertie introduced us, she dug something out of the bag, calling it a stethoscope, and positioned it to listen for the baby's heartbeat. I couldn't figure how the strange device could hear such, but I didn't want to interrupt with questions. I'd try to remember to ask Bertie about it later. It sure would be something to hear my baby's heart beating while he was still inside me.

Rhoda closed her eyes, saying a contraction was upon her. I watched everything, pondering what it would feel like when it was my body preparing for birth. So far, Miz Dunn's labor didn't seem too bad.

When the contraction ended, Bertie moved the end of the stethoscope all over Rhoda's belly, stopping here and there, then moving on. A frown formed on her brow, growing deeper with each placement.

"Bertie?"

Bertie looked at Rhoda. I saw worry on her face.

"Is somethin' wrong?"

Bertie stood and draped the instrument around her neck. "When's the last time you felt the baby move?"

Rhoda cradled her belly protectively with her hands. "He was movin' last night. I couldn't sleep 'cuz it was so hot in the house. Earl set one of the boys' cots outside for me and I dozed some." She indicated three child-size wood-frame beds across the room. "The baby's been quiet this morning though. Sleepin', I 'spect."

Another contraction came and went. It must not have been too strong, for Rhoda barely seemed to take notice, her stare fixed on Bertie.

"My baby's all right, ain't he, Bertie?" Fear tinged her words.

"Let's not jump ahead of ourselves now."

Bertie briefly glanced my way. Something in her eyes told me she wished I hadn't come along. I didn't understand what was happening, and I started to feel nervous.

"We need stronger contractions." Bertie dug through her bag again until she came to what she sought. She took out the small vial. "This is black cohosh. You've used it before?"

Rhoda nodded. "Ma gave it to me and my sisters when we started our flows. Helped with cramps some."

"It's good for inducin' labor, too." Bertie turned to me. "Fetch a cup of water for Miz Dunn, please."

When I returned with the drink, Bertie offered me a look of encouragement. "You're doin' fine." I nodded my appreciation, but my nerves were still a-jangling. I just didn't know why.

Bertie added several drops of the tincture to the water. After Rhoda drank it, we settled in to wait.

"Earl took our two older boys to my sister's house on his way to fetch you." Rhoda lay back against a stack of pillows. "But Jeffrey Earl wouldn't go. Said he wanted to stay here and play with his new brother."

"Earl has him in the barn, I believe." Bertie glanced out the open door.

I followed her gaze, but all I could see was forest and clear blue sky. Nary a leaf stirred in the hot sunshine, and the house felt stuffy and warm.

"I'll sure be glad when this heat is done and cool returns to the hills," Bertie said.

Rhoda agreed, then closed her eyes.

The contractions slowly grew stronger over the morning hours. By noon, Rhoda was in full labor, yet Bertie still looked worried each time she used her stethoscope to listen for the baby.

While Rhoda dozed, Bertie motioned me outside.

"I fear somethin's not right with Rhoda's babe."

I gave a slow nod. "I know. You ain't actin' happy."

Bertie sighed. "I can't find a heartbeat. She also hasn't felt the baby move today."

Instinctively my hands shifted to my own belly. "What does that mean, Miss Bertie?"

"It means we need to pray for the best outcome but prepare for the worst."

We held hands and asked the Lord to be with Rhoda and the baby. "Thy will be done, Father," Bertie said.

I thought about her words when we returned to the house. Surely God's will was to save Rhoda's baby, wasn't it?

Earl came and went, taking blankets and food to the barn with him on his last trip once it became clear night would fall without the baby's arrival. I noticed Bertie didn't mention her fears to him, but he seemed aware that something was amiss.

"I'll be near if . . . if she needs me."

Well after midnight, things grew tense inside the cabin. Rhoda moaned and thrashed with each contraction, now less than a minute apart. I had sheets and hot water ready, as Bertie had instructed, but I couldn't stop fear from growing inside me. Was this what childbirth would be like for me? When Rhoda cried out, I grasped her hand and didn't flinch as the laboring mother squeezed so hard it cut off the circulation to my fingers.

The baby finally came out in a rush of blood and green-tinged water, sometime in the wee hours of morning. The tiny boy was perfectly formed, yet his skin was gray and beginning to peel. There was no life in him, nor would there be.

Rhoda, half-delirious, lifted her head. "Is he . . . ?"

When Bertie held the little thing up for his mother to see, a wail like nothing I'd ever heard emerged from the brokenhearted woman.

I stood frozen. I wanted to rush from the house, away from the sight of the dead baby. Away from the terrible sound coming from his mother. But then my eyes found Rhoda, her face full of pain and loss. Her child was dead, and there was nothing she could do to bring him back.

I fell to my knees next to the bed and took the sobbing woman in my arms. She clung to me, and we wept together.

Movement told me when Bertie cut the umbilical cord, and I looked to see her carefully wrap the body in a blanket.

"I'll take him."

Earl stood in the open doorway, his face drawn. He'd no doubt heard his wife's grief.

Bertie carried the lifeless infant to his father. "I'm sorry, Earl. He . . ." She didn't finish.

Earl simply nodded, reverently accepted the bundle, and exited the cabin.

Rhoda's sobs continued. Bertie gave her something to help her sleep, and soon an eerie, heavy silence filled the cabin instead of the joyful sound of a newborn's cries.

I looked over at Bertie. She appeared completely spent.

"Are you all right, Miss Bertie?"

"I feel responsible for what happened," she said, her face a mask of grief. "I last saw Rhoda a month or so ago and everything was fine. Maybe I should've come sooner to make sure all was well."

The babe in my womb kicked. "Didn't Rhoda say she felt the baby move when she went to sleep outside on the cot last night?"

Bertie glanced to the small beds across the room. I followed her gaze.

The frames were made from thin wooden supports, with canvas stretched across.

"If Rhoda rolled onto her side," she said, more to herself than to me, "with her belly pressed into the rail, it may have cut off the umbilical cord."

We would never know. What mattered now was helping the mother through the loss.

The image of the dead baby, however, wouldn't leave me.

"I'm scared, Miss Bertie," I whispered. "I'm scared God's gonna take my baby the way he took Rhoda's. I done wrong, but my baby ain't done nothin'. Rhoda's boy was so small and helpless. How could God do that to him?"

Bertie held me the way I'd held Rhoda.

"God's ways aren't our ways, child. Sometimes it's impossible for us to understand why things like this happen. Other times, he makes it clear. Like when there's somethin' not quite right with the baby." She sighed. "But as hard as it is to accept, we have to trust that God knows best."

We sat in silence for a long time, each lost in our own thoughts.

"Is Rhoda's baby in heaven with God?" I whispered.

"Yes." Bertie spoke that one word with a confidence I needed to hear. "He's in heaven with his Papa."

I sniffled. "I hope that brings comfort to his pa and ma."

Bertie's arms tightened around me. "So do I, sweet girl. So do I."

Ten

REESE ENDED HER VISIT WITH JEAN. She assured the expectant mother all was progressing well with the baby.

"Try to stay off your feet as much as possible." She glanced to Jean's swollen ankles as they walked to the door of the bus-home. "I'm not overly concerned about the swelling at this point, but we do need to keep an eye on it."

Jean placed her hands on her tummy. "I won't be able to see my toes before long, swollen or not," she said with a laugh. "Resting with my feet up throughout the day sounds wonderful."

Reese waved goodbye and headed for the VW. She'd been concerned about Walker's abrupt exit from the bus but going after him hadn't seemed necessary. Some men simply weren't comfortable around pregnant women. Even though her visit with Jean hadn't required an examination, she guessed seeing the expectant mother's large belly had been a bit much for the singer.

When she reached the car, however, it was empty.

Reese scanned the wooded area surrounding the bus.

Had he gone for a walk?

She glanced at her wristwatch. They needed to get back on the road. Her plan was to get to the Sevier County courthouse after lunch and inquire about reserving a room for tomorrow where she and Walker could pore over birth records. She'd packed an overnight bag with toiletries and two changes of clothes, estimating they wouldn't need more than a day, two at the most, to sort through the documents.

After storing her midwife bag in the trunk, she leaned against the driver's door and waited. And waited.

Where was he?

Another glance at her watch.

"Mr. Wylie?"

No answer.

"Walker?" she called louder.

Nothing.

Reese blew out a breath. She hoped he wasn't lost. What would his manager say if she had to confess she'd misplaced his famous client somewhere in the Appalachians?

After a quick survey of the surroundings, the woods directly opposite the bus seemed the most likely direction he would have gone. She wasn't entirely certain how much land the hippies occupied, but it stood to reason Walker was still within their borders. If she couldn't locate him, she'd get Jean's husband to help.

She grabbed a thermos of water from the back seat and headed into thick brush.

There weren't any signs of him.

"Walker?"

Still no answer.

A whisper of fear began in the pit of her stomach, overtaking her frustration.

He was safe, wasn't he?

An animal trail led deeper into the woods. Reese followed it and prayed she didn't run into a foraging bear or hungry cougar. It occurred to her she should say the same prayer for Walker.

It wasn't long before the sound of water reached her. A stream, no doubt. The mountains were full of waterways, large and small. Some even led to glorious waterfalls.

"Mr. Wylie?"

She'd just turned to follow a different trail when she heard him.

"Over here."

Relief washed through her. She picked her way through the tangle of wild shrubs and came to the banks of a pretty creek. There he sat, watching the water as it gently tumbled over boulders and fallen tree limbs.

"Thank goodness I found you. For a minute there I thought I was going to have to call the forest rangers."

He didn't respond to her joke. In fact, he didn't move at all.

Reese bit her lip. "Are you okay?"

He gave a slight shrug. "I don't know what I am. I don't know what I'm doing here. Maybe this whole thing is a really bad idea."

She hesitated, uncertain how to handle the situation, especially if their visit to Jean had triggered something in him. She stepped off to his left and sat on the grassy bank. Not next to him but close enough to have a conversation . . . if he was willing.

"I can't pretend to know exactly what you're going through," she said, her gaze fixed on the flowing water too. "I think all of us— adopted children, I mean—have to work things out in our own way."

Long minutes went by without a response. A cool breeze stirred gold and red leaves in the surrounding trees, while a squirrel across the stream ignored its human audience and continued to hide acorns for the coming winter. Reese hoped the beauty and peace of this place would ease Walker's troubled spirit the way words couldn't.

Finally he turned to her. "That's just it. I don't see this thing *working out.*" He paused and eyed her. "What's your story? How did you *work things out?*"

His tone made it clear he didn't believe it possible.

"My story is fairly common. I'm the result of an affair my birth mother had with a married man."

Those words used to awaken deep shame in her heart. Thankfully, they no longer did. She'd long ago come to terms with a truth she had no power to change.

"Wow. Sorry."

She nodded her appreciation. "My parents—my adoptive parents—adopted me when they were in their forties. My birth mother was the daughter of my dad's college buddy. He knew my parents hadn't been able to have children of their own, and one Saturday afternoon he showed up at our house and asked if they'd adopt me." Reese recalled the day Mom told her the whole story and how they'd cried, hugged, and cried some more. "My mom said she took one look at me and knew I was meant to be her daughter. She named me Reese Esther—Reese after a great-aunt she'd loved and Esther after Queen Esther in the Bible because she was adopted."

"And you lived happily ever after." His words dripped with sarcasm.

"I've had a good life." Reese returned her attention to the peacefulness around them. "But it hasn't always been easy. After I learned the truth about my birth parents, I struggled with anger issues. I went through the same stages of grief you're experiencing now."

"Grief?"

Reese nodded. "I knew my family was different. Most of my friends knew the details about the day they were born, and many of them had siblings. My parents were older, but that didn't bother me because I loved them, and they made sure I was loved in return. But when I was thirteen years old, the word *adopted* became something to be ashamed of. Kids at school teased me. One day I'd had enough. I came home and told Mom I wanted to know the whole story, even the parts that are shameful."

She thought back to that day, remembering the anger, the sadness. "It took some time for me to process it all. Not just because I was still a child, but because there's a lot of emotion tied to our identities, whether we realize it or not. I didn't know who I was anymore. I'd lost myself, my family. I'd even lost my past and my future, if that makes any sense."

Forest sounds filled the gap of silence between them.

After a while, Walker heaved a sigh. "Oddly enough, I know exactly what you mean. I have no idea who I am anymore. I keep wondering who I was supposed to be, you know?"

Reese saw pain etched in his face, and her heart went out to him. She wanted to assure him he *was* who God created him to be, but now wasn't the time for what might seem like platitudes. "Anytime you want to talk about it, I'm here for you." When he didn't take her up on the offer, she said, "I'll understand if you'd rather not go to Sevier County today. There isn't a rush. Those documents will be there whenever you're ready."

"Will I ever *be* ready?" He picked up a stone and flung it into the water. "I've never been a quitter. I set goals, then work hard to achieve them. But this—" he shook his head—"I don't know how to move forward, yet I can't go backward in time either. This thing, this *adoption*, happened to me, but I have no idea how to deal with it." He faced her. "If you think finding some obscure midwife will help put this behind me, then let's do it. But if it's going to open a crazy Pandora's box to the past, I'd rather skip it."

Reese knew she had to be honest with him. "I wish I could tell you that the feelings you have right now will go away once you know the facts about your birth and adoption. Knowing the full story definitely helped me process things and gave me a sense of control I'd lacked, but all these years later I still have days when I wish I wasn't adopted. When I long to have a family related by blood. But that will never happen. That's not my story. To dwell on it, to let it drive me into depression, doesn't help. Instead, I focus on the good parts. God blessed me with amazing parents who love me unconditionally. I am who I am today because of them."

She stood, sensing he could use some time alone to sort things out. "I'll wait for you back at the car. Whatever you decide is fine."

When Reese reached the VW, Jean and Patrick sat on the steps to the bus, where they watched their two young children play in the dirt with carved wooden farm animals.

"We were beginning to worry about you," Jean said as Patrick stood. "Is everything cool?"

"We went for a little walk. I hope that's okay."

"Can't blame you for wanting to get into nature on a day like this," Patrick said.

They chatted about the perfect autumn weather and laughed at the children's antics, but Reese kept an eye on the woods. Finally Walker emerged, his face drawn. She introduced him to Patrick, said goodbye to the little family, and she and Walker made their exit.

They bounced over the rutted path in silence. When they came to the main road, Reese let the car idle, uncertain whether she should head west or return to Piney Ridge.

Several cars whizzed past while she waited.

"I need to finish this," Walker finally said. "No matter the outcome."

When Reese met his gaze, she saw confusion and frustration remained, but she also saw a glimmer of determination.

A step in the right direction.

She pulled the car onto the road and headed toward Sevier County.

⚘

Walker opted to wait in the car while Reese went into the historic building that housed the Sevier County courthouse. He knew he should accompany her, being that this trip was about his whacked-out, complicated life, but a strange paralyzing feeling washed over him the moment they reached the parking lot.

What secrets from his past were hidden within those redbrick walls?

It wasn't long before Reese reappeared. When she climbed into the car, his throat tightened, and he couldn't voice even a simple question. It felt as if his very existence hinged on what she'd learned inside.

"We have an appointment tomorrow morning at nine o'clock with the archives director," she said, clearly pleased.

He swallowed past the lump. "Cool."

She glanced at her watch. He'd done the same thing moments before she arrived, so he knew it was a little after three.

"I inquired about area motels," she said. Her face turned a becoming shade of pink. "I'm told the Old Black Inn is a nice place to stay."

Walker grimaced. "*Old* Black Inn doesn't exactly scream luxury accommodations."

"Old Black is a mountain here in the Great Smokies." She grinned. "This isn't Nashville, Mr. Wylie. Clean sheets and hot water are the most luxury you can expect."

Walker looked out the window as she drove down streets lined with quaint businesses and pleasant homes. Small-town America had never interested him. He much preferred a fast-paced place to live and play. But he had to concede the lack of traffic and crowds was exactly what he needed just now.

The motel lived up to Walker's expectations—old—but Reese's as well—clean. Their rooms were adjacent but thankfully not interconnecting. The last thing he wanted was to give Reese the wrong idea about him—although at this point he wasn't even sure what that might be—but it would be best to keep their relationship on a business level.

At six o'clock, he knocked on her door. She hadn't changed clothes, but then neither had he.

"I checked the phone book in my room," she said as they walked to her car. "There are several listings for families with the last name Jenkins, but no Berties. I didn't think it was appropriate to call the people listed at this point, but if we don't have success at the courthouse tomorrow, we might have to resort to cold calls."

Walker hoped not. The fewer people who knew they were searching for the midwife, the better.

"The desk clerk claims the Old Black Café has really good food," Reese said once they were back in the car. She was clearly attempting to hide a grin.

Walker rolled his eyes in mock exasperation. "What is it with you and old things?"

She chuckled. "I thought we could drive around, see the sights. Maybe we'll run across a restaurant that meets your high standards, Mr. Wylie."

"Sounds like a plan." Walker hesitated. "Listen, if we're going to spend the next couple days together, I'd rather you called me Walker. It's less likely to draw attention."

Her eyes softened in a nice way. "As long as you call me Reese."

"Deal."

They cruised around town and found a place serving steaks and barbecue. Reese had packed a picnic lunch of chicken salad sandwiches and potato chips to eat on the drive to Sevier County, but knots in Walker's stomach had kept him from eating much. Now he found himself half-ravenous.

While they waited for their food, Walker studied Reese from across the table. "You know all about me thanks to gossip magazines, but I know next to nothing about you."

Her face flushed pink again, something Walker was starting to enjoy.

"There's not much to know."

"Sure there is." He leaned back in his chair. "For starters, how'd you become a midwife? That isn't exactly a common occupation."

Her shoulders relaxed. "After high school, I studied nursing. I was in my third year when I attended a birthing for the first time." Her brown eyes glimmered. "It was the most amazing, miraculous thing I'd ever witnessed, and I knew I wanted to be part of that again and again. Once I graduated, I got a job at the Knoxville hospital as a labor and delivery nurse."

Something in her voice changed.

Walker put his elbows on the table and studied her. "You weren't happy there."

"How can you know that?"

He grinned. "Take my advice. Don't ever play poker. Your face gives everything away." He grew serious. "Why didn't you like working in a hospital?"

She didn't answer right away. "It's not that I didn't like it. I loved my job. Helping women through one of the most important events of their life is a privilege. But when a woman chooses to deliver her baby in a hospital, there are a lot of rules and regulations to contend with. Some of them, unfortunately, distract or even impede the beautiful and natural experience of childbirth."

Walker drew back, confused. "I don't understand. Isn't it better for women to be in a hospital environment to have a child rather than at home? I imagine all kinds of things can go wrong that would require medical intervention."

"Yes, things do sometimes go wrong, but no, it isn't always better for a woman to give birth in a hospital. It's far more likely the mother will be given some type of drug to either help induce labor or take away the pain of the contractions."

"And that's not good?" Walker asked, trying to understand.

"Obviously I have no idea the pain level we're talking about, but from what I've always heard, it gets pretty intense."

Reese nodded. "It does, but the contractions prepare the body to give birth. The mother should be fully aware of what's happening so she can push the baby out when it's time. Drugs dull her senses and can slow down labor. I've also seen too many women subjected to surgery when it wasn't entirely necessary in my opinion."

"But what about emergencies?" Walker countered. "How do you handle it when something goes wrong?"

"Thankfully there have only been two cases where I've had to transport a patient to the hospital because of complications, and both turned out well in the end." Her face revealed her earnestness. "I don't have anything against hospitals. I just wish they weren't quite so rigid when it comes to childbirth. Happily one rule *has* changed, and that is to allow fathers in the birthing room. Before that, they were forced to stay in the waiting area until the baby was settled in the nursery."

Walker remembered something from the newspaper write-up. "The article said you also do volunteer work with kids in the foster care system."

A sad smile formed on her lips. "There are a lot of children who, for various reasons, end up wards of the state. They often go from one foster home to the next, waiting for a 'forever family' to adopt them. As a single woman, I can't be a foster parent, but I can give them my time. I help with homework, babysitting, things like that. If my parents hadn't adopted me, I might have ended up in the system too."

Her words struck Walker in the gut.

If Warren and Annie Wylie hadn't adopted him, his story could have gone in a completely different direction.

Their food arrived, and while Reese chatted with the waitress, Walker took a moment to watch Reese without her being aware.

He admired her passion, he realized. In truth, he admired her. Not too many people would offer to help a total stranger the way she'd done so willingly. Sure, they had the connection of adoption, but Walker knew it went deeper than that.

Reese Chandler truly cared about people.

"Thank you," he said after the waitress left them to their meal.

She looked confused. "For what?"

"For coming with me."

Their gazes held for a long moment. A soft smile parted her lips.

"You're welcome, Walker."

Eleven

OCTOBER ARRIVED ON A BITTER WIND.

"I wouldn't be surprised if we have snow before the leaves are off the trees," Bertie said, surveying the autumn-colored landscape as she and I worked in the herb garden. Bertie wanted us to harvest the last of the life-giving plants before frost destroyed them.

"I like snow," I said, arching my back. My swollen belly felt heavy and looked huge despite the oversize dress I wore along with Rubie's go-to-meetin' coat. It still amazed me there was a baby growing inside me, gettin' bigger every day.

"Snow has its purposes, but it can sure bring a load of misery, too."

I studied the golden glory around us, envisioning the forest covered in snow. "True, but it sure does make the world seem fresh 'n' new when it's covered under a blanket of white, all still and peaceful-like."

Bertie smiled. "That's pretty enough to be a poem."

"Miss Rubie says I should try writin' down my thoughts, but I ain't no good at stringin' words together. Not like the folks who write the books she reads to me. They have a way of bringin' ever'thing to life in my mind, like a picture show. I couldn't do that."

"How will you know unless you try? Besides, there's all different kinds of poets and poetry. It's like these plants, each with its own purpose. That's how God made us—different, with our own strengths and things we're good at."

"Like you knowin' how to doctor folks with plants."

Bertie nodded. "Yes, but you're gettin' real good at knowin' which herb is for what sickness. It'll be no time at all before you're as knowledgeable as me."

We continued to work in the garden, relishing warm sunshine on our faces even as the air carried a warning of the changing seasons.

After a while, I started to hum a song I'd made up the previous day. The words and tune just sorta settled on me while I made diapers from the soft material Jennie brought home last week.

"What's that you're singin'?" Bertie asked. "It's pretty."

I felt my face flush. "Oh, it ain't nothin'. Just a little ditty I thought up."

"Well, you'll have to sing it for us tonight after supper while we sit round the fire. I 'spect our pleasant evenin's on the porch are numbered."

Another stretch of companionable silence passed before I sat back on my haunches and massaged my belly, my thoughts on the baby inside. I couldn't wait to meet him, but I wouldn't let my mind think about the process it would take to bring him into the world. Not after what I'd witnessed in the Dunn cabin.

"Somethin' ailin' you? You got cramps?" Bertie gave me her full attention.

I shook my head. "Nothin' like that." I shrugged. "I've just been thinkin' 'bout the baby a lot. I don't want him growin' up without a pa."

Over the last weeks, I'd begun to refer to the baby as a boy. Bertie told me not to get my hopes up so there wouldn't be disappointment, but I couldn't picture a tiny girl inside me.

I met Bertie's gaze. "What if Amos's ma don't tell him 'bout the baby? You and the sisters have so many wonderful stories 'bout your pa. How he loved his family and God. It makes me sad for the baby to think of him not havin' someone like that to teach him."

Bertie sent me a look of compassion. "Our papa was one in a million, to be certain. I sometimes wonder if that's why Jennie and I chose not to marry. The other girls, they would've married had it worked out. But Jennie and me, we never gave much thought to becomin' wives. We were content to live here, with Papa and Mam."

My sadness intensified, thinking of how much I wanted to be Amos's wife. "Amos and me, we loved each other. Can't see me lovin' nobody else."

Bertie set her trowel down. "Dear one, you have many years ahead of you. The life my sisters and I live is a good one, but it can be lonely. None of us has the responsibility of children, so we can't fully know what it's like to worry over a young'un." She reached across the bed of sassafras, thyme, and mint. I grasped her outstretched hand with cold fingers. "Let's leave the future to the Lord, hmm? He knows the plans, the whys, and the hows of it all."

I nodded, but my melancholy lingered, even after we'd finished our work and retreated to the warmth of the cabin, where Jennie fussed over our chilled faces. Later, once a satisfying dinner of collard greens with bacon and corn bread dumplings was enjoyed by all, we settled in the gathering room.

Amelie and I sat on the cot, where she helped me work out a difficult pattern on the small quilt I was sewing for the baby. I'd never done much sewin' except for buttons or tears in my little brothers' overalls. But Amelie was a patient teacher, and I felt a bit of pride as the soft blanket took shape.

"Songbird," Bertie said from her place near the stone fireplace, "why don't you sing us that song you was hummin' out in the garden today. It sounded as pretty as the birds."

The other sisters looked up from their various occupations—Jennie from shelling the last of the peas, and Bonnie from embroidering a set of pillowcases for their niece, Chad's daughter, who was soon to marry.

I shook my head. "It ain't a real song. Just somethin' I made up."

"We'd love to hear it, dear." Rubie put a ribbon in the book she'd been reading and closed it.

The other sisters voiced their agreement until I gave in. I laid my quilting aside and stood.

"All right, but like I said, it's just a little ditty I came up with . . . for the baby." I placed a hand on my big tummy and closed my eyes, envisioning the tiny life inside.

"Sweet babe of mine, so perfect in every way.
 Who will you become?
Sweet babe of mine, I wait for the day
 when I'll watch you run and play.
I don't know how to be a ma,
 and you may never know your pa.
But you've got a Papa, and so do I,
 Sweet babe of mine,
 Sweet babe of mine."

Stillness followed as my voice faded into the crackle and pop of the fire.

When I opened my eyes, I found tears on the wrinkled cheeks of the sisters.

"That was beautiful, child," Bonnie said, her lips trembling.

"Songs like that are words that come from deep inside the

soul," Rubie said. "Words that can't simply be spoken. They must be sung."

Bertie rose from her place and came to stand next to me. She laid a hand on my cheek. "Don't believe the lie that you're not a poet . . . and a songwriter. God has given you a talent, dear girl. You've been singin' hymns and mountain songs for us every night for weeks, and we've enjoyed them immensely. But this song . . . this is different. You reached down into your heart and put what you found there to music. That's a rare gift."

Her words warmed me. They must've pleased the baby too because he gave a firm kick. I smiled and looked down at my belly. "He moves a lot when I sing to him."

Bertie hugged me, laughing when the baby kicked her, too.

"Perhaps he'll be a sportsman instead of a singer," she said with a wink.

I returned to my seat, pondering the future of my child. "I'd be mighty proud for him to have so much book learnin' he can do anythin' he wants."

Hours later, when the cabin was quiet and the women were abed, I lay awake, my mind and heart full. Oh, how I prayed that every one of my dreams for my child would come true.

Indian summer, or so it was called, returned to the mountains after two days of frosty weather. Warm sunshine spilled from brilliant-blue skies, and the need for a fire in the evenings vanished as quickly as it had arrived. Still, Bertie and her sisters knew the signs and began their yearly chores to prepare the farm and animals for winter.

"Brothers Tom and Chad will come tomorrow to butcher the hogs," Jennie told them at breakfast the next day. "We need to have things ready and prepare the smokehouse for the meat."

Hog butchering day was a busy one, what with hauling wood,

MICHELLE SHOCKLEE ✿ 109

boiling cauldrons of water, and cleaning up the mess once the meat was sectioned, washed, and salted. Bertie was grateful Papa's sons continued to help them, even though both men had families and farms of their own.

"Miss Jennie," Songbird said, uncertainty in her voice, "what 'bout me? Should I take to the woods for the day so's your brothers don't see me?"

Jennie's perpetual frown dipped even further. "To be honest, I hadn't considered such. I 'spect it might be a good idea to keep you out of sight while they're here."

Bertie looked to Jennie. "I figure it's time our brothers know 'bout Songbird. If we want her child to have the blessing of godly men in its life—" she glanced at Songbird and gave a nod—"then our brothers and nephews must be made aware of the situation."

Rubie, Bonnie, and Amelie offered words of agreement until Jennie raised her hand to silence the chatter.

"If we're to make it known that we have a young mother livin' with us, then we best agree on the story and details we'll share." She tapped the cover of Papa's Bible, still lying on the table after she'd read from it a short while ago. "God wouldn't wish us to lie, even to protect someone we cared about. But I also don't believe we're required to reveal the entirety of the circumstances that brought Songbird to us." Her face softened slightly when she looked at the girl.

"Agreed." Bertie's mind whirled with what to tell folks. There could be no mention of Songbird's pa or the shooting. If he learned she was still alive, there was no telling what he might do. "We'll simply say that Songbird's family isn't able to help her with the child, therefore she's become our ward. There is no untruth in that."

Her sisters concurred.

"But," Jennie said, "if Tom or Chad suspect more to the story and ask questions, we must be honest with our brothers."

With that settled, plans for the morrow commenced. It would be a day full of hard work, with three hogs needing to be butchered, but somehow knowing they'd taken steps to further Songbird's place of belonging in their home brought an air of celebration to their preparations.

Tom and Chad arrived before the sun had time to peek over the mountains the following morning. There was no surprise in their eyes or suspicions raised when Songbird was introduced, despite her obvious nervousness. They simply greeted her with polite nods and continued to the barn. There wasn't time to stop and ponder over a young pregnant girl their spinster sisters had taken in.

Truth be told, it wouldn't be the first time the Jenkins sisters welcomed someone in need into their home. Papa and Mam never turned away a hungry or wayward stranger, and neither did their daughters. Over the years, they'd had many interesting folks spend time in their simple mountain cabin. Brother Brown, the pastor of their tiny church, often sought help from the sisters when someone came to him, asking for assistance.

The weather turned out perfect for butchering—cool but not cold. Overly warm days also weren't desirable because it made the job miserable, especially for those manning the fires and cauldrons of boiling water. Tom and Chad took the noon meal of cold chicken, cheese, and biscuits with the women on the porch and found pleasure in entertaining everyone with stories about growing up in the large family, clearly delighting their young guest. Bertie suspected Songbird hadn't had much joy since her ma's passing. It brought a smile to her heart to know babe and mother would benefit by having the Jenkins men to look up to in the years to come.

Daily chores awaited them after their brothers left. Songbird usually chipped right in, but the long day had taken its toll on the expectant mother. She looked pale and worn-out.

When she made to follow Bertie out to the chicken coop, Bertie shook her head. "No, dear one. You stay here. You've had a long day."

"So have you," the girl countered. "I'll just come—" Before she could finish the sentence, she doubled over. "Ohhh!"

Bertie dropped the egg basket and grabbed Songbird to keep her from falling.

"What is it? Are you havin' pains?" She placed a practiced hand on Songbird's belly. It felt hard all over. "Is this the first?"

Songbird shook her head, her breathing heavy.

When it was over, the girl slowly rose up, a look of guilt in her eyes. "I been feelin' 'em 'bout the last hour or so."

Bertie gave her a stern look. "You should have told me."

"I didn't want to bother you when we was so busy." She shrugged. "'Sides, they weren't too painful till just now."

"Let's get you to bed." Bertie took Songbird by the arm and led her back into the house.

Rubie was making her way to the door to go milk the cow when she saw them. "What's wrong?"

Bertie continued to lead Songbird to her cot. "She's havin' contractions," she said matter-of-factly. At Rubie's gasp, Bertie added, "It could be false pains, but we'll have to wait and see."

Rubie hurried to the kitchen. Soon the five sisters were gathered around Songbird, asking questions and generally making a ruckus.

"Quiet down, Sisters." Bertie huffed. "I can't think with all this chatter." She turned to Songbird. "Now, turn over onto your left side. It'll help slow down the contractions if it's not your time yet. When did you last use the outhouse?"

"A little while ago, but it wasn't much." Songbird grunted as she awkwardly rolled onto her side.

"Dehydration can sometimes bring on labor," Bertie said, "and

I 'spect you haven't been drinkin' enough today, what with all the busyness. Bonnie, fetch her some water."

Jennie helped Bertie tuck pillows behind Songbird to help her rest more comfortably.

"Best get on with your chores, Sisters." Bertie settled in a chair nearby. "We'll know soon enough if this baby is determined to make his appearance today or not."

"But you said it's still a month fore he should come, Miss Bertie." Panic filled Songbird's voice and eyes as she glanced over her shoulder. "He can't come yet. I . . . I ain't ready."

"I know, dear one," Bertie said calmly. She hoped her tone would soothe the frightened mother. "But sometimes babies can't be stopped if they're a-comin'. Let's wait and see what happens in the next hour, shall we?"

Rubie came forward and laid a gentle hand on Songbird. "Lord Jesus, your Word tells us all our days are written in your book before we take our first breath. Be with this child—these, your children—and let your perfect timing give us peace. Amen."

"Amen," the sisters echoed.

With reluctance, the women departed until the cabin was quiet again. Bertie began a mental list of everything she'd need if they were to welcome the little fellow this evening. She always had a bag ready with tinctures, tonics, and sterilized instruments needed for labor and delivery, but an early baby could come into the world with underdeveloped lungs, low birth weight, or even unexpected physical deformities.

"I'm scared, Miss Bertie," Songbird said. Quiet tears followed her admission.

Bertie moved from her chair to the edge of the cot and rubbed Songbird's back. "I know you are, sweet girl, but bringing a child into the world is a wonderful gift from God to a woman. It's a beautiful experience."

"I keep thinkin' 'bout the Dunn baby." Fresh sobs shook her. "What if my baby dies? I couldn't bear it."

"Shush, now." Bertie rubbed the frightened girl's arm. "Have you felt the baby movin' today?"

Songbird nodded.

"That tells me he's fine."

Two more contractions came, although not as strong as the previous one. Bertie used her stethoscope and was pleased to hear the baby's steady heartbeat. To ease Songbird's fears, she let the girl listen to her child's heart and grinned when Songbird marveled at the sound.

The sisters gathered in the kitchen and spoke in hushed tones so they wouldn't disturb Songbird. When an hour had passed and the contractions slowed, Bertie breathed in relief.

"I can't be positive, but I don't believe we'll meet your wee one tonight."

Songbird closed her eyes. "Thank you," she whispered.

After the girl drifted off to sleep and Bertie told her sisters the good news, they agreed to turn in for the night. It had been an exhausting day.

Bertie stayed downstairs, however, to keep an eye on Songbird. It was near midnight when the girl roused. Bertie helped her use the chamber pot and brought her some bread and butter since she'd fallen asleep without eating her supper.

"Miss Bertie," Songbird said, her quiet voice the only sound in the still house, "I have somethin' to ask you."

"What would that be?"

Earnest hazel eyes met Bertie's. "When my baby does finally come, I'd like to name him Amos Joshua, after his pa and yours. Would that be all right with you and the sisters?"

The question caught Bertie by surprise. Moisture clouded her vision. "Dear one, we'd be honored. So would Papa."

Songbird settled back into the pillows. Her eyes drifted closed. "I'm glad God brought me here, Miss Bertie. Y'all have become my family."

Bertie reached to pull the covers over the girl, her heart overflowing with motherly love. "I'm glad God brought you here too, child," she whispered. "Gladder than you know."

Twelve

THE SEVIER COUNTY COURTHOUSE wasn't exactly a happening place.

A stolid-faced gentleman met Walker and Reese promptly at nine o'clock in the deserted lobby and introduced himself as Mr. Hogan, the archives' director. He led them down one tiled hallway, then another, ending at a tiny, windowless room where nearly a dozen cardboard boxes were stacked on the floor next to a small table with two folding chairs. In quick fashion, he went over the rules—*don't damage the documents* and *don't take them out of the room*—then bid a hasty goodbye, closing the door behind him as he made his exit.

"Here we are," Reese said. She clearly tried to infuse cheer into the words.

It didn't work.

Walker groaned inwardly. The same questions he'd asked himself since climbing into her car the previous day rolled through his head.

Is this a waste of time?

Do I truly want to find the midwife who tended my birth?

Do I truly want to find my birth parents?

"I don't necessarily have a plan of how to go about this," she said, studying the boxes, oblivious to his inner turmoil. "Mr. Hogan says these are copies of the original documents that were sent to the Office of Vital Records in Nashville. They aren't official. When I explained we wanted to search for a midwife rather than birth information, he agreed to let us look at them."

"There sure are a lot of boxes," Walker observed.

"I asked him to provide records for the year written on the note, 1943, as well as five years before and five years after, just in case Bertie Jenkins didn't attend many births. We'll each take a box and start going through the records if that's okay with you."

Walker shoved his hands into his jeans pockets. "What will we do if we find what we're looking for?"

The question hung in the air for a long moment.

A look of compassion filled Reese's eyes. "That will be entirely up to you. There's no guarantee we'll find any information about the midwife. All of this—" she indicated the containers—"is just a starting point. Nothing more."

Once again, she was right on the money with her answer.

Reese took off her sweater and draped it over the back of a chair. She picked up a box, lugged it to the table, and opened the lid. "I've helped my friend Bill look through court records in the past. While it does seem like you're looking for the proverbial needle in the haystack, it's quite satisfying when you actually discover what you're searching for."

Walker would take her word for it. He didn't relish digging through stacks of musty papers but followed her example and sat down with a box of yellowed documents from 1943.

As he lifted the lid, it occurred to him there should be a piece of paper in one of these boxes with his name on it. Not Walker Wylie, but his *real* name. Such a document, however, didn't exist. The children listed on these birth records had been given names and most likely went home to live with their parents. Parents who hadn't given them away.

He took out the first sheet of paper. Typed words—*full name*, *place of birth*, and so on—were followed by blanks filled in with scrawling handwriting. Walker didn't bother to look at the name of the child or their parents or any of their private data. The only information his eyes sought was in the bottom right corner in the section titled "Affidavit of Attendant at Birth."

> I hereby certify on oath that I was the attendant at the
> birth of . . .

He skipped over the name.

> And that the facts stated in the certificate attached hereto
> are true and correct to the best of my knowledge and belief.

The signature of the attendant wasn't Bertie Jenkins.

A breath he hadn't realized he held pushed past his lips.

He moved on to the next birth record with a little less trepidation thumping in his heart.

The hands on the clock above the door seemed in no hurry as they slowly ticked off the morning hours. Walker and Reese said very little to each other as they made their way through the boxes.

By one o'clock, Walker was hungry and discouraged.

He tossed the document he'd been perusing onto the table. Like the jillion others he'd read, this one didn't contain the name they sought. "We're wasting our time. I'm starting to doubt the woman even exists. Bertie Jenkins is probably a fake name just like my birth date."

Reese looked up from the paper in her hands. "We've only gone through four boxes. My guess is Bertie Jenkins didn't fill out a birth record for every delivery she attended. They weren't required by law until the 1930s, but even then, mountain people tend to be leery of the government. Remaining anonymous is often important to them."

She paused before adding, "It wouldn't make any sense, to me at least, for the name of the midwife on the letter to be false. Why bother? Why not just leave it blank rather than make up a name?"

Walker considered her words. "I see what you're saying, but isn't it strange that we haven't come across her name on any of these documents?"

Reese gave him a patient look. "Things are done a little different in the mountains. Depending on where Bertie Jenkins lived, she may not have been able to come to the courthouse and fill out the necessary paperwork each time she delivered a baby."

Her explanation didn't reassure Walker. In fact, his discouragement intensified.

"And what if we don't find her name in any of these boxes?" Walker stood and ran his fingers through his hair, frustrated with the entire situation. "What then?"

"I don't know," she answered honestly. "But let's not give up yet. Do you want to get some lunch before we keep looking?"

Food wouldn't alleviate his discouragement, but it might help his mood.

They left the courthouse and walked a couple blocks to a quaint mountain-themed café. After ordering burgers and fries, Walker asked the question he'd wondered about since learning Reese was adopted.

"Have you tried to find your birth parents?"

She didn't seem offended, but a shadow passed over her features. "When my birth mother signed the adoption papers, she made it clear to my parents she wanted to forget I existed. She had a lot of bitterness against the man she'd had the affair with. He denied he was my father. Mom always thought my birth mother believed he'd divorce his wife, marry her, and we'd live happily ever after. When that didn't happen, she wanted nothing to do with me." Reese sighed. "Every now and then I think about contacting her, just to see if time and maturity have changed her mind. But the thing is, she knows who adopted me. My parents have lived in the same house since before I was born. If she wanted to meet me, she could."

Their food arrived, and they ate in silence before Reese continued.

"In the three years since I opened my practice in Piney Ridge, I've delivered a few babies that were given up for adoption by their young mothers. It isn't an easy decision to come to, but they each have reasons why they don't feel they can raise their child. I would've been a painful reminder to my birth mother of a time in her life she'd rather forget. I hope she went on to live a happy life. I did."

Walker appreciated her honesty. "It can't be easy knowing your birth mother could find you if she wanted." He shook his head. "I still don't understand how a woman can give up her baby. I mean, she carries it for nine months. I read once that some kind of bond is formed between an expectant mother and her child during pregnancy. If that were true, you and I wouldn't be sitting here."

"The bond is real, trust me." Reese swirled a long french fry in the dollop of ketchup she'd squeezed onto her plate. "But circumstances play a huge role in it, too. Not every woman who becomes pregnant is ready to be a mother."

Walker scoffed. "That sounds like an excuse to 'play but not pay.'"

"I suppose for some it is," she said, frowning, "but not for everyone. Take my birth mother, for instance. She shouldn't have been with a married man, obviously, but what about him? My birth father was a jerk who took advantage of a teenage girl and cheated on his wife. He most definitely wanted to 'play but not pay,' wouldn't you agree?"

She was right, of course. "I see what you're saying, but—"

"But what?"

Walker shrugged. "This is all still new to me. You've had time to sort things out. To come to terms with . . . with what happened to you. I'm not ready to give anyone a pass just yet, no matter the circumstances."

"I understand how you feel, but believe me when I say it isn't easy for any mother to give up a child they've just given birth to, no matter their reasons. That decision lasts a lifetime." She paused and seemed to consider her next words carefully. "I've met some birth mothers who say they think about the child they gave up nearly every day. Most would still give the baby up, but some wish they could go back and do things differently."

Walker wondered if his birth mother would agree. Would she keep him instead of handing him off to a pastor who handed him off to Walker's folks? If so, what would his life be like now?

They finished lunch and returned to the courthouse. Reese had reserved the room until four o'clock, so they had less than two hours to sift through the remaining records.

Walker took the lid off the box dated 1946. With little enthusiasm, he took out one paper after the other and read through names that meant nothing to him. Until . . .

He stilled.

The copy of the document in his hand was smudged in places, but the neat signature of the attendant was unmistakable: *Alberta Mae Jenkins*.

"I think I just found her." He hadn't realized he'd spoken out loud until Reese jumped to her feet and circled the table.

"You found her?"

Walker handed her the paper, stunned that he might have just located the midwife who attended his birth thirty years ago.

"Alberta Mae Jenkins. That could definitely be Bertie Jenkins."

Reese scanned the other information on the document. "Her address is only listed as Sevier County, Tennessee, but she attended the birth of a baby boy whose parents, Earl and Rhoda Dunn, lived on Bear Creek Road."

The cheeseburger Walker ate for lunch sat heavy as his stomach clenched. "Now what?"

She returned to her chair and studied the document. "Well, the Dunn baby was born in January 1946. The family may or may not live in the same area—" she looked up—"but it might be worth trying to locate them to see if they know the whereabouts of Alberta Mae Jenkins and if she's one and the same person as Bertie Jenkins."

From the moment they'd stepped into this room in the courthouse basement, Walker had struggled with what he would do if they did indeed find what they were looking for.

Did he want to move forward with the search for information about his birth parents?

Or would it only lead to heartache or, worse, more anger?

Reese must have taken his silence as his decision because she offered a look of understanding.

"We've found what we came for, Walker. Or partially, at least. Maybe you should go home and think about what your next steps should be."

Walker scrubbed his face with his hands. "You don't know how much I'd like to do exactly that." He looked across the table to her. "To go back to Nashville and resume my life. I'm supposed to be on tour promoting my new record, but my life imploded. Or that's how it felt, anyway. Everything came to a crashing halt." He shook his head. "If I leave now, I won't come back here for answers. And if I don't get answers, I can't move on with my life."

His ramblings probably didn't make sense, but nothing made sense right now.

"Then, if I understand what you're saying," she said, caution in her voice, "for you to have some sort of resolution and get back to your life, we need to try to find Bertie Jenkins."

It sounded so simple, yet it was a life-altering decision.

The silence in the tiny room stretched as Walker weighed his options. He meant what he said to her—if he walked away now, he wouldn't come back. What that spelled for his future, he didn't know, but it left him frightened in a way he'd never experienced.

"I've come this far," he finally said, dread in each word. "If I don't see this thing through, I know I'll regret it."

"Okay." She glanced at her watch, then took out a pencil and small notebook. "Let me jot down this information; then we'll see if we can find a map of the area. It's almost three o'clock, so we still have several hours of daylight left."

Walker appreciated her sensitivity. She didn't judge, express a strong opinion on the matter, or fire off a dozen ill-timed questions the way Vanessa had done. Reese simply accepted his decision and proceeded to help however she could.

They exited the courthouse a short time later, armed with a map of Sevier County they'd obtained at the visitor information desk. Bear Creek Road wasn't far from the small community of Cosby Run, and Reese suggested they start there. Someone was bound to know something about Bertie Jenkins or the Dunn family.

They left town and headed south on a narrow two-lane road into the foothills of the Great Smoky Mountains. Tall trees dressed in autumn golds, reds, and oranges lined the highway, with a crystal-blue sky overhead. Walker couldn't help but wonder if his parents had traveled down this same road once upon a time. Did they still live in the area? Would this journey into the hills end with a reunion of some kind?

So many questions. Not enough answers.

Cosby Run consisted of a handful of stores, a couple of gas

stations, and not much else. Reese pulled into the parking lot of a store that advertised everything for a dollar.

"I'll run in and see if anyone knows Bertie or the Dunns." Reese reached to open her door, but Walker couldn't simply sit in the car this time.

"I'm coming too."

The store was a hodgepodge of merchandise, with everything from toiletries to hardware items.

"Can I help you folks find something?" A woman wearing far too much makeup eyed Walker with unmistakable interest from her place behind the counter.

He glanced at Reese, wishing they'd stopped at a different store. The last thing he needed was for someone to recognize him. He pulled down the bill of his ball cap.

Reese didn't take the hint and instead moved toward the woman. "We're looking for some people who lived in this area thirty years ago. Maybe you'd recognize the names?"

The woman's deep-red lips lifted in a coquettish grin while her eyes remained on Walker. "Sure thing. Who ya lookin' for, darlin'?"

Her flirtatiousness wasn't welcome. "Bertie Jenkins. She was a midwife."

Walker's terse answer, along with the word *midwife*, no doubt, caused the woman to draw back. Her eyes darted from Walker to Reese's slim figure, then back.

"Jenkins is a common name round these parts," she said with less enthusiasm. "There's at least a dozen families up yonder in the hills, all Jenkins kin." She leaned forward, offering Walker a glimpse at her low-cut neckline.

He averted his gaze.

"What about the Dunn family? They lived on Bear Creek Road back in the forties," Reese said, drawing the woman's attention away from Walker.

"Sure, I know the Dunns. His pappy settled their place in the 1800s. Dunns have lived there ever since." She squinted in thought. "Seems like one of their boys took over the place some years back and built himself his own cabin, but the elder folks is still livin' in the original homestead."

Reese met Walker's gaze, a gleam of hope in her brown eyes. He raised his brow in agreement.

"What's your business with the Dunns and this here midwife?" the woman asked. Suspicion replaced the interest she'd shown earlier. "I don't wanna bring no trouble to them—'specially not from outsiders nosin' around."

Walker wondered if she'd feel differently if he'd returned her flirtation.

"You needn't worry, ma'am." Reese offered a friendly smile. "I'm a midwife as well and would like to meet Ms. Jenkins. She delivered a friend of mine many years ago. The Dunns were some of her clients."

The woman didn't appear completely convinced, but Reese somehow managed to finagle directions to the Dunn place before they bid her farewell.

"You're really good with people," Walker said when they were back inside the VW. "I wouldn't have been so patient."

"It's part of the job." She grinned. "I've had to calm down many soon-to-be fathers and convince eager grandparents to leave the birthing room because they're a distraction. I find that anything said with a smile and kindness goes a long way."

Walker glanced at his watch. "It's too late to try to find the Dunn place today. It'll be dark soon. Wandering around the mountains at night probably isn't the smartest plan."

"I was thinking the same thing. We can come back first thing in the morning."

"I hate to take up more of your time. Aren't you needed back in Piney Ridge?"

She shook her head. "None of my expectant mothers are due right now. Besides, a good friend, Dr. Kocen, and I have an arrangement to handle each other's cases when we're unavailable. I gave my clients his number should they have any issues come up while I'm gone."

The sun had just slipped behind the mountains when they reached the Old Black Inn. After a long day, a quick bite at the café seemed best. The desk clerk had been right. It was good country cooking.

"I'll see you bright and early in the morning," Reese said when they reached their respective doors. "I hope you can get some sleep."

Walker nodded, but there was something he had to say.

"I want you to know how much I appreciate what you've done—what you're doing—for me. There's no way I'd be here, tracking down strangers, if it weren't for you."

Her expression softened in the dusky light. "I'm glad I'm here." A shy smile parted her lips and she bid him good night.

Walker entered his room and was soon stretched out on the bed. He wouldn't say it had been a good day, but it also hadn't been nearly as bad as he'd feared. Finding the elusive Bertie Jenkins's name on the Dunn child's birth certificate was fortuitous, he supposed. Tomorrow could be the day he got answers to his many questions about his origins.

But unlike the rolling wave of apprehension that prospect first brought him in the days after learning of his adoption, the thought of finding the midwife who'd attended his birth settled on his psyche with something that felt akin to hope.

Hope for normalcy.

Hope for the future.

For the first time in weeks, he slept peacefully all night long.

❧

"Top of the World" by the Carpenters played on a small transistor radio at the far end of the Formica counter in the Old Black Café. A handful of patrons sat around the room—some on stools at the counter, some at tables and booths—while the aroma of coffee, bacon, and burnt toast permeated the air.

Walker waved to Reese, who was already seated at a booth near a window where golden sunshine spilled over the faux wood laminated tabletop. The edges of her dark hair were still damp and curled on her forehead in an attractive frame.

"Good morning," she said as he slid onto the vinyl bench opposite her.

"Morning. I hope you slept well."

"I did. How about you?"

He gave a slow nod. "Surprisingly I slept better last night than I have in weeks. Months, even."

"Must be the mountain air."

The waitress took their orders—the farmer's breakfast for Walker and a ham-and-cheese omelet for Reese—and left them each with a mug of steaming coffee.

Walker glanced out the window to the tree-covered mountains that filled the spectacular view. This part of the state truly was beautiful, no matter the season. It had also become quite popular, with the Great Smoky Mountains National Park drawing millions of visitors each year. Sleepy towns like Gatlinburg and Pigeon Forge weren't so sleepy anymore.

"Are you ready for today?"

He returned his attention to her. "I'm as ready as I'll ever be. Finding the Dunns is our first order of business, right?"

"Right . . . if that's still what you want to do. I know the decision to move forward isn't easy."

"It isn't," Walker said, wishing there were a different path he could take to finding peace for his soul, "but it's what I *have* to do. I've also been thinking about what I'll do if we don't locate the Dunns or Bertie Jenkins. Ray knows a private investigator in Nashville. He might be able to dig up information on them that we can't."

She nodded and took a sip of coffee. "I checked the telephone book in my room again. I looked up the name Dunn, but there weren't any listed."

"I did the same. Seems odd since their family has lived here for years."

"You'd be surprised at how many modern conveniences, like telephones, these mountain people *don't* have. Some of my clients live in cabins without electricity or indoor plumbing."

Walker shook his head. "Why would anyone want to live like that?"

Reese chuckled. "I'm not sure I'm the best person to answer that question, because I could never do it. But like the Amish and their shunning of things we think essential to living, a lot of mountain people embrace the old ways."

The waitress brought their food, refilled their cups, and left a ticket on the table before moving on to a group of new customers.

A song by the Beatles came over the radio, bringing a memory with it.

Walker grinned. "Back when I was in college, some of my buddies and I formed a band, determined to become as famous as the Fab Four."

"Is that when you got into music?"

"Sort of. We were pretty green, but we managed to get some gigs at weddings and hotels." He grew thoughtful. "But then the US entered the war, and we decided to join the Army."

Surprise lifted her brow. "I didn't realize you served in Vietnam."

"I didn't." Walker shrugged, recalling those days of shame and disappointment. "While I was in basic training at Fort Benning, I tore my rotator cuff. We were on a nighttime march in the rain carrying sixty-pound packs on our backs when a bunch of us slipped down a hill. I tried to brace myself, but my shoulder took all my weight. I was discharged and wasn't allowed to reenlist, even after I healed."

Empathy shone in her eyes. "At least you tried. You didn't dodge the draft like a lot of people."

"I don't blame those guys for doing what they believe is right, but I wanted to fight for my country." Walker thought back to the day he arrived home from Georgia, beaten down and discouraged. "I was embarrassed I couldn't finish basic with my buddies. Pop told me how he'd wanted to join the military after Pearl Harbor was attacked but couldn't because he was deaf in one ear. He said there are lots of ways to serve without being a soldier. That's when I started playing USO shows. Ray had just finished his tour of duty when he came to a show. We hit it off right away." He grinned. "Ray is determined to make me into the next Elvis Presley."

She studied him a lengthy moment, seemingly unimpressed by such a lofty ambition. "Is that what you want? To be as famous as Elvis?"

Walker pondered the question. "I suppose on some level, it is. I mean, every musician wants a long and successful career like his. But . . ." He paused, searching for the right words to explain the confusion going on inside him. "With everything that's happened in the last four months, I'm not sure of anything anymore. Losing Pop. Finding out I'm adopted." He shrugged. "My life is pretty messed up right now. It's hard to know what tomorrow holds, let alone the future."

Reese met his gaze. "I'm a firm believer that God can take the bad things that happen in life and turn them into something posi-tive and good. Just look at your military experience. Your injury closed one door but opened another."

Walker had never seen his shoulder injury as anything other than a setback, but she was right. Look where life had taken him since that day.

A question pricked his mind.

Could he look at his adoption through the same lens?

Time would tell.

They finished their meal, with Walker insisting on paying the bill, then climbed into the VW and headed into the mountains.

✒

Bear Creek Road wasn't a road at all.

Ruts-'n'-Rocks Trail would have been a more appropriate appellation for the washed-out path that wound up a steep hill. The only indication it might possibly end at someone's home were the dangerously leaning utility poles they passed, with wires that dipped nearly to the ground before they disappeared in thick brush.

Reese let the car idle as she and Walker surveyed the precarious-looking route. "You're sure this is it?"

Walker studied the map they'd obtained at the courthouse the previous day. "I'm not sure of anything out here, but according to this map, this is Bear Creek Road."

"Do you think my car can make it up that?"

The look on his face mirrored her doubts. "It's iffy, at best. We can walk the rest of the way if you don't want to chance it."

Reese considered their options. "We're not even sure how far it is to the Dunn place. It could be on the other side of the mountain, for all we know. On the other hand, I'd hate to get the car stuck. Who knows how far we'd have to walk to find a telephone to call a tow truck." She tapped the steering wheel with her index finger. "It looks like we're walking either way."

"How about we get to the highest point we can and see if there's a house or just more road? Then we can reevaluate."

It sounded like a good plan.

They stowed their belongings in the trunk, locked the doors, and started up the jagged path. The breeze felt crisp and clean. Birds fluttered and trilled in treetops high above them, where leaves of gold, red, and brown danced in morning sunshine.

"You have to admit, it's beautiful up here." She took in a lungful of air. "I mean, smell that. So fresh and earthy."

Walker smirked. "Earthy? That's mold and mildew you smell. Rotting leaves and animal . . . stuff."

Reese laughed. "You're not much of an outdoorsman, are you?"

"Nope. I'm a proud city dweller." He grew thoughtful. "Pop took me camping once when I was about ten. He wasn't much of an outdoorsman either, but we managed to stay alive and not get lost. Funny, I haven't thought about that camping trip in years."

They walked for a good mile. Up one hill, down another. The road never improved, convincing Reese they'd made the correct choice to leave the car where it sat.

"Who's taking care of your dog?" Walker asked after several silent minutes.

The memory of Oreo's muddy paw prints on the front of Walker's shirt surfaced, and she cringed. "Kathy, my neighbor, dog-sits when I'm away from home. Her little boy, Ryan, loves to play with him. By the way, I'm really sorry Oreo messed up your shirt."

Walker chuckled. "Oreo? I guess I know why you came up with that name."

"Actually—" Reese grinned—"I love Oreo cookies. When I went to the animal shelter to choose a dog, I picked him because of his coloring."

"Lucky dog."

She smiled. "Do you have pets?"

He shook his head. "My life is too crazy. Especially now."

He grew quiet, and Reese let the subject drop.

She thought back to her telephone conversation with Kathy last night. When she'd taken Oreo over to her friend's house on the morning she and Walker drove to Sevierville, she'd simply said she was helping a friend with some research. But now that the quick trip had been extended, she had to come clean with her friend about what she was doing and with whom.

"Walker Wylie?" Kathy had shrieked. "*The* Walker Wylie? You've been holding out on me, Reese Chandler."

Reese laughed and quickly explained about Ray contacting her, although she couldn't tell her friend the specifics of their conversation. When Kathy assumed Walker needed her skills as a midwife for his girlfriend, Reese cleared things up.

"It's nothing like that, Kath. Honestly, I'm not sure I'll be much help, but I think he just needs a friend right now."

Gratefully, Kathy didn't press for more details.

When Reese and Walker reached the top of the next hill, she let out a breath of relief. "Thank goodness, there's a house."

They made their way across the overgrown yard. A smaller cabin stood some distance away, tucked in a grove of trees. A faded pickup truck sat in front.

All was quiet when they gained the sagging porch of the larger house, where several wooden chairs with peeling paint lived. A lone window was curtained, giving them no hint at what awaited inside.

Reese exchanged an apprehensive look with Walker before she knocked on the door.

At first it seemed no one was home. After a long moment, however, footsteps sounded. Soon, a stooped, gray-haired woman opened the door. Her weathered face revealed surprise.

"Land sakes, I thought you was one of my grandkids playin' a trick on me." Her expression went from surprise to suspicion. "What can I do for you folks?" She glanced behind them. "How'd you get up here, anyways?"

"Ma'am," Reese began, "are you Mrs. Dunn?"

The woman nodded.

"My name is Reese, and this is my friend Walker. We're sorry to disturb you, but we're looking for someone and were told you might know where she lives."

Wariness deepened the crevices on her face. "Who would that be?"

"Bertie Jenkins. She was a midwife back in the 1940s. I'm also a midwife, and I'd hoped to meet her. She delivered a friend of mine many years ago."

The scowl on Mrs. Dunn's face eased some. "Sure, I know Bertie. She tended ever' one of my birthin's." She paused as her gaze grew distant. "Even little Samuel's. Won't never forget that day. Bertie and that little gal who come with her were so kind, but there weren't nothin' anyone could do."

Reese didn't know what happened to little Samuel, but she recognized the look of loss on the mother's face.

"Haven't seen Bertie in ages though." The woman looked out to the hills. "'Spect she and Rubie are still livin' at the old Jenkins place, but I can't be certain."

Reese glanced at Walker. The concern she found in his eyes matched her own. It hadn't occurred to her that Bertie Jenkins might not be alive.

"Would it be possible to get directions to her home?" Walker asked, an urgency in his voice Reese hadn't heard before.

Mrs. Dunn considered him. "I can tell you folks how to get there from here, but you ain't never gonna find it. Ain't no road signs, like in the city. Just stumps 'n' cricks 'n' hollers."

Frustration crossed Walker's face. "We have a map in the car down the hill. I'd be happy to get it and maybe you could show us where Ms. Jenkins lives."

"Like I told you, young man," Mrs. Dunn said, "there ain't no road signs. I doubt your map would be any help. Bear Creek and a handful of others are the only named roads. The rest is just mountain trails."

Reese sensed Walker's growing desperation. They needed to come up with a solution to the problem. "Is there someone available who could show us the way? We'd be happy to compensate them for their trouble."

Mrs. Dunn tugged her knit shawl tighter across thin shoulders, seeming to consider Reese's offer. "My boy Jeffrey Earl lives just yonder." She pointed to the small house they'd seen in the trees. "He ain't workin' at the loggin' company today. Busted his arm last week huntin' wild hogs. He might be willin' to show y'all where the Jenkins place is."

"We'd appreciate it, ma'am," Walker said, visibly relieved.

Jeffrey Earl was summoned when his mother used a sturdy stick to bang loudly on a pot that hung from the front porch rafters. When he arrived, with his arm in a cast and a cagey look on his face, Mrs. Dunn introduced everyone and told him the plan. When he began to balk, she mentioned the monetary appreciation.

Jeffrey Earl's demeanor changed. "Why, sure, I can show you folks how to get to the Jenkins place."

They bid Mrs. Dunn goodbye, with her asking them to give Bertie her regards if they found the midwife, and loaded into Jeffrey Earl's 1950s Chevy pickup. He drove one-handed, giving little care to his passengers as the vehicle flew over rocks and ruts, all the while chattering about them being the only visitors they'd had up on Bear Creek Road in a coon's age.

Reese sat in the middle of the bench seat and had to lean toward

Walker to avoid being in the way of the floor-mounted gearshift. She banged into his shoulder multiple times as they bounced down the hill, but she didn't have any choice.

Thankfully, they arrived at the VW in one piece. When Jeffrey Earl volunteered to drive them to the Jenkins homestead, Reese said, "I'm not sure how long we'll stay. Do you think my car can make it there safely?"

Jeffrey Earl considered the small vehicle and shrugged. "I s'pose. Them roads in that part of the mountains ain't as pitted as ours."

With that settled, Reese and Walker climbed into the car. Thankfully, Jeffrey Earl's prediction of road conditions was correct, and the little car easily kept up with his wild driving.

"Mrs. Dunn was right," Walker said after they'd taken a half-dozen lefts and a half-dozen rights. "We would have never found Bertie Jenkins's home."

Jeffrey Earl's truck eventually came to a stop at a Y in the road. A small, whitewashed church with a graveyard stood nearby.

Reese rolled down her window when he approached.

"That there road'll take you to the Jenkins place." He pointed to the lane that branched off to their right. "It's 'bout a mile, give or take. Can't miss it."

"Thank you very much, Mr. Dunn. We truly appreciate it." She offered her hand.

He glanced at it but didn't move to shake it. "Uh, you said there'd be somethin' for my troubles."

"Of course." Walker quickly exited the car, came around to meet Jeffrey Earl, and handed him some bills. Jeffrey Earl seemed pleased, and the two shook hands.

"Nice meetin' you folks. If y'all need more help, lemme know." He waved and returned to his truck.

Walker climbed back into the VW. He and Reese waved again as Jeffrey Earl made a U-turn and flew past them in a cloud of dust.

When the air cleared, Reese took a deep breath. "Well, this is it."

Walker nodded, but his gaze remained focused on the path that disappeared into the trees, a solemn look on his face. "Yeah," he said quietly. "This is it."

Reese wished she had some words of wisdom for him, but nothing came to mind that didn't sound trite. She simply put the car into gear and started up the path that might very well lead to the one person who held the answers Walker needed.

Thirteen

AFTER SONGBIRD SCARED THEM with signs of early labor, Bertie insisted the girl remain on bed rest until the baby arrived—early or not.

"But, Bertie," she'd complained, a pretty pout on her face as Bertie fluffed pillows and straightened blankets, "I'll get bored just layin' here."

Bertie'd put her hands on her hips and worked up a stern look. "A bored mama is the price I'm willin' to pay for a healthy, full-term babe."

Songbird complied, albeit grudgingly, and kept to her bed or a chair in the weeks that followed the hog butchering. The contractions still came from time to time, but Rubie would lay her hands on Songbird's taut belly and pray until they ceased. Someone might suggest the contractions were false cramps women had prior to real labor, but Bertie'd been a midwife for decades and knew the difference. She'd never witnessed labor come to a stop the way Songbird's did when Rubie prayed.

The sisters took turns entertaining the young patient throughout the long days, bringing her books and flowers and such to make her smile. Jennie went off to Cosby Run one morning and returned with a writing tablet and a dozen pencils, claiming Songbird needed to work on her poetry and songs. Their older sister's complete turnaround where Songbird was concerned still amazed Bertie. Like the Good Book said—nothing is impossible with God.

As the days passed, Songbird became more restless and uncomfortable.

"I'm gettin' so big, Miss Bertie," she said one morning after a sleepless night. "I can't hardly lay still no more. The baby kicks and squirms so much, like he's fightin' to get out. It surely must be time for him to come, don't you think?"

"I do. Let's see what this little fellow has to say about it."

Bertie took the stethoscope from the birthing bag she kept near Songbird's cot these days, ready the moment labor commenced. She'd told Rubie just yesterday they were past the danger point and the baby's lungs should be fine now if he decided to make his appearance.

Rubie simply smiled. "Yes, Sister. I know." It occurred to Bertie then that her sister hadn't prayed over Songbird's large belly the last few days.

Bertie listened to the baby's steady, strong heartbeat for a full minute. Then she listened to Songbird's heart as well as her internal organs. Bertie wasn't a doctor, but she'd tended enough folks to know when things inside the body weren't quite right. Gratefully, everything sounded normal.

After examining Songbird, she determined the girl's body was unquestionably preparing for birth.

"I wouldn't be surprised if you weren't holding your wee one within the week."

Bertie thought her happy declaration would bring a smile to the young mother, but panic washed over Songbird's face instead.

"I . . . I'm scared, Miss Bertie," she whispered, her chin trembling.

Bertie's heart went out to the girl. So young to be facing such a life-changing event.

She pulled the chair closer to the cot. It was time to have *the talk* Songbird had been avoiding.

"Childbirth is the most natural thing a woman can do, dear one."

Fear-filled eyes met hers. "I remember Pa's wife screamin' when she was havin' her babies. She said terrible things to Pa. I was s'posed to be in the barn with the young'uns, but I snuck to the door and listened. It sounded awful." She looked away. "Then there's Miz Dunn and—" She shuddered.

"Oh, sweet child, you mustn't think of those things." She grasped the girl's hand and coaxed her to meet her gaze. "Childbirth is painful, yes, but it's also beautiful. Think about your own ma. She went through the pain to get you, her precious daughter."

A small smile touched her lips. "Mama loved babies. Said she'd have a dozen if the Lord'd give 'em to her."

Bertie leaned forward. "That sounds like a woman who was willin' to face the hard, painful things about childbirth to get to the good part: a sweet babe in her arms."

Songbird visibly relaxed. "I wish she was here."

"I know you do."

"But I'm glad you'll be tendin' me."

Bertie squeezed her hand. "I am too, dear one."

For the next hour, Bertie explained what would happen to Songbird's body once labor fully commenced. The girl asked questions, but the fear she'd shown earlier edged away with the wonder of it all.

"I hope he comes on my birthday," she said with a yawn.

Bertie had been organizing her birthing bag but stilled. She looked at Songbird, whose eyes grew heavy.

"Your birthday? When is that?"

Songbird snuggled into the pillow with another yawn. "Tuesday."

With that, she drifted off to sleep.

Bertie, however, sprang to her feet and hurried to the kitchen. Saturday chores were no different from any other day of the week, so she knew she'd find at least one sister in the kitchen.

It was Jennie.

"Sister," she said, aflutter with her news. "Songbird has just told me something extraordinary."

Jennie gave her a look of disapproval from her place at the stove, where she stirred an enormous pot of apples they'd peeled and cored the day before. After the fruit cooked down and was mashed with sugar, Jennie would fill a dozen or more jars and put them in the cellar so they could enjoy the bounty from Papa's orchard all winter.

"What in tarnation, Alberta Mae? You look as if you're about to burst."

Bertie ignored the scolding. "Tuesday is Songbird's birthday."

Her sister's scowl vanished. "Tuesday?"

"Yes, and we must have something special for her. Don't you agree?"

Jennie didn't answer directly. The sisters typically didn't celebrate birthdays. It seemed rather pointless at their ages. But Songbird was still a child, even if she was to become a mother any day.

"What do you have in mind?" Jennie asked, surprising Bertie. Her older sister rarely sought the opinions of others.

"Well," Bertie said as she slid onto a chair at the worktable, "I s'pose we should have a cake." She glanced at the pot Jennie was stirring. "We could make a stack cake. You'll have plenty of fresh applesauce."

Stack cake was a family favorite, although it was usually reserved for Christmas and Easter.

Luckily, Jennie didn't disagree. "That's a fine idea. And we'll roast a couple chickens and bake some yams."

Rubie, Amelie, and Bonnie arrived for the noon meal, and the sisters continued to discuss the birthday celebration while Songbird slept.

"What about a gift?" Bonnie asked. "We could make her a new dress or buy a hat at the mercantile."

"Seems like it should be more meaningful," Bertie said. "Something from our hearts."

The sisters sat around the table deep in thought when Rubie gave a little gasp. "I know what we should give her."

Four pairs of eyes turned to her.

"A Bible of her own."

Bertie grinned. "Of course." It seemed so obvious now.

It was decided that Rubie and Bonnie would go directly to town and see about purchasing the Book for their young friend. If their small mercantile in Cosby Run didn't have one in stock, perhaps Brother Tom would be willing to drive the sisters to Sevierville.

After the women departed, Bertie tiptoed into the gathering room to check on Songbird. The girl slept peacefully, as did the babe, it seemed. She chuckled softly. Apparently the wee one already had his days and nights mixed up.

She bent to place a light kiss on Songbird's forehead.

"I love you," she whispered.

Bertie couldn't wait to see Songbird's face when they surprised her with a celebration on her birthday.

⁂

Tuesday arrived, bringing bright sunshine and a cool breeze.

Both of which worked perfectly with the sisters' plan to keep Songbird from the house that afternoon while party preparations were underway. It had been ages since such excitement filled the Jenkins home, and they each had a difficult time containing their smiles and whispers so Songbird wouldn't become suspicious.

But the poor child was so heavy and exhausted, nothing beyond the impending birth occupied her thoughts. Not even Jennie's unusual activity of plucking two hens from the coop or Rubie's task of decorating the table with a large bouquet of fall leaves were enough to gain her curiosity.

Bertie helped her into the chair beside the cot so she could eat a bowl of grits with butter and cream, but the girl fidgeted so much she nearly spilled her breakfast.

"My back sure is achin' this mornin'." She sat up as straight as she could, grimacing. "Must've slept sideways or somethin'."

Bertie's ears perked up. A backache was a sure sign labor wasn't too far-off. "I'll make a warm compress after you've had somethin' to eat."

Songbird nodded, but it was obvious she was distracted and uncomfortable. After a few bites, she gave up. "I ain't too hungry, Miss Bertie. Sorry."

"No need to apologize, dear. Your body is preparing to deliver a baby. Losing your appetite is perfectly normal."

Bertie glanced toward the kitchen, where Jennie was busy putting the finishing touches on the stack cake she had made last night after Songbird fell asleep. Bertie hoped the girl would feel like eating the feast they'd planned for her birthday. Roasted chicken, baked yams, turnip greens with ham, and stack cake were foods usually reserved for days when they had company or even a holiday. Celebrating Songbird's special day seemed a perfect time to enjoy a sumptuous meal.

Bertie carried the near-full breakfast dish to the kitchen and found her sister bent over the cake, carefully arranging dried slices of apple on top. It reminded Bertie of the many years she and her sisters watched Mam make the delicious, stacked dessert. It was so familiar to each of them, she reckoned they could make it with their eyes closed.

Make the dough. Separate into five equal parts. Pat into eight-inch circles and bake until the edges are golden brown. When the cakes were cool, the baker layered them with sweet apple filling. They'd cover the cake and let it sit overnight to enhance the gooey deliciousness.

"It looks wonderful, Sister." Bertie went to the basin and washed the bowl. "Mam would be proud."

Jennie didn't look up from her work. "I want it to be special, just for our girl."

Bertie hid her smile at the endearing reference. Her older sister wouldn't appreciate the teasing that was on Bertie's lips, but it was nice to know Jennie had been as captivated by Songbird as the rest of them.

After the noon meal, Bertie coaxed Songbird outdoors. "The sun is warm, and you need some exercise. Lying abed for so many weeks has your muscles lazy."

They wandered down to the garden and puttered in the herb boxes. Songbird continued to rub her back, but she didn't want to sit on the stump of a large tulip tree Papa cut down when he built the homestead all those many years ago.

"It feels good to walk." She lifted her face to soak in autumn sunshine. "I'll sure 'nough be glad when I can carry this babe in my arms and not my belly."

They remained outside for an hour or so, enjoying the glorious day, until Songbird began to grow weary. She declined Bertie's offer to make a comfy place on the porch where she could nap and instead moved slowly to her cot. She was asleep within moments.

When Bertie entered the kitchen, her sisters were gathered around the table, working on the special dinner in various ways.

"I won't be surprised if she goes into labor soon," Bertie said, joining them. "She's showin' all the signs."

"Won't it be wonderful to hear the little one?" Rubie said as she rolled out biscuit dough to go on top of the greens. "Newborns have such a sweet way of cryin', almost like a kitten mewling."

Bonnie chuckled. "I don't 'spect his cryin' is what I'm lookin' forward to the most." She glanced at Rubie. "I was seven years old when you were born, but I still remember the first time I held you. There's nothin' as precious as a baby in your arms."

As the supper hour neared, their excitement mounted.

Bertie surveyed their efforts with pleasure.

The table was set with Mam's finest dishes and two tall, tapered candles in silver holders that once belonged to Granny Jenkins. A dinner fit for a queen, including the stack cake, warmed on the stove, and the special gift sat on the table at the place of honor. The book's black leather cover looked remarkably different from Papa's tattered Bible, whose cover and pages threatened to fall to pieces each time they opened it.

Bertie prayed Songbird's Bible would someday appear just as worn and loved.

➤

I woke to delicious smells, and my stomach growled in response.

When I opened my eyes, I found Bertie beside the cot, her smile wider than usual. "You look rested."

I glanced at the clock on the wall, surprised by the late hour. "I slept so long I'll never get to sleep tonight." With a yawn and a stretch of my arms, I slowly sat up.

Bertie walked with me to the outhouse, chattering on about nothing in particular. When we returned to the house, all was quiet, which seemed odd. Preparing supper was usually a noisy affair. Perhaps the sisters didn't want to disturb my sleep.

I followed Bertie into the kitchen.

"Happy birthday," the four women gathered around the table called out.

I could only stare at them, my mouth hanging open. "How . . . how . . . ? I didn't have any idea you all was doin' this." My eyes filled. "I'd nearly forgotten it was my birthday."

"We didn't." Jennie motioned me to the head of the table, a place Jennie herself usually occupied. "You're the guest of honor today."

Everything looked so pretty, I couldn't believe it was all for me. "I ain't never had a birthday party before. Mama sometimes had us a special doodad when we were kids, but after she passed . . ." I shrugged. "No one remembered or cared 'bout my birthday."

Once I was seated, I noticed a Bible next to my plate. It looked brand-new. "Miss Jennie, did you get yourself a new Book? It sure is pretty." I picked it up and offered it to Jennie.

I'd never seen Jennie smile so big. "It ain't mine."

Confused, I took in each of the sisters, only to find them all grinning. After a moment, understanding washed over me. I looked at the book in my hands.

"Is this for me?"

"We couldn't think of a thing better to give you than God's Word," Rubie said.

After several moments of staring at the cover where the words *Holy Bible* were written in gold letters, I carefully opened the book, slowly turning crisp, new pages.

"Thank ya," I said softly, mostly because my throat felt all choked up.

I looked up, first meeting Bertie's watery gaze and then to each of the women gathered around me. Women I'd come to love. "I've never had nothin' as beautiful as this. I'll treasure it always."

After the sisters sang a rather off-key rendition of the birthday song, with plenty of giggles and poking of their neighbor when a bad note rose loudly, the celebration began. Much to their delight, my appetite returned, and we enjoyed the special meal. I even had a second helping of Jennie's yummy stack cake.

We lingered in the kitchen after the dishes were washed and the leftover food put in the cellar to stay cool. The sisters shared memories of childhood birthday celebrations and nearly got into an argument when they couldn't agree on the best stack cake recipe.

The clock, however, told us the day was nearing an end.

"We best turn in." Jennie rose. "Tomorrow will be here afore we know it."

They all slowly got to their feet, chattering about what needed to be done on the morrow. I stood too but gasped when I felt a gush of warmth between my legs.

When I looked down, there was a puddle of water at my feet.

Fear washed over me.

My eyes darted to Bertie. "Miss Bertie?"

Bertie hurried over and clutched my shaky hand, unable to keep a smile from her lips.

"Dear one," she said, excitement shining in her eyes. "Your babe is on its way."

Fourteen

AFTER SEEING THE DUNN PLACE, Walker was better prepared for the ancient-looking cabin they encountered at the end of the dirt path.

Reese maneuvered the car across a potholed, open yard and parked a short distance from the house. A dog, as gray around its muzzle as the weathered logs of the dwelling, rose from his spot in the sunshine and ambled toward the VW.

Walker's gut churned with nervousness as he studied the aged residence.

The first thing he noticed were two enormous rock chimneys—one on the front of the cabin and one off to the side. Serious labor had gone into the construction of them. Surprisingly, they appeared sturdy and showed no signs of drooping despite the probability of their being in place for many decades.

A covered porch occupied the right corner of the building. From Walker's place inside the car, it looked jam-packed with everything from an old-fashioned spinning wheel to what appeared to be a butter churn. Vegetation grew in disarray along the base of the log walls—various shrubs, rosebushes without blooms, plants that looked like assorted herbs—and vines with bright-red leaves climbed the porch railing and posts.

Thick pieces of tree trunk in odd shapes and sizes lay haphazardly about the yard. An axe leaned against a sagging picket fence nearby, waiting for someone to turn the pieces into firewood. Several empty galvanized pails and a half-dozen garden tools lay on the ground here and there, seemingly forgotten by the last person to use them.

Not far from the house stood what looked to be a barn of sorts, long and narrow, also made from weather-beaten logs. Dozens of rust-covered shovels, hoes, and scythes hung from nails on the rough-hewn walls, along with ropes, harnesses, wagon wheels, and a hodgepodge of farming equipment Walker couldn't identify. Most appeared as antiquated as the building itself. A hand pump and wooden animal trough completed the scene.

A scene that came straight out of the 1800s.

Time, it seemed, stood still in this part of the mountains.

"What are we doing here?" he muttered. He turned to Reese, who'd been silent since they arrived. "This is nuts, you know. Look at this place. It's like we've traveled back to a different century or something."

Reese offered a look of compassion. "You've come this far, Walker. Let's see if Bertie Jenkins is home. If at any point you want to leave, we will, no questions, no judgment."

How did she always know what he was thinking?

Leaving was exactly what he wanted to do.

After another glance at the house, he inhaled a deep breath and blew it out. "All right. The sooner we get in there, the sooner we can put this behind us."

They exited the car. Cool mountain air wafted around them, along with *earthy* scents Reese loved. The dog, who'd patiently waited for them, sauntered over, tail wagging. Not exactly a watchdog, it seemed.

Reese bent to scratch the animal on its head, then joined Walker at the base of the porch. Three large, flat rocks were positioned as steps, leading to a space crowded with even more items than Walker noted from the car. A table held a dozen empty clay pots along with small gardening tools. A bench as well as several straight-backed chairs offered seating, although some held buckets, shoes, and other smaller items. A homemade broom leaned near a door, and pots, hats, and tools hung from hooks and nails on the wall.

"There are two doors," Reese whispered. She glanced between identical entrances on either side of the porch. "Which one should we try?"

Walker shrugged. "The house isn't that big, so I don't think it matters."

Reese mounted the stone steps and approached the nearest door. She rapped three times and waited.

Nothing.

Walker glanced around the yard. He didn't see a vehicle, so perhaps Bertie Jenkins was away.

Reese knocked again. "Hello? Is anyone home?"

No one answered.

Disappointment washed over Walker, surprising him.

He didn't know what he expected to discover about himself at this cabin hidden in the Appalachians, but if Bertie Jenkins wasn't home, he'd never find out.

Reese stepped down from the porch and joined him. "Maybe we should look around. She might be nearby."

Walker shook his head, defeated. "Let's just leave. I'm sorry I wasted your time coming all the way out here. This is just one big wild-goose chase."

Reese bit her lip, but true to her word, she didn't argue.

They made their way back to the car with the dog trailing behind. Just as Walker opened his door, the breeze carried the distant sound of conversation to them.

"Did you hear that?" Reese turned in the direction from where it came. "I think there's someone over that way."

Walker looked to where she pointed, past the barn, to what appeared to be the edge of an orchard.

"Shall we see who's there?"

Her eager smile broke through Walker's discouragement. "Are you always so optimistic?"

She grinned. "Yes."

Walker chuckled, closed the car door, and followed her down a worn footpath. The dog perked up and, with a burst of energy, sped past them to lead the way.

The voices grew louder once Walker and Reese passed the barn and entered the orchard, where row upon row of fruit trees grew.

"I don't think this is a good idea, Sister," came a woman's voice. "What'll I do if you fall off that ladder?"

It seemed to come from deeper into the orchard. The dog headed that direction, with Walker and Reese following behind.

"Papa worked in his orchard when he was older than we are," another female said, although her voice was somewhat muffled. "Besides, who'll pick the apples if we don't? The boys have school. We can't let good fruit go to waste."

The dog barked a greeting when he reached a plump woman wearing an old-fashioned dress and a bonnet that completely hid her face. She was looking up into the branches of a tree where a tall wooden ladder disappeared into golden leaves. The hem of yet another outdated dress and a pair of dust-covered, high-top shoes—could they be handmade?—were all that was visible of the other woman. A small pushcart on two wooden wheels sat nearby, half-full of ripe apples.

"Well, hello, Shep." The woman on the ground bent to pat the dog before she took notice of Walker and Reese. She jerked, clutching her chest. "Good gracious, you young people startled me."

Before Walker or Reese could respond, the woman in the tree tossed down three apples, barely missing the other woman's head.

"What did you say, Rubie?" she called.

"We have visitors, Sister." The woman squinted to get a better look at Walker. "Do I know you?"

Walker guessed her to be somewhere in her late seventies or early eighties. He was certain they'd never met. "I don't believe so, ma'am."

The woman on the ladder muttered and carefully started down the rungs. "You best not be pulling my leg just to get me down, Sister, or I'll—"

She reached the ground and lifted the bill of her own large bonnet. "Well, I declare. You weren't tellin' a story. Hello. Where did you folks come from?"

Reese smiled. "My name is Reese, and this is my friend Walker."

"I'm Bertie, and this is my sister Rubie. We're all that's left of the Jenkins sisters."

Reese's eyes widened, and she exchanged a look with Walker.

Walker's heart thrummed, and his mouth went dry. The woman's brow rose as he continued to stare at her. Finally he found his voice. "Bertie Jenkins, the midwife?"

The woman's face revealed surprise at Walker's question. "Yes, I used to tend births, but I'm too old for that now. Is that what you're a-wantin'? A midwife?" Her keen gaze gave Reese a once-over.

"No, ma'am," Reese said as her cheeks flamed. "We've actually come to talk to you about a birth you attended thirty years ago."

This information gave the woman pause. Her gaze went back and forth between them before it settled on Walker. The intense study that ensued made him feel like a specimen under a microscope.

"Yes, I'm sure I know you." Rubie smiled and seemed content with her conclusion, although she offered no information on the possibility of their prior meeting.

After another stretch of silence, Bertie broke eye contact with Walker. "You folks come on up to the house and you can tell me your story."

The dog must have understood her meaning, because he rose from where he'd plopped down and started back in the direction they'd come.

Rubie bent to lift the handles on the wooden cart.

Walker stepped forward. "May I help?"

The woman grinned and relinquished the task to him.

"Our nephews—great-nephews, actually—help with fall harvest," Bertie said as the women fell in behind Walker and the cart. "But they're in school today. The almanac says frost is comin', and Papa never left fruit on the trees to ruin."

The two sisters had to be in their eighties, so Walker wondered if she meant her husband rather than her father.

Reese remarked on the beautiful scenery around them, putting her people skills to work.

"Papa and Mam homesteaded here after the war," Bertie said as they made their way past the barn. "He and Mam's pa built a simple one-room cabin with a sleeping loft. Papa added on the kitchen and porch after the babies started a-comin' and they needed more room."

Walker set the cart down, certain now Bertie's "Papa" was indeed her father, especially if the war she referenced was the Civil War. He studied the log home. "Is this the original house?"

Bertie and Rubie both nodded.

"Papa and Mam raised eleven young'uns here. My sister and I have lived here our whole lives."

The interesting conversation worked to briefly distract Walker from the reason he and Reese were there, but once they grew silent, his anxiety level increased.

Did this elderly woman hold the information he sought?

Would anything she had to say help him come to terms with his adoption? Or would it send him into a tailspin, as he feared deep down?

"Come on in and we'll have a cup o' tea." Bertie led the way up the stone steps to the door Reese had knocked on earlier. Rubie followed, moving a bit slower than her sister.

Reese met Walker's gaze while they waited their turn, her brow raised, as though asking, *"Do you want to stay?"*

Walker gave a slight shrug followed by a nod in answer. The mixed message was exactly how he felt.

He followed Reese onto the porch and immediately ducked his head, coming within an inch of giving himself a concussion. The ceiling itself wasn't much more than six feet high. Not a good situation for someone as tall as Walker.

When they entered the house, he and Reese came to a dead stop.

He'd thought the porch held an astonishing number of belongings, but the sheer volume of objects in this room—a room he guessed was the main cooking and eating area—was astounding.

Another spinning wheel, identical to the one on the porch. A dozen or so chairs of varying sizes. Even the rafters of the low ceiling were filled with baskets, bundles of dried herbs, flowers, and all manner of cooking utensils. Both sisters removed their bonnets and hung them on a row of hooks with similar head coverings and coats. An interior doorway opened into the adjoining room, where Walker saw a second stone fireplace and a small bed with a quilt spread across it. There was no telling what else occupied the room out of his line of vision.

"Have a seat." Bertie motioned them to a long, worn table at the center of it all. Not a crumb rested on its surface nor on the plank floor, he noted. Despite the clutter, the home appeared clean and well-kept.

Although an enormous fireplace dominated one wall, Bertie

moved to an old-fashioned blackened stove in the corner. It reminded Walker of something out of a Western movie. This stove, however, wasn't a prop. It appeared to be what these sisters used every day to cook meals on.

Bertie opened a door on the front of the iron appliance and tossed in a couple small pieces of wood. Surprisingly, they caught fire right away even though Walker hadn't noticed any flames.

"Sister, shall we serve the last of the cherry tarts?" Rubie asked. She turned to Walker and Reese. "Papa's cherries never disappoint, especially when our niece puts them into tarts."

Walker watched the women bustle about the kitchen, working in sync. He wondered about their own families. Neither mentioned husbands or children. Had they truly never lived anywhere other than this ancient cabin?

The thought was dumbfounding.

Once the table was laden with floral teacups, matching plates, and a larger plate stacked with a half-dozen delicious-looking tarts, the sisters joined Walker and Reese.

It had been hours since their early breakfast at the café in town. Despite his nerves, Walker reached for one of the desserts but stilled when Rubie bowed her head, followed by Bertie, and finally Reese. He quickly withdrew his hand, feeling like a naughty child.

"Father, we thank thee for the new friends you've brought to our table. May the bounty of our land, although just an afternoon treat, bring nourishment to our bodies. In Jesus' name, amen."

Bertie passed the plate of tarts to him after the brief prayer. Humor danced in her eyes, convincing him she'd seen him reach for one. "Where are you folks from?"

Walker took a tart, then handed the plate to Reese. "I live in Nashville."

"I grew up in Knoxville, but I live in Piney Ridge now," Reese said. She looked at Walker, then back to Bertie. "Walker and I are just friends. Business associates, in a way. We actually haven't known each other very long."

Bertie's face revealed a hint of puzzlement over the rambled explanation, but she let it go.

"Piney Ridge. Isn't that where Cousin Fred's daughter and her family live, Sister?"

Rubie looked thoughtful. "I do believe you're right. Fred was a cousin on Mam's side of the family," she added, giving names, ages, and descriptions of their relatives. When Reese admitted she wasn't acquainted with the family, Rubie determined they needed to rectify that posthaste.

While they bantered back and forth about the Piney Ridge area, Walker felt Bertie's eyes on him. After the teacups were empty and the tarts tucked away in their bellies, Rubie yawned and excused herself with an apology.

"I think I'll lie down while you folks talk. That apple pickin' wore me out." She disappeared into the adjacent room.

When Walker returned his attention to Bertie, he found her studied gaze on him once again.

"Now, why don't you tell me about the birth I tended way back. When did you say it was? Thirty years ago?"

Reese looked at Walker, a question in her eyes. He knew she'd happily explain the situation, but it was time for him to take matters into his own hands.

"Yes, ma'am."

His heart raced.

This very moment was the reason he sat in a stranger's ancient log house, deep in the mountains, hoping she would remember.

"I recently learned I'm adopted. My mom, well, the woman who adopted me, has a letter signed by you, Bertie Jenkins, that says I was born here in Sevier County. I hope you can give me more information about . . ." He swallowed. "About my birth."

He doubted very many, if any, of the babies she'd helped bring into the world came searching for her years later. Yet there was no indication the explanation of his presence at her table caught Bertie by surprise.

"A letter signed by me, you say."

Walker nodded. He'd brought the letter with him, but it was in his bag in the car. Until he was certain she was the midwife who'd signed it, he'd keep the letter to himself.

The wrinkles on her forehead deepened. "What does this letter say?" she asked, something akin to caution in her voice.

"It's quite brief, really. A healthy baby boy was born in Sevier County in 1943."

He waited for her reaction.

Bertie didn't even blink.

After a long silence, she narrowed her eyes on him. "Thirty years is a long time. I tended lots of births back in those days. I'm an old woman now with an old woman's memory." Her gaze intensified. "What is it you want to know?"

The direct question hit its mark, like an arrow piercing a bull's-eye.

What *did* he want to know?

A dam broke somewhere deep inside. A flood of emotion that had been building from the moment he learned he was adopted released and spilled forth.

"I want to know who my mother was. And my father. Why did they give me up for adoption? Was I not good enough for them? Not perfect enough? How could they just give me away and never come find me?"

As he put to voice the questions that had lived inside him since the day after Pop's funeral—questions that fueled feelings of rejection, doubt, and fear—anger stole over him and took their place.

"I know women have legitimate reasons to give up a child," he said, glancing to Reese, who'd remained quiet through the conversation, "but I have a right to know why it happened to me."

He leveled a firm look at the woman across the table.

"If you're the midwife who tended my birth, then you're the only one who can help me find the answers I'm looking for. I need you to tell me why my mother didn't want me."

Fifteen

BERTIE HAD NEVER SEEN so many nervous women in one room.

"What should we do?" Jennie wrung her hands and looked as frightened as Songbird, who stood in the middle of it all with wide eyes.

"Boil water? Yes, yes, we need boiling water!" Bonnie exclaimed, already moving toward the hand pump and basin.

"I'll get the blanket we made for the baby. We don't want him to get a chill." Amelie hurried to the trunk in the corner, tripping over the hem of her skirt in her haste. Thankfully she caught herself before landing on the floor.

Rubie's head had bowed the moment Songbird's water broke, and her lips moved nonstop in silent petition.

"Sisters," Bertie said, her voice authoritative, bringing everything to a halt. "Let's get Songbird into a fresh nightdress and settled in bed. It'll be hours afore the wee one makes its appearance. There's plenty of time to get things in order."

A sense of calm followed her words, and the women set about preparing for the impending birth with more confidence.

Songbird allowed Bertie to examine her after she'd donned clean clothes and rested against a stack of goose-down pillows.

Bertie nodded with satisfaction at what she saw. "Yes, you're well on your way to havin' this baby. Your body has more work to do to open up though." She washed her hands in the basin of warm water Bonnie had ready. "How are you feeling, dear?"

Songbird rubbed her big belly with both hands. "I'm painin' some, but it ain't bad. 'Bout like my monthly times, I s'pose."

"Remember what we talked about." Bertie didn't wish to frighten the girl, but she needed to remind her the worst of it was still to come. "The pains will gradually increase, gettin' things ready for the birth. When they start comin' faster and harder to manage, I'll be here to talk you through 'em."

Songbird's eyes filled with moisture. "How can I thank you enough, Miss Bertie? I ain't scared, knowin' you're here with me."

Bertie patted her arm. "Precious girl, it's always an honor to tend a birthin', but 'specially for someone so dear to my heart."

Over the next hours, Songbird's labor progressed just as Bertie hoped. The sisters came and went, bringing fresh water for the basin, towels, and the occasional cup of lavender tea to help Songbird relax in between contractions.

By midnight, the pains were coming within a few minutes of each other, not giving the young mother much time to rest and prepare before the next one was upon her.

She moaned and grimaced as her body worked to bring her child into the world. "Ohhh." Fear filled her eyes. "I can't do this no more, Miss Bertie. I can't do it. It hurts too bad."

Jennie took a cool, damp cloth and gently mopped Songbird's face while Bertie peeked beneath the sheet. Bonnie, Amelie, and Rubie poked their heads into the room from the kitchen, worry in their eyes. No one wanted to go to bed until the wee one arrived, safe and sound.

Bertie nodded when Songbird's tired, pain-filled eyes met hers. "Yes, you can do this, dear one. In fact, you're doin' it. I can see the top of the baby's head." She placed her hand on Songbird's hardened belly. "Now, when you feel the urge to push—remember what I told you it felt like? When you get that sensation, go right on and push."

Songbird indicated she understood and closed her eyes.

The very next contraction brought her upright.

"Oh, oh, Miss Bertie." She didn't say more before she grabbed her bent knees and pushed with everything she had.

"That's it," Bertie said, keeping an eye on the mother as well as the slowly emerging head of her baby. "Take a break when you need it, but you're doin' just fine. Everything looks good."

Songbird breathed heavily but rallied at the next contraction.

"Jennie, get behind her and help her sit up," Bertie directed.

Her sister's face had gone pale, but she did as she was instructed. It occurred to Bertie that her elder siblings hadn't seen the birth of a baby since Mam labored in this very room nearly fifty years ago. Rubie attended births with Bertie in the early years, but even she watched with wide eyes from a short distance away. And although they'd had plenty of critters born on the homestead throughout the years, the arrival of a tiny, helpless human was something Bertie would always consider nothing short of a miracle.

Songbird continued to push, but still the baby didn't come. After a solid hour, she was exhausted. Bertie'd seen babies take a full twenty-four hours to make an appearance, so she wasn't overly concerned. Songbird was a very young and very small mother. While it was impossible to know how much the baby weighed, he could be larger than what her body could easily manage.

There were other reasons, of course—far scarier reasons—that could prevent the baby from exiting his cozy home, but Bertie wouldn't let her mind go there. Not yet anyway.

The contractions were now so close, there wasn't time for Songbird to catch her breath. Jennie held up the girl's sweat-dampened, limp body while Bertie tried to help move the baby downward by massaging Songbird's belly.

Slowly but surely the baby's head began to emerge.

"I see him," Bertie said after Songbird collapsed into Jennie after a long, hard push. "One more good push, dear girl. You can do it."

With a primal growl, Songbird squeezed her eyes closed and rose to meet the challenge.

The dark-haired head of her child came forth. His face, however, was deep blue.

Bertie immediately saw the cause.

The umbilical cord was looped around his neck.

"Hold on now, Songbird." She worked to free the baby. "Don't push just yet."

"Is he all right?" Songbird cried, fear in her wide eyes. "He ain't dead, is he?"

"No, child," Bertie said. "He's gonna be fine. Just got tangled up in his cord, is all. I've got him fixed up now, so give me one more big push and let's get him into your arms."

Determination replaced fear.

Songbird grabbed her knees and pushed with all her might, screaming as her son emerged from her body.

"He's here!"

Bertie didn't stop to celebrate but began rubbing the plump little boy's back and feet with a towel to encourage him to breathe.

"Come on, sweet boy. Give Bertie a howl."

She rolled him onto her forearm, with his tummy down, and ran her finger inside his mouth to clean out secretions and clear his air passageway. When he remained silent, she smacked him on his behind for good measure.

A lusty wail was her reward.

Songbird's joyful cry blended with her son's.

"He's a mighty handsome boy," Bertie said as she laid the babe on his mother's chest, then cut the cord with a knife and tied the ends with string.

Songbird's exhaustion seemed to vanish and pure wonder shone in her eyes. "He's so beautiful," she declared as she took him in her arms. "The most beautiful thing I ever did see."

The baby's whimpers stopped at the sound of her voice, and the two studied one another. Songbird barely seemed to notice when her body finished the birthing process and delivered the placenta.

The sisters, who'd watched from the kitchen doorway, came forward with happy smiles.

"They say when a baby takes its first breath," Rubie said, her voice full of reverence, "the little one is declaring the very name of God."

"Amen," Jennie said.

Bertie glanced at the clock and saw it was past three in the morning.

"Little Amos Joshua just missed arrivin' on your birthday." She took the wee boy from his mother. "Let's get him cleaned up and wrapped in that pretty blanket you made for him."

While Bertie tended the baby, the sisters took care of removing soiled sheets and tidying the area. When all was done, Songbird settled in with the babe in her arms.

"He'll be wantin' to nurse soon," Bertie said, a warm, content feeling deep in her soul as she watched the sweet pair.

After the clock struck four times, Jennie, Bonnie, Amelie, and Rubie reluctantly climbed the ladder to the loft and went to bed, although not for long. The animals needed tending at sunrise, no matter the women's lack of sleep.

Songbird giggled through the lesson Bertie gave her on how to breastfeed her son. Her milk wouldn't come in for another day or two, but there was enough to satisfy the wee one. Soon, they were both asleep.

Bertie, worn-out now that the excitement and anticipation of the birth was over, sank onto the chair next to the cot. Her eyes filled with grateful tears as she gazed at the beautiful sight of mother and child, both safe and resting peacefully.

"Thank you, Lord," she whispered.

There wasn't need to say more.

It felt as though thirty years melted away, and Bertie was in this very room with Songbird, watching her nurse her newborn son.

A son who now sat across from Bertie, all grown-up and angry.

Angry at Songbird for not keeping him. Angry at Bertie for knowing his secrets. Maybe even angry at God for letting it happen.

Bertie knew who Walker was the moment he mentioned the note she'd written all those years ago, yet she couldn't let him know she remembered. She couldn't tell Songbird's boy everything that took place before and after his birth. Every detail brought pain with it. Heavy, crushing pain she had no desire to revisit, nor did she wish to pass the agony onto Songbird's child.

But didn't he deserve to know the truth? It was his story, too, after all.

Bertie studied the young man across from her. If she found the courage to share about those long-ago events, would he be strong enough to carry the heavy burden that came with it? The deep regret and disappointment that knowledge would surely bring?

What should I do, Father? What should I do?

In quick answer, Bertie remembered something that might buy her some time to figure out what to tell Walker.

"I kept a book with names and dates and such of all the babies I helped bring into the world." She scratched her chin and pretended as though she had to think hard on the subject. "Sometimes I made notes about the family. But it's been years since I tended a birth. It may take a few days to recollect where I put that little book."

Walker frowned. "A few days?"

Bertie indicated the vast array of belongings that surrounded them. "Your guess is as good as mine on its whereabouts. Could even be out in the barn or down in the cellar." Which was true. She wasn't certain where the record book was stored.

Locating it, however, wasn't necessary for her to tell Walker about his birth. About his mother and why he now sat across from Bertie, asking questions. She remembered every beautiful, heartbreaking detail as though it happened yesterday.

But that story, secreted away deep in her heart, wasn't one she was ready to part with. At least not until she learned more about the man Songbird's boy had become.

Walker's face took on a look of disappointment. He'd come a long way, looking for answers. Bertie felt guilty for not coming clean right away, but she needed time to think. To pray. To figure out what to tell him. The tale was messy, and her gut warned that he wasn't ready to hear the full truth.

Not yet.

"We've got plenty of room," she said. "You folks are welcome to stay the night and help look for the record book. I'm too old to go climbin' round in the loft or cellar."

When it appeared Walker might balk at the suggestion, she gave a great show of rubbing her arthritic knuckles. "It's hard for Rubie and me to get much done these days. If you've got time, I'd be much obliged for you to stay. You have me curious, and I'd like to see that book again."

Indecision crossed Walker's face. Bertie watched closely, gauging the earnestness of his desire to learn the truth about his birth. If he left now, she felt certain she'd never hear from him again.

And that would leave her heartbroken for a second time.

He turned to Reese, who'd been listening to the exchange without comment.

What was their relationship? Bertie wondered. Reese claimed they hadn't known one another long, but it seemed strange that she'd come all the way out here with someone who wasn't important in her life.

"I can't ask you to stay," he said to Reese. "I've taken too much of your time as it is. I'll hang out with these ladies and see if we can locate that record book. I'd appreciate it if you'd let Ray know where I am. He can send a car."

Bertie's heart skipped with gladness hearing his decision, although she kept her joy to herself. "There's a cot yonder in the barn where our nephews sometimes sleep. You'll be comfortable there."

"If it's okay with the two of you," Reese said, "I'd like to stay and help. It's the weekend, and I don't need to be back in my office until Monday. I'd enjoy learning more about your midwife practice, Miss Bertie. I'm a midwife myself."

It was Bertie's turn to be surprised. "Well, I'll say. I'd enjoy chattin' with you, but like I said, it's been a coon's age since I tended a birth. Some folks," she said, recalling Ramsey Alister's callous words from long ago, "thought I was past being a good midwife when I was still in my fifties."

She chuckled to herself.

She'd heard through the grapevine Ramsey was sure sorry he hadn't listened to Bertie after he got a whopping bill in the mail for the hospital's services, which included a surgery Bertie felt unnecessary. The Ramsey baby girl grew up to be a lovely young woman, which, in the end, is what everyone—even those hospital doctors—aims for.

"I hope I'm still delivering babies when I'm in my fifties,"

Reese said, drawing Bertie out of the past. "I can't think of anything else I'd rather do."

Bertie gave a nod of satisfaction. "That's how I felt back then, too."

With it decided that both Walker and Reese would stay overnight, they set about getting the guests settled: Walker in the barn and Reese up in the sleeping loft that was no longer used. The ladder was too steep for Bertie and Rubie to navigate safely, and they instead slept in the gathering room near the fireplace, where Mam and Papa once slept. Old bones, it seemed, required plenty of warmth on chilly nights.

While Walker and Reese unloaded their belongings from the small red car, Bertie worked on a plan of how to go about things. She needed to keep Walker busy while she discovered who he'd become over the last thirty years.

Was he the kind, caring sort, as his mother had been? Or was he selfish and arrogant, like his grandfather? Would he respect the painful decisions that had to be made many years ago, or would his anger keep him from seeing the past with fresh eyes?

These were questions Bertie needed answers to before she'd know whether she could trust him with the story of his birth or send him on his way, with no more understanding of who he was than when he'd arrived.

Rubie awakened and clapped her hands when Bertie told her the plan.

"I'm glad you came." She reached up to pat Walker's scruffy cheek the way she did their young nephews'. "You're a sweet boy."

Whether or not her sister suspected Walker's identity, Bertie couldn't guess. Over the years, Rubie's mind had become slow and confused at times. Bertie wouldn't reveal the truth to her sister just yet, lest the secret become too difficult to keep.

Once their guests were settled, everyone convened in the kitchen.

"Where should we start?" Walker asked, seemingly eager to begin the search. His gaze slid over the many items in the room.

"The garden."

Bertie forced herself to keep a straight face when Walker's registered bewilderment at her answer.

"Did you bury the book?" he asked.

Bertie let a small chuckle escape. "The only thing buried out yonder are some turnips that need diggin' if we're to have greens 'n' roasted turnips for supper."

Walker frowned, but from the corner of her eye, Bertie saw Reese cover a smile with her hand.

While Rubie went to feed the chickens and gather eggs, Bertie led Walker and Reese to the large garden just down from the house.

"We grow everything we need here on our land." She heard pride in her voice but felt no shame because it wasn't pride in her hard work. It was knowing she and her sisters had carried on Papa's and Mam's dream long after they'd gone to their heavenly home. "Papa always said if he couldn't grow somethin' or make somethin' himself, he didn't need it."

Walker looked skeptical. "You can't grow a car in a garden."

Bertie laughed. "We've never owned a car, so I s'pose Papa is still right."

Walker glanced back to the house, his eyes searching. After a long moment, he asked, "Do you not have electricity?"

"No need," Bertie said. "We have candles made from lard and lamps that use homemade oil instead of kerosene. We go to bed and get up with the sun, so 'lectricity wouldn't do us much good."

Walker shook his head. "I had no idea there were people in the United States who still lived like this."

He made it sound as if their way of life was a bad thing.

"Now, hold on there, young man." She pushed the wide brim of her bonnet off her face so she could meet his gaze. "*This* is a good life. Always has been. We've never had a day when we didn't have a fine roof over our heads and food in our bellies. We work hard, and we're honest, God-fearin' folks. Our way of doin' things may be different from you, but different don't mean wrong."

"I'm sorry," he said, seemingly sincere. "I didn't mean to offend you. Apparently I have a lot to learn about life in the mountains."

Satisfied with his apology, Bertie reached for the hoe leaning against the fence. "I ain't offended. Learnin' is something we never stop doin'. Now let's dig up some turnips."

"You'll have to show me what to do," Walker said as she handed him the tool. "I've never dug turnips before."

Bertie couldn't resist patting his stubbled cheek the same way Rubie had earlier.

"I know, dear boy," she said, her heart opening to let him in even as caution warned her to tread with care. "You don't need to worry. Bertie will teach you everything you need to know."

Sixteen

MOTHERHOOD WAS MORE WONDERFUL than I ever imagined.

It had been a week since my son made his entrance into the world, and all I wanted to do was hold him and stare into his beautiful eyes. I never knew such a powerful love existed, but when I mentioned that to Bertie, she reminded me that's how God loves us, his children.

"Isn't he the prettiest baby you've ever seen, Miss Bertie?" I asked.

Bertie had just come in from milking the cow to find me bathing the baby in a basin of warm water. The tiny boy squirmed and made noises only a newborn can make but otherwise seemed to enjoy the bath, his second in as many days.

"He's mighty handsome, to be sure." Bertie came up beside me and admired the wee one. "Best not linger though. There's a chill in the air today."

I nodded, but my attention remained on my son. "Josh likes baths. I put some lavender oil in the water like you said. It makes him smell good."

"Amos Joshua may like the warm water, but he won't be too happy if he takes a cold." Bertie's eyes shone with love. "It does my heart good to hear his name though. Two of our nephews carry their grandpa's name, but I feel sure Papa would be especially pleased that this tiny fella will always be known as Joshua."

I smoothed Josh's dark hair with my wet hand. "He looks like Amos when his hair is slicked back like this. I'd tease Amos, tellin' him he used so much pomade, a fly would go skatin' across his head if it tried to land on him."

Bertie picked up a soft towel from the counter and held it out. "I see a lot of you in Joshua too. He's got your eyes for certain."

I lifted the baby from the water and let Bertie wrap him up, snug and content.

"I've been thinkin'," I said, touching Josh's cheek with my finger. He turned, working his sweet little mouth. He'd be hungry soon.

"Thinkin' 'bout what?" Bertie asked, her eyes on the baby, and his on her.

When I didn't answer directly, Bertie glanced at me. "Thinkin' 'bout what?"

I'd given this decision a lot of consideration, yet I knew Bertie wouldn't be pleased with my idea.

"I want Amos to know he has a son."

As I'd anticipated, Bertie frowned. "Amos is in Europe, fightin' Hitler. There ain't any way for you to contact him. It's doubtful his mother would pass on the news."

I sat at the table and wound a thread that had come off the towel around my finger. "I thought, maybe . . ." I bit my lip.

Bertie's frown deepened. "It ain't like you to be mysterious. Go on. Spit it out, child."

"I thought maybe I could write a letter to his sister." I needed the older woman to understand how important this was to me. "Millie was a friend. She could mail a letter to Amos, lettin' him know 'bout Josh. She might even be glad to know she's got a nephew."

The baby fidgeted, turning his mouth toward Bertie. A sure

sign he was hungry. Bertie passed him to me and watched as I settled him at my breast.

Her face bore her concern when she sat across from me. "I understand you want Joshua's pa to know about him, but this don't seem like a good idea. Are you certain you want his people to know where you are? Amos's ma already said she don't believe her son is the baby's pa."

I looked down at Josh, my heart full of love. "She wouldn't say that if she could see him. She'd take one look and know he's Amos's son."

"What if Millie doesn't believe you?"

I gave a helpless shrug. "Then I'll have to wait till the war is over and find Amos myself."

Bertie reached across the table. I grasped hold of her hand.

"You and Joshua will always have a home with us," she said.

I nodded. "I know. I don't mean to be ungrateful—"

"You ain't bein' ungrateful, child."

"It's just that . . ." I shrugged again. "I miss Amos." My eyes filled, and a tear dripped onto the baby.

Bertie had warned me new mothers were often emotional, what with all the hormones, exhaustion, and changes, but I knew my longings went deeper than that. I missed the man who'd fathered my sweet babe. Amos deserved to know he had a son.

Finally Bertie nodded. "If you want to send Amos's sister a letter, we'll take it to the post tomorrow."

Relief washed over me. "Thank you, Miss Bertie. I just know Millie will be glad to hear the news 'bout Josh."

After the baby finished nursing and was fast asleep in the cradle Jennie found in the attic, I sat down to compose the letter to Millie. She was a year older than me, but we'd become fast friends after Amos and me started courtin'. She'd had a beau too, and sometimes the four of us would go down to the crick and swim.

When the letter was finished and sealed in an envelope, I couldn't help but feel a surge of excitement as I envisioned Amos's face when he heard the good news.

Someday soon, God willing, we'd be a family.

⚞

Reese helped Bertie wash and cut the leafy heads of turnip plants while Walker hauled dusty wooden crates down from the loft.

"It'll be easier to go through 'em down here in the gatherin' room," Bertie said when she assigned the task to him. Reese, however, couldn't help but wonder if it was more to keep him busy than anything else.

He'd done a fair job in the garden but working outside in the dirt definitely wasn't his thing. He'd groused about the bugs, the dirt, and the smells, especially when he learned the sisters used manure to fertilize the plants. Reese belly-laughed when he started singing the theme song to the TV show *Green Acres*, imitating Eva Gabor's Hungarian accent and declaring himself more like her character, Lisa Douglas, than her farmer-husband, Oliver.

"New York is where I'd rather stay. I get allergic smelling hay."

Even now, the memory made her grin.

"I'm pleased to hear you're a midwife," Bertie said from her place at the stove, where she filled a huge pot with water and chicken broth. "I ain't never met a midwife who wasn't from round here. Are your kin mountain folk?"

Reese smiled. "No, ma'am. I studied nursing in school. The first time I saw a baby born, I knew I'd found my calling."

Bertie nodded. "That's just how I felt. Mam midwifed for our people and took me with her when I was just a girl. Been tendin' births ever since."

"How many babies have you delivered?"

"Mercy, I ain't got no idea." She threw a couple pieces of wood into the firebox of the stove and closed the door. "If we find that record book I kept, we can tally 'em. I 'magine I missed some here and there, but for the most part, I kept good track of 'em." She paused. "Even those that didn't turn out the way I hoped."

The comment drew Reese's attention. The subject of infant loss wasn't often discussed among the midwives she knew. "You lost a baby?"

Bertie gave a slow nod. "Three, over the years, although that don't count miscarriages. I lost a mama once, too. Couldn't stop her bleedin', no matter what I did."

"I don't know what I'd do if I lost a baby or a mother," Reese said. "Childbirth is such a beautiful miracle, but I sometimes forget all the things that can go wrong."

"It's important to remember we ain't in control. Losing a baby or a mama doesn't take God by surprise."

Reese considered the truth in the simple statement, yet it was a difficult concept to accept. "But how do you comfort a woman who's just lost the child she carried in her womb?"

"You don't," Bertie said matter-of-factly as she stirred a handful of dried herbs into the pot. "That ain't your job. There ain't nothin' you can say that will take away that mama's hurt. Only God can heal it."

They worked in silence for long minutes.

"It's hard to understand, you know," Reese said. "We help bring new life into the world. Death shouldn't be part of that picture."

"I hope you never have to carry that burden," Bertie said, her voice soft.

Reese hoped so too.

Walker entered the room as they chatted. Bertie pointed to the basin of soapy water. "You can wash your hands there and help get the turnips ready to roast."

Reese almost laughed out loud when Walker grimaced after

Bertie returned her attention to the pot on the stovetop. Apparently turnips weren't his favorite.

"We'll bake some corn bread, too. Nothing tastes better with turnip greens than hot corn bread with fresh butter."

Rubie came in from the chicken coop with nearly two dozen eggs. The sisters decided hard-boiled eggs should be added to the menu and set about heating more water.

"We don't get too many visitors these days," Bertie said as she set the table for four with floral-patterned dishes like the ones she'd used earlier for the tarts. "But back when Papa and Mam were alive, this house fairly burst with folks comin' and goin'."

"Remember our sweet girl, Sister?" Rubie smiled at Walker.

Bertie, however, frowned and shook her head at her sister. When she found Reese watching her, she seemed to force a smile. "We've had lots of sweet girls and boys stay with us through the years. Our brothers and Sister Catie married and have families nearby, so there's always been young'uns come to visit."

"How many brothers and sisters did you have?" Walker asked, a bit of longing in his voice. Reese understood. Being an only child could be lonely at times.

"There was eleven of us in all. Sisters Jennie, Bonnie, and Amelie lived here with Rubie and me after Papa and Mam passed on. None of us ever married."

"The five of you lived here alone?" Walker's voice revealed his surprise. "How did you manage the farmwork without help?"

Bertie glanced at Rubie, who grinned, before returning her attention to Walker. "Young man, we've been doin' farmwork our whole lives. Papa had four sons but seven daughters. Two of our brothers died as young men, and we lost a sister when she was just a wee girl. There was always work that had to be done. Everyone in the family pitched in."

When all was ready, they sat down to what turned out to be

a delicious meal. Even Walker admitted that although he'd never eaten roasted turnips, they weren't as bad as he'd expected.

"Is your mama a good cook?" Bertie asked.

He nodded, a hint of sadness in his eyes. "Mom loved to cook for Pop and me. She'd make our favorites." He swallowed. "Pop passed away four months ago. I learned about my adoption the day after his funeral. Our family attorney felt it was important I know about it, especially since the adoption wasn't exactly conventional."

Bertie studied Walker from across the table. Compassion filled her eyes. "I'm sorry for your loss."

"Thank you. It's been hard. I just wish Pop and Mom would've talked to me about the adoption."

Reese heard frustration in Walker's words.

"Secrets always have a way of being found out eventually," Bertie said, a faraway look in her eyes.

After the dishes were washed and put away, Rubie stayed at the kitchen table to read from her papa's Bible while Bertie, Walker, and Reese gathered around the wooden boxes Walker had brought down from the loft.

"There ain't no tellin' what we'll find in these," Bertie said. "Lots of old, forgotten things, I imagine. Hope you kids don't mind sortin' through it."

"Not at all." Reese rubbed her bare arms. She still wore the T-shirt she'd put on earlier in the day when the air was warmer, but this room was noticeably chillier than the kitchen had been.

Bertie took note. "We best get a fire goin' if we don't want to catch cold. It turns nippy once the sun dips below the hills."

With expertise, Bertie took firewood from the stack next to the rock hearth and had a nice blaze going in no time at all. "I'll make us some chamomile tea to warm our bones while we dig around in these. Start wherever you please."

After she left the room, Reese looked at Walker. "How are you feeling about all this?"

"To be honest," he said, his voice lowered, "I'm wondering if Miss Bertie just wants some free labor."

Reese chuckled. "You did look a little uncomfortable out in the garden earlier."

His mouth tipped in a lopsided smile. "I told you I'm no Oliver Douglas. I'll take singing for a living over a hoe any day." The smile faded. "But now that we've found Bertie Jenkins, I want to know more about where I came from. If locating that record book helps get me to that end, then I'm willing to do whatever it takes."

His gaze held hers. "I'm glad you're here, Reese. I couldn't do this without you."

Warmth spread through her, but she forced herself to ignore it. Developing a schoolgirl crush on the famous singer wasn't a good idea. They were too different. He was a city boy with a movie-star girlfriend. When they returned to their lives, he'd forget about Reese Chandler. It was best to keep that in mind.

"I'm happy to help. Truthfully, this has been an eye-opening experience for me. Even though I'm adopted, I never had to go through anything like what you're dealing with. It's reminded me that every adoption story is different. I should thank you for letting me come along."

Bertie arrived with the tea. "Rubie's gettin' tired, so if you folks don't mind, we'll start on the boxes tomorrow."

Disappointment crossed Walker's face, but he nodded. "I'll see you ladies in the morning," he said, taking his tea and a lantern with him.

Reese watched him leave the cabin.

"He's a handsome fellow," Bertie said from behind her.

When Reese turned, she found the woman studying her. "He

is," she responded, feigning disinterest, "but he's definitely not my type. Besides, he has a girlfriend."

Bertie eyed her. "I've lived long enough to know not everything is as it seems."

They bid each other good night. Reese made her way up the ladder to the loft, but when the house was quiet and dark, she lay in the lumpy bed, wondering what Bertie meant.

Seventeen

A ROOSTER'S CROW WOKE WALKER while it was still dark outside.

He groaned and rolled onto his back. Despite Bertie's insistence that the cot in the barn's loft was comfortable, his stiff muscles said otherwise. It was cold out here, too. He hoped the Jenkins sisters had coffee. He was going to need a whole pot to make it through the day.

With a yawn, he stared up at the plank ceiling, where slivers of dawn's pink light were barely visible through the cracks. The sound of munching came from below, and Walker remembered a black-and-white cow lived in the stall below him. He must've become used to her pungent odor sometime during the night because he could no longer detect it in the chilly air.

That thought, however, reminded him there was no getting used to the stench that came from the outhouse behind the cabin. How the sisters tolerated it was beyond him. Maybe he'd take advantage of the woods and bypass the smelly shack all together.

He chuckled.

What would Ray say if he could see Walker now?

He quickly sobered when Vanessa's face flashed across his mind's eye.

What would *she* think if she knew he'd slept in a musky barn, deep in the Appalachians, while searching for information about his birth family at the ancient home of the elderly midwife who'd delivered him?

If someone had told him four months ago this would be his life, he'd have said they were nuts.

Now, Walker was pretty sure *he* was the one who'd gone nuts.

And Vanessa would agree.

He thought back to yesterday morning when he'd tried to call her before he left the motel. After the phone rang a dozen times, he'd hung up. He wasn't even sure she was in the country. She was shooting a new movie, with some of the scenes taking place in Morocco. Walker and all his issues were probably the last thing on her mind.

With a hint of guilt, he recalled the relief he'd felt when she hadn't answered the call. Their last conversation made it clear she didn't understand what he was going through. How could she? She was the apple of her daddy's eye and looked just like her mother.

But her insensitive remarks—"You need to move on, Walker," and "I can't be around you when you're so moody"—reminded him that as much as he cared for Vanessa, he didn't need that kind of negativity in his life right now.

His thoughts drifted to Reese.

Last night she'd made it clear their relationship was strictly about locating his birth information. Business and nothing more. Did she at least consider him a friend? Walker wasn't certain. Which, in the long run, was probably just as well, even if his ego got a little bruised in the process. As much as he appreciated her help, he'd make sure he kept his distance.

The rooster crowed again.

Who needed an alarm clock when you lived on a farm?

A short time later, Walker entered the cabin and was greeted with laughter and the smell of fried bacon.

"Good mornin'," Bertie said as she flipped flapjacks on a griddle built onto the stovetop. "We were just wonderin' if you were up yet."

"I don't think your rooster would let anyone sleep late." He turned to find Reese watching him from her place at the table. "Good morning."

"Morning." Her shy smile intrigued him. Maybe they were friends after all.

"How'd you sleep?" Bertie drew his attention. "Didn't I tell you that cot in the barn was comfortable?"

"You did at that."

Rubie approached with a mug of steaming black coffee.

"You must've read my mind, Miss Rubie. Thank you." He accepted the drink with gratitude.

"Our girl didn't care for coffee, but men usually like a cup or two in the morning before chores. Now that you're grown-up, you'll want coffee too."

She moved off, humming softly.

Rubie was an odd little woman, Walker decided. Not only had she declared she knew Walker prior to yesterday, but she'd referred to "our girl" several times with little explanation of who she spoke of. According to Bertie, Rubie had never married or had children.

"After chores are done, we'll get to lookin' for that book," Bertie said. She placed a platter loaded high with fluffy cakes on the table. Rubie followed with a plate of crisp bacon. A small crock of butter and a bowl of syrup completed the spread.

"Chores?" Walker wondered if his statement about Bertie wanting free labor was closer to the truth than he first thought. He was anxious to find the record book and move on to the reason why he and Reese were there in the first place.

Bertie nodded to the window that looked out to the barn. "Critters need to be fed. Stalls need cleanin'. Daisy needs milkin' if you're of a mind to try your hand at it."

Walker heard Reese snicker. He had to admit the image of him milking his roommate was outrageous.

"I'll pass on that, but I'll help with the other chores," he said. While he planned to pay the sisters for his and Reese's room and board, farmwork wasn't exactly something he'd bargained on.

When they were seated at the table, Rubie prayed over them and the food, asking the Lord to bless their boy and his friend.

"Papa planted maple trees just past the orchard," Bertie said as she handed the bowl of warm syrup to Reese. "All these years later we're still enjoyin' syrup and sugar from 'em."

Their life fascinated Walker. "You've never wanted to live anywhere else?"

Bertie seemed to ponder the question. "I s'pose when I was younger, I had an itch to see what was beyond our mountains. But Jennie'd decided to be an old maid and take care of Papa and Mam in their golden years. She talked me and Bonnie into doin' the same." She glanced at Rubie, who seemed lost in her own thoughts. "After a while, it was just the five of us girls here. Didn't seem right to go off and leave the work to my sisters."

Having never had siblings, Walker couldn't fully understand that kind of sacrifice. "I don't think I could've lived here all my life. It's beautiful, but there's so much world out there to see. So much life to be lived."

Bertie's keen gaze landed on him. "Livin' life ain't about seein' and doin'. It's about lovin' and takin' care of those who've been put in your path. God gave us this land to tend, just like he says in the Good Book. I don't need to travel the world to find satisfaction with the life he's given me."

Walker disagreed, but he also didn't want to insult Bertie. Her choices were just that: hers. Living out his days on a farm deep in the mountains wasn't a life he would ever choose.

A shocking thought burst into his mind, and he nearly choked on the bite of pancake he'd just taken.

If his birth mother hadn't given him up for adoption, would the life Bertie just described have been *his* life? Would he have grown up in a cabin much like this one, with no electricity, no indoor plumbing, no modern conveniences? What about his education? Would he have attended college and gone on to become a country music singer?

The realization that his life would have been completely different stunned Walker.

A tremor of terror raced through him.

Had he lived a lie for thirty years? Was he supposed to be someone else entirely? And if so, *who*?

The women's conversation moved on to other topics. Reese and Bertie discussed various herbs that were useful in childbirth, but Walker didn't participate. He couldn't shake the uninvited feeling that his adoption had forced him to become someone he was never intended to be.

When the meal ended, Walker assumed they'd clean things up, then head outside. But neither Bertie nor Rubie rose from their seats. Instead, Bertie took the worn Bible he'd noticed beside her plate and opened it.

"Papa always started the day with the Word. We've carried on that tradition all these years." She turned thin pages until she came to the passage she'd settled on. "The Psalms have always been our favorite, isn't that right, Sister?"

Rubie gave a sweet smile.

Bertie cleared her throat. "'O Lord, thou hast searched me, and known me. Thou knowest my downsitting and mine uprising, thou understandest my thought afar off.'"

She continued to read how it's impossible to hide from God, no matter where we go. Walker, however, couldn't concentrate on Bertie's reverent voice. Their previous conversation left him feeling—

"'I will praise thee; for I am fearfully and wonderfully made.'"

That last phrase caught his attention.

"'My substance was not hid from thee, when I was made in secret, and curiously wrought in the lowest parts of the earth.'"

She kept reading, but Walker stopped listening.

Had she chosen that passage on purpose? Clearly the author—was it King David?—wrote about a baby being formed in its mother's womb. Walker hadn't considered his life before he was born, and frankly he didn't want to think about it now. He already felt overwhelmed with the realization of how different everything would be if he hadn't been adopted. What his birth parents did to create him was strictly off-limits in his psyche.

When Bertie closed the book, Rubie offered another strange prayer about "their girl" and "their boy" and how God's plans are perfect. Walker didn't know if she was lucid or talked nonsense, but he supposed God knew.

After the kitchen was cleaned, they prepared for the day.

When the two elderly women went for their bonnets, Reese approached Walker, concern in her eyes.

"Is everything okay? You seem a little . . . tense."

Walker knew she would understand if he tried to explain what was going through his head, but he didn't want to talk about it just now.

"I'm fine."

Her eyes told him she didn't buy it, but she didn't press. "Okay. I thought you might be worried Bertie was going to make you milk the cow."

Her teasing worked magic on his moodiness. "I wouldn't want

to take that pleasure away from you, Miss Chandler. Daisy is all yours."

Bertie arrived while she was still laughing.

"Laughter is good medicine for the soul," she said from beneath the wide bill of her homespun bonnet. It tied beneath her chin and had a flap down the back to keep the sun off her neck. She handed a similar head covering to Reese. "You best put this on lest you get a burn."

When Walker chuckled under his breath, Bertie turned to him. "And you can wear Papa's hat."

She moved to take a bedraggled, moth-eaten felt hat from a hook on the wall. After a swat to remove the layer of dust, she handed it to him.

There was nothing to do but wear it. "Thanks."

With their headgear in place—Walker was certain they looked like they'd just come from the set of the television show *Gunsmoke*—they headed outside into a glorious fall day.

Bertie led Daisy from her stall. A quick lesson had Reese milking the cow as though she'd grown up on a farm. Walker and Bertie left her to it and moved on to the unpleasant task she'd assigned him.

"Muckin' out stalls ain't hard." She handed him a shovel. "Just load the manure and soiled hay into the wheelbarrow and take it yonder behind the garden. We'll need it come spring plantin'."

Walker surveyed the nasty piles scattered about his roommate's stall and grimaced.

Bertie continued with her instructions. "After you're done here, there's Kit Junior's stall next door—he's our mule—and two on the end where our nephews kept their horses when they were here Sunday. You can let Kit roam while you're cleanin'. He won't go far."

She patted Walker on the shoulder before leaving him alone in the stall.

He heaved a sigh.

How did mucking out the barn become part of the deal? He'd come to this remote place for answers, not a lesson in how to dispose of animal poop.

With resignation, he carefully picked his way around the small space and stood in the safest spot he could find. He'd need to watch his step. He didn't want to end up ruining his brand-new Chuck Taylor sneakers.

Reese appeared in the opening to the stall after he'd filled the wheelbarrow for the second time. She carried a pail full of fresh milk.

"How's it going?"

He leaned on the shovel. "I told you she just wanted free labor."

She chuckled. "Maybe. But it's kind of fun. I've never spent time on a working farm before."

"Neither have I, and now I know why."

His wry tone made her laugh, which pleased him. Walker hoped he'd read her wrong last night because he really did enjoy her company.

"I better get back to work before the boss comes to check on me."

He turned just as Reese shouted, "Watch out!"

Too late. His shoe sank into something squishy. Walker closed his eyes. "Is it as bad as I think it is?"

"It is."

He opened one eye and found her fighting back laughter. "Go on. Let it out."

She did. Her giggle was infectious, and soon Walker was laughing too.

"You two kids sound like you're havin' a good time." Bertie had arrived, a smirk on her face. Then she frowned when she saw Walker. "Oh, my."

"I'm not sure I'm cut out for this job." Walker removed his foot from the messy pile. He tried to clean it on hay lying about the stall, but most of it stayed where it was, stuck to his formerly favorite sneaker. As soon as he got home, he'd trash these.

"Nonsense. Everyone steps in dung on a farm. Go on, now. Finish the job. Reese 'n' me will let the milk set out so it'll sep'rate from the cream. Maybe I'll teach you kids how to churn butter before you leave."

She headed back the way she'd come. Reese gave a little shrug and followed.

Walker looked at his shoe again and blew out a breath full of frustration.

If he didn't know better, he'd think Bertie was purposely keeping them from looking for the record book. Or, like he kept saying, she'd seen an opportunity to get some no-cost help around the homestead and snatched it. Either way, his patience was thinning.

For the next hour, he shoveled, wheeled, and shoveled some more. When the task was complete, he felt rather proud as he admired the clean stalls filled with fresh-smelling hay.

"All done?"

He hadn't heard Bertie come in. She stood behind him. "I am. What do you think?"

She didn't glance at the stall but kept her eyes on him. "I think I could make a farmer out of you yet."

He laughed. "Never, but I appreciate the vote of confidence."

She told him where to store the shovel and wheelbarrow, and together they left the barn. Sunshine spilled over the mountains in the distance, and the fresh air on the breeze was welcome after shoveling manure all morning.

"Tell me about Nashville," Bertie said as they headed to the house. "What do you like about livin' in the city?"

He glanced at her. "You've never been there?"

A strange look passed over her face. "Just once, but I wasn't there long."

"Nashville is a terrific place. There's always something happening. Concerts at the Grand Ole Opry. The symphony. Plays. Clubs down in Printers Alley with great food and music. A couple weeks ago the city hosted a celebrity golf tournament with a lot of famous musicians, athletes, and actors." Walker didn't mention that he'd been one of the honored guests, too. "Mickey Mantle was even there."

"Who's he?"

Walker's jaw dropped. "You don't know who Mickey Mantle is?"

When Bertie shook her head, he said, "He's one of the greatest baseball players to ever play the game."

"Hmm. I reckon I've probably read his name in the paper if he's as good as you say," she said, as unimpressed with Mantle as Walker had been with mucking out stalls.

Walker told her about the dinner parties his parents hosted and the concerts they attended. "I remember the last time Pop and I went to the Opry at the Ryman. We went to hear his favorite singer, Merle Haggard. Haggard went from being a man in and out of prison, bent on ruining his life, to becoming a bestselling country singer. Pop always said Haggard knew more about life than most people."

"Sounds like your pop was a wise man."

Walker nodded. "He was, but . . ."

"But what?"

Walker's emotions about Pop were complicated and heavy with the pain of loss. With a shrug, he finished his thought. "I wish he'd been wise enough to understand I should have been told about my adoption. He went to his grave with the secret."

They reached the porch, and Bertie turned to him. "Why do you reckon that is?"

Walker had asked himself that very question a hundred times over the past four months. "I don't know. To protect me. To protect him and Mom. Or maybe it was shame. Maybe he didn't want anyone to know I wasn't really his son."

Bertie frowned. "What do you mean, you weren't his son? Sounds like he spent his life raisin' you."

"You know what I mean. I wasn't his biological son."

She gave him a hard look. "Biology don't make a man a father. The heart does. Lots of men have biological kids, but they ain't no good as fathers 'cause their heart ain't in it."

Walker watched Bertie climb the rock steps to the porch and mulled over her words.

Pop had been a terrific dad—there was no question about that. Walker couldn't have asked for anyone better. Sure, his career as a real estate mogul kept him busy, but Walker couldn't remember ever feeling neglected or unloved.

His mind went back to the day after Pop's funeral. Mom tried to explain why they'd kept the truth from him, but Walker wouldn't listen. Everything he'd ever believed about himself shattered with the word *adoption*. Like a mirror smashed into a thousand pieces, leaving the reflection distorted. He no longer knew who he was, and he still didn't, four months later.

His gaze swept the mountain homestead.

The quest to find answers brought him to this remote place in the hills, but so far, he hadn't learned anything he didn't already know. Bertie Jenkins was most likely the woman who'd delivered him, but he had yet to learn the identity of his birth parents or the circumstances that led them to give him up for adoption. Blisters on his hands and a ruined pair of sneakers were all he had to show for his time with the Jenkins sisters.

Questions filled his mind.

Would Bertie remember the details he so desperately needed to know? Did the record book offer answers? Or would he and Reese drive away from here as ignorant of where Walker came from as when they'd bounced up the rutted mountain road in her VW?

"You comin'?" Bertie stood in the doorway to the cabin, watching him.

For a moment, Walker wondered if he should just turn around and head back to Nashville. Why waste everyone's time digging through Bertie's family belongings, looking for something that might or might not jog her memory about Walker's birth?

But if he walked away now, he might never be free of the feelings of rejection and abandonment that had weighed him down since he'd learned he was adopted.

And more than anything else, that reality terrified him.

It left him little choice.

"I'm coming."

Walker stepped onto the porch and followed Bertie inside.

Eighteen

IT HAD BEEN TWO WEEKS since I'd mailed the letter to Amos's sister.

Every day, I waited for a response.

"Amos sure is gonna be surprised when he hears 'bout Josh," I said.

The chubby baby lay on the cot, fist in his mouth, while I changed his soiled diaper. Bertie sat nearby mending a tear in the hem of her skirt. She'd stumbled in the garden yesterday when her foot caught on a loose rock. Later, Jennie had scowled when she noticed the dirty, dangling fabric.

"Alberta Mae, you need to be more careful. Those big feet of yours never had much grace."

After Jennie returned to the kitchen, Bertie'd stuck her tongue out at her sister's retreating back. It made me giggle, which in turn made the baby at my breast coo.

Bertie pulled the needle through the fabric. "Amos shouldn't be surprised, considerin' he's sure to know how babies are made."

I picked up Josh, my face hot with embarrassment. "You know what I mean, Miss Bertie. He didn't have no idea I's carryin' a baby when Pa moved us to Tennessee." I settled in a rocking chair and gazed down on my son. "But I reckon the minute he lays eyes on this boy he'll know Josh is his."

My certainty that Amos would accept the baby worried Bertie. She'd asked all kinds of questions before we put the letter to Millie in the post.

What if the responsibility of being a father wasn't something Amos wanted?

What if he called me a liar and rejected the child as his own mother had done?

Or worse than all of that, what if he came back from Europe with a bride as some soldiers were doing? What then?

So many things could go wrong with the happy future of my dreams, but I just kept praying God would work everything out for Joshua and me.

"I hope you're right, child," Bertie finally said.

Another week passed, but no letter arrived.

"I can't understand why Millie hasn't written," I complained for what seemed the hundredth time over the past weeks. "She's sure to guess I'm anxious for Amos to know about his son. If she'd write and tell me where I can reach him, I could send a letter myself."

Bertie and I sat at the kitchen table, peeling carrots, potatoes, and turnips in preparation for the big Thanksgiving dinner we'd enjoy tomorrow at Sister Catie's in Sevierville. Bertie said Catie had the only house big enough to accommodate the growing Jenkins clan, plus Catie liked to show off the modern amenities her husband installed in the house. Early this morning, Brother Tom drove Jennie, Bonnie, and Amelie to town to lend a hand with preparations, but the day was dreary and cold, and Bertie thought it best if Joshua and I stayed indoors.

"Maybe Millie didn't get the letter," I continued, worry trying to take hold inside me. I glanced to the cradle near the fireplace, where a toasty blaze warded off the November chill in the air and kept Josh warm as he slept. "Do you reckon them Army folks would tell me how to reach Amos? It's sort of an emergency, don't you think? A soldier should know he has a son waitin' for him back home."

Bertie shook her head. "It ain't likely. I think it best you stop frettin' over things. Too much frettin'll cause your milk to sour."

New worry filled me. "It can? I wouldn't want to do nothin' to harm Josh."

Bertie's face reflected regret over her words. "Aw, now, I don't mean it. You're a good mama to that child. I just think you need to leave things in God's hands and wait to see how he works it out."

I knew she was right, but waiting was hard.

We continued the meal preparations in silence for a time before I glanced up.

"Miss Bertie, are you ever sorry you didn't have children?"

Bertie seemed to ponder her answer. "There were times, when I was a young woman, I felt like I'd missed somethin' important by not marryin' and havin' babies. But lookin' back, I wouldn't change things. Sister Catie has five children, and our brothers each have a houseful. There was plenty o' wee ones to love on."

Josh stirred in the cradle, although he didn't cry.

"You're lucky to have such a lovin' family," I said. "That's what I want for Amos, Josh, and me."

Bertie offered an understanding smile. "I want that for you, too, dear girl."

The conversation turned to Thanksgiving. Bertie told stories about the holiday meals they'd shared here in the cabin when her ma and pa were still alive. When the baby fussed, I nursed him while Bertie fixed a simple lunch of fried eggs and corn bread.

We'd just finished putting things away when the sound of car tires crunching over rocks reached us.

"That must be Tom bringin' Jennie and the girls home." Bertie moved to the window. "Hmm, that ain't Tom's car. Looks like a couple." She took her coat from its hook. "I 'spect they're travelin' for the holiday and got lost. I best see where they're headed."

She hadn't reached the door when a man hollered from outside. "Hello the house."

I gasped.

It couldn't be.

"What's wrong?" Bertie glanced at the babe in the cradle, but he'd dozed off.

I didn't answer. Instead, I rushed to the window and peeked through the curtain. A small cry escaped my lips, and I fell back, pressing into the log wall.

"No, no, no."

"Child," Bertie said, alarm in her voice, "what is it? What's happened?"

My body trembled with fear. "It's Pa," I hissed. "He's found me. He's found us."

"Hello the house," came a second call.

Hot panic washed over me.

I couldn't let Pa know I was here. I couldn't let him find my son.

"He'll kill me, Miss Bertie," I whispered, my frantic gaze darting to the cradle. "And Josh, too."

Terror widened Bertie's eyes. "Dear Lord," she breathed. "What should we do?"

I searched the room for somewhere to hide, but Bertie ran to the fireplace and took down a rifle that hung above the mantel.

"I haven't fired Papa's gun in years," she said, turning it over in her hands. "I don't even know where we keep ammunition. The only reason we needed a gun in the house was to shoot wild game or scare off a critter. The boys do all the huntin' these days."

I stared at her. "What are you gonna do, Miss Bertie?"

She didn't answer the question. "You stay inside with Joshua and keep quiet. Bar the door behind me. If things go wrong, take the baby and get down in the cellar." She indicated the trapdoor in the floor in the corner. "Stay hidden till Jennie and the others get here."

I opened my mouth to protest, but Bertie didn't wait. She turned and marched to the door. "How dare that man come lookin' for you. He tried to kill you and the child. I'll be hanged if I let him anywhere near you."

I stood in frozen terror as I watched her leave the cabin. I knew Pa wouldn't take kindly to a stranger telling him what to do.

After I put the bar across the door, I tiptoed to the window. Careful not to disturb the curtain, I peeked out the corner. I noticed two things right away. Pa was armed with the very rifle he'd used on me, and there was a woman in the passenger seat, although it didn't look like Vera.

"What do you folks want?" I heard Bertie say. She must've pointed the gun at Pa because he held up one hand.

"Now hold on there, lady. I ain't here to cause no trouble. I'm lookin' for my daughter, is all."

"And who might that be?"

"Evelyn. Evelyn Harwell. I heard she was stayin' with y'all."

Evelyn.

I'd never told the sisters my real name. After being known as Songbird for five months, it felt odd hearing my given name.

"I don't know any Evelyn," Bertie said.

Pa reached into his coat pocket and took out a piece of paper. "I got a letter here that says different. Says she and her kid are here."

My heart sank.

How had Pa gotten hold of the letter I sent to Millie?

"I want to see them. Now." He raised his gun and aimed it at Bertie.

I knew he wasn't foolin'. I couldn't let any harm come to her. I ran to the door, lifted the bar, and rushed onto the porch. "Don't shoot, Pa."

Bertie didn't take her eyes off the man but spoke to me. "I told you not to come out, child. Stay behind me."

I did, but I didn't stay silent. Seeing my father again brought up all kinds of ugliness inside me. "You ain't welcome here. I ain't got nothin' to say to you."

"Aw, now, don't be like that, Evelyn. I've come to bring you home. The boys and Vera miss you."

I scoffed. "That witch only misses me 'cuz I ain't there to cook 'n' clean."

Pa's face grew stony. "Don't talk 'bout your ma like that."

"She ain't my ma," I screamed, furious that he would insult Mama like that. "And you ain't my pa. You tried to hurt me and my baby. You got no cause to come here. I want you to leave!"

Just then the passenger door to the car opened. A woman wearing a worn coat and a black pillbox hat with a short veil stepped out.

It took a moment, but recognition suddenly struck me.

"Miz Cole?" I moved out from behind Bertie, shocked at finding Amos's ma here. "Miz Cole, you came."

"Millie got your letter," the woman said. Her tone sounded sweet, not cold and snobbish as it had been the day Amos took me to meet her. She hadn't liked me any more than Pa had liked Amos. That's when he and I started meeting at our secret place. "I'm sorry you felt you had to write to her instead of me about the birth of your son."

I frowned, confused. "You didn't believe me when I said the baby was Amos's. You told me not to write to him anymore."

"I know, and I'm very sorry. I was wrong. Can you forgive me, dear?"

I stared at her. She believed me? She believed Josh was Amos's boy?

Pure joy burst within my heart. I moved to step off the porch, but Bertie reached to hold me back.

"I don't trust them, child," she whispered. "Somethin' ain't right."

I laughed, nearly giddy with happiness. "Everything is wonderful, Miss Bertie. Don't you see? Amos's ma believes me." I turned back to Miz Cole. "Does Amos know 'bout Josh? Is he comin' home soon? I can't wait for him to meet his son."

Miz Cole didn't answer. She didn't smile. In fact, she looked downright ill.

A knot of fear began to form in my belly. "Miz Cole? Is Amos all right? Has he been injured?"

Tears filled the woman's eyes and her chin trembled. She simply shook her head and covered her face with her hands.

"Miz Cole?"

Pa answered instead. "Amos is dead, girl."

The air and everything around us stood still in that terrible moment.

I tried to process what had just happened, to make sense out of Pa's emotionless words, but my mind couldn't catch hold of anything solid.

Bertie reached for me, but I pushed her away.

"No," I said, shaking my head. I glared at Pa. "You're lyin'. You never liked Amos. Why would you come here and tell me such horrible lies?"

"It ain't a lie, child." Miz Cole wiped her nose with a hankie.

I stared at her, my breath coming hard. I didn't want to hear what she had to say, but I couldn't look away.

"The telegram arrived in September. My boy, my Amos, died somewhere in Italy. They didn't even send him home. Just buried him in an I-talian grave."

I didn't move.

I didn't breathe.

Amos was never coming home. He'd never hold me in his

strong arms again. Joshua would never know his pa. Amos didn't even know he *was* a pa.

Something inside me shattered. Something that, instinctively, I knew would never be whole again.

The keening started low and sorrowful in my belly where Amos's son had hidden for nine months. It grew and rose higher in my throat, building and building, until my entire body shook with grief. My knees gave out and I felt myself falling, but I didn't care.

Bertie caught me just before I hit the porch floor.

"Amos, Amos." The ache in my heart went deeper than any pain I'd ever felt before. I'd grieved when Mama passed on, but this was different. Me and Amos had become one. We'd made a child. I couldn't live without Amos.

Bertie gently took me in her arms, crooning words of love and comfort, and I cried even harder. "Oh, Bertie, he's dead. My Amos is dead."

Bertie wept with me, holding on to me as tightly as I held on to her.

When the sorrowful wave ebbed, my weeping slowed, but I stayed in Bertie's arms.

What would I do now? Every dream, every hope for my future, was gone.

"May I see the baby?"

Amos's ma stood near the porch, her face splotchy and wet with tears.

When I met her gaze, genuine sorrow filled her eyes. "May I see Amos's son?"

I stared at her a long time. I couldn't imagine the grief she must be experiencing. I'd only loved Amos a few short months, but he'd been her son for eighteen years.

I knew what Amos would want.

"Yes," I said.

A frigid breeze rustled bare branches in the trees.

"I don't trust your pa," Bertie whispered in my ear, "but it's too cold to bring Joshua outside."

I nodded my understanding.

Bertie looked at Miz Cole. "Y'all come inside out of the chill." When Pa stepped forward, she narrowed her gaze on him. "Leave that gun there or don't come in."

He frowned and seemed taken aback by her commanding voice. "Ain't no cause to be unfriendly-like, now."

"A bullet hole in your daughter's shoulder is plenty o' cause."

Miz Cole looked between them, confusion on her face. "What do you mean?" She turned her attention to me. "What is she talkin' about? Are you injured?"

I gave Bertie a pleading look and shook my head. "I'm fine," I said. "There was . . . an accident, but I'm fine now."

I hurried to the door, with Miz Cole following behind, but Bertie didn't move. I looked back to see her rifle aimed at Pa again, almost daring him to cross her.

Finally he leaned his gun against the car and slowly walked toward us.

"She ain't yours," he said to Bertie when he gained the porch, his voice low, menacing. "And neither is that kid o' hers." With that, he brushed past Bertie and followed Miz Cole into the house, ignoring me completely.

"Keep your distance from that man," Bertie said, warning in her voice.

When we entered the house, we found Pa and Miz Cole near the cradle.

"He's beautiful," Amos's ma breathed. Tears welled in her eyes again. "He looks just like Amos when he was a baby."

I went to stand on the other side of the cradle, my grief so raw it was hard to breathe. The sight of my sleeping son was like one of Bertie's salves. "I think he looks like Amos too."

"May I hold him?"

I hesitated, casting a glance to Bertie, who stood sentinel, the rifle still in her hands. She gave a brief nod.

I carefully took the sleeping baby from his warm bed. He didn't protest, but he did stretch and yawn, causing his grandmother to laugh.

"Oh, he's darlin'." She opened her arms to receive the baby.

Seeing the woman's tears and knowing Joshua was her dead son's only child broke my heart afresh.

I glanced over to Pa, uncertain. "Here's your grandson, Pa."

His face remained unmoved. "Just another mouth to feed, like I told you. What are you gonna do now, girl? His pa is dead. You can't stay with this old woman forever."

"Yes, she can." Bertie glared at him. "She and the babe are welcome to stay as long as they need a home."

His jaw clenched. "I told you she ain't yours. Evelyn ain't but fourteen years old."

"I'm fifteen now, Pa."

He smirked. "Fifteen, then. Still a child in the eyes of the law. I'm her pappy, and I say what happens to her."

My heart thundered with fear. I looked at Bertie. "I want to stay with you and the sisters, Miss Bertie."

"Of course you can, child." Bertie moved to put her arm around my waist. "Ain't no reason you and Joshua need to go anywhere."

"Joshua?" Miz Cole glanced up from the baby and frowned. "He should be named after his father."

Annoyance rolled through me. Not long ago the woman had denied her son's paternity.

"His name is Amos Joshua," I said, "after his pa and Miss Bertie's papa."

"What in tarnation?" Pa bellowed, startling the baby. Joshua let out a tiny wail. "You named the boy after someone you don't even know? What 'bout namin' him after me, the man who took care o' you all your life?" His angry gaze landed on Bertie. "I see what's goin' on here. You're wantin' my girl to stay on and take care of you in your old age. I 'spect you've already got her cookin' and cleanin' for you. Well, you ain't gonna keep her. Evelyn, you're leavin' with me."

He moved to snatch the baby from Miz Cole. Little Josh, who'd settled back down, cried out at the rough treatment.

"No, Pa!" Panic filled me. "You said yourself you don't want another mouth to feed. Let me and Joshua stay here. I want to."

He glanced at Miz Cole as Joshua continued to whimper. A look I couldn't define passed between them.

Amos's ma lifted her chin. "Evelyn, your pa and I think it's best if the baby comes home with me."

Bertie gasped. "No."

I stared at Miz Cole, confused. "You want me and Joshua to live with you?"

The woman's mouth firmed. "No, child. You're young, with your whole life in front of you. You don't need to be saddled with a baby. What man will marry you if you've got a child already?"

"I don't understand." Her words didn't make any sense. "I ain't gonna ever marry. Not with Amos gone. It's just me and Joshua now."

"I'm sure you want what's best for the baby, don't you?" Miz Cole once again used that hard tone she'd spoken with the day we first met. As though I was just a stupid girl from the hills. "And the best thing for Amos's son is for me to raise him."

The full meaning of her words hit me. "You want me to give you Joshua? He's *my* son. I love him. You can't have him." I stomped to where Pa stood, but he held the baby out of my reach.

"You little fool." He snarled like a mad dog. "You never was too smart. Look at the trouble you got yourself into with that boy. Miz Cole is willin' to pay us cash money for this kid, and I ain't about to let you ruin things."

I gaped at him. "You sold my son?" My angry gaze whipped to Miz Cole. "You think you can buy my son?"

The woman turned away.

I reached for Joshua. "Give him to me, Pa. Give me my son."

He backed away. "The law says you're still a child. *My* child. And you got to do what I say, and I say you ain't fit to raise this baby."

"I'm his ma."

"You ain't nothin' but a fool girl who got pregnant. If Amos was still alive and married up with you, that'd be different. But he's dead. He ain't comin' to rescue you."

Tears swam in my eyes at his harsh reminder, but I didn't back down. "Give me my son, Pa."

When I reached for the baby again, Pa gave me a hard shove. I stumbled and fell to the floor, and my head slammed against the wooden planks. My vision blurred for a moment, and I thought I would pass out.

"We're done here." Pa turned to the door. Miz Cole hurried to follow.

I struggled to stand, but a wave of dizziness knocked me down again. "No," I screamed, fighting to get to my feet. I couldn't let them leave with Josh. I knew if I let them carry my son from this cabin, I'd never see him again.

"Hold it right there."

Bertie's angry voice brought Pa and Miz Cole to a halt. She lifted her papa's rifle and aimed it directly at Pa's head.

"You take one more step and it'll be your last."

Nineteen

THE FACT THAT HER HANDS DIDN'T SHAKE amazed Bertie, considering she'd never held a gun pointed at a living soul before. It helped knowing there wasn't a live round in the chamber.

At least, she hoped not.

"You're crazy, lady. You can't shoot us both." Songbird's pa sneered, his yellowed teeth bared.

"You're right." Bertie remained calm, praying the man believed her bluff. "But I can blow a hole through your head like it was a pumpkin. I doubt Miz Cole would give us much trouble after that."

Fear flashed in the man's eyes.

"Hand the baby to Amos's ma." She used the rifle to motion the frightened woman to take the baby.

The man glanced at the gun once more before relinquishing Joshua. Thankfully, the tiny boy had quieted, although his puckered brow told his confusion.

When Mrs. Cole had Joshua safely in her arms, Bertie kept the gun trained at Songbird's pa but spoke to the woman. "Give Joshua to his mama."

The woman hesitated, looking between Joshua, Songbird, and Papa's gun.

When she didn't move, Bertie glared at her. "I said, give the baby to his mama."

Songbird remained seated on the floor, but she held out her arms for her son.

"Please, don't do this," Mrs. Cole begged as she passed the baby to his mother. "I'd take good care of him. You can come see him whenever you want. You can even live with us and be his ma. Just please, please, don't keep him from me. He's all I've got left of Amos."

"He's all I've got left of Amos, too," Songbird said, anger in her voice. "And you was willin' to buy him like he was a sack of flour."

Remorse washed over the woman's face. Whether from their failed kidnapping or true regret over her ill-conceived plans, Bertie didn't know.

"Now, back away," Bertie commanded. She hadn't changed the aim of the weapon, but her eyes darted between Songbird's pa and Mrs. Cole, lest one of them make a lunge for the gun.

When Mrs. Cole returned to her place, Bertie moved in front of Songbird and the baby.

"You folks ain't welcome here no more." She narrowed her eyes. "Go on back to the hole you crawled outta and don't never show your faces round here again."

Mrs. Cole sobbed. "Please, Evelyn, please."

"Goodbye, Miz Cole," Songbird said.

The woman's face revealed her heartbreak, but Bertie couldn't feel sorry for her. She'd come here with the intention of stealing Songbird's child without thought to the young mother's pain.

Bertie watched the woman stumble toward the door, her sobs echoing in the room. After Mrs. Cole's exit, Bertie's attention returned to Songbird's pa. Anger had turned his face dark and ugly.

"You'll be sorry you done this." His lips curled in a snarl when his glare landed on Bertie. "The law says that girl is still a child.

And since I'm her pa and you ain't nothin' to our family, the law's on my side."

His rage fell on Songbird next. "You can come with me now and be done with this, or I swear I'll have the sheriff lock up this ol' woman. Either way, you ain't keepin' that brat."

Songbird gasped. "Bertie ain't done nothin' but help me. You shot me, Pa. You tried to kill me. What will the sheriff say 'bout that?"

He scoffed. "I don't know what you're talkin' 'bout. Makin' up stories, like you al'ays done. Ain't no one gonna believe I shot my own daughter. You was messin' around with a married man and his woman shot you. Just ask my wife. She saw the whole thing."

The man's vileness sickened Bertie. "You lyin' piece of dung. Get outta my house before I shoot you 'n' call the sheriff to come haul off the body. There's two witnesses that'll say you tried to kill your daughter, which is the truth. Won't matter if it happened some months back. Who's gonna tell him otherwise?"

The man seethed. "You think you're smart, don't you? You're gonna regret the day you got mixed up with that good-for-nothin' girl of mine." He moved to the door but turned to spit on the plank floor at Bertie's feet. "Take a good look at that kid of yours," he said to Songbird, "'cuz you ain't never gonna see him again after tomorrow."

"You might think twice before you haul the authorities up here." Bertie smirked. "I 'spect they'll be mighty interested in that still of yours. I've known Sheriff Matt a long time. He don't cotton to moonshiners in his jurisdiction."

The man's face paled. His glare shot to Songbird. "Runnin' your mouth again, ain't you? Mark my words, girl. You'll be sorry." He turned and stormed out of the house.

Bertie kept several paces behind him as he left the cabin and stomped to the car. Mrs. Cole sat in the passenger seat, her face in her hands. Songbird's pa aimed a vulgar gesture at Bertie, then climbed into the vehicle and slammed the door. The engine revved, and the car tore out of the yard so fast, a thick cloud of dust billowed in the chilly air. When it cleared, the vehicle was gone.

She waited outside several minutes to be certain the unwelcome visitors didn't try to double back. The sisters would have to lock their doors until things settled down. Bertie considered going to the sheriff herself, since she didn't think for a moment a moonshiner who'd tried to kill his daughter would seek help from the law. When Jennie and the others returned, they'd discuss their options.

Growing chilled, Bertie made her way back into the warm house.

She found Songbird sitting in a chair, nursing the baby. Silent tears flowed down her cheeks.

"They're gone." Bertie slid the bar in place behind her, making it impossible for someone to open the door from outside. She did the same in the adjoining room. When she returned, she said, "I best find ammunition for this gun. I sure wouldn't want your pa to come back and call my bluff."

Songbird didn't look up.

Bertie opened a drawer in the dresser near the door and rummaged through it. "Ah, here's a box of bullets."

"I can't stay."

The quiet words stilled Bertie. She turned to look at Songbird. "'Course you can stay. I told you, they're gone. I 'spect that's the last we'll see of 'em, too. Your pa ain't gonna risk gettin' caught with a moonshine still. He was tryin' to fool us same as I was tryin' to fool him with a gun that ain't loaded."

But Songbird shook her head. "You don't know my pa. He's done bad things to folks who's crossed him." She met Bertie's gaze. Despair filled her eyes. "I can't put you and the sisters in danger by stayin'."

Raw fear swirled through Bertie that had nothing to do with the girl's father. She set the gun against the wall and went to stand beside Songbird's chair.

"Listen to me. We've been takin' care of ourselves for nigh on twenty years or more. We've fought off bears and cougars and rattlers. Had broken bones, sickness, failed crops, and a fire in the hills that woulda taken the farm if God hadn't sent a south wind and rain."

She knelt beside Songbird so the girl could look directly in her eyes. "One angry pa don't scare me. In fact, I'm so riled I could string him up by his toes and dangle him out yonder on the big oak."

A faint smile brushed Songbird's lips, but it was quickly replaced with a troubled frown. "But what he said 'bout the law and me still bein' his daughter. Is he right? Can they make me go with him? Can they take Joshua away from me?"

Bertie sat back on her haunches. "I don't know the answers, child. But I do know we Jenkins sisters will do everything we can to make the sheriff and anyone else who comes askin' understand what your pa did and why you can't go back."

Songbird nodded and looked down at the sleeping baby in her arms. "I felt kinda sorry for Miz Cole." A tear slid down her cheek. "I can't hardly believe Amos is dead, but she wouldn't lie 'bout somethin' like that."

They sat in silence. Bertie knew the girl would grieve the loss of Joshua's father for a long time, maybe forever. Both Rubie and Amelie still mourned the loss of their fiancés even though nearly thirty years had passed since the men had died in the logging accident. At least Songbird had a beautiful, living, breathing reminder of the young man who'd given his life in service for his country. That was a legacy little Amos Joshua could be proud of.

The sound of a car brought them both alert. Bertie scrambled to her feet and grabbed the gun.

Doggone it. Its chamber was still empty. She'd just have to keep up the pretense of an angry ol' woman with a loaded weapon and see if the fool dared cross her.

Heart thundering, she went to the window and stole a peek. Tangible relief washed over her. "It's Brother Tom, bringin' the girls home." She hurried to remove the bar across the door.

Bertie nearly wept when she heard Jennie's voice, barking out orders to the others as they came into the cabin. Her sisters twittered on about their day, the food, the dishes, talking at once as they removed their coats and hats.

"We'll need more firewood if we're to get half a dozen pies baked today." Jennie sent Bertie and Songbird a quick nod but kept moving toward the kitchen. "I reckon y'all have had a quiet day of it. Well, that's 'bout to change. Catie's girls are sick with the sniffles and can't help with the dinner, and the boys are still out huntin' a turkey, if you can believe it. Papa and Mam never let things wait till the last minute when they was in charge of hostin' the Thanksgiving meal. Can't understand Catie's thinkin', knowin' we're all comin' to her place on the morrow. We told her we'd make the pies on top of everythin' else we're cookin'."

Her monologue ended abruptly when she looked back at Bertie. Jennie's usual frown drooped further down her face as her gaze went from Bertie to Songbird, neither of whom had moved since the women entered.

"What's wrong? You both look like the world's 'bout to end." Her attention focused on the baby in Songbird's arms. "Is Joshua sick?"

Bertie shook her head and leaned the gun against the wall.

"Why do you have Papa's gun?"

"Come, sit down, Sisters," Bertie said, a grave tone in her voice.

Bonnie, Rubie, and Amelie's chatter quieted.

Jennie huffed. "You best spit it out, Alberta Mae. I can see on your face somethin' bad has happened."

When the women were seated, Bertie took a deep breath. "Songbird's pa was here." At the gasps around the room, she put up her hand to silence any questions. "He had Amos's ma with him. They brought news."

Bertie glanced at Songbird, who stared at the baby, her throat convulsing.

"Amos was killed over in Europe back in September. He ain't comin' home."

Both Amelie and Rubie clutched their hearts. The sad news no doubt reminded them of the day they'd learned about the tragedy that took their fiancés.

Jennie continued to stare hard at Bertie. "From what I know 'bout those two, they ain't the compassionate type. They came here wantin' somethin', didn't they?"

Jennie was no fool. Bertie could never hide anything from her oldest sister.

"Amos's ma wants Joshua. She was even willin' to pay cash money for him."

Horror washed across each of her sisters' faces.

"I hope you told that woman where she could put her money," Jennie said, her remark completely out of character. She glanced at Songbird, then back to Bertie. "What else ain't you tellin' us?"

"Pa says I got to go back home," Songbird said, her voice shaky. "Says I can't keep Joshua neither, so I might just as well give him to Miz Cole. He says the law'll make me do what he wants 'cuz he's my pa and I ain't of age yet." She burst into tears and clutched the baby to her, causing him to let out a small cry at being awakened. "I'd rather give Joshua to strangers than let Amos's ma have him."

Each of the sisters' faces reflected the shock and dismay Bertie knew her own face bore. She proceeded to tell them the entire harrowing tale of Songbird's pa's arrival, Mrs. Cole's tears, and the threats made before Bertie ran them off with Papa's rifle.

"I promised Songbird we'd do everythin' possible to make sure she don't have to go back home with that man."

Bertie expected Jennie to agree but worry deepened the lines on her sister's face. "Her pa is right. Under the law, a fifteen-year-old gal ain't a grown woman yet. Don't matter that she's a ma now. She ain't married, so that means she's still under his authority."

Songbird's eyes widened. "Are you sayin' I got to go back home and give Joshua to Miz Cole?"

"We ain't gonna let that happen," Bertie said, angry at Jennie for stating such. "You don't know any more 'bout the law than I do. No lawman is gonna make that girl return to a father who shot her. Let's not forget 'bout that."

"I ain't forgotten," Jennie said defensively, then added, "but I 'spect it'll be her word against his."

Songbird's chin trembled. "Pa said his wife would tell the sheriff I was messin' round with a married man and it was his woman who shot me."

The gravity of the situation hung in the air.

"We can't let this happen, Sisters." Bertie glanced around the room, determined to do something—anything—to help their girl. "Maybe we can hide Songbird and Joshua till this blows over."

"Hide them? Where?" Bonnie asked.

"The cellar," Amelie said, glancing to the door cutout in the plank floor in the corner.

"They can't live in the cellar," Jennie growled. "It's almost winter."

"There's plenty of huntin' and trappin' cabins in these parts." Bertie glanced out the window. "Wouldn't be hard to find one up in the woods where that hateful man wouldn't know to look."

"We'd take them food and blankets and firewood," Rubie added, her face full of hope.

"Sisters," Jennie said, her firm voice commanding everyone's attention. "I know you want to help. I do too." She glanced at Songbird, who'd remained silent during the discussion. "But if her pa brings a lawman with him next time, we got no choice. We can't interfere with the law."

Bertie gaped at Jennie. "I can't believe what I'm hearin'. You'd just let them take our girl? You'd let them take Joshua? I'm ashamed of you, Eugenia Jenkins. I thought you cared about Songbird, but I reckon I was wrong."

Jennie's face grew dark. "Don't you dare say I don't care 'bout them." Her eyes filled with moisture as she looked at Songbird. "I love them like they was my own. But—" she returned her attention to Bertie—"we're five old spinster ladies, livin' up here in the mountains alone. What do you think we could do against lawmen if they was to come here, lookin' for her? Or what if her pa comes without the law but brings his kin? I don't want nothin' to happen to Songbird or baby Joshua any more than you do, but how can we protect 'em? Hidin' in the forest ain't no life for a young gal and a baby."

Her words doused the angry fire in Bertie like a bucket of cold water poured on a runaway flame.

As much as she hated to admit it, Jennie was right.

What could the sisters do if Songbird's pa followed through with his threat and brought the sheriff with him next time? Or took the law in his own hands? Hiding the young mother and child in the woods was a temporary solution, but how long could that go on?

"Then we have to come up with a different plan," she said, determined not to give up. "We've got plenty of relatives 'n' friends in these mountains. Someone's bound to be willin' to help us."

The other women nodded their agreement, but Jennie remained unmoved.

"That'd just put more people in danger. We can't ask folks to get involved in this."

Hopelessness began to creep in, trying to take root in Bertie's soul.

She looked at Songbird, who stared down at the baby.

"We can't give up," Bertie whispered. There had to be a way out of this mess.

Heavy silence hung in the room.

Finally Songbird looked up, tears in her eyes. "There ain't nothin' I can do to stop Pa. When he's got his mind set on somethin', he don't back down. He won't stop lookin' for me and Josh, and I won't put y'all in any more danger."

She took a deep breath and seemed to steel herself with resolve.

"I can't keep Josh. He won't be safe with me." Sorrow-filled eyes met Bertie's. "You said folks adopt children that ain't theirs. That's what Joshua needs now. He needs new folks who'll love him and take him far away from Pa."

As her sisters' gasps and shocked voices filled the room, Bertie stumbled backward. She clutched her chest while intense, sharp pain soared through her.

But Bertie wasn't suffering a heart attack.

Her heart, she knew, had just shattered into a thousand pieces.

Twenty

THE STRONG ODOR OF MOTHBALLS filled the gathering room.

"This old trunk hasn't been opened in years, I 'spect," Bertie said when Walker lifted the lid of a large chest in the corner near the rock fireplace, releasing the sour smell. "I sure thought that record book woulda been easier to find. It's only been twenty or so years since I used it last."

Walker's frustration with the woman and the search was close to reaching his breaking point. They'd been at this for hours, with only a short respite for a noon meal of ham sandwiches and fresh milk. They'd sorted through boxes of photographs, letters, her father's farm record books, and even a diary one of the sisters kept. They'd climbed around the dusty attic, although the only items stored there were some broken chairs, a three-legged stool minus one leg, and a handmade cradle. Bertie had paused to run a hand lovingly over its smooth wood, a faraway look in her eyes, before she turned and ducked through the small doorway that opened into the loft.

Reese glanced his way from where she and Rubie sorted through one of three wooden crates Walker had carried up from the cellar. The dank space was located directly beneath this room, but even with the trapdoor open, Bertie declared it too cold and instructed

Walker to haul the boxes upstairs. The sky outside had turned gray, with a strong northern wind, and Bertie predicted winter weather was coming. Walker hoped not, considering he and Reese were leaving tomorrow. This madness couldn't go on indefinitely. Reese needed to get back to her clients, and Walker had to get back to his life, whether he received answers to his questions or not.

"Granny Simms made this quilt." Bertie drew his attention to a handmade bedcovering, sewn with squares that must've been colorful years ago but were now faded and tattered in places. "Mam wasn't much of a seamstress, but Granny had a steady hand. She and Grandpa lived east of here, over the next hill. After Papa served in the Union army, he bought our land from Grandpa when he was courtin' Mam." She chuckled as she smoothed the fabric. "Mam said Grandpa quoted a price so high, she just knew Papa wouldn't pay it and would go find himself another gal to court. But he didn't blink. Took out his wallet and gave Grandpa cash money on the spot. That's when Mam knew she loved Papa."

She set the quilt aside and looked at Walker. "You got grand-parents?"

He nodded. "Mom's folks live in Memphis, so we see them often, but Pop's family came from Virginia. They're both gone now, but I remember going to visit them in the summers when I was a kid."

His answer seemed to satisfy her, and she continued with the search. When the trunk was emptied and there was no ledger, Walker helped return the items to their hiding spot. "Are you sure you kept the record book? Maybe it got thrown out."

Bertie chuckled. "Look around you, son. Does it look like we throw anything away?"

The wry words held truth.

She was slowly getting to her feet when Rubie squealed like a young girl.

"Sister, look." She pointed to Reese, who had just pulled a small book from a box.

"Is that what I think it is?" Walker asked, afraid to let his hopes rise yet feeling them swirl in his gut anyway.

Bertie made her way across the room, but she didn't reach for the book right away.

"I sure don't recall puttin' it in the cellar. That seems like somethin' Jennie woulda done. She was always gettin' on us for leavin' our things out. 'There's a place for everything, and everything in its place,' she'd say. You may not believe that's true—" she glanced about the room, jam-packed with belongings that hadn't been used in years—"but even when all us kids were livin' at home with Mam and Papa, we knew where to find what we needed."

She took the book from Reese and stared at the plain brown cover. "Lots of memories are recorded in these pages. Most are good. Others not so much."

She moved to one of the rocking chairs and settled in. Walker tagged along like a schoolboy waiting to hear his mother read *The Hobbit* for the first time.

Bertie took a deep breath and met his gaze. "I know you want what's written in this book to help jog my memory of when you were born, but I want you to understand somethin'. Whatever happened back then don't change who you are now."

Walker nodded. "I know."

"Do you?"

He wasn't sure what she was getting at. "I'm ready to hear whatever you have to say."

She didn't appear convinced.

Bertie turned to the first page, filled with neat handwriting. "I wrote down nearly every birth I tended in this book. 'Course, I'd accompanied Mam for a dozen or so, but I was just a girl then. Wasn't a midwife yet." She glanced at Reese. "We didn't go to school to become a midwife in those days. We learned it from our mas, who'd learned it from theirs. Mountain folk don't trust outsiders much, so most every community has their own midwife. I always felt honored our neighbors trusted me to bring their babes into the world."

Bertie turned several pages, perusing the names listed there. She'd comment about so-and-so's baby and what he or she grew up to become.

Walker shifted his stance from one foot to the other, anxious for her to come to the name that brought him on this journey. A stranger's name. How he would feel to hear it for the first time wasn't clear.

More pages turned and more shifts of Walker's feet brought Bertie's attention to him. "You're as fidgety as a squirrel huntin' an acorn. Pull up a chair. This is gonna take some time."

He did, but it didn't keep him from tapping his foot on the plank floor. "Didn't you record the births in order?"

She nodded but didn't look up. "I s'pose so."

Walker kept himself composed, even as his impatience intensified. "Wouldn't it be better to search the pages with births from the year you believe I was born?"

"I s'pose it would," she said, sending him a patient look. "But I ain't seen this book in a long time. Surely you can afford an old woman a few minutes to reminisce along the way to where we're goin'."

The mild scolding did its job.

"Yes, ma'am." Walker settled against the chair.

Bertie continued to exclaim over this baby and that baby, she and Rubie each sharing a memory here and there. Walker was surprised to learn that Rubie had tended births with her sister for a while.

"Mam got sick 'bout that time," Bertie said. She sent her sister a sad smile. "Rubie took wonderful care of our mother until the Lord took Mam home."

Walker thought of Pop.

He wished he'd been home more the last year of his father's life, but neither of his parents let on that Pop was terminally ill. He was tired and lost weight, but Walker never imagined cancer was raging inside of him. Instead, Pop encouraged him to chase his dream. By the time Mom tearfully confessed what was happening, Pop was on so much medication to dull the pain, he barely knew Walker was home.

Bertie continued to peruse the book. The hands on the wall clock crept along. It had just chimed three times when she grew still.

"Here it is. The record of your birth."

Walker swallowed hard. "What does it say?"

She handed the book to him. "Second from the top."

He silently read the brief entry.

Amos Joshua, son of Songbird. Born October 27, 1943, at 2:15 a.m. Mama and baby healthy. Guess he weighs about seven pounds. Cord around neck at birth.

Confusion swirled through Walker as he stared at the unfamiliar names in the ledger.

"'Amos Joshua, son of Songbird.' Is that my mother's name?"

Bertie nodded. "We called her Songbird."

"I think it's lovely," Reese said.

Walker stared at the date Bertie wrote in the ledger thirty years ago. The same date as on the note his parents received from the mountain preacher. "This can't be right. This says I was born on October 27, 1943." He faced Bertie. "That isn't my birthday. I was born on February 12, 1944."

Bertie took the ledger back and studied the entry before answering. "I'm sure I wrote down the correct date. I remember because you were born the day after Songbird's birthday."

Questions raced through Walker's mind.

"If this is accurate and I was born in October, why would my parents celebrate my birthday in February? My military records and school records all have the February date on them. It doesn't make any sense unless—" He paused as a startling thought pushed its way forward.

Had the pastor who brought a baby to his parents somehow mixed Walker up with another child? What if the note describing Walker's birth was meant to go to a different couple? What if it belonged to a different baby boy?

"Unless what?" Bertie asked, her frown deepening.

Walker glanced to Reese, who looked as confused as he felt, then finished his sentence.

"Unless I'm not Songbird's son. Maybe I'm not Amos Joshua after all."

❧

Bertie met Walker's gaze, unruffled by his doubts. "'Course you're Amos Joshua. I wrote the note that brought you here with my own hand. The very same note Brother Brown gave to your parents at the church in Nashville."

Walker wasn't convinced. "What do you know about the pastor? Could he have been involved in a scheme to sell babies? I've read about stuff like that happening back in those days."

"It wasn't anything like that, I can tell you for certain." Bertie sighed. Clearly the time had come to tell him the whole story, but she didn't know where to begin the tragic tale.

Did she tell him about Songbird's pa shooting her when she refused to abort her baby? Should she start with Songbird's relationship with Amos, including his death in the war? What about his own grandmother offering to buy him, like he was a thing to own rather than a child to love?

Bertie wasn't certain he was prepared to hear any of it, yet he had a right to know where he came from, whether he was ready or not.

"I first met your mama in the summer of '43," she said, her mind traveling back in time. That hot June day seemed a lifetime ago, yet the memories came alive. "The day was warm. I was sittin' on the porch when Clem started barkin'." She glanced toward the window. Although Bertie couldn't see the woods where Songbird hid, the image of the girl lying on the ground, bleeding, was as clear as if it had just happened.

"A teenage girl was out yonder," she said, pointing in the direction of the corncrib. "She was by herself. Her pa had moved the family from North Carolina to Tennessee that winter. She'd had a beau back home, but her pa didn't approve of the boy. Even though she knew it was wrong, she wanted Amos to know she loved him, so they . . . well, she lay with him."

Walker's frown deepened. "If she and my father were in love, why didn't she just marry him?"

"It wasn't as simple as that," Bertie said. "They were just kids. By the time she knew you were on your way, she and Amos lived in different states. She didn't have money for bus fare, so she wrote him a letter. Told him she was expectin' and that he should come and fetch her."

"Let me guess. He had no desire to be a father," Walker said. "Let's just cut to the chase here. I was given away because neither of my parents wanted me. It doesn't matter that they were teenagers."

"'Course it matters. She was barely more than a child herself when she came to live with us."

Walker stared at Bertie. "My mother lived *here*?"

Too late she realized she'd slipped up. "I . . ." Her shoulders slumped before she gave a feeble nod.

Confusion, quickly followed by anger, crossed his features. "I knew it. I knew something was off, with all the chores and searching for that book." He stood, his chair teetering before it righted. "You've known all along who I am and who my parents were, haven't you?"

Bertie locked eyes with the young man. "Yes, I knew who you were soon after you arrived."

"Then why didn't you just come out and tell me who my mother was? Why all this secrecy and stalling?"

"Because," Bertie said, praying he'd understand, "I needed to know if I could trust you with the story or not. I wanted to know what kind of man Songbird's boy had grown into."

"Trust *me*? That's rich." He shook his head. "Whether or not you trust me doesn't give you the right to keep information from me. You were the midwife who tended my birth. All I want to know is what happened that day and why my mother didn't keep me. Can you tell me that?"

With a heavy sigh, Bertie nodded. "I'll tell you what you want to know."

Walker didn't move to take his seat again.

"Your mama was injured when she came to us. She'd been shot in the shoulder . . . by her pa."

Reese gasped, but Walker's expression remained stony.

"When he found out she was carryin' you, he wanted her to drink a tonic that would make her lose the baby. Songbird refused. He got his gun and said if she wouldn't get rid of the baby, he'd do it himself."

Thick silence filled the space between her and Walker. She knew the information must be painful to hear, but his anger kept him from reacting to it.

"What happened after she came here?"

"We took her in and tended her shoulder. Once she was healed, we knew we couldn't send her back to her pa. She lived with us until you were born."

Surprise washed over his face. "Are you saying I was born *here*, in this cabin?" His gaze swept the room before returning to Bertie.

She nodded. "You arrived in the early hours of October 27, 1943. The day after Songbird's fifteenth birthday."

"Fifteen?"

"She was a sweet, gentle child who found herself in a situation she couldn't handle on her own."

"A situation she shouldn't have been in." His tone offered no forgiveness. "No fourteen-year-old girl should be sleeping with her boyfriend."

"You can cast judgment if you like, but it don't change the fact that you're the result of what she did."

He frowned. "What about my father? Where was he in this? You said my mother wrote him a letter."

"That's right, she did. But Amos's ma got the letter, because Amos had enlisted in the Army and was in Europe by then."

"My birth father was in World War II?" At Bertie's affirmative nod, he said, "That's ironic. Pop was deemed 4-F. He had the mumps as a kid, and it left him deaf in one ear." After a pause, he added, "He also couldn't have children."

What Walker called irony Bertie saw as destiny.

"Did Amos's mother—my grandmother—tell him about me? About my mother being pregnant?"

"I don't think so," Bertie said. He didn't need to know the woman denied he was her son's child at first. "But it didn't matter in the end."

"Why wouldn't it matter?"

She knew her next words would wound him, but he deserved

to know the truth. "Because Amos was killed in the war. He never came home."

Walker took a step backward, his face twisted. "He died? Without even knowing I existed?"

Bertie wasn't sure how to answer. "God has a way of makin' us aware of things, important things, down deep in our souls. Whether or not Amos knew he was a father, no one can say, but I'm sure he would've been proud to have a son."

"How can you say that? You didn't know him. He slept with a fourteen-year-old girl. That's not something a man of honor does."

Bertie heard bitterness in his words. "It's true I didn't know Amos," she said, feeling the need to defend the young man Songbird had loved. "I'm not sure how old he was when he met Songbird. But one mistake don't make him a bad person. Everyone makes mistakes."

"That's it in a nutshell, isn't it?" Walker gave a humorless laugh. "I'm a mistake. I should have never been born." He turned to Reese. "You're a mistake too. Our parents didn't want us."

"I don't agree, Walker," Reese said. "Our birth parents are the ones whose actions were wrong, but that doesn't make us a mistake. I remember when one of the kids at school called me a foul name. I didn't know what it meant and asked Mom. After she explained the definition, she said something I will never forget: 'There's no such thing as illegitimate children. Every child is planned by God.'"

Bertie nodded. "Your mama was right." She looked at Walker. "God made you for a reason, son. You were conceived by God before you were conceived by your parents. He decided *when* you would be born, *where* you would be born, and *who* your parents would be. Your existence may have surprised your ma, but it didn't surprise your heavenly Father."

He scoffed. "I'm a songwriter, Miss Bertie. Pretty words are meaningless. That stuff about God making me for a reason is a load of—" He shook his head, his jaw clenched. "You can't convince me God thought it was a great idea to let a fourteen-year-old girl get pregnant and then get shot by her own father when she wouldn't abort me. You can't convince me my father dying in the war and my mother giving me up for adoption is some wonderful plan God concocted."

His words hung heavy between them. They held truth, but it was distorted by his anger.

"You're right. The circumstances of your conception wasn't God's design, but you *are* here because he willed it." Bertie prayed he would have ears to hear. "Your mama chose life for you because she loved you. If Songbird hadn't wanted a baby, she could have easily taken the tonic her pa offered. Some women do choose that sad path. Thankfully, our God forgives when we repent and gives those mamas the promise of seeing their child again in heaven. You shouldn't judge your mama for doin' everything she could to keep you safe, son."

For a moment, she thought he might consider her words. But his expression never softened. Instead, he strode to where his jacket hung on a peg. "I'm done. I got what I came for. I don't want to hear any more about the messed-up family I come from. Let's go, Reese."

Tears sprang to Bertie's eyes. She'd failed him. She'd failed Songbird.

"Walker, can't we—?" Reese began, but he cut her off.

"I'm done. I'm ready to go." He threw on his coat and moved to the door.

Reese remained where she sat. "I'm not leaving. Not like this."

His face grew hard. "Need I remind you this isn't about you, Miss Chandler? I hired you to find the midwife who attended my birth. You've done your job. Now I need you to drive me down this mountain so I can get back to my life."

His raised voice echoed in the small room.

Rubie whimpered from where she'd been dozing on the cot. Bertie moved to stand beside her sister, feeling responsible for Walker's anger yet unsure how to fix it.

"I said I'm not leaving." Reese stood, went to where her jacket hung, and retrieved a set of keys from the pocket. She held them out to him. "Take my car. I'll find my own way home tomorrow."

Impatience colored Walker's face. "Don't do this, Reese. Just come with me. We're done here."

She shook her head and folded her arms. "Goodbye, Mr. Wylie. If you'd have your manager return my car, I'd appreciate it."

They stared at each other for several ticks of the clock. Finally Walker snatched the keys, turned, and stalked out the door. He gave it a hard slam for good measure.

The three women remained where they were. Outside, the car's engine revved. A moment later, the crunching of rocks told them Walker truly was leaving.

Bertie met Reese's troubled look. "You should've gone with him, dear. He probably shouldn't be alone, considering all he's been through today."

"Maybe," Reese said. She sank onto a chair. "But he made me so mad. How dare he take out his frustration on you."

"His ma and pa ain't here. I'm the only one he could get angry with."

Rubie kissed Bertie's hand, then rested her cheek on it. "Our boy will be back."

Bertie squeezed her sister's hand. "Let's hope so."

Rain pelted the tin roof.

Bertie glanced out the window, where dark clouds filled the frame. "I 'spect we're fixin' to get a taste of winter. The almanac said we'd have us an early cold spell."

"I hope Walker gets down the mountain okay." Reese's face

spoke her worry. "He'll probably head home to Nashville. That's a long drive in bad weather."

Bertie went to the young woman and took her hand. "How 'bout we pray for him?"

Rubie joined them.

"Lord," Bertie began, her voice a wobbly whisper, "take care of our boy."

Twenty-One

MY HEAD THROBBED, but it was nothing compared to the cutting pain in my heart.

I couldn't keep Josh.

That terrible awareness hit me so hard and so fast, it took my breath.

But I knew it was true. My son wasn't safe with me. Pa would do whatever it took to get Josh. I'd seen evil burning in his eyes when Bertie forced him to give the baby up. We were all in danger.

But Bertie refused to listen.

"I ain't afraid of your pa." She paced the gathering room. "I ain't afraid of the law, neither. If we go to the sheriff ourselves, we can tell him 'bout your pa shootin' you and wantin' to force you to drink poison that'd kill your baby and maybe even yourself. Our family has been in these parts long before your pa arrived. The Jenkins name means somethin' round here."

Rubie, Amelie, and Bonnie nodded in agreement, but Jennie's serious expression didn't change.

"That's why I have to leave," I said, drawing everyone's attention. My eyes implored Bertie to hear me out. "Y'all have been so good to me 'n' Josh. I don't know what I would've done if I hadn't found your place. But Pa'll raise a ruckus, I know he will. He'll tell lies 'bout me and 'bout you, too. He won't stop. Not till he gets what he wants. And I won't let Amos's ma have my son neither. The only way to protect him from them is to give him to someone else. Someone who lives far away from here."

The lasting implications of my statement hung in the silence of the room.

Could I do it? Could I give my son away?

"She's right, Bertie."

Bertie didn't turn to look at Jennie. I knew she didn't want to see the truth on her oldest sister's face. I didn't either, yet what other choice was there?

"There's got to be another way," Bertie said, her loud voice startling Josh.

He let out a cry and turned to me for comfort. I lifted my blouse and he quieted.

"What will that child do without you?" Tears spilled down Bertie's cheeks. "You're his mama."

I looked down on the baby at my breast, his eyes half-closed in contentment. I wanted to give him the world, but I was barely more than a child myself. "You said God adopts us and makes us part of his family." I looked up, my eyes filling too. "We gotta pray that God'll give my Joshua another mama who'll love him as much as I do."

Bertie dropped to her knees in front of my chair, her body shaking with sorrow. Soon, all the sisters were gathered around us. No doubt the old cabin hadn't heard such sorrowful weeping since Papa Jenkins passed on to his heavenly home twenty years earlier.

When all grew quiet again, Jennie was the first to rouse.

"I'll go down to the church parsonage and fetch Brother Brown. I 'spect he and the missus won't go to their son's house in town for the holiday till tomorrow." Her voice quavered. "We'll need help if . . . if this is what must happen."

I swallowed hard, wishing things could be different but knowing they couldn't. "Thank ya, Miss Jennie."

She nodded and moved to get her bonnet. "If the parson ain't home, I'll ride to Tom's and ask him to drive me to town."

Jennie put on her coat and left through the kitchen. I imagined Kit wouldn't be too happy to leave his warm stall. I appreciated both Jennie's and Kit's sacrifice.

"I'll make us some tea." Bonnie disappeared into the next room, with Amelie following behind.

Rubie moved to a quiet corner of the gathering room and closed her eyes, her lips giving evidence of silent prayers going up. I knew I'd need them if I was to follow through with this.

I raised Joshua to my shoulder and gently patted his tiny back. Bertie hadn't moved from her place on the plank floor.

"Miss Bertie," I whispered, glancing to the kitchen, then back. There was something she needed to know. Something that might help her understand my decision. "I ain't never told no one this, but after Pa tried to make me drink the tonic, I got to thinkin' that he might've done the same to my ma. She was expectin' another baby when she died. I thought she was just sick, but now I'm wonderin' if Pa done somethin' to her."

"Oh, child." Bertie clutched my hand with both of hers. "You don't need to see that man again. No matter what happens, we'll make certain he'll never bother you again."

"But you see why I can't stay. There's no tellin' what he might do."

Bertie pressed her lips before nodding. "I do, but that don't mean we have to give up. I'm holding out hope we can think of a way to keep both you and Joshua safe but together. Maybe Brother Brown will have an idea."

I didn't respond. I knew letting Joshua go was best for him. He deserved a loving family, with a ma and a pa and brothers and sisters. Without Amos, I couldn't give him that.

"I think I'll put Joshua in his cradle, then lie down upstairs." I rose from the chair, hopelessness making even that simple movement an effort. "I'm plumb worn-out."

"'Course you are, dear one." Bertie stood too, her movements stiff after being on the hard floor for long minutes. "We'll talk more after the preacher gets here."

I carried my son across the room, his tiny head on my shoulder. The faint scent of lavender on his skin brought tears to my eyes. I knew I'd always think of Joshua whenever I smelled the fragrance.

With a kiss on his warm cheek, I tucked him into the small bed. My feet felt heavy as I climbed the ladder to the loft and lay down on one of the neatly made beds.

Why, God? Tears slid down my face into my hair. *Why did Amos have to die? Joshua needs his pa. I need him too.*

I rolled onto my side and buried my face in the pillow. "Oh, Amos," I sobbed. "What am I gonna do without you?"

I lay there a long time, remembering the moment I first saw Amos at the mercantile. His gentle spirit. His laughter. I thought about the day we made our son. I knew I should be sorry for it, but I wasn't. Not when I knew I'd never be his wife. I dared not think about how he died and instead pictured him in heaven, his smile eternal.

"Rest in peace, my love," I whispered.

But there was no peace for me. Not with the life-altering decision I had to make.

My heart twisted with raw pain at the thought of giving my son away. The very idea made me sick to my stomach, yet it was the only way to keep him safe. Pa, and even Miz Cole, I suspected, wouldn't give up easily. If Pa followed through with his threat to get the law involved, I'd have no choice about what happened to my son. I couldn't allow that. At least this way, I was the one making the decisions.

Low voices came from the gathering room, where the sisters awaited Jennie's return. I hadn't heard Joshua fuss, so I guessed he must still be asleep. Despite my exhaustion, my mind wouldn't be still.

I rose from the bed and settled at the small writing table near the window. A drawer held paper and pen. For a long moment, I stared at the blank page, wondering how to tell my son I was sorry I couldn't keep him and assure him I loved him more than anything.

With trembling fingers, I began to write.

> *Sweet babe of mine,*
> > *So perfect in every way.*
> *Who will you become?*
> *Sweet son of my heart,*
> > *You may not understand,*
> > *It's because of love I must let you go.*

˪

Jennie returned to the homestead an hour later. After putting Kit in the barn, she came inside, her nose red from the cold. Songbird came down from the loft, her face wan, and everyone gathered in the kitchen, where a warm fire burned in the rock fireplace.

"Well?" Bertie said, impatient yet fearful to hear what her sister had to say. She almost hoped the parson hadn't been home, thus giving her time to think of a way to prevent the tragedy that barreled toward them. So far, however, nothing practical had surfaced, but she wasn't giving up.

"Brother Brown understands the seriousness of the situation." Jennie looked at Songbird, her usual frown appropriate for the conversation. "After I told him the story, we drove to the mercantile so he could use the telephone to call his cousin who's a pastor in Nashville. The man said he knows of a childless couple and believes they'd be happy to adopt Josh."

Thick, sorrow-laden silence hung in the air.

"I asked him to give us time to talk things over, but he'll be here soon. Says he can drive you to Nashville tonight."

Bertie gasped. "Tonight?" Her gaze darted to Songbird. "Surely you don't need to leave tonight."

The girl's wide eyes stared back, full of fear. "I . . . I don't know."

"Brother Brown and I are in agreement that we need to act quickly," Jennie said, her mouth firm. "If Songbird's pa makes good on his threat, he might show up anytime. I don't think any of us want to put ourselves or Songbird and little Joshua in danger. That man has already tried to kill his daughter once. There ain't no tellin' what he's capable of now that he's riled up."

The gravity of her words was reflected on each of their faces.

They knew she was right.

Bertie wanted to collapse on the floor and thrash out her anger like a child throwing a tantrum.

"It ain't fair," she hissed. "Why'd that man have to come here and ruin everythin'?"

Only God had the answer, but he seemed distant and silent.

"We best get Josh's things together," Jennie said.

No one moved.

"What about Songbird?" Rubie asked. "Where will she go, Sister?"

"Brother Brown said there's a place in Knoxville that helps women . . . like Songbird."

Her meaning was clear.

"Songbird ain't like those women," Bertie said, angry Jennie would even consider such a thing. "She's a sweet girl and a good mama to her baby."

Jennie sent Bertie a glare. "I didn't say she wasn't. Brother

Brown said it's a home for girls who don't have family to help 'em. They teach 'em things so they can go out and get a job and such."

Bonnie forced a smile as she looked at Songbird. "Knoxville ain't so far away that you couldn't come visit."

The decision, however, rested solely with Songbird. All eyes turned to her.

"Thank ya, Miss Jennie. I 'preciate everything you done to help work things out for Joshua and me." She moistened her lips and took a shaky breath. "I think this is for the best."

The sound of a car entering the yard gained their attention. Jennie went to the window.

"It's Brother Brown." She turned to face Songbird. "He'll be a-wantin' your answer."

The girl nodded.

At the parson's knock on the door, Jennie let him in. The gray-haired man greeted each sister but without his usual smile and chatty conversation. When Jennie introduced him to Songbird, compassion filled his eyes.

"Dear child, I'm sorry to hear all that you've been through."

Bertie moved to stand next to Songbird and wrapped her arm around the trembling girl's waist. "She's a good girl, Brother Brown. As sweet as they come."

The gentle man nodded. "I don't doubt it."

Once they were seated around the kitchen table, he came right to the point of their meeting.

"Jennie has informed me there is an element of danger if you and your son remain here with the Jenkins sisters."

Songbird looked down at her hands, shame on her face. "Yes, sir. My pa, he tried to kill me when I wouldn't get rid of my baby. I 'spect he's so fired up mad that I wouldn't give Joshua to Amos's ma, there ain't no tellin' what he might do." She glanced around the table. "These ladies have been so kind to me—"

Tears choked her, and her shoulders shook with sobs. "I can't . . . I can't let anythin' happen to them." She met the parson's gaze. "If you're still willin', I'd like you to take me and Joshua to Nashville . . . tonight."

Bertie covered her mouth lest she scream at the injustice of it all.

How could God let this happen?

How could she let go of her girl? Of little Joshua?

"If that's what you wish," Brother Brown said, "then we need to be off. It's a long drive to the city, especially at night."

Songbird's face crumpled. "It's not what I wish, but it's for the best. For everyone."

Bertie sat in a daze as her sisters rose to action.

Bonnie got out bread and ham and began making sandwiches for the journey.

Amelie quietly set about packing the tiny nightdresses and diapers she and Songbird had lovingly sewn for Josh.

Rubie helped Songbird pack a bag of the things she'd acquired since coming to the homestead, including the new Bible she'd been reading to Joshua every day.

Jennie went up to the sleeping loft and came down with a small leather pouch. Bertie suspected it held money.

In all the commotion, only Bertie heard the tiny noises coming from the cradle near the fireplace. She stood and found Joshua staring up at her. He let out a soft coo that melted her heart.

"Come here, sweet boy," she whispered, lifting the wee one into her arms. She hadn't realized she was crying until a tear landed on his dimpled fist.

Dear Lord, please let us keep him. I can't let them go.

She held him close, her arms clutching him to her chest, as though daring anyone to take him from her.

"It's time, Bertie." Jennie stood beside her all too soon.

Bertie's hold on the baby tightened. "I'm goin' with them," she announced, surprising herself as well as everyone in the room. She had no idea when she'd decided such a thing, but it made perfect sense.

"I don't think that's wise," Brother Brown said, a slight frown on his weathered face.

"Please let her come with me." Songbird stepped forward, wearing Amelie's coat, Rubie's hat, and Bonnie's gloves. She met Bertie's gaze, her eyes conveying her fear. "I don't think I can do this without her," she whispered, her voice tremulous.

Bertie gazed at the girl who'd become a daughter. A daughter who needed a mother's strength to lean on now. "I'll help you through this, child."

Songbird gave a tearful nod of thanks.

Preparations for the journey were nearly complete when Bertie realized they'd need some sort of documentation to accompany Joshua to his new family.

"I best write a letter, tellin' them when and where he was born."

Songbird pressed her hand to her lips and nodded.

Bertie began to write the baby's name on a sheet of paper, but Songbird stopped her.

"His new ma should give him a name." She glanced to where Jennie stood holding the baby. "He'll always be Amos Joshua to me, but the couple in Nashville may have a family name they like better."

Couldn't Joshua at least keep his name? Bertie railed. A name that had so much meaning? Surely the people who adopted him wouldn't mind. But Songbird was insistent.

Bertie crumpled the first letter and began again. *Baby Boy was born . . .*

With a heavy heart, she signed her name and stuffed the note into the bag of his belongings.

When Bertie and the baby were bundled against the cold, and

Songbird's and Josh's things stored in the trunk of Brother Brown's car, it was time to say goodbye.

Each of the sisters gave Songbird a tight hug and kissed the baby's sweet head, tears flowing down everyone's cheeks.

"We'll miss you, child," Jennie said, her voice thick with emotion. "Write to us and let us know how you're doin'." Songbird nodded and started to turn away, but Jennie tugged her back. She took Songbird's face in her hands and whispered, "I love you."

Bertie looked on in amazement. In all her years, she'd never heard Jennie say those words to anyone, not even to Mam or Papa.

Stars shone in the inky sky as they made their way outside.

Brother Brown opened the door to the back seat. Bertie climbed in first, then reached for the baby in Songbird's arms. After she relinquished him, the girl turned to face the sisters.

"I'll miss you all. I'll never forget you."

With that, she climbed into the car next to Bertie, her body shaking with quiet sobs.

Pastor Brown closed the door and came around to the driver's seat. He looked back at Bertie and Songbird, then closed his eyes. "Father, give us safe passage. May your will be done when we arrive."

The car's engine roared to life. Although it was dark outside, Bertie looked back as they drove across the yard.

Muted light came from the windows of the old log home. She could just make out the silhouettes of her sisters, arms linked, holding each other up even as their broken hearts threatened to bring them to their knees.

None of them, Bertie realized, would be the same after this day.

Twenty-Two

WALKER COULDN'T SEE THE RUTTED ROAD through the pouring rain, but that didn't stop him from ramming the gas pedal on Reese's VW to the floorboards.

He had to get off this mountain.

Reese and the Jenkins sisters must think him insane the way he'd behaved, shouting and slamming doors, but he couldn't remain in that house another minute. Not after everything Bertie divulged. Learning about his messed-up birth family nearly pushed him over the edge, and he couldn't take any more.

A fourteen-year-old child for a mother?

A grandfather who'd wanted him dead?

It was too much.

A flash of lightning briefly illuminated the muddy path ahead. A moment later the VW hit a deep rut and nearly had Walker airborne. He braked hard, sending the small car into a skid. It took all his strength to fight the steering wheel, but thankfully he got it under control before the car plowed into the creek that ran alongside the narrow trail.

The vehicle came to a jerky stop.

Walker inhaled a gulp of air, his heart pounding along with

the *thump*, *thump*, *thump* of the windshield wipers. He exhaled noisily.

"What are you doing, Wylie?" he muttered. "Trying to kill yourself?"

He leaned his head against the driver's window, the glass chilled from the cold air outside. The weather had turned miserable. Anyone with half a brain would be indoors, sitting by a warm fire, drinking some of Bertie's herbal tea.

He heaved a sigh.

There was no way he was going back. Even if he could swallow his pride after the way he'd stormed out of the house, he had no desire to set foot in that cabin again. The shock of discovering he'd been born there still hadn't worn off.

Rain continued to beat against the small car.

Walker reached into the back seat for the map. He had no clue how to get to Nashville from here. He didn't even know how to get to the small community of Cosby Run, since they'd started from the Dunn cabin the day they arrived at Bertie's place. Frustrated, he tossed the map behind him and hoped he'd eventually find someplace to get directions.

Taking things more slowly, he maneuvered the car down the rest of the trail until he reached a fork in the road. Another flash of lightning revealed the path to the right disappearing up a steep incline. Definitely not the direction Walker wanted to attempt in the rain.

He steered the car to the left.

The headlights landed on a small church a short distance from the road. A house stood nearby. Walker vaguely remembered passing it when Jeffrey Earl led them to Bertie's. However, no light shone through the windows of either building, so there wasn't any point stopping to inquire about directions to town.

He'd just pressed the gas pedal when a flash of color darted down the steps of the church. Walker slammed the brakes again and squinted, trying to see what it was, but he'd lost it in the shadows.

It couldn't be an animal. Not with such bright colors.

Maybe he was seeing things.

He chalked the vision up to his stressed-out brain and hit the gas. The sooner he was off this mountain, the better for his sanity.

He hadn't gone ten feet when blurry colors appeared directly in the middle of the road.

Walker swerved, barely missing whatever it was. He pumped the brake and whirled around to look through the small rear window.

Had he hit it? He hadn't felt the car bump anything.

Another flash of light across the sky revealed the colors in a heap on the muddy road.

Walker stopped the car, opened the door, and climbed out, shielding his eyes from the drenching rain.

"Hello?"

No answer.

Was this a ploy to rob him? Maybe he should just get back in the car and leave. The last thing he needed was for someone to mug him and steal Reese's car.

"Help," came a weak voice through the rain.

He glanced around but only thick, dark woods met his eyes.

If the lump on the road was truly someone in need, he couldn't drive away. The temperature was steadily dropping, and tiny bits of ice were now mixed with the rain.

An oath crossed his lips.

Resigned, Walker jogged over to the colorful mound and saw it was a woman.

"Are you hurt?" he hollered over the din of the rain.

She lifted her head. Long pale hair hung drenched and limp, and big eyes met his.

"I'm . . . I'm havin' a baby."

Walker's stomach sank to his feet with her words, and he stared at her in horror. "Now?"

She nodded, clutching her huge belly beneath the bright, flowery dress plastered to her body. No shoes protected her bare feet nor was there a jacket in sight.

"What are you doing out here in the middle of a storm?"

Answering questions was probably the last thing she wanted to do, considering her situation, but Walker still wasn't convinced this wasn't some kind of hoax.

"I thought the preacher would be here," she shouted, nodding to the church. "But it's locked up tight. I hoped he'd take me to the hospital."

As if to emphasize her need, the girl doubled over, groaning as she did.

Walker wiped water from his face with both hands, as if that would help him see the situation more clearly.

What should he do?

There were two choices . . . but only one to choose.

"Let's get you into the car." A loud clap of thunder nearly drowned him out.

She looked up, wariness in her eyes. "I don't have money to pay you."

"I don't need your money." He reached out a hand.

After a moment of hesitation, she placed icy fingers in his. Walker tugged her to her feet. As they slowly made their way to the car, he realized her entire body was shivering.

Once she was settled in the passenger seat, he took off his jacket and threw it over her. He closed the door and made a dash for the driver's side. Out of the rain, Walker turned the key at the same time he asked, "Where should I take you? I'm not from around here, so you'll have to give me directions to the nearest hospital."

The girl's face scrunched up before she could answer. She grabbed her belly, breathing heavily.

A sinking feeling washed over Walker.

He'd never get her to a hospital in time, even if he knew how to get there. He had no experience with childbirth, but even he recognized the need to get her somewhere fast if he didn't want her delivering the child in the front seat of Reese's VW Beetle.

He looked out the rain-washed window to the mountain he'd just come down.

Another oath fell from his lips.

When she glanced at him, he schooled his frustration. "I know someone who can help you."

Big eyes stared at him, but she nodded. "Okay. Hurry."

He didn't need to be told twice.

Walker strong-armed the gearshift to get the car moving and headed back in the direction he'd come. He tried to avoid the deepest ruts in the road, but it was nearly impossible, considering he could barely see the mountain trail. The girl yelped and squeezed her eyes shut when the tires bounced over a large rock.

"Sorry," he said.

It took an eternity to reach the Jenkins homestead, or at least that's how it seemed. If Walker didn't know this was the only road leading to the cabin, he might've thought he'd become turned around and gone the wrong way.

The log home finally came into view, golden light from the windows sending out a warm welcome on a cold, dreary night. Someone moved aside the curtain and peeked out, but he couldn't tell if it was Bertie, her sister, or Reese.

Walker parked the car as close to the porch as he could and sounded the horn. When the door to the cabin opened, he leaped out into the freezing deluge and ran around to the passenger side.

"Let me carry you," he said to the shivering girl.

She didn't argue. When he scooped her up, she wrapped her arms around his neck and hung on. Ice and rain pelted them as they crossed the space between the car and the house.

Walker gained the porch and looked up to find Reese standing in the open doorway. Their eyes briefly held but there was no time for words. Once inside, he carefully laid the girl on the cot near the fireplace in the gathering room.

"I found her on the road," he said, trying to catch his breath. "Down by the church. Preacher wasn't there. She's . . . she's . . ."

"Having a baby," Reese supplied.

Bertie moved into his line of sight. "You done right bringin' her here."

Shame for his previous behavior rolled through Walker, but now wasn't the time for apologies.

"Let's see what we've got," Bertie said. She sat on the edge of the cot where the girl lay shivering under the blanket Reese had spread over her. Bertie gently took the girl's hand and started rubbing it. "We best get you outta those wet things, child."

The girl shook her head and started panting. "No . . . time. Baby . . . coming."

Reese moved to stand beside Bertie. "We better check to see how close she is to delivering."

Bertie agreed. "You go on and take charge. My eyes don't see as good as they used to."

Reese lifted the blanket.

Walker suddenly realized what was happening and turned his back. "I'll wait in the kitchen," he said, striding quickly in that direction.

Shep lay on a rug near the fireplace. His eyes took notice of Walker's entrance, but otherwise he didn't move.

Rubie stood at the stove and poured hot water from a kettle into a cup. She smiled at Walker as though nothing out of the ordinary had occurred. As though he hadn't stormed out of the cabin like an angry teenager.

"I knew you'd come back. Tea?"

He gave a sheepish smile. "Thank you, Miss Rubie."

She patted his arm, then frowned. "You're soaked through." Without another word, she retrieved a blanket from the gathering room and draped it over his shoulders.

Bertie appeared in the doorway as Rubie filled more cups with tea. "I 'spect we'll have us a wee one within the hour. We'll need more hot water, sheets, and some warm things for the babe."

While Rubie went in search of the items, Bertie's gaze landed on Walker.

Guilt washed over him. "Bertie, I—"

She raised a hand. "There'll be plenty o' time to sort things out later. Right now, we've got us a baby on the way."

Walker nodded. "What can I do to help?"

"Seems to me you saved Naomi from deliverin' her baby out in the cold. Ain't nothin' more needs doin' than just sittin' here and gettin' yourself warm."

"Naomi? I didn't even think to ask her name, it was so crazy finding her in the middle of the road."

Reese called to Bertie then and she returned to the other room. Walker couldn't see what was going on, but he could hear everything. The girl on the cot alternated between groans and panting breaths while Reese and Bertie spoke encouraging words to her.

"That's it. You're doing great," Reese said. "When you begin to feel the urge, go ahead and push."

"Ol' Bertie is gonna get a few things ready for the delivery now," Bertie said, followed by a rustling noise. "You'll be holdin' your wee one in no time at all."

Walker felt uncomfortable remaining inside the house during the birth, but going out to the barn in this weather was out of the question. He'd simply stay in the kitchen and try to focus on something besides what was taking place in the next room.

That, however, proved impossible.

Naomi's moans grew louder.

"I can't do this," she sobbed. "It hurts too much."

Reese spoke in a soft, calming voice, and although Walker couldn't hear the words, Naomi seemed comforted, and her sobs quieted.

Walker closed his eyes, suddenly-exhausted from everything that had transpired that day. Being back in the cabin, with a young mother giving birth, certainly wasn't where he'd expected to find himself. Yet the red-hot anger that swirled through him when he'd stormed out the door was gone.

Movement next to him brought his eyes open. Rubie sat in the chair beside him and placed a worn Bible on the table.

"It could be a while fore the little one arrives," she said, turning pages. "I always think of Psalm 139 when a babe is on the way."

She began to read aloud while Walker listened.

It was the same passage Bertie had read that morning. This time, however, the words didn't disturb him as they'd done before. The thought of God seeing him and knitting him together in his young mother's womb sparked a feeling of awe rather than disgust. Sure, Songbird hadn't been more than a child herself, but if the story Bertie told him was true, Songbird truly had loved Walker's father. What if Amos had come home from the war? Would his birth parents have married as Bertie thought? Had other children? Walker remembered wishing he had siblings as a young boy. Life as an only child could be lonely at times.

"I see the head crowning." Reese's voice reached him from the other room.

"Give a good push now," Bertie instructed.

A long, guttural sound came from Naomi.

Rubie rose and disappeared into the gathering room.

"That's it," Reese said. "One more big push."

Suddenly faraway voices filled Walker's head. Faint, yet he could make out the words.

"That's it, Songbird. One more push and your son will be here."

Was he remembering his own birth? It seemed crazy to think so, but he closed his eyes anyway, listening.

Bertie's voice announced the arrival of a healthy boy.

"He's so beautiful," came a soft reply. *"The most beautiful thing I ever did see."*

Naomi's scream brought him back to the present.

Without thought to what he was doing, Walker stood and moved to the doorway, as if drawn to the miraculous event taking place on the other side of the log wall.

Was this what it was like the day he was born in this same cabin? Excitement and wonder tingling in the air?

The gathering room glowed with yellow lantern light. Naomi sat up on the cot, her knuckles white as she gripped her knees. Bertie sat behind her and rubbed her back while Rubie stood next to them, her lips moving in silent prayer. Reese sat on a stool at the foot of the bed, watching the miracle of birth unfold beneath a sheet loosely draped for privacy.

"The head is out," Reese said after Naomi gave a great push, her face turning deep red.

From his vantage point, Walker couldn't see the baby, but he could see Reese. He watched in amazement as she worked, helping a new life enter the world.

After Naomi gave one last push, the howl of a newborn filled the room.

"It's a girl. You have a daughter." Reese laughed and cried at the same time.

Tears flowed down Naomi's cheeks, but a radiant smile transformed her entire face. With gentle expertise, Reese wiped the baby with a towel, cut the cord, then laid the tiny girl in her mother's eager arms.

Naomi gathered her daughter to her and kissed her wet little head. "She's perfect."

"What will you call her?" Bertie asked.

"Stormie, since she came with the rain. Stormie Claire, after my ma."

"That's a right fine name."

The women oohed and aahed over the baby, pronouncing her the most darling thing they'd seen in a coon's age. Walker thought little Stormie looked a bit puffy and red, but still, he now understood what Reese was talking about when she said every birth was a miracle.

He returned to the kitchen, leaving Naomi and little Stormie to bond, but he couldn't sit still. His mind was too full of the truth.

Thirty years ago, he came into the world in this very cabin. His mother—Songbird—had been a young woman like Naomi, pregnant and alone until Bertie rescued her. She'd been a child herself, but she'd chosen life for him. She'd protected him when her own father threatened to kill him. What happened after he was born and why she gave him up was still a mystery, but Walker no longer blamed her.

The anger he'd been carrying around for months flowed out of him. In its place, welcome peace.

He sat down at the table and picked up Joshua Jenkins's Bible, still open to the Psalms.

"I will praise thee; for I am fearfully and wonderfully made."

Walker was still reading when he heard Reese's worried voice from the next room.

"Naomi?" Reese called. "Naomi?"

"She's going into shock," Bertie said.

Walker rushed to the doorway in time to see Naomi's arms go slack and her eyes roll back in her head. Bertie lunged for the baby before the little girl tumbled off her mother's chest.

Rubie hurried over and took the infant so Bertie could help Reese.

Before Walker knew what was happening, a gush of dark blood flooded the floor at Reese's feet. He could only stare in horror.

"Dear Lord in heaven," Bertie gasped. "She's hemorrhaging."

Twenty-Three

"THERE'S TOO MUCH BLOOD." Reese's panicked voice rent the air. "The placenta looked intact, but now I'm wondering if I missed something."

Bertie heard fear and second-guessing in Reese's voice. Although her own heart raced, they needed to stay calm if they were to save Naomi's life. "Let's focus on gettin' the bleeding stopped. You elevate her feet. I'll see if I can get her uterus to contract."

While Reese rushed to remove pillows from beneath Naomi's head and pile them under the unconscious mother's feet, Bertie began to knead Naomi's abdomen, using vigorous motions. If there was indeed something still in the uterus—part of the placenta or a blood clot—the muscles wouldn't contract like they needed to in order to constrict the blood vessels. The new mother was in grave danger if they couldn't stop the flow.

Minutes ticked off the clock.

Reese checked Naomi's blood pressure. Her own face was nearly as pale as the mother's when she met Bertie's gaze. "Her heart rate is going down, Bertie. Her pressure is plummeting. What do we do? There isn't time to get her to the hospital."

Bertie could only stare at Reese as a terrible memory from long ago pushed its way into her mind.

A young woman not much older than Naomi had died because Bertie couldn't stop the bleeding. She'd been devastated, the guilt nearly too heavy to carry. Ever since Mam took her to that first birthing and shared the secrets of being a midwife with Bertie, she'd had an air of confidence that bordered on pride. Losing that young mother forced Bertie to recognize she had no control over the outcome of any birth she tended. The experience left her humbled and shaken.

Now, as she looked at Naomi's pale face, those feelings rose to the surface once again.

In the next moment, the mother stopped breathing.

"We're losing her," Reese cried. She rushed to begin mouth-to-mouth resuscitation.

Time dragged as Reese alternated between pumping Naomi's chest and breathing several short puffs into her mouth. All Bertie could do was watch, feeling helpless and useless.

Naomi didn't respond to the lifesaving efforts. She lay motionless on the cot, as though her spirit had already seeped from her.

Somewhere behind Bertie, the baby let out a tiny wail.

"Dear Lord," Bertie whispered, "please don't let little Stormie lose her mama. Please."

Reese wept as she frantically worked to pump blood into Naomi's heart. "She can't die. She can't."

Bertie sank to her knees. Unable to help. Unable to pray. Feeling as powerless as she had all those years ago. Life and death belonged to the Lord, she knew, but it was hard to understand sometimes.

After another minute, Walker moved to Reese's side and put his hands on hers. "She's gone, Reese." The soft words were not what any of them wanted to hear, yet it was true.

Reese stilled, her breath coming in gulps. Her body sagged, and she fell into his arms, sobbing.

It was Rubie's voice, strong and sure, that brought Bertie's head up.

"'The hand of the Lord was upon me, and carried me out in the spirit of the Lord, and set me down in the midst of the valley which was full of bones.'"

With the baby in her arms, Rubie crossed the room and stood beside the cot, not a trace of fear or confusion on her face.

"'And he said unto me, Son of man, can these bones live? And I answered, O Lord God, thou knowest.'"

Bertie recognized the words from the book of Ezekiel. She watched as Rubie gently laid Stormie Claire on her mother's chest. Then Rubie smiled.

"'Thus saith the Lord God unto these bones; Behold, I will cause breath to enter into you, and ye shall live.'"

The door flew wide then, pushed by the frigid wind, and banged against the wall, startling everyone. Walker hurried to close it.

When Bertie's gaze returned to Naomi, she found the mother's cheeks pink, the deathly pallor gone. Scrambling to her feet, she stood next to Rubie. Her sister simply grinned.

What happened next left Bertie speechless.

Naomi's eyes fluttered open. Taking a deep breath, she filled her lungs in a way Reese's efforts could not.

Little Stormie let out a cry, and her mama reached a hand to quiet her.

With a peace-filled smile, Rubie gazed down on the mother and child.

"'And ye shall know that I am the Lord.'"

⁓

Bertie watched Naomi nurse her newborn daughter for the first time, rejoicing over the miracle that had taken place. God had given little Stormie back her mama, plain and simple. Bertie couldn't answer the question of why other mamas and babies died. Today, she would simply be grateful for the two beautiful lives he'd placed in her care.

"Miss Bertie," Naomi said, her eyes drooping, "I'd like to get word to my mama about Stormie Claire. I'm sure she's worried. After me and my boyfriend argued, I tried to get to her house but got lost. Do you have a telephone I can use?"

Bertie chuckled. "I know you young people can't live without a telephone or electricity, but we don't have neither. There's a neighbor down the road who lets us use his call box when there's a need. Reese was plannin' to go down there in the morning to call her friend. I'm sure she'd be more'n happy to contact your ma."

Bertie glanced across the room to where Rubie slept. It was well after midnight, and her sister hadn't been able to keep her eyes open another moment after the excitement settled.

But Bertie knew she couldn't sleep until Joshua—or Walker, she should say—heard the whole story of his birth and his mama's sacrifice.

She found him and Reese seated at the table, mugs in their hands.

Reese stood. "Would you like some chamomile tea, Bertie?"

"That'd be nice."

Once Bertie was settled with her drink, she said, "It's been quite a night."

Reese retook her seat next to Walker. "When I worked at the hospital, we had a mother die shortly after giving birth. The circumstances were different, as she had a serious medical condition, but the doctor did everything he could to save her. I'll never forget how devastated he looked when he had to stop CPR." She glanced at Walker. "That's how I felt when you made me stop. Helpless. Hopeless."

They sat in silence for a time.

"Do you really believe we just witnessed a miracle?" Walker asked. He turned to Reese. "Maybe your chest compressions got her heart started and it just took a while for her lungs to kick in."

Reese shook her head. "I don't think so. She had no pulse."

"Rubie doesn't want any credit either," Bertie added. "She just spoke words that came right out of the Good Book."

"So what you're saying is, we have no logical explanation for what took place in this cabin tonight." Walker looked at Bertie.

"Nothin' we humans can explain," she said.

"Wow."

"Exactly," Bertie said. "As old as I am, you'd think my faith would be as strong as my sister's. But Rubie has always had more trust and understandin' of God's ways." She glanced toward the gathering room. "Naomi doesn't remember a thing," she said, her voice lowered. "I figured it best not to tell her just now. Don't want to frighten her."

"But we know what we saw," Reese said.

Bertie gave a firm nod. "There ain't any doubt in my mind that God breathed into that girl just as sure as he breathed into those dry bones back in Ezekiel's day." She turned to Walker. "I'm more certain than ever the Lord sent you down that mountain so you'd find Naomi."

Bertie sipped her tea. After a difficult day and an eventful evening, they all needed a good night's sleep. She knew, however, that there were things that must be said, and now was as good a time as any.

"I 'spect you have questions for me."

When Walker nodded, it was Joshua looking back at her.

"I want to know about my mother. About Songbird. What was she like?"

Warmth spread through Bertie as she looked at the boy she loved. "She was a sweet child. Pretty, too. You have her eyes."

"I do?" He seemed pleased by this information.

"I 'spect your pa must've been tall, 'cause Songbird was a little thing." Bertie's mind traveled back to June 1943. "After her wound healed, she stayed with us 'cause she had no place to go. Her ma had died some years back, and her pa wasn't much of a father, as you can guess. I'm not ashamed to admit she was like a daughter to me." Bertie's voice quavered with emotion. "I loved your mama. And I loved you, too."

Bertie told him about the night he was born and how each of the Jenkins sisters adored the tiny boy. She shared how Jennie's heart softened when Songbird gave her own heart to Jesus and how Songbird's coming to the homestead brought joy and laughter.

"Her bein' here was good for our souls," Bertie said. "It felt right havin' you and her part of our family. We wanted her to stay with us forever."

"Why didn't she?" Walker asked.

The heartache Bertie had tried to keep buried all these years resurfaced, and tears blurred her vision.

"She loved us too much to stay."

Twenty-Four

WE DROVE THROUGH THE LONG NIGHT.

Bertie and I hadn't spoken much since we left the homestead. At first, she tried to convince me to get some sleep, but I couldn't. I simply held Joshua and wept silent tears, whispering secrets to my son that neither Bertie nor the parson could hear over the car's noisy engine. Sometime after we passed through Knoxville, Bertie fell asleep.

I must've dozed off at some point too because I woke to find a million twinkling lights from Nashville ahead, seeming to magically appear in the inky blackness. I used to tell Amos I wanted to run away to the city and get as far from Pa as I could. Amos would always promise to take me there once we married.

"We'll have us a good life, Evie," he'd say with a smile that warmed me to my toes. "We might even head out West. Would you like to see the Pacific Ocean, Evie?" Then he'd tell me about the giant white whale he'd read about in a book called *Moby Dick* and tease me about being eaten by the monster.

A tear left a wet trail down my face.

Amos was gone. We wouldn't have a life together in the city or out West.

As I looked through the window, Tennessee's capital sprawled before me, but I wanted nothing more than to be back in the safety of the sisters' simple cabin tucked deep in the mountains. The city and everything it offered was no longer a refuge for me. Instead, it would play a role in the devastation of my heart.

Brother Brown steered the car through quiet streets. When we passed a store that had pilgrims and turkeys in a lit display, I remembered today was Thanksgiving. Families all over the country would gather to count their blessings and enjoy delicious food, laughter, and rest. I wondered if the Jenkins sisters would go to Catie's house for the holiday meal as planned. Something told me a quiet day at the homestead would most likely be their choice, considering all the upset with me and Joshua leaving.

Downtown Nashville was a sight to behold, and I wished Amos were here with me. I couldn't believe there were so many tall buildings in one place. We crossed a wide, dark river and Brother Brown stopped the car in front of a redbrick structure. Although the sky was still dark, with just a hint of morning on the eastern horizon, light shone through the building's stained-glass windows.

Bertie awoke when the parson shut off the engine. "My goodness, I sure didn't mean to go to sleep. Are we there?"

"This is the church where my cousin is pastor." Brother Brown met my gaze. "When I called him from the gas station in Knoxville, he said he'd meet us in the sanctuary."

Bertie glanced at me, a look I couldn't quite figure in her eyes. "We'll wait here while you go inside to see if everyone has arrived. Songbird and I have some things to discuss."

Brother Brown's face revealed his sympathy. "I understand."

He took his hat from where he'd laid it on the passenger seat, exited the car, and disappeared into the building.

When he shut the door, Josh's eyes opened. He stretched and yawned where he lay in my lap.

"We don't have much time." Bertie shot a look back to the building just as Joshua began to fuss.

"I best feed him before . . ." I didn't finish the sentence. My chin quivered as I lifted my blouse to feed my son for the last time. Bertie had tucked a packet of herbs into my bag that would help my milk dry up faster, but I doubted I'd be able to bring myself to use them.

"Listen to me," Bertie said once the baby quieted. "I have an idea. I've been thinkin' on this since we got into this car."

Her excitement confused me. "What idea? What are you talkin' about, Miss Bertie?"

"I'm talkin' about you not givin' Joshua up for adoption."

My body sagged. "We already decided it was for the best. Pa—"

"I ain't concerned with your pa, and if you agree to my plan, we don't need to worry 'bout him anyway."

I stared at her. "How?"

"I'll stay here in Nashville with you 'n' Josh. We'll get us a place to live. I'm too old to find work in a city, but I can stay home and take care of Joshua once you get a job."

It sounded beautifully simple yet utterly impossible.

"I can't ask you to do that, Miss Bertie. Your life is back on the farm with the sisters."

"You ain't askin'," Bertie said, peeking out the window again. "I'd be plumb tickled to take care o' you two."

For one hope-filled moment, I considered her idea.

"What kind of job could I find? I ain't never worked, 'cept for house chores and such. Don't guess anyone'd want to hire me, just being a kid and all."

"We'll cross that bridge when we get there. In the meantime, we need to tell Brother Brown you've changed your mind." A light behind us grew brighter, and we both turned to see the parson exit the building and stride toward the car. "Here he comes now."

I covered myself and the baby with a blanket. Brother Brown climbed back into the car and turned in the seat to face us.

"My cousin was correct," he said. "A couple who attend this church are very interested in adopting Joshua. God didn't bless them with children of their own. They're here, inside." He offered a look of compassion as his eyes met mine. "They seem like nice people."

I stared at him, my heart racing. Bertie wanted me to tell the parson I'd changed my mind. I didn't know how the three of us would survive in a city as big as Nashville, but Bertie seemed confident.

I looked down, and although I couldn't see Josh's face, I felt him drawing nourishment from my body. I was his mama. The only person on earth who could claim that honor. The woman who waited inside the church wanted to be his mama, but God had given this little boy to me. How could I let him go? To never again hear the sweet noises he made? Hear him say his first word? See him take his first steps?

Yet what kind of life could I offer Josh? No pa. A teenage mother. Poverty, at best.

What Bertie read the day I came to Jesus sprang up in my mind. *You received God's Spirit when he adopted you as his own children. Now we call him, "Abba, Father."*

If adoption into his family was God's perfect plan for us, could it also be the plan he had for Josh?

I glanced at Bertie. She gave me an encouraging nod, one meant to convey her assurance that all would be well once the three of us settled in Nashville.

Papa, help me do what's best for Josh.

After a long moment, I returned my attention to the parson. "Thank you, Brother Brown. We'll be in soon as Josh has finished nursin'."

The man agreed and exited the car.

"Why'd you tell him that?" Bertie asked, confusion on her face. "We don't need to meet those folks. You 'n' me 'n' little Josh'll find us a place to live tomorrow. Till then, we'll ask the parson to take us to an inn."

I didn't want to hurt Bertie, but I knew in my heart I needed to do what was best for Josh.

"I can't be a ma, Miss Bertie," I whispered, my chin trembling. "Not without Amos here to help raise Josh. A little boy needs a pa. He needs a man to teach him and to look after us. I know you mean well, but it's best to let the couple yonder in the church take him home with them."

"Oh, child," she said, a look of fear in her eyes. "Don't do this."

I squeezed my eyes closed, the pain in my heart nearly unbearable. "Josh needs more than I can give him, Miss Bertie. Can't you see? I'm sorry."

I didn't look at Bertie again. I wouldn't be able to go through with this if I saw the raw pain I felt certain was on her face. She didn't say more, and I was glad.

I laid Joshua on my lap and changed his wet diaper. When I finished, I wrapped him in the blanket I'd sewn for him. For long minutes, I stared into his precious face, memorizing every detail. How I wished I had a photograph of him. Even a drawing.

When I finally faced Bertie again, she reached to put a hand to my cheek. "I'm proud of you, child. You're not giving up your son 'cause he's an inconvenience or a burden. I see now I was wrong to ask you to keep him. This is the hardest, most selfless act any mama could do."

Tears blurred my vision. "Thank you."

She heaved a sigh. "Let's go on in and meet the couple."

I shook my head. "I can't, Miss Bertie. I can't see them lookin' at Joshua with longin' in their eyes. Will you take him inside for me?"

Bertie frowned. "It don't seem right for you not to meet the folks who'll be raisin' your son. You don't have to linger. Just long enough to see 'em, should you wonder 'bout 'em later."

I gazed at my son. A tear dropped onto the blanket. "I want to remember him like this. Here, in the car, he's my son. In there, he's theirs."

Bertie took my hand in hers and squeezed. "You're a good mama. Josh is a lucky boy to be so loved. Your ma would be proud of you, too."

"I love you, Miss Bertie." I needed her to understand. "Other than my ma, I ain't never loved no one like I love you."

Bertie sniffled. "I love you too, dear one."

She opened her door and slowly climbed out. "I'm stiffer than an old mule after sittin' in this car for so long. I don't relish the drive back. Maybe we can ask Brother Brown to let us stretch our legs every so often."

I didn't respond. I knew they planned to stop in Knoxville and get me settled at the home for young women the parson had recommended. He said he often drove to the town and wouldn't mind if Bertie tagged along to check on me. I wished I could go home with Bertie, but my presence on the homestead put them in danger.

Bertie went to the trunk of the car to retrieve the hand-sewn bag with Josh's things while I gathered my courage. I thought back to the day I realized I was pregnant. I'd been scared, but I'd also been excited. Amos and me hadn't planned to make a baby that day in our secret place, but God wasn't surprised. He'd known Joshua even then, before I was aware of the life growing inside me.

I looked down at mine and Amos's son. He'd fallen asleep and looked like a tiny, perfect angel.

"Papa, please take care of him," I whispered. Tears threatened, but I wouldn't let them come. I had to be strong for Josh. "Let the folks waitin' inside this church be good to him and love him."

I placed a long, lingering kiss on his head. My lips moved to his ear, where I whispered, "I love you more than you will ever know, Amos Joshua."

Bertie waited on the sidewalk. My arms felt like lead as I opened the car door, kissed Joshua one last time, and handed my son to her.

"Tell them he's a good baby. Tell them he likes it when I sing to him. Maybe his new ma will sing to him, too."

"I will, child."

"Tell them—" Sobs choked me. I shook my head and turned away. "Please, just go. I can't watch."

Crippling anguish nearly brought me to my knees as I stumbled back to the car. It was as if some unseen knife dug deep into my being, all the way to my very soul, ripping away everything that I held dear.

How could I live without my son? Without Amos? They'd been my reason to exist. I almost wished Joshua and me had died when Pa shot me. Then we'd be with Jesus and Amos.

But I didn't wish it. I couldn't.

Josh was a miracle sent from God. His heavenly Papa had plans for him.

And I realized, if God had plans for my son, then I had to believe he had some for me, too.

Was I brave enough to find out what they were?

❧

Bertie glanced at the door of the church, the unknown couple on the other side of the wood.

Could she walk in there and give this child, whom she loved with everything that was in her, to strangers? Hadn't God brought Songbird and Joshua to her for safekeeping? Were they making a tragic mistake? A mistake that would last a lifetime?

She glanced back to the car. Songbird sat in the back seat, her head in her hands. Their girl was going to need a lot of love and care to help heal from the pain of giving her son up for adoption. Bertie suspected that kind of grief never fully went away. But time and perhaps new love would offer joy in place of the heavy sadness one day.

Just then the sun peeked over the river. Golden light spilled across the water, lighting up the world and chasing away shadows of night. A new day dawned, bright, crisp, and beautiful.

A single ray of light fell on Josh, illuminating his angelic face. Bertie's breath caught.

She didn't hear God speak to her, but she was suddenly aware of his presence in that light. Warm and comforting. Powerful and all-knowing. As if giving her assurance everything would be all right despite how it looked. Despite how it felt.

"Thy will be done, Lord."

Bertie didn't linger another moment for fear she wouldn't be able to accomplish the heartrending task entrusted to her. With a deep breath, she walked into the church. Brother Brown waited in the foyer, compassion on his face when she entered.

"Songbird couldn't . . ." Bertie's throat tightened. She simply shook her head.

"I understand." He motioned to a door behind him. "My cousin and the Wylies are waiting in the sanctuary. They seem like good, caring folks, Bertie. They live here in Nashville, and my cousin has known them for several years."

Bertie let the parson talk, telling what he knew of the people who would take Joshua away from her. Away from Songbird.

When he grew silent, she came to a decision.

"I can't be the one to give him to them," she said, her voice thick. "I don't want him to think I don't love him."

Empathy filled the parson's face. "I'm sure he knows how much you love him, Bertie. His mother, too. God is a devoted Father. He'll watch over Joshua."

"I know," Bertie whispered.

As Songbird had done, Bertie kissed the baby's forehead, then whispered words of love in his tiny ear. When she handed the precious bundle to the parson, inexpressible peace washed over her. The kind of peace that passeth all understanding. The kind that was unexplainable but was as real as anything she'd ever experienced.

"We'll wait in the car," she said, setting the bag of Josh's things on the floor.

"I'll be there shortly."

Bertie opened the door to the sanctuary and held it for him. As he walked into the quiet, spacious room, she saw a neatly dressed couple seated on the front pew. Another man stood nearby. When they saw Brother Brown enter, the man and woman rose.

As Bertie watched from the doorway, the woman's face lit up when the parson approached, her eyes fixed on the baby in his arms.

"He's beautiful," she said, tears spilling from her eyes. "May I?"

Brother Brown carefully placed Joshua in the woman's eager arms.

She stared at him a long moment, then bent to kiss the baby's forehead, whispering something Bertie couldn't hear.

Tears blurred Bertie's vision as she quietly closed the door on the tender scene, but the peaceful feeling she'd experienced moments ago remained.

Josh would be loved; she was certain of it. God would watch over him.

Songbird needed her now.

As Bertie walked to the car, she noticed the trunk stood open. She must've forgotten to close it when she retrieved Josh's bag.

After she shut it, she went to Songbird's door. The girl might want to stretch her legs before their long drive back to Knoxville.

The car, however, was empty.

Bertie glanced around. The city of Nashville was quiet. No one was out and about on the holiday.

Where could Songbird be?

She looked back inside the car.

There on the seat where the girl should be lay a sheet of paper. Bertie picked it up.

Sweet babe of mine,
So perfect in every way.
Who will you become?
Sweet son of my heart,
You may not understand,
It's because of love I must let you go.
Sweet child of God,
I'll never hear you laugh nor watch you grow,
But there is One who can.
Until the day when we meet again,
I'll keep you here, O beloved son,
Forever within the memories of my heart.
Always remember, you are perfectly loved.

A note at the bottom of the song read: *Thank you for everything, Miss Bertie. I will never forget you.*

Bertie didn't need to look in the trunk to know that Songbird's bag was no longer there. She didn't need to search the streets, thinking the girl had wandered off and become lost.

With heartbreaking certainty, Bertie knew the truth.

Her Songbird had flown away.

Twenty-Five

THE STORY WASN'T PRETTY.

Bertie sat across the kitchen worktable from Walker and Reese and prayed his heart was ready for the truth.

"Amos's ma came here with false intentions the day she told Songbird that Amos died in the war."

Walker blinked. "What do you mean?"

"That woman came for one purpose: to get you. And she brought Songbird's pa along to help."

Confusion filled his eyes. "Are you saying she wanted to take me away from my mother?"

Bertie nodded. "She'd lost her only son, and she wanted you, his only son, to come live with her. But . . ." She paused.

Should she tell him everything?

"But?"

"She and Songbird's pa made some sort of deal before they got here. Amos's ma would pay him money, and he'd make sure Songbird gave you up. At fifteen, Songbird was still a child in the eyes of the law, under her pa's authority. She wasn't married, so they figured she had no say in the matter. When she refused to cooperate, her pa threatened to bring down the law on her. He even threatened me and my sisters if we interfered."

Walker's face registered shock. "That's the wildest thing I've ever heard. My own grandmother was going to kidnap me?"

"The thing is, Songbird wouldn't'a kept you from her. She woulda let Amos's ma see you whenever she wished. But the woman hadn't approved of Amos courtin' Songbird in the first place, so she sure didn't want Songbird raisin' his son."

"What happened? I obviously didn't go live with my grandmother."

Bertie filled in the missing details. How she herself held a gun to Songbird's pa—Walker's grandfather—and how Amos's ma had a change of heart when she realized their foul plan had failed. She told him about Songbird's pa's plot to discredit his daughter's claim that he'd shot her by telling the authorities a lie, corroborated by his wife, a supposed witness to the crime.

"It sounds like I didn't miss a whole lot by not knowing at least two of my grandparents, but I still don't understand why Songbird chose to leave and give me up for adoption."

Old scars tugged at Bertie's heart at the remembrance of the raw pain she'd known the day Songbird and Joshua disappeared from her life.

"After Amos's ma and Songbird's pa left, Songbird feared he'd come back and carry out his threat to get the law involved. Or worse. She said he wouldn't stop till he'd gotten what he wanted. You have to remember: she knew her pa and what he was capable of. I kept tellin' her I wasn't afraid of that man, but Songbird wanted to protect us. She wanted to protect you."

Walker rubbed his whiskered jaw. It reminded Bertie of how Papa used to tug on his long beard when he was thinking on something serious.

"So my mother gave me up for adoption . . . to keep me safe?"

"She did." Bertie reached over and laid her wrinkled hand on his. "She loved you. More than she loved her own life. She'd been protectin' you from the moment she knew you existed. If we hadn't found her hidin' in the woods, there's no tellin' what might have happened to the two of you."

"The woods," Walker said, his expression indicating a light bulb had gone on in his head. "Ever since I learned I was adopted, I've had dreams—nightmares, really—about being left in the forest, alone."

"The woods saved yours and Songbird's lives. If she hadn't hightailed it into the hills when her pa was tryin' to kill her, you'd both be dead." Bertie sighed. "I'm ashamed to admit I tried to talk Songbird out of leavin'."

"Why would you be ashamed of that?" Reese, who'd been listening quietly, asked. "You loved them both."

"Yes, I loved 'em, but I wanted 'em to stay because that's what was best for *me*. I couldn't let 'em go."

Walker placed his other hand on Bertie's.

She topped the stack and looked into eyes that reminded her of her girl. Emotion rose to the surface. "I've never regretted not gettin' married or havin' young'uns of my own. But after Songbird came to us, I convinced myself God brought her here to be my daughter." A tear slid down her cheek. "When you were born, I was over the moon 'cause I had a grandson."

She didn't know if her confession was appropriate or not, but it was the truth.

Walker didn't respond right away, and Bertie feared she'd said too much. He probably saw an old mountain woman spouting nonsense, not someone he wanted in his life.

"After what you've just told me about my grandfather and grandmother," he said, a twinkle of teasing in his eyes, "I'm pretty certain you would've been a great improvement."

Her worry disappeared with his words, and she chuckled with relief. "Hmm, now I see what you were like as a boy. Gettin' into all sorts of mischief, I 'spect."

He grinned. "You have no idea."

She sobered. "The day your mama gave you up was the worst day of my life."

"Can you tell me about it? If it's too difficult, I'll understand."

"It's part of your story," Bertie said, sniffling. "You deserve to know it." She pulled her hands from the stack, took a hankie from her pocket, and wiped her nose. "After your grandparents left, your mama declared she couldn't keep you. She feared her pa would force her to give you to Amos's ma. Like I said, I tried to convince her otherwise, but Jennie knew better. She went to fetch the parson, a kindly man, and he drove you, your mama, and me to Nashville."

"I wondered how I ended up in the city."

Bertie shared the whole, heart-wrenching story of their last night together. When she came to the part about finding the car empty, her voice broke.

"Songbird had taken her bag from the trunk of the car, and . . . I never saw her again."

All kinds of emotion flashed across Walker's face. Shock. Confusion. Sadness.

"Why would she run off like that?" he asked.

Bertie'd had thirty long years to try to understand it herself, yet she still bore the pain of that day deep in her soul. "Brother Brown had suggested she stay in a home for wayward girls in Knoxville, but I think she feared her pa would eventually find her. In the city, she could disappear. The thing is, her pa never did show his sorry face round here after I run him off. Years later we heard he was caught runnin' moonshine. Don't know what became of him."

Bertie wiped her nose again. "After I discovered Songbird was gone, I was desperate to get my girl back. I couldn't lose you both on the same day. Brother Brown and I drove around the city for hours, but—" Her chin trembled, and she didn't continue.

Instead, Bertie rose from her seat. "There's somethin' I need to show you."

She took Papa's Bible off the shelf. After she returned to her chair, she opened it and removed a folded sheet of paper, yellowed around the edges, and handed it to Walker.

"'Sweet babe of mine, so perfect in every way,'" he read aloud. "'Who will you become? Sweet son of my heart, you may not understand, it's because of love I must let you go.'"

"That's beautiful," Reese said.

Walker looked up after he finished reading. "Did my mother write this?"

Bertie nodded. "She left it in the car. For you."

Twenty-Six

WHILE FOLKS ENJOYED THANKSGIVING DINNER with their loved ones, I wandered the cold, lonely streets of Nashville.

I wouldn't let myself think of all I'd left behind when I ran away from the church. The very thought of Joshua in the arms of his new ma crushed me until I was sure I'd die. Then there was Bertie. Her heart surely broke when she found me gone, but it was for the best. If Pa showed his face at the Jenkins place again, they could honestly say they didn't know where I was. I'd do whatever I needed to keep the people I loved safe. Even if it meant disappearing from their lives.

And that's exactly what I wanted to do.

Disappear. Forget. Leave my old life behind and begin anew.

The problem was, I didn't know how to go about it.

Due to the holiday, no businesses were open. I passed darkened stores and shops and tried to remember their location so I could come back the next day and inquire if they needed help. I didn't know how long or how far I walked, but I eventually came to a large building with five rows of windows and eight enormous columns gracing the entry. Mama once told me about the time she and her parents stayed in a fancy hotel in Raleigh when she was a girl, and I guessed this must be the kind of place she'd described. Folks in fine clothes came and went, laughing and enjoying the day of thanks.

A bitter wind sent a chill racing down my spine. I tugged the collar of Amelie's coat tighter. Maybe I could sneak into the hotel without being noticed, just to warm myself for a spell.

Swallowing hard, I clutched my bag close and walked inside, trying to blend in with the other folks. The spacious entrance where I found myself was like nothing I'd seen, and I stood and gaped at the scene.

Black-and-white checkered floors flowed like a river as far as I could see. Polished dark wood covered the walls and high ceiling. An enormous light with thousands of tiny glass jewels hung over it all, where it shimmered and cast miniature rainbows everywhere. Men, women, and even children milled about the big room, while some traveled up and down a grand stairway that led to a second floor that was open so folks could peer down from the banister that circled the opening. Music and delicious aromas drifted down, reminding me I hadn't eaten since the previous day.

"May I help you?"

The male voice startled me.

I turned to find a stern-faced man in a dark suit glowering at me, obvious disapproval behind his wire-rimmed glasses. He had an air of authority about him, and I reckoned he worked at the hotel.

"I, um, was hopin' to . . . that is, I need to ask about—"

"As I thought," he said, interrupting me. He took me by the elbow and none too gently hauled me toward the door I'd just come through. "You'll need to leave. The Maxwell House Hotel does not tolerate vagabonds or beggars."

People around us stared as we passed. I felt my face flame.

"I'm not beggin', sir. I just need a job."

We'd nearly reached the door when a woman's voice echoed through the spacious room.

"Unhand that girl, Mr. Crawford."

The man skidded to a halt, causing me to nearly lose my balance. We both turned to find an older woman in a black dress striding toward us, the click of her heels echoing in the now-silent room. All eyes were upon us.

I snuck a look at Mr. Crawford's face. He seemed nearly as put out with the woman as he was with me.

"This is none of your concern, Miss Nichols. Unless she is one of your strays." He released my arm with a grimace. "If that is the case, you know the rules."

The woman glanced at me, and although she didn't smile, I felt kindness in her gaze. "What is your name, dear?"

I stood mute, weighing how to answer. If I gave my real name, would she or the hotelman alert Pa somehow? I couldn't risk it. Songbird, however, didn't sound real, and I figured they'd know I was lying.

The woman's brow arched, and the man's scowl deepened.

I opened my mouth, and all on their own, words came out. "Birdie. Birdie Jenkins."

The lady seemed satisfied. "Miss Jenkins, my name is Priscilla Nichols, and I reside here at the Maxwell House. May I buy you a cup of tea?"

Mr. Crawford turned his glare to Miss Nichols. "I will not tolerate this. When you rented a room, you were informed of our policies. The hotel will *not* provide accommodations for—" his eyes landed on me—"girls like her."

I swallowed. He couldn't possibly know about Joshua or Amos or Pa, yet shame and guilt filled every inch of me.

"I best leave," I whispered. I appreciated the woman's offer, but I didn't want to cause her any more trouble.

"Nonsense. It isn't against hotel rules to enjoy some refreshment with a new friend." She sent the man a pointed look. "Your assistance is no longer needed, Mr. Crawford."

They faced off for an extended tense moment before the man huffed, frowned, and finally whirled on his heel and stomped away.

I didn't know what to make of Miss Nichols as she led me to the opposite end of the lobby. A small shop boasted a plaque above the door that read *Harriet's Tearoom*, and was decorated with flowers, lace, and white-wicker furniture. Only one of the small tables was occupied, with two women deep in discussion. Miss Nichols and I took the corner table, where she ordered tea, finger sandwiches, and cake.

While we waited for our food, she lifted her chin and narrowed her gaze on me. "I believe you have a story to tell."

I felt my eyes widen, and my appetite fled. Would she send me away if I didn't share all the particulars that brought me to this place?

"You have nothing to fear from me, Miss Jenkins. We all have things in our lives we'd rather no one knows." She offered a small smile. "I simply want to help, if I can."

Our tea and refreshments arrived. My stomach rumbled despite my nervousness.

"Let me tell you my story," she said as she filled a plate with delicious-looking delicacies and handed it to me. "Then, if you're willing, you can tell me about yourself."

While I ate, trying not to act like a pig at a trough, Miss Nichols told how she, as a young woman, arrived in Nashville with her parents for the Tennessee Centennial Exposition. Here at the Maxwell, she met a handsome Italian man and his younger sister, who found themselves caught in a sinister plot. Miss Nichols didn't give the details of what happened next, but she ended up staying in Nashville and founded a home for wayward girls.

"So you see," she said with a sad smile, "I've seen much and heard many stories, but one thing that remains true in them all, including my own, is that God has a plan and purpose for each of us."

Her words reminded me of Bertie's declarations of God's love.

I bit my lip. I sensed this woman genuinely wanted to help, but could I trust her with my miserable tale?

Her kind eyes told me I could.

It poured out of me. All of it. Mama. Pa. Amos. Josh. Me running away from Bertie. The desperate need for a job.

When I came to the end, I thought she might appear shocked, but only compassion rested on her face.

"You've had more than your share of sorrow, to be sure." Her eyes squinted and she tapped a finger to her chin in thought. "I've just dined with a gentleman who is president of a large insurance company here in Nashville. They also operate the WSM radio station." At my blank look, she added, "That's the station that plays music from the Grand Ole Opry."

I'd heard that show a time or two on Amos's family's radio.

She stood. "Wait here a moment, dear. Let me see if Mr. Craig is still in the dining room upstairs."

I felt exposed sitting in the tearoom alone, but the other ladies and employees didn't even look my way.

Miss Nichols soon returned with a finely dressed older gentleman. I scrambled to my feet, unsure of what was happening. I hoped she hadn't shared the private things I'd told her in confidentiality.

"Miss Jenkins, this is Mr. Craig. Mr. Craig, this is my friend, Miss Birdie Jenkins."

The man shook my hand. "Miss Nichols tells me you're in need of a job."

I nodded, unable to speak.

He glanced at Miss Nichols. "My wife and I have long been admirers of the work Miss Nichols does here in the city. Just this evening we discussed how we could become more involved." He returned his attention to me. "It seems our prayers have been answered. If you're willing, Miss Jenkins, I have a proposition for you. We are in need of someone to clean the offices of several businesses, including our insurance company and radio station. We also own a boardinghouse, and if it suits, you may have a room there in exchange for help with cooking and cleaning."

I stared at the man, unable to believe what I was hearing.

Miss Nichols chuckled. "I do believe we've taken Miss Jenkins by surprise."

I turned to her. "Is this . . . is this real?"

"It is, my dear. All you need say is yes."

"Yes!"

Miss Nichols and Mr. Craig smiled. "It's settled then."

Within the hour, after I'd bid Miss Nichols an emotional goodbye, a man in a dark suit drove Mr. Craig, his wife, and me to a two-story house where warm yellow light spilled from the windows. Mr. Craig introduced me to Mrs. Dabney, a sweet woman who reminded me of Bertie. She quickly had me settled in a tiny room behind the kitchen where a soft bed all my own awaited my exhausted body.

As I lay in the darkness, tears flowed down my face into my hair.

I missed Bertie and the sisters terribly. I knew they would ask God to watch over me, and he was. The evidence was all around. Yet I ached deep inside for my baby, my son. Even now, my breasts filled and released the nourishing milk he needed.

I wiped my face hard and tried not to think about Joshua and his new life as someone else's son.

"I don't know how I'll make it without him," I whispered, bringing on fresh tears. "Without Amos."

One day at a time.

I didn't know if it was God's voice I heard or Bertie's or even Mama's. But a shaky peace settled on my soul with the simple truth.

I didn't have to know what the future held. Not for me and not for Josh. I just had to trust God's plan, like Bertie and Miss Nichols said. That was something I could do.

One day at a time.

Twenty-Seven

WALKER STARED AT THE WORDS SONGBIRD WROTE thirty years ago. Words about him and how much she loved him.

"I wish she could see you now," Bertie said, wiping her nose with a handkerchief. "You were such a tiny thing the last time we saw you."

"I had no idea she'd disappeared in Nashville. Your note said I was born in Sevier County, so it never occurred to me she could be in the city. I can't help but wonder if we've crossed paths and didn't know it."

Bertie put her wrinkled hand on his, hope shining in her eyes. "Maybe you could find her."

Walker didn't respond right away.

Did he want to take this search to the next level? To try to locate his birth mother?

"I don't know. I honestly didn't think we'd find you." He looked at her. "I'm glad we did. I'm grateful to know where I came from even if the story wasn't exactly what I expected. But looking for my mother . . . well, that's completely different."

Bertie studied him. "Are you afraid of what you might find?"

He shrugged. "Maybe. What if I'm a part of her life she'd rather forget? I'm not sure I want to face that kind of rejection. Opening the door to the past isn't always a good idea."

Bertie's lips puckered, and she narrowed her gaze on him. "Tryin' to outrun pain in this life is useless. It always catches up to you, no matter how far you run. Numbin' it don't work either. Seems to me facin' our fears is the best way to move forward. You wouldn't want to live with regret."

"Think about the song, Walker," Reese said. She picked up the paper with Songbird's handwriting. Her eyes drifted over it before she looked at him again. "The woman who wrote these words isn't a woman who didn't care."

He considered the statement. "Even if I wanted to find Songbird, I wouldn't have any idea where to begin searching. I don't even know her real name."

"Evelyn." Bertie gained his attention. "Evelyn Harwell. That's what her pa called her the day he came to take you away. We hadn't known it until then. We called her Songbird 'cause of her sweet voice."

"Evelyn Harwell," Walker repeated. Knowing his mother's full name brought an unexpected surge of hope with it.

"After Songbird learned Amos died," Bertie said, "she declared she'd never marry, but I hope she did. I wouldn't want to think of her going through life alone, especially after all that happened."

"If she did get married, her name would be different," Reese added, "but marriage records aren't sealed. It might be possible to look for her using the same method we used to find Bertie."

Walker glanced between the two women. "You two aren't going to let this go, are you?"

Reese and Bertie exchanged a grin.

Walker put his hands in the air. "I can't argue with both of you pouring your wisdom into me. I give in. I'll look for Evelyn Harwell. I don't know what will happen if I find her, but . . ."

"But what?" Bertie asked.

He met her gaze. "But if I don't try, I'll always regret it."

"Tell me 'bout your family," Bertie said. "Did your folks adopt other children?"

Walker shared about his parents and the life he'd lived as their only son. He described the well-appointed home he'd grown up in, the schools he attended. He told them about church camp and summer vacations on North Carolina beaches. The more he talked, the more he realized the truth of his earlier statement.

He'd truly had a good life.

And it wasn't lost on him that every single detail he'd just shared would have been completely different if his birth mother had kept him and raised him here in the hills of Tennessee. If he hadn't become the son of Warren and Annie Wylie, he wouldn't be Walker Wylie.

Who would Amos Joshua have grown up to be? he wondered.

"I never thought I'd say this, but . . . I'm glad I was adopted." He looked at Bertie. "If Songbird had stayed here with you and your sisters, I'm sure I would've been loved and well cared for. But if I hadn't been adopted, I would've missed out on the life—a really great life—my adoptive parents gave me."

Bertie patted his hand. "There's no shame in bein' grateful for the family God gave you, son. Family don't always mean blood kin."

Walker was beginning to understand that truth.

"Reese said you make your livin' singin'." Curiosity shone in Bertie's eyes.

Walker nodded. "I've been fortunate. Some of my songs have topped the charts." He didn't mention how his career stalled when he'd sunk into a deep depression after learning about his adoption.

"Isn't that somethin'. Makes me wish we had a radio," Bertie said, beaming with unmistakable pride. "Your mama had such a sweet voice. She'd be mighty proud to know you inherited some of her talent."

A strange sensation washed over Walker at the thought of his birth mother being proud of him. He'd held such a grudge against her since learning of his adoption, thinking she'd given him up because of selfishness. But after everything Bertie had told him, he saw Songbird in a new light.

"It's an odd feeling to know I have a mother out in the world whom I've never met. She's a stranger."

A look of love filled Bertie's countenance. "Oh, but you did know her. You were part of her while you were formed in the secret place for nine months. And after you arrived, she spent ever' moment carin' for you. Mm-hmm, you knew her. And those memories are still there, inside your heart. God brought you home, Joshua. Trust him for the next part of your story."

The clock chime told them it was late—or early, depending on how one looked at it.

Bertie yawned. "We best get some shut-eye." She rose slowly on stiff legs. "I'll check on Naomi and the wee one fore I turn in. It's too cold for you to sleep in the barn," she said to Walker. "You can spread that tick mattress in the corner there in front of the fire."

Reese stood as Bertie disappeared into the adjoining room.

"It's been quite a day." She turned toward the wide-stepped ladder that led to the loft above the kitchen. "There are some extra blankets upstairs. I'll toss them down."

"Reese," Walker said, gaining her attention. There was so much he wanted to say, yet he wasn't sure where to start. "I need to apologize for the way I acted earlier. You were right to be angry with me."

Her face softened. "There's no need to apologize. This hasn't been easy for you. It's a lot to take in at once."

He jammed his hands into his pockets. "Yeah, but I didn't have to behave like an angry bull."

She chuckled. "True."

He gazed into her chocolate-brown eyes. "I don't know how to thank you, Reese. You're the reason I'm standing here, in the very house where I was born. I know more about myself than I ever have because of you. You were willing to accompany a grouchy, rude stranger on a quest he didn't believe in."

Her eyes glistened. "It's been an honor to be part of this. Your adoption story is so beautiful. I hope you find Songbird, Walker. From everything we've heard, I think she must be a very special woman."

"So are you."

Their eyes held for a long moment. An overwhelming desire to kiss her filled Walker, and he took a step forward just as Bertie reentered the kitchen.

"Naomi's hungry," she said, heading to the stove without glancing their way. "I'll fry a couple eggs, then go to bed. You young'uns want anything?"

Reese turned toward the steps. "No thank you, Bertie." When her eyes met Walker's again, a shy smile was on her lips. Lips he wished he was kissing right now. "Good night, Walker."

"Good night." He watched her climb the ladder. A moment later, two quilts dropped over the loft rail.

"Hope I didn't interrupt somethin'," Bertie whispered as he picked them up.

Walker shook his head and went to retrieve the thin mattress. "Just thanking her for putting up with me."

Bertie chuckled but didn't say more as she cooked the simple meal, blew out the lantern, and bid him good night one last time. He heard Reese's soft footfalls above him and Bertie's murmurs from the next room; then the house grew quiet.

Walker rolled onto his side and stared at flames licking a thick log Bertie had added before she left the kitchen. What a day! His mind was so full of everything that had taken place, it was hard to focus.

One thing was certain.

He wasn't the same man who'd walked into this cabin two days ago.

Considering he'd thought his life destroyed after he learned of his adoption, it was rather surprising to feel such peace settle in his soul now that he knew the facts. Now that he knew his birth parents hadn't rejected him.

"God," he said, his quiet words only for the Almighty's ears. "I don't know how it's all going to work out, but I trust you. If it's your will, I'd like to meet Songbird." He paused, emotion tightening his throat.

"I want to meet my mother."

~

I celebrated my sixteenth birthday alone in the tiny room at the back of the boardinghouse. Just as I hadn't told anyone my real name, I'd also left out other details, like how old—or young—I was. Mr. Craig and Mrs. Dabney seemed pleased with me and the work I did, and I didn't want anything to make them think they'd made a mistake in giving me a job and a place to live.

The Bible Bertie and the sisters gave me sat on the bedside table. I picked it up and held it against my chest, remembering the beautiful day I'd enjoyed last October in the Jenkins homestead. As long as I lived, I would never forget their kindness. I longed to return to the hills, but I knew I couldn't. I had to stay away and trust that the Lord would keep the women safe from Pa.

The day after my birthday, I walked to Centennial Park and celebrated Josh's. I couldn't imagine my tiny son was already a year old. I sat on a bench near the lake and wept as I envisioned him learning how to walk and talk. Did he still look like Amos? Was he happy?

"'Sweet babe of mine,'" I sang softly, my eyes closed. "'So perfect in every way.'"

Love for my baby boy poured out with every word, every tear.

When the song came to an end, I whispered, "Take care of him, Papa. Take care of my Josh."

Weeks passed. By the time a new year arrived, contentment settled over me. Not happiness, because I wasn't sure I could truly be happy again, but the heaviness that had weighed me down since I ran away from the church lifted. Even Mrs. Dabney noticed.

"I like seeing you smile," she said one day while we worked side by side in the boardinghouse kitchen making chicken and dumplings, a favorite of the dozen tenants. She had flour on her nose, and when I teased her about it, she dabbed some on mine.

Spring soon arrived and with it came a fresh batch of songs on the radio. My favorite was "Into Each Life Some Rain Must Fall" by Ella Fitzgerald. I sometimes felt she was singin' about me, and I knew all the words by heart. Bob, the voice of WSM, grinned every time he saw me coming, because he knew I was going to beg him to play it.

I was mopping the tiled hallway outside his glass-enclosed soundproof studio one day when he did just that. While music came from a speaker above the studio door, I pretended the mop handle was a microphone and belted out the lyrics. Bob of course couldn't hear me, but he laughed and gave silent applause when the song ended.

When I turned to continue my mopping, I found Mr. Wilson, the radio station manager, watching me from the doorway to his office, arms folded across his big belly.

Heat rushed through me at being caught horsing around when

I was supposed to be working. "I'm sorry, Mr. Wilson. It won't happen again."

But the man didn't look angry. "You've got a good voice."

"Thank you, sir."

He squinted his eyes and pursed his lips. "We're looking for a new gal to sing jingles for commercials." He paused and gave me an intense study. "Mr. Craig's never told me much about why a kid like you is living on your own here in Nashville, but you're a hard worker. What would you think about trying out for a job singing on the radio?"

The mop fell out of my hand. All I could do was stare at Mr. Wilson. "Me? Sing on the radio?" My heart thundered just thinking about such.

He chuckled. "I'm not saying you'll become a star of the Grand Ole Opry someday, but I think you'd be a nice addition to the group of singers and writers we already have on board."

Mama's words from long ago popped into my head.

"God blessed you with a gift, Evelyn. Your voice is as sweet as a songbird."

She'd sure be proud if I ended up singin' on the radio.

"I'd like to try, Mr. Wilson," I said, thrilled and terrified at the same time.

As I went back to mopping, I couldn't help but whisper, "Thank you, Papa."

For the first time in a long time, the future held a tiny spark of light.

Twenty-Eight

REESE WOKE EARLY THE NEXT MORNING to the delicious aroma of frying bacon.

Although the lone window in the loft revealed the sky outside was still inky, the soft glow from a lantern and low voices from below told her Bertie, Rubie, and Walker were already awake.

She sat up and stretched. A chill lingered in the cabin, but warmth from the kitchen fireplace drifted to the rafters as she hurried to dress.

Bertie said something Reese couldn't make out, followed by Walker's deep chuckle.

Butterflies stirred in Reese's belly at the sound.

Last night, she was certain Walker was going to kiss her before Bertie returned to the kitchen. Even now, the possibility of such a thing happening sent a wave of excitement mixed with fear racing through her. She was falling in love with him, as crazy as that sounded, and that scared her because their friendship would come to an end today. Walker would call his manager to send a car for him, and he'd disappear from her life in the same way he'd entered it. Letting her feelings go beyond friendship with the singer was foolish enough. A kiss would have been disastrous to her heart.

Best to keep her emotions under wraps in these last hours they were together and part ways with no expectations.

Walker glanced up from his place at the table as she carefully made her way down the ladder. A mug of steaming coffee sat in front of him.

Reese pushed a cheerful smile to her lips. "Good morning."

"Good morning."

"Something smells good." She passed by him and went to where Bertie and Rubie both worked at the big stove—one sister tending the bacon and the other flipping flapjacks. "How can I help?"

"Mornin'. You can get the table set," Bertie said, nodding to the stack of plates and cutlery on the counter. "Little Stormie Claire had us awake early. I'm surprised you didn't hear her. That sweet gal sure has some lungs on her."

"I must've been tired because I never heard a sound."

She carried the plates to the table, keeping a good amount of space between her and Walker as she set them out.

"If it's okay with you," he said, "I thought we could drive to the general store to make our calls after breakfast. Ray will want to send a car to pick me up as soon as he can get one here. I figured it would be easier for a driver to meet me at the store rather than try to find this place."

Regret washed over her at the thought of him leaving. If only things had been different. "I'm sure you're anxious to get home."

His gaze held hers. "Honestly, I wouldn't mind staying longer. I'd like to hear more about life on the homestead and learn how to milk a cow." He winked at Bertie when she sent him a grin. "But I need to get back to Nashville. I need to see my mom. I'm not sure how she'll feel about my plan to search for Songbird, but I hope she'll be happy for me."

Reese put aside her reservations about their relationship and reached to place her hand on his arm. "I hope so too, Walker. I really do."

The four of them enjoyed a filling breakfast of fried eggs, bacon, and flapjacks drowned in maple syrup. Naomi surprised them by slowly making her way into the kitchen with the baby cradled in her arms. Everyone oohed and aahed over the tiny girl, then laughed when she hiccuped. The sound startled the little one, and they were treated to the sweet mewling of a newborn.

After the dishes were washed and put away and the Word read, Reese and Walker donned their coats. Reese planned to stay one more night, just to make sure all was well with Naomi and the baby. She also knew Bertie and Rubie would be sad to say goodbye to Walker and hoped her company would help.

"Tell Mama that me and Stormie Claire are just fine," Naomi said once she'd written down her mother's name and telephone number. "And that I'm sorry I worried her."

Reese nodded. "I'm sure she'll forgive you the moment she knows the two of you are safe."

Naomi turned to Walker. "Thank you for helping me. God surely must've sent you."

Walker hugged Rubie goodbye, smiling when she patted his cheek. Then he turned to Bertie. "I promise to come visit," he said, his voice thick.

Bertie's eyes glistened. "I'm gonna hold you to it." She wrapped frail arms around him, her head barely coming to the middle of his chest. "You'll always be our boy," she choked. "Mind if I call you Josh sometimes?"

Walker's arms tightened around the elderly woman. "I'd like that. And I hope it's okay with you ladies if I call you Grandma Bertie and Aunt Rubie."

"Nothin' would make us prouder, isn't that right, Sister?"

Bertie stepped back, her gaze intent. "You'll tell us if you find our Songbird?"

"I will."

Bertie took a slip of paper from her skirt pocket. Reese recognized it as the page with Songbird's writing.

"Take this with you," she said, handing it to Walker. "You won't need it to prove who you are should you find her. Your mama will know you the minute she lays eyes on you. But she might want to see it and remember."

Walker took the paper, his throat working to contain his emotions. "Thank you for everything you did for her . . . and for me."

A tear rolled down Bertie's cheek, but she smiled anyway. "I sure am glad you came lookin' for me."

They all made their way to the porch. A cold breeze rustled nearly bare branches in the oak trees, and the Tennessee sky was painted with the colors of dawn.

Reese waved to the women huddled together on the porch and climbed into the car. As she turned the key in the ignition, she watched Walker give one last hug to each of the sisters before he, too, got into the car.

"Leaving is harder than I thought it would be," he said, his eyes on the log house. "This is where my life began."

As Reese turned the VW around and headed down the mountain, she glanced at him. "They really love you."

He gave a solemn nod. After a silent moment, he said, "For the past four months, I believed I wasn't given a name when I was born. Now I know that wasn't true. I'm Amos Joshua." A slight smile tipped the corner his mouth. "Josh."

The car bounced down the dirt trail, splashing in holes filled with rainwater from the previous night's storm. When they reached the main road, Walker pointed to the church off to their left.

"That's where I found Naomi."

Reese glanced at the whitewashed building as they passed by. "She's right, you know. God put you here to help her."

He gazed at the building. "I guess the saying 'God works in mysterious ways' is true. I shouldn't have stomped out of the cabin like I did," he said, turning to her. "But I'm glad I was able to get Naomi somewhere she'd be safe and warm, especially knowing how close to death she would come."

Following the directions Bertie gave them, they continued to wind their way through the woods until the small community of Cosby Run came into view just as the sun peeked over the mountain. Reese parked in front of the general store, and they both entered the old-fashioned mercantile. The smell of burnt coffee, leather, and aged wood permeated a space lined with shelves overflowing with items for purchase. The clerk pointed to the back of the store when Walker asked about a pay phone.

Reese stepped into the telephone booth first, shoved coins into the slot, and dialed Naomi's mother's number. The poor woman wept when she heard that her daughter and granddaughter were safe and well. She knew the area and felt certain she could find the Jenkins cabin. Next, Reese called Kathy even though it was early. She told her friend about Naomi and how she felt the need to stay with Bertie and Rubie one more night. Kathy assured her Ryan and Oreo were having a grand time and not to worry.

Reese hung up the phone receiver a minute later and exited the booth. Walker came over. "It's all yours."

He switched places with Reese and closed the folding door. Reese wandered the store, but nothing caught her eye. When Walker finished his call, she made her way back to him.

"Ray's hiring a car and driver out of Knoxville. He said it should be here in a little over an hour."

Reese tried not to let her disappointment show. "I'm happy to wait with you," she volunteered, hoping to delay the inevitable.

But he declined. "I don't want to take up any more of your time." His eyes caressed her face. "I meant what I said last night, Reese. There's no way I can possibly thank you enough for what you did for me."

"I'm glad it turned out well. I'll be praying for you as you move forward with the search for Songbird."

"Thank you." His gaze held hers. Would he say more?

Reese was the first to look away. "I better get back and let Naomi know her mom is on the way to get her and the baby."

Walker nodded. "I plan to visit Bertie and Rubie as soon as I know something about Songbird." He chuckled. "I still think it's crazy they don't have a telephone. Maybe I'll have one installed so I can call and check on them."

Reese grinned. "I think they might be open to that. Anything for their Josh."

They made their way outside to where the VW was parked.

Reese opened the car door and turned to face Walker, determined not to cry. "I'll have to buy one of your records and find out what the hoopla is all about."

He gave a half-hearted smile at the teasing. "Goodbye, Reese. Have a safe trip home."

"You as well."

She climbed into the car and started the engine. Walker took a step backward, an unreadable expression on his face. When she waved to him, he gave a single nod.

"Goodbye, Walker Wylie," she whispered.

With her vision blurred by tears, Reese headed the small car back up the mountain. She'd just returned to the cabin when Naomi's mother arrived.

The woman immediately took charge of her daughter and granddaughter. She thanked Reese and Bertie for all they'd done but didn't linger. In a matter of minutes, she had the new mother and baby tucked in a blanket in the back seat of her Ford station wagon. Bertie thought it best not to mention the miracle just now, although she advised Naomi to take things slowly until she regained her strength. Bertie would write a letter to her in the coming weeks and explain how God had breathed life into both her and Stormie Claire on the same day.

After the excitement of the past few days, the old log home felt deserted when Reese, Rubie, and Bertie settled in the gathering room.

"I can't hardly believe God brought Joshua back to us," Bertie said, staring into the fire burning in the fireplace. She looked at Reese. "How'd he find you?"

Reese shared the story of Ray contacting her after reading the newspaper article and Walker's resistance at first. "He was angry. At everyone, I think."

"It's a shame his folks didn't tell him 'bout bein' adopted sooner," Bertie said. "Mighta been a whole lot easier on him if they had."

"But he might not have come home, Sister." Rubie sat in a rocking chair with her eyes closed. Reese thought she'd drifted off, but clearly she was listening. "The Lord worked things out for his purposes."

"He did indeed." Bertie grinned. "Imagine our Joshua singin' on the radio. Makes me wish we had one of those music boxes."

Rubie was soon snoring softly in her chair.

"I reckon you'll miss our Joshua too," Bertie said, gaining Reese's attention.

Heat flooded Reese's face at the knowing look in Bertie's eyes. "I . . . we . . . we're just friends. I barely know him. He has a life in Nashville, and mine is in Piney Ridge."

The woman looked skeptical. "I might not have been courted by a beau, but I've got eyes in my head. I interrupted somethin' last night, and I'm awful sorry I did."

"Nothing happened, Bertie." Reese shifted in her seat. "Walker was simply saying thank you for helping him."

Bertie's keen gaze softened. "Tell me the truth. You have feelin's for him, don't you?"

Unbidden tears sprang to Reese's eyes, frustrating her. "It doesn't matter if I do. He has a girlfriend—a beautiful woman who stars in movies, no less. He lives in Nashville and is a famous singer. I live in backwoods Piney Ridge, Tennessee, where I spend my time driving around the hills, delivering babies. We have absolutely nothing in common. A relationship would never work between us."

She hadn't meant to spill her heart out, but there it was.

A look of compassion came to Bertie's face. "I see I stuck my nose in business that don't concern me. You'll have to forgive me for upsettin' you."

Reese wiped her eyes. "You didn't upset me, Bertie. I upset myself." She paused, wondering if she should trust the older woman with the truth. She needed to talk about it to someone. Kathy would listen, but she wouldn't understand the situation as well as Bertie. "I do care for Walker. In fact, I think I was beginning to fall in love with him, as ridiculous as that sounds. We just met."

"I don't think it sounds ridiculous. If I hadn't known better, I would've thought you'd known each other for years."

Reese chuckled. "You wouldn't say that if you'd seen us that first day."

"Pigheaded, was he?"

"Very."

They shared a laugh; then Bertie asked several questions about Walker's music and his life. Reese told her everything she knew, although she left out information that was strictly gossip.

"I'm proud of the man our boy has become," Bertie said. "If

he'd stayed here in the mountains with us, there's no tellin' what his life woulda been like. I hope he would've still made somethin' of himself, but we'll never know. God had other plans for him."

Reese enjoyed spending the afternoon with the two sisters. She and Bertie talked shop, as Bertie called it, and exchanged stories about the births they'd attended. Reese laughed at the funny tales the sisters shared about their large mountain family and admired their sincerity when Bertie said she wouldn't change a thing despite the oft-lonely life they'd led.

After supper, they agreed to turn in. It had been a long, emotional day, and Reese planned to leave early the next morning.

"I'm glad you came to us, Reese," Bertie said, giving her a warm hug. "I hope you won't forget us."

Reese shook her head. "Never. Besides, I need advice about how to be a good midwife. I hope you won't mind if I come for a visit every now and then."

A deep chuckle rumbled in Bertie's chest. She reached up and patted Reese's cheek.

"You're a good girl."

The simple compliment was one Reese knew she would always cherish.

Twenty-Nine

WALKER SAT IN HIS JEEP IN THE DRIVEWAY of the stately home on Granny White Pike, with morning sunshine warming the chilly October air. A wave of emotions swirled through him.

Guilt at how poorly he'd treated his mom the past four months.

Worry over how she'd take news of his journey to locate his birth mother.

Sorrow that Pop wasn't inside, ready with a joke and a hearty laugh.

He heaved a sigh.

So much had changed since the day Mom handed him the note Bertie wrote thirty years ago. *He'd* changed. Was changing still. And with God's help and the help from his new friends, the changes weren't as frightening as they'd seemed four months ago.

He squinted through golden light and studied the well-built two-story house, with its wraparound porch, professionally mani-cured yard, and pool with a diving board out back. Comparing it to Bertie's simple mountain cabin wasn't fair, nor was that his intention. Both dwellings held a special place in his heart. He'd begun life in one and lived life in the other. He'd grown into a man under Pop and Mom's steady, faith-filled guidance. When he told

Bertie he was grateful he'd been adopted by Warren and Annie Wylie, he meant it. Not because of the material blessings he'd been given—things he might not have experienced had Songbird raised him—but because his parents loved him. They'd chosen him. He was their son in every way that mattered.

The front door to the house opened.

Mom took hesitant steps onto the covered porch, her hands clutching her throat.

Swallowing hard, Walker exited the Jeep and closed the distance between them. It felt odd to be nervous about coming face-to-face with the woman who'd raised him. The last time he'd seen her was the day she handed him the note from Bertie Jenkins and tried to explain why she and Pop kept his adoption a secret. He hadn't wanted to hear her out and left.

"Hi, Mom."

"Hi, Son."

Walker stepped forward and wrapped her in his arms.

"I'm sorry," he whispered. "I'm so sorry, Mom. Please forgive me."

Her grip tightened around his waist. "Oh, Son," she choked. "I'm the one who needs your forgiveness." She pulled out of his embrace to meet his gaze. "I only wanted to protect you. I never meant to hurt you. I never meant—"

Her slight body shook with regret.

"I know you didn't, Mom. You and Pop were—are—the best parents. I couldn't have asked for anyone better."

Her hand went to her heart. "I've been praying so hard for you, Walker. That God would help you see past our mistakes and failures and know that he had a plan for you. Why he chose such imperfect people to accomplish it, I'll never know." She took a handkerchief from her pocket and wiped her nose.

Walker put his arm around her shoulders and tucked her into his side. "I know that now, Mom." Slowly they made their way to the front door. "It took me a while to figure it out. It took a trip into the Smoky Mountains to help me see it."

Mom stopped and stared up at him, surprise in her eyes as she searched his face. "You went looking for your parents?"

Walker heard fear in the question.

He squeezed her shoulders. "Let's go inside, and I'll tell you all about it."

Mom insisted on making him breakfast when he admitted he hadn't eaten anything that morning. His stomach had been in knots, anticipating Mom's reaction to his news about Bertie and Songbird. Now, sitting at the same kitchen table where his world had been upended four months ago, Walker felt the dust of his life begin to settle.

It was good to be home.

After eating his fill of scrambled eggs and hash brown potatoes with onion, Walker cupped his hands around the warm mug of coffee Mom had just refilled. She sat across from him with her own mug, only hers hadn't been touched.

"I've always wondered about the woman I saw the day Pastor Brown brought you to us," she said, a faraway look in her eyes. "Was she Bertie Jenkins, the woman who wrote the letter?"

Walker nodded and, from the beginning, told her about his journey to find Bertie. When he described the eclectic home he and Reese found in the hills, he smiled. "I was born there."

"Oh, Walker," Mom said, chin trembling. "I'm so happy for you. It must've been difficult to not know where you came from, who your family was."

His mind went back to the day after Pop's funeral. "When you told me I wasn't yours and Pop's biological son, I lost my identity. I didn't know who I was. If I wasn't Walker Wylie, son of Warren and Annie, who was I?"

"But you *are* our son—you know that, don't you?"

"I do, Mom, but I also had to come to grips with the fact that I'm also the son of someone else. Someone I don't even know."

Her brow tugged into a frown. "I wish we'd asked more questions the day you came to us. Who were your parents? Why couldn't they keep you? But we'd prayed for a child for so many years, we were overwhelmed with joy and fell in love with you the moment we saw you. It didn't matter where you came from. In fact, it felt like you'd dropped out of the sky, a sweet bundle sent to us from heaven. Of course, in our minds we knew there was a young woman and man who'd made the difficult decision not to keep you, but our hearts buried those unhappy thoughts. We took you home and raised you as if you were our own child. You were *our* son. That was what mattered."

After hearing about Songbird's painful decision to give him up, Walker had a better understanding of what his parents must have felt when he came into their lives.

"You've loved me my entire life. I can't hold that against you."

Mom sighed. "We should've been honest with you. I wanted to tell you about the adoption when you were old enough to understand, but Warren begged me to keep the secret hidden. He carried shame over his inability to father a child. He was so proud of you and wanted everyone to believe you were his biological son. The night Pastor Brown brought you to us, you and I went to stay with my parents in Memphis for several months. I don't know that our ploy fooled everyone, but when we returned to Nashville, no one questioned a newborn baby the size of a four-month-old."

"That's why you changed my birthday," Walker said, the mystery of the different dates finally solved. "Who else knew? Besides Grandma and Grandpa?"

"I think my sister always suspected the truth, but we never talked about it. She lived in St. Louis by then, with her own family. Warren and I didn't tell any of our friends in Nashville.

No one at church knew except Pastor Brown. Once we brought you home, it was the most natural thing to let everyone believe you were ours."

"I guess it would've been hard to reveal the secret after so many years." He wouldn't judge his parents. Not after everything they'd done for him.

"But don't you see? It didn't feel like a secret." She shrugged. "We were a family, brought together by God. I can't imagine being any happier as a mother if I'd given birth to you. You're my son."

A memory from his time in the mountains surfaced. "Bertie says family doesn't always mean blood kin."

Walker finished telling the story, ending with the midnight trip to Nashville, Songbird's disappearance, and Bertie's heartbreak.

"I can't explain what I'm feeling right now," Mom said. "To hear everything that happened just one day before you became our son is . . . shocking. I'm horrified to know what Songbird went through. She truly loved you, Walker. She truly loved her son. I wish she could see you now. She'd be so proud of the man you've become. I hope you're able to find her."

Walker lifted her hand to his lips and kissed her knuckles. "I love you, Mom."

"I love you, too, Son."

After promising to return for dinner—his favorite: meat loaf and mashed potatoes—Walker headed home. Cruising down Granny White Pike, he flicked on the radio, feeling lighter than he had in months. He'd ended his rocky relationship with Vanessa, and just yesterday he'd given Ray the green light to reschedule the tour for next spring. Although his bandmates hadn't known the reason he'd canceled, they'd waited patiently while he was MIA the past four months. They'd all be glad to get back to the music.

The radio announcer's voice filled the Jeep.

"*Here's a new one off the soundtrack for the movie* Perfectly Loved. *Fellas, my wife cried through the whole film. Don't say I didn't warn you.*"

Walker chuckled. He'd read a review about the movie—*sentimental drivel* is what the critic called it—but Mom mentioned she'd seen it with a friend and enjoyed the story of a pregnant woman diagnosed with cancer and the difficult choice she makes to postpone treatments to save the life of her baby. Being that action films were more his style, Walker doubted he'd see the movie, drivel or not.

A woman's voice, lovely and soft, began singing.

"*Sweet babe of mine, so perfect in every way.*
    Who will you become?
Sweet babe of mine, sweet son of my heart.
    Will you remember my voice?
Precious child of my dreams, I pray one day you understand,
    I would never leave if I had a choice."

Walker reached for the knob and turned up the volume. He couldn't recall hearing the song before, yet the lyrics sounded oddly familiar.

"*Sweet babe of mine, sweet babe of mine,*
    Until the day when we meet again
Always remember,
    You are perfectly loved."

The song ended.

"*What did I tell you, folks,*" the announcer said. "*It's a tearjerker, for sure. That was Evelyn Jenkins singing, by the way.*"

Walker stared at the radio.

Evelyn Jenkins?

His heart began to race as his mind traveled back to Bertie's cabin and the poem Songbird left on the seat of the car before she disappeared in the city. Hadn't the lines been similar?

A car horn sounded behind him.

Walker looked up to find the traffic light had turned green. He mashed the gas pedal and practically flew the rest of the way to his apartment, completely baffled by what he'd just heard. After taking the stairs two at a time, he fumbled with the key but finally gained entry.

The yellowed paper lay on the dresser in his bedroom. He snatched it up.

Sweet babe of mine,
  So perfect in every way.
  Who will you become?
Sweet son of my heart,
  You may not understand,
  It's because of love I must let you go.
Sweet child of God,
  I'll never hear you laugh nor watch you grow,
  But there is One who can.
Until the day when we meet again,
  I'll keep you here, O beloved son,
  Forever within the memories of my heart.
Always remember, you are perfectly loved.

He read it a second time, unable to believe what his eyes were seeing. The words weren't identical to those he'd just heard on the radio, but they were close enough to presume they'd come from the same source.

He sat on the edge of the bed and stared at the note Songbird had penned thirty years ago.

The similarities could not be coincidence. Had she copied it from somewhere? A book of poetry perhaps?

Bertie said Songbird was the author. His mother had even sung the song to him after he was born. It had to have been written by the same person who wrote the lyrics to "Perfectly Loved." Yet the version he'd just heard on the radio was sung by someone named Evelyn Jenkins.

His heart thundered as the only possible explanation exploded in his mind.

Evelyn Jenkins and Evelyn Harwell were the same person.

Had he just heard his birth mother on the radio, singing about *him*?

The very idea was preposterous, yet what other explanation was there?

Walker strode to the kitchen and picked up the telephone receiver. There was only one person he could talk to about this. Only one who could help him sort it all out.

He quickly dialed Reese's number and prayed she was home.

❧

It had been two weeks since Walker heard "Perfectly Loved" on the radio. When he'd told Reese about it, she sounded as shocked as he'd felt.

"It has to be her," she'd said. "When Songbird disappeared in Nashville, she wouldn't have used her real name. She wouldn't have wanted her father to have any way to find her. It would make sense if she changed her name to one that meant something to her: Jenkins."

They'd talked for over an hour, discussing what Walker's next move should be.

"Ray has some contacts in Hollywood," Walker said, beginning to put a plan together in his mind. "Maybe they can track down Evelyn Jenkins and find out who she is."

"I'll be praying for you, Walker."

Reese's soft, heartfelt words continued to bring him comfort. Just knowing she was on his side made all the difference as he waited for Ray's contact to locate Evelyn Jenkins.

Walker was just returning to his apartment after a morning run when he heard his telephone ringing. He quickly unlocked the door and made a grab for the receiver before the caller hung up.

"Hello?"

"Geez, it's about time, Walker. Where have you been?" Ray didn't bother with a greeting, nor did he give Walker a chance to answer. "We found her."

Walker's heart skidded to a stop, or so it seemed. "You found her?"

"Yep. My contact had to do a little digging, but he wanted to be certain he had the right woman. Evelyn Jenkins is actually Evelyn Seymour. Her husband is a big-time movie producer. His company was involved in *Perfectly Loved*. Seems he used his position to get his wife's song on the soundtrack."

Ray kept talking, but Walker wasn't interested in the motives of movie executives and the Hollywood favor system. He needed to know one thing.

"Is she from Tennessee?" he asked, interrupting Ray's stream of words.

"She is, buddy," Ray said. "She married this guy back in the late forties after he discovered her singing jingles for radio in Nashville."

Walker's heart started pounding against his chest. "Do you have a phone number?"

"I'll do you one better. I have a phone number *and* an address in Malibu."

Walker jotted down the information, his handwriting shaky and barely legible. He hung up the telephone a minute later and stared at the paper.

He'd found her.

The realization was astounding.

This was the moment he almost hadn't dared to imagine when he set out on this journey of discovery a little less than a month ago. So much had changed in that short time, but one question—the question that put the most fear in his heart—remained the same as it had from the day he learned he was adopted.

What if his birth mother wanted nothing to do with him?

What if, like the woman who gave birth to Reese, she'd rather forget her child even existed? Could he deal with the emotions of that outcome?

He thought about Bertie. She believed, even after thirty years of silence, the young woman who gave birth to him still loved him. Hadn't Reese come to the same conclusion when he told her about the song on the radio? Why Songbird never returned to the cabin or tried to find him remained a mystery, but until he heard her story, he would never know the truth.

Was he ready to face it?

With a deep breath, Walker picked up the telephone receiver again.

There was only one way to find out.

Thirty

I woke long before the sun appeared over the horizon, only one thought on my mind.

Josh.

My Amos Joshua would be here, in my home, in just a few hours.

Awe washed over me anew as I recalled hearing his deep, hesitant voice on the telephone three days ago. When he asked for Evelyn Jenkins, I knew.

"I think I might be your son," he'd said, caution in every word.

Even now, I felt each emotion that flooded me in that moment. Shock. Joy. Terror.

I'd waited for this day for so many years—envisioned what we would say to one another so many times—I should have been ready with a practiced response. But I wasn't ready. I could barely speak. Barely comprehend Joshua had finally found me.

In the end, I didn't confirm or deny his suspicions. That all-important conversation couldn't take place over the telephone. Instead, I invited him to Malibu, and he accepted.

Without waking my husband, I slipped into my robe and quietly padded onto the deck, the sound of the Pacific Ocean a soothing balm to my nerves. The breathtaking view from our hillside home never failed to bring peace to my soul, no matter what was going on in my world. I curled onto a lounger with a blanket and breathed in salty air as shades of pink and purple painted the sky and water.

So many questions would be answered today. Questions I'd asked for thirty long years.

Did Joshua have Amos's easygoing nature?

Had he had a happy childhood?

Could he forgive me for giving him up for adoption?

I closed my eyes, the simple prayer I'd whispered a million times or more since that painful day on my lips.

"Father, I trust you. Give me grace to trust you more."

I'd had to trust God the day I handed Joshua to Bertie, never to see him again. All through the years I'd prayed for my little boy, hoping with everything in me that one day I would see him again. But time passed and the longing for my son remained unanswered. Even as reminders of God's faithfulness were all around me, I had to confess hearing Josh's voice on the telephone three days ago was the one blessing I'd waited a lifetime for.

I still found it amazing to discover my son was the singer Walker Wylie. Frank had Walker's new album in his study, and as soon as our brief telephone conversation ended, I'd rushed to find it. The black-and-white photograph on the cover revealed a handsome man looking into the camera, his expression serious. I wept when I saw Amos's nose and mouth on our son.

"Here you are."

I turned to see Frank step onto the deck, dressed and ready to go to his office in downtown Los Angeles.

I stood. "Let me get you some breakfast." I'd given Judy, our housekeeper, the day off, to ensure privacy for Walker and me. Whatever was said between us wasn't for anyone else to hear.

"No time. I need to run by the studio anyway and check on our new project. You know craft services always has more food than the film crew can eat."

I nodded.

Frank took me in his arms. For a man in his midsixties, he was still as strong and lean as he'd been when we met all those years ago at the WSM radio studio in Nashville when I was a "jingle girl."

"You okay? I can cancel my appointments for the day if you want me to stay home."

I closed my eyes and rested my cheek on his chest. "I'm just nervous." I tilted my head to look up at the man who'd been my rock for nearly twenty-five years. "But thank you for offering."

Frank kissed me goodbye and disappeared into the house. A short time later I heard his new "toy"—a 1973 Corvette convertible—thunder down the hill toward Pacific Coast Highway.

A glance at the clock told me I had two hours before Walker would arrive. After showering, I donned the simple outfit of turquoise slacks and a matching knit sweater I'd decided upon last night after going through nearly everything in my closet. As I studied my reflection in the mirror, it occurred to me that the woman who stared back wasn't the same teenage girl who'd given birth to a baby boy in a backwoods cabin, deep in the heart of the Appalachians.

When my son and I faced each other today, it would be as strangers.

At exactly ten o'clock, the doorbell rang.

My heart nearly beat out of my chest as I pulled open the heavy wooden door and gazed upon my son for the first time in thirty years. "Hello."

"Hello," he said. "I'm Walker Wylie." He stuck out his hand.

When I placed mine in his, it was as if an electric current ran through me. As though a connection that had been severed long ago was once again restored. Had he felt it too?

My eyes drank in every detail, from the top of his dark-haired head to his boots-clad feet. A proud smile lifted the corners of my lips. "You're taller than I imagined."

He appeared as if he wasn't sure what to say.

"Please, come in." I moved aside so he could enter the house.

I led the way to my favorite room in our home—a spacious living room with floor-to-ceiling windows that looked out over the ocean. It was my haven, a special place I wanted to share with my son.

I directed him to a chair, then settled on the sofa. Earlier, I'd placed a tray with a coffee carafe, cups, and blueberry scones on a low table between us.

"Coffee?" I asked, trying to calm my racing nerves. No doubt he was anxious too.

Walker declined the offer of refreshments. I didn't partake either.

"You have a beautiful home," he said, glancing out to the ocean, then back to me. "I've visited Malibu several times in the last couple years. It has an interesting history."

I appreciated his attempt at small talk. "Frank, my husband, fell in love with this house the minute he saw it. It was built in the thirties when movie stars first started coming up here, and he'd always admired the Spanish-style mansions that lined the hills."

When I fell silent, we stared at one another. There was no need to declare the obvious.

Walker was my son, and I was his mother.

"This feels rather surreal. Almost like one of Frank's movies," I said. "I've always prayed this day would arrive. On your eighteenth birthday, I told Frank you were now free to look for me. I didn't know how God would accomplish it, but I never gave up hope."

"You remembered my birthday?" He seemed surprised by this information.

"Every year."

Walker's brow furrowed. "My folks—Warren and Annie—they didn't tell me I was adopted." His tone held an apology rather than anger. "I didn't find out until Pop passed away last June."

I pressed my fingers to my lips as relief washed over me with his words. For thirty years I feared my son hated me, but the truth was far less dramatic.

He hadn't known I existed.

"I suppose I can't blame them," I said. "Revealing you were adopted might have caused you pain and confusion growing up."

He nodded, but his frown remained. "I know they meant well, but I wish they'd told me the truth a long time ago."

I had a million questions about his life, past and present, but first I had to know something.

"May I ask how you found me? I never told anyone my real name after I moved to Nashville. Frank is the only person who knows my story."

He reached into his coat pocket, took out a folded paper, and handed it across the space between us. "This is the note Pastor Brown gave my parents. It's signed by Bertie Jenkins, the midwife who tended my birth."

I gasped. "My goodness, I'd forgotten all about this letter." I read the brief missive, memories of the day it was written spilling into my heart. "Dear, dear Bertie. It was her idea to include a note to your adoptive family."

"I met her."

I stilled and met his gaze. "Bertie?"

He nodded. "A friend and I tracked her down through old

birth records at the county courthouse in Sevierville. She still lives in the same cabin . . . where I was born."

I stared at him, thinking of the woman who'd been like a mother to me. "This is extraordinary. I've thought about Bertie so many times through the years. I wondered if she was still alive. If she remembered me. I can't believe you found her."

Walker filled in the details of the day he and his friend arrived at the cabin. He admitted his shock at discovering he'd been born in such a rustic place. With warmth in his voice, he shared how Rubie called him "their boy" and how Bertie knew who he was right away.

"I still don't understand," I said, trying to fit the pieces of the puzzle together. "I didn't tell Bertie my real name. She and the sisters called me Songbird. I liked it because it let me forget who I really was."

Walker reminded me about Pa coming to the cabin. "Bertie said he called you Evelyn."

I shut my eyes against the images of that dark day. Pa's selfish greed cost me my son. It had taken many years and many prayers of repentance to put aside my burning hatred and forgive him.

I faced Walker again. "Your grandmother named me Evelyn. She was a sweet, beautiful lady who deserved a better life than the one she was given. I started using my real name after we moved to California to honor her."

Walker took a second piece of paper from his pocket. "Without this, I don't think I would have found you. Bertie said you left it on the seat of the car the day you gave me up for adoption."

I didn't reach for it. I knew what was written on that page. "It broke my heart to write those words," I whispered, my chin trembling.

Walker laid the paper on the coffee table. "This song led me to you."

A long moment passed before I understood. "You heard 'Perfectly Loved' on the radio."

"I did."

Oh, Papa, only you could have worked this out for our good.

I wiped my nose on a handkerchief. "Frank brought home the script for the movie, knowing I like to read them before filming starts. Even though he didn't want me to work after we were married, he's always valued my opinion. I've even suggested a handful of changes to scripts over the years that have been implemented."

My mind traveled back to the day I read about a pregnant woman determined to save her baby, no matter the cost to her own life.

"This script—this movie—made me think of you. Of us. Of how I was willing to do anything to make sure you were safe." I offered a shaky smile. "I hadn't sung the song I wrote for you in years, but every word came back to me that day. Frank convinced me to record a version of it for the soundtrack. I think somewhere deep inside I hoped you would hear it."

I gazed at the handsome young man known as Walker Wylie, but all I saw was my Josh. Here in my home, looking so much like Amos, with questions in eyes that matched my own.

He deserved to know the truth. A truth I hadn't spoken in a very long time.

"I would have kept you if I could have," I whispered. "I was just a child myself. Bertie offered to help, but I knew I couldn't raise you without Amos. Do you know about Amos?"

He nodded. "Bertie told me everything."

"Everything?"

"Everything she knew."

Shame washed over me, thinking of all the terrible secrets the word *everything* covered. "Then you know about the highly dysfunctional family you come from."

"I don't blame you for your father's actions. I know you went through a lot to keep me safe."

I looked at Josh, remembering it all. The pain, the fear, the heart-wrenching decision. "You were worth it."

"What happened after you arrived in Nashville?" he asked, curiosity rather than judgment in the question. "Bertie looked for you, but you'd vanished."

"That was exactly what I wanted to do. I wanted to disappear. Evelyn Harwell no longer existed. When someone asked my name, I told them it was Birdie Jenkins, a play on the nickname the sisters had given me and a tribute to the woman who'd loved me like a daughter."

Memories resurfaced from where I'd buried them. I took a deep breath and met Josh's gaze again.

"All of that seems a lifetime ago. I'm certain Bertie's prayers for me reached heaven, because the very day I arrived in Nashville, I met a kindly woman who introduced me to the owner of a local radio station. Mr. Craig was his name. He hired me to clean their offices and gave me a place to stay. One day while I was mopping, I sang along with the song playing over the speakers, and the manager of the station heard me. He asked if I'd be interested in singing jingles for commercials."

I smiled, thinking back to the day my life changed. "That was my big break, so to speak. I quit my cleaning job and started singing for several different stations. That's how I met Frank. He produced radio shows in New York City but was in Nashville on business. He came by the station where I was recording a little ditty about laundry soap. I hadn't dated anyone except Amos, but Frank's maturity and stability appealed to me. We were married three weeks later, and I moved to New York. We eventually came out to California so Frank could work in movies."

"You never had more children?" Walker asked.

The question used to leave me raw inside. Time, however, healed my longings for a family. "Frank had been married before he met me. He has a daughter, but they're not close. He was more interested in building his career than in raising children. That's one of the reasons his wife left him." I glanced out to the ocean. "Before we married, he told me he didn't want more children. Couldn't have more, in fact. I was only twenty years old at the time and didn't fully understand the implications of that."

I looked at Walker. "I've often wondered if I could have loved another child as much as I'd loved you. In the short time we had together, you were my whole world. It may sound selfish, but I don't know that I could've given myself to another child the way I gave myself to you."

"Did you ever try to find me?"

I heard hope in his voice and knew my answer would disappoint. "I didn't. In my mind, you were safest without me in your life. But I never forgot you. Not a day went by that you weren't in my prayers."

Walker reached into his pocket again. "My mom, Annie, wanted you to have this."

"It's you." I stared at the black-and-white photograph of him as a tiny baby. "That's exactly how I've always remembered you."

"Mom said it was taken a couple days after I came to live with them."

"So many times I wished I had one picture of you. Just one." I clutched it to my heart. "Thank you. Please thank your mother for me."

"I will." Walker smiled. "She'd like to meet you someday."

"I'd like that, too."

We talked for the next three hours, filling in the blanks of the past thirty years. I told him all about Amos, and Walker expressed pride in his father's service to our country. He in return told me about his parents, his friends, and how he got into the music business.

Frank arrived home and we ate lunch on the deck overlooking the beach. He couldn't get over the fact that Walker Wylie was my Joshua and told Walker to have Ray contact him about recording a song for his next movie. With a wink at Walker, I teased my husband about nepotism.

When the sun hung low over the ocean, it was time for him to leave.

"I hope you'll come see us often," I said, my arm linked with my son's. Frank wouldn't hear of Walker taking a taxi back to the city and had insisted on hiring a limo. The driver waited beside the big black car in the circular driveway. "Now that I have you back in my life, it's going to be hard not to hound you to come for a visit."

Walker grinned. "No hounding necessary. In fact, you'll probably get tired of me stopping in every time I come to California."

"Never."

Walker wrapped his arms around me in a tight embrace. I could have held him forever.

I pressed my ear to his chest, listening. After a long moment, I smiled up at him. "I remember the first time I heard your heartbeat before you were even born. Bertie let me listen with her stethoscope. It's an answer to prayer to hear it again."

"I love you, Mom," he said, emotion in his voice.

Tears sprang to my eyes. "I've waited a lifetime to hear those words." I laid my hand on his cheek and gazed into my Josh's beautiful hazel eyes. "I love you, too, Son."

Walker climbed into the back seat of the car and the limo pulled away from the mansion. The last thing I saw was my son waving goodbye, the promise of seeing each other again in both our hearts.

Deep, abiding peace settled in my soul as I stood in the empty driveway. The ocean roared, seagulls called, and the sky filled with glorious golds, reds, and blues, bringing the extraordinary day to an end.

"Thank you, Papa," I whispered. "Thank you for bringing my Joshua home."

Thirty-One

REESE STEERED HER VW BEETLE TOWARD HOME, reflecting on the
past twenty-four hours.

Twins!

Adrenaline still pumped through her veins as she recalled the
excitement from the delivery that took place in the wee hours of
morning. Moriah Waggoner's labor had gone like clockwork, with
no complications or hiccups. Identical twin girls arrived tiny but
healthy, a double blessing for the new parents.

Reese carefully maneuvered the car onto her street, grateful to
see that the town's one snowplow had gone through the neighbor-
hood after yesterday's storm. Kathy said Ryan was ecstatic when
snow started falling after breakfast, but Reese had worried she
wouldn't be able to get out of her driveway should Moriah go into
labor. Thankfully, when the call came at noon, the snow hadn't
turned to ice yet. Now she couldn't wait to tell Kathy about the
twins, especially since her friend recently shared her own good
news of another baby on the way. Reese would have to tease Kathy
about the possibility of Ryan getting two baby brothers for the
price of one.

A red vehicle Reese didn't recognize sat in front of her mailbox when she pulled into the driveway. A family with several teenagers had moved in across the street last month just in time to celebrate their first Christmas in their new home. The vehicle no doubt belonged to one of their friends. She might have to politely ask the kids not to park in front of her house since it also served as her business. A client wouldn't be able to read her sign or address from the street.

She parked the VW next to her house and pulled the parka-style hood of her coat over her head. Although the snow had stopped falling shortly after the twins' arrival, a bitter wind continued to chill the bones of anyone who dared go outside.

Loaded down with her purse, an oversize midwife bag, and several books she'd checked out from the library last week, Reese exited the car. She'd run into the house and deposit her things, then head over to Kathy's for a cup of hot chocolate and to hear what mischief Oreo and Ryan had gotten into while she was gone.

Taking tiny, cautious steps on the slippery sidewalk, she slowly inched to the porch. She'd almost reached it when she heard a car door slam. Footsteps crunched in the snow.

"Oh, hey." She turned to see who'd gotten out of the vehicle, but the fur trim on the hood of her coat dipped over her eyes. Loaded down as she was, she couldn't push it up, and all she saw were a pair of boots coming toward her. "I'm wondering if you could park somewhere else. You're blocking my sign."

A chuckle sounded. "I'd be happy to move, but I *was* hoping we could take a ride together."

Reese dropped the midwife bag and jerked off the hood.

Walker stood in front of her, grinning and more devastatingly handsome than she remembered. Clean-shaven, hair neatly trimmed, dressed in jeans, a black turtleneck sweater, and a leather jacket.

All she could do was gape at him.

They'd spoken on the telephone almost weekly over the past two months, especially after Walker heard the song "Perfectly Loved" on the radio. Reese cried when he shared about his emotional visit with Songbird, once again thanking Reese for her role in helping to find his birth mother. They reminisced about their time in the mountains with Bertie or talked about what was going on in their lives—writing new music for his upcoming tour and the new babies she delivered—yet none of their conversations led Reese to believe he wanted anything beyond friendship. Even though Kathy assured her that he and Vanessa were no longer dating—"According to the magazines, she's seeing the costar of her new movie"—Reese forced herself not to get her hopes up each time he called.

Now he stood in her yard, looking quite pleased with himself.

"What are you doing here? Where'd you come from? How are you?"

He bent to retrieve her bag, unruffled by the barrage of questions. "I came to see you; I drove in from Nashville; and I'm doing really well . . . except for being cold at the moment."

"Oh, goodness, of course. How rude of me. Come inside. Can I get you some coffee? Or maybe hot chocolate?"

Reese knew she sounded like a babbling idiot, but she couldn't get over the fact that he was there. She quickly turned away so Walker wouldn't see her face, which felt like it was on fire with embarrassment. She started for the house—

And belatedly remembered the ice on the walkway.

Her feet flew out from beneath her.

Books sailed through the air. Her purse stayed with her, held by the strap, but her arms flailed in a useless struggle to stay upright. Just as she braced for a hard landing on the snow-covered ground, Walker yanked her up. She crashed hard against his chest, forcing an *oof* out of them both.

Before Reese could remove herself from his arms, ferocious

barking sounded. She glanced over to find Oreo tearing across the small yard between her house and Kathy's. Ryan stood in the open doorway to his home, his little-boy laughter egging the dog on.

"No, Oreo," Reese shouted, but the dog had already launched himself at Walker, sending the three of them to the ground.

Snow, mud, and wet dog fur filled Reese's view as she sprawled on her back.

"Hi, Oreo," Walker mumbled.

She couldn't see him, being that Oreo was sandwiched between them, but she heard a smile in his voice.

"Nice welcome, buddy. Seems every time we meet, there's mud involved."

Reese giggled and pushed herself to a sitting position. Walker did the same, while Oreo's entire body wagged with his delight as he tried to lick each of their faces.

"Are you guys okay?"

Kathy hurried toward them as fast as she could manage in the snow with Ryan on her hip.

"I'm so sorry, Reese," her friend said when she reached them. "This rascal wasn't supposed to let Oreo out until we had the leash on him." Her attention went from Reese to Walker. "My apologies to you too, sir—" Her mouth fell open, and her big blue eyes bugged. "Walker Wylie? Oh, my gosh, Reese! It's Walker Wylie."

Walker smiled good-naturedly, but Reese wanted to dig a hole and crawl into it. What would he think about all this madness?

"You must be Reese's friend Kathy. I'd shake your hand, but . . ." He held up his mud-covered fingers. "Reese has nothing but good things to say about you."

It was Reese's turn to stare at him.

He remembered her stories about Kathy?

Walker got to his feet, then helped Reese up. Oreo bounced around Walker's legs as though they were best friends now.

"I've offered Walker some coffee," Reese said, her attention on Kathy. She couldn't look at Walker, with his mud-covered clothes. Was his leather jacket ruined? "You're welcome to join us."

The look in her friend's eyes said she'd like nothing better than to spend the afternoon chatting with the singer, but Ryan started to whine about being cold and hungry.

"I better get this guy fed and down for a nap," Kathy said, disappointment in her voice. She turned to Walker. "For the record, I love your music. Reese has become a fan, too."

Walker thanked her and offered to autograph her album covers. Kathy eagerly accepted and said she'd bring them over later.

After she and Ryan headed back through the melting snow, Reese found Walker's gaze on her, a big grin planted on his face.

"So you've been listening to my music. What'd you think?"

She couldn't help but laugh. "Fishing for a compliment, are you?"

Oreo barked from the door, wanting inside. "I think he's got the right idea. May I?" Walker extended his arm. "We wouldn't want to end up flat on our backs again."

After retrieving the books, Reese linked arms with him. "I'm sorry about Oreo . . . and the mud."

"Mud washes off. No harm done."

When they reached the porch, Reese picked up the towel she kept by the door for the very purpose of drying off Oreo before letting him inside. Walker politely removed his muddy boots even before Reese had a chance to remove hers.

Once inside and settled on the sofa in her cozy living room with mugs of hot chocolate, Walker brought her up to date on his New Year's trip to California. "I've asked Evelyn to come to Nashville in the spring. Mom talked me into giving a concert to benefit the Family House in April, and I'm hoping Evelyn will sing a duet with me. I'd love for you to meet them both."

Reese happily accepted the invitation, then studied him. "You seem more at peace with life than when we first met."

Walker nodded, his gaze intent. "I am. And I owe you a debt of gratitude for helping me get to this point."

When Reese started to protest, he reached to grasp her hand. "Reese, I'm serious. I would have never found Bertie and Songbird if it weren't for you. I'm not sure where I'd be if you hadn't volunteered to help me. To be a friend when I needed one." His thumb caressed the top of her hand, sending warm tingles up her arm. "I'm not the same man I was a few months ago. Chasing fame and fortune, thinking I'm somebody just because my songs are on the radio. This experience has opened my eyes in a lot of ways. It's opened my eyes to God and what his plans are for me."

Reese tightened her grasp on his hand. "Walker, I'm so happy for you."

He reached for her other hand. "I know I was a jerk when we first met, but I'm hoping you might be willing to give the new and improved Walker Wylie a chance."

His words made her heart leap. "I'd like that."

In the next moment, Reese melted into his arms. His lips met hers, sweet and tender. Everything a first kiss should be.

"If you have time," he said when he drew back, his arms still around her, "I hoped you, me, and Oreo could take a drive. I'm thinking about buying a place up in the hills. I'd like to show it to you."

Reese gasped. "You're leaving Nashville?"

"I'll keep my apartment in the city, but the mountains are in my blood. I want to get to know that part of me." He caressed her cheek, sending delicious sensations swirling through her as their gazes held. "But mostly I want to get to know you."

Their lips met once again, full of gentle passion and promise.

Epilogue

BERTIE GLANCED OUT THE WINDOW for the umpteenth time.

Where were they?

"Sister, do sit down," Rubie said. "Staring out the window won't make them get here any quicker."

Bertie sent a look of annoyance to her sister, who sat near the fireplace, calmly working on a stocking in need of darning. Rubie's poor eyesight, however, prevented her from truly mending the sock well, and Bertie knew she'd have to redo the work when her sister was napping.

"Josh said they'd be here at noon." Bertie glanced at the wall clock again. Two more minutes and both hands would be straight up on twelve.

Rubie chuckled. "Papa always said patience wasn't a Jenkins trait. I 'spect he was right. You're 'bout to wear a path in the floor with your pacin'. Best save your energy so you're not worn to a nub when they get here."

Bertie wasn't in the mood for Rubie's wisdom and remained where she could see the yard. She should have tidied it up, she realized belatedly. Yesterday Shep had gotten into the pile of wool Bertie'd stored in the barn after the boys sheared her small flock of sheep, and now pieces of white wool clung to bushes and fence posts like snow.

The clock struck twelve. The yard remained empty.

Bertie's shoulders sagged.

She'd waited months for this day to arrive. Years, really. They'd had a long, bitter winter, with the roads in and out of the mountains closed to traffic for weeks on end. Brother Tom's oldest grandboy owned a big vehicle that could get through snow and such. The day after Christmas he'd brought Bertie and Rubie enough supplies and staples to see them through the lonely months until the roads were passable once again.

Thankfully, hints of spring finally began to appear. A bird's nest here. A flower there. Snow melted. Mountain rivers and streams filled.

The best thing the warmer weather brought, however, was Joshua.

Bertie chuckled, remembering the day he stepped out of his pretty red vehicle and announced, quite adamantly, that he was going to have a telephone installed in the Jenkins cabin as soon as a telephone company truck could make it up the mountain.

"I won't go through another winter worrying about the two of you up here," he'd said.

Neither Bertie nor Rubie objected.

Just last week, a big truck arrived with some nice young men who'd mounted a forest-green telephone right there on the wall beside Papa's hat. Bertie had to admit it was a fine day when she heard Josh's voice on the other end of the contraption.

The sound of tires crunching over gravel brought her back to the present.

Bertie fastened her eyes on the road just past the yard, her breath stalled in her lungs.

A moment later, a long, black car rolled slowly into view.

"They're here, Sister." Her voice quavered with—

What was this emotion rushing through her?

Excitement? Anxiousness? Fear?

She hurried to pull on her coat, her fingers fumbling with the buttons, then helped Rubie with hers. By the time they reached the porch, a fancily dressed man exited the front of the car and went around to open the back door.

A moment passed before Joshua climbed out. He called out a hello to Bertie and Rubie, then reached a hand to help Reese from the car. She waved and stepped aside. An older woman emerged next, her smile genuine as she nodded a greeting to the sisters. It had been thirty years since Bertie saw Josh's adoptive mom, but she remembered that long-ago day at the church in Nashville as if it were yesterday.

Bertie clutched Rubie's cold hand, more nervous than she'd been in all her eighty-three years.

Finally a lovely woman stepped from the car.

Bertie gasped.

Songbird.

She looked nothing like the child they'd found in the woods with a bullet hole in her shoulder, yet Bertie would have known her anywhere. No longer wearing homespun, she looked elegant and refined in a pale-blue pantsuit and matching coat.

Questions tumbled through Bertie's mind.

Had their Songbird changed over time? Would she still be their girl?

While the others waited near the car, Songbird came forward with a hesitant smile.

"Hello."

"My goodness, look at you." Rubie nodded her satisfaction. "You're all grown-up."

"It's wonderful to see you again, Rubie."

Songbird's gaze shifted to Bertie then.

Time seemed to melt away, and it felt as if her girl had never left. Had never disappeared from their lives. Had never broken Bertie's heart.

"I've missed you, Bertie," Songbird whispered, her eyes welling with tears. "I'm sorry I didn't come back."

How many prayers had Bertie said through the years, asking God for this very moment? How many tears had she shed, wondering if she'd see her girl again?

She looked over to where Joshua stood with one arm around his mom and the other around Reese. On his last visit he told them he planned to propose to Reese soon, assuring Bertie he'd send a car to drive her and Rubie to the wedding at his property in Piney Ridge, hopefully sometime in the fall.

More evidence of answered prayers.

God had been faithful. Through the silent, lonely years when it seemed he wasn't listening. Through the pain and sadness, wondering why things had to happen the way they did. He was there, all along, preparing this day. Reminding each of them he was a good, good Father, adopting everyone who believes in Christ into his family where all would be loved and cherished for eternity.

Bertie stepped off the porch and opened her arms.

Songbird flew into her embrace.

"Welcome home, sweet girl. Welcome home."

A Note from the Author

I FIRST LEARNED ABOUT THE WALKER SISTERS of the Great Smoky Mountains in 2018. My husband and I took a trip to see the fall foliage, and I came home eager to write a novel about five unmarried sisters who lived their entire lives in the cabin their father built in the 1800s. While *Appalachian Song* is inspired by the Walker sisters, it is a fictional tale with fictional characters born in my imagination.

The Walker family—John and Margaret Jane and their eleven children—lived on a 122-acre farm in Little Greenbrier Cove, not far from Gatlinburg, Tennessee, that John purchased from Margaret's father in 1866. Six of the seven daughters—Margaret, Polly, Martha, Louisa, Hettie, and Nancy—never married and remained on the family farm until their deaths. It's unlikely we would have ever heard of the Walker sisters had Congress not approved authorization of a new national park in 1926, which became the Great Smoky Mountains National Park. The congressional authorization allowed Tennessee and North Carolina to start raising money to purchase nearly half a million acres. With most of the land privately owned, families were approached and asked to sell their homes and move outside of the park boundaries. The five remaining Walker sisters, however, refused to leave their mountain homestead, even amid threats to annex their land. President Roosevelt officially dedicated the park in 1940, and thousands of visitors flocked to the beautiful area. The sisters knew it was time to give up their fight and reluctantly negotiated a deal. They received $4,750 for their land and were granted permission to continue living in their cabin for the rest of their lives. I chose not to include this story line in the book because it belongs exclusively to the real Walker sisters. Instead, I placed the Jenkins homestead in an area of the Smoky Mountains that was not owned by the government.

The sisters' story, however, continues to intrigue. Because their property became part of the national park, new restrictions meant they could not farm, hunt, or raise livestock. They'd often said their land provided everything they needed to live, but after the park opened, all that changed. When park visitors made their way to Little Greenbrier Cove, the sisters would welcome them and sell their handmade products, such as fried apple pies, crocheted doilies, and children's toys like tops and whimmy diddles. Louisa even wrote poems that were available for purchase. In April 1946, the sisters were featured in the *Saturday Evening Post*, giving the world a glimpse into their mountain lifestyle. They would continue to greet visitors until only Margaret and Louisa remained. The two elderly women asked the park superintendent to remove the Visitors Welcome sign, and they lived out their days away from the public eye. Margaret died in 1962 at age ninety-two, and Louisa stayed in the house until she died on July 13, 1964.

The Walker sisters' cabin still stands in the park today, along with the original springhouse and corncrib. I did my best to bring the homestead to life in the book, keeping with the realities of living with no electricity or indoor plumbing. I also studied photographs that allowed me to see what the interior of the cabin looked like when it was occupied by the sisters. One research book briefly mentions the sisters caring for a baby boy who was the son of a relative. I turned that nugget of history into Walker Wylie's story.

The historic site of the Walker homestead is a relatively easy one-mile hike from the Little Greenbrier schoolhouse that John Walker and his sons helped build. Both the cabin and the school served as inspiration for scenes that take place in *Appalachian Song*, and if you are ever in the Gatlinburg area, I encourage you to visit them. The towns of Cosby Run and Piney Ridge are fictitious, so don't look for them on a map, but you can visit the redbrick Sevier County Courthouse in Sevierville where I had Walker and Reese search through birth records. There are also several beautiful, whitewashed churches in Cades Cove, a short drive from the Walker sisters' cabin, that inspired the church I placed near Bertie's home. You can find pictures of these historic buildings and other interesting images related to the book on my Pinterest page: https://www.pinterest.com/shocklee8455/appalachian-song/.

Until the middle of the twentieth century, midwives attended most births in Appalachia. Like Bertie, these women learned the skills from their mothers and grandmothers, earning them the nickname *granny women*. Margaret Jane Walker's mother was a midwife and taught her daughter. It's unclear if any of the Walker sisters carried on the tradition. As it became more common to give birth in a hospital, midwifery declined. Today there are very few granny women left. They are the last of their kind, aged and unable to practice legally due to restrictive legislation. Certified midwives like Reese, however, continue to serve mountain communities.

Hippie communes in Tennessee really did exist. There are also hundreds of stories about moonshiners (I've even been to an old, abandoned moonshiner's shack) and the fascinating people who made (and make) their home in the hills and hollers of Appalachia. Although the characters in the book are fictional, they are based on research into life in Tennessee during the 1940s and 1970s.

Adoption is at the heart of *Appalachian Song*. Three words kept coming to mind as I wrote the story: **I choose you.** My extended family and many of my friends' families have been blessed through adoption. Yet as beautiful as it is to see a child find their forever home, there is a mother and a father who gave up the privilege of raising their child. Thankfully, Father God sees all of this—every tear of joy and every tear from heartache. As Bertie tells Songbird, God's perfect plan for mankind is one of adoption. Romans 8:9-16 reminds us that God adopts us as his own children when we put our faith in Christ, giving us the freedom to call him, "Abba, Father." My hope is this truth will resonate with each and every reader and that you will know God as your Papa.

Thank you for choosing to read *Appalachian Song*. It is an honor to share this story of hope with you.

Acknowledgments

IT WOULD NOT HAVE BEEN POSSIBLE for me to write a book about adoption and the emotional journey adoptees and their families (birth and adoptive) go on had I not had so many beautiful examples of it in real life. While their stories are not mine to tell, I want to acknowledge some of the people who inspire me and therefore influenced the book: David, Becky, Jacob, John, Lori, Maggie, Rachel, Robert, Sherry, Brian, McKenna, and Chasity. I've watched God work out his plans and purposes through each of you. May he continue to bless you and your families with peace, love, and joy.

To my husband, best friend, field trip buddy, chauffeur, and hero of my heart: Brian, you are my gift from God. I love that our adventure to the Great Smoky Mountains led us to the Walker sisters' cabin and inspired this book. Where to next, my love?

As I wrote *Appalachian Song*, I couldn't help but thank God for blessing me with two amazing sons. Taylor and Austin, although you are young men, you will always be my babies. Erica, you've become the daughter of my heart, and I can't wait until it's official! Thank you, each of you, for your love and encouragement.

I'm grateful to have so many family members and friends come alongside me, cheering me on as I pour my heart into writing books for the Kingdom. Thank you, truly. Your love and support mean the world to me.

It is said that the ideal editor brings out the best in a writer. I agree wholeheartedly! Thank you, Jan Stob and Erin Smith, for your insights, your encouragement, and your patience as I wrote and rewrote (and rewrote!) this story. I am honored to work with such talented, Christ-loving women. Huge thanks must also go to Karen Watson and the entire team at Tyndale House Publishers. What a joy it is to be part of such an amazing, hardworking, dedicated publishing family. I look forward to our next projects together.

Many thanks to my agent, Bob Hostetler. I count it a blessing to work with you, and I appreciate everything you do on my behalf.

Thank *you*, faithful readers, for your many emails and messages that let me know how my books have touched your hearts. Thank you for recommending my books to friends, family, coworkers, book clubs, and online groups. I've enjoyed meeting many of you at in-person events, virtual book club meetings, and on social media. If we haven't met yet, I hope we will soon.

Although I've known Jesus my entire life, I didn't truly grasp the depth of love Father God has for us, his children, until I became a mother. It's amazing to know that God's love is so deep, so rich, and so complete, that he was willing to do whatever was necessary to make sure we spend eternity with him. To make sure that sin and death would not win. When we are adopted into God's family through faith in Christ, we become his heirs of his glory (Romans 8:17). And for that, I am eternally grateful.

Soli Deo gloria.

Discussion Questions

1. Bertie Jenkins spends more than forty years as a midwife, calling it "her God-given gift." How does she respond when people in her community begin to question her abilities? Is the criticism fair? What lessons can you take from Bertie's doubts and faith?

2. The Jenkins sisters find Songbird in their yard, injured and afraid. What similarities do you see between the sisters' actions and the parable of the Good Samaritan (Luke 10:30-37)? When Songbird asks Bertie why God would help her, a sinner, what does Bertie say? What comfort does that response give you?

3. Walker Wylie has a crisis of identity after learning of his adoption as a baby, feeling like he's lost both his past and his future. What do others tell him about who he is and who he was made to be? What would you say to Walker?

4. Bertie's eldest sister, Jennie, isn't initially very welcoming to Songbird. What makes her reluctant to allow Songbird to stay? What does Jesus say about the sick and the sinner? (Read Matthew 9:9-13.)

5. Reese Chandler acts as an adoption advocate. How does she define the word *advocate*? How successful is she at being an advocate in this story? Are there important issues or causes where you are or can be more of an advocate? What would that look like?

6. *Appalachian Song* is set in part in 1973, months after the Supreme Court ruled on *Roe v. Wade*, which deemed unduly restrictive state regulations of abortion unconstitutional. Walker notes that "arguments for or against abortion had been abstract and distant . . . until now." Describe a time when an issue became more real for you—maybe after going on a mission trip or collecting supplies for an organization in your community. What makes you fired up to champion a cause? Why is it important to engage with important issues facing society, even when they don't directly affect you?

7. Though the Jenkins sisters believe Songbird is a gifted poet, the teen tells Bertie, "I ain't no good at stringin' words together. Not like the folks who write the books." Do you think Songbird ever believed she had a natural talent? Do you ever doubt your own abilities but take a chance anyway? What happens in those moments?

8. While grief is often associated with death, Reese describes going through the stages of grief over her adoption, even though she always knew the truth of her story. What might she be grieving and how could that be considered a "death" of sorts? When have you been surprised by grief not related to a physical passing? Does knowing the different stages of grief (shock, denial, anger, bargaining, depression, testing, and acceptance) provide clarity or comfort?

9. When Walker learns his birth father died without knowing about him, Bertie offers this comfort: "God has a way of makin' us aware of things, important things, down deep in our souls." What do you think of this idea?

10. As Walker learns about the circumstances of his conception and the ways Songbird's family tried to prevent him from being born, he has a hard time believing God had something good planned. What do Reese and Bertie tell him about "illegitimate children" and God's design? What does Psalm 139:16 say?

11. Reese and Bertie help deliver a young mother's baby together—the miracle of childbirth. Then Rubie prays over the young woman to stop her hemorrhaging, and Walker wonders if what happened next was actually a miracle. What do you think? How do you define miracles?

12. Bertie tells Walker: "Family don't always mean blood kin." What does family look like for Bertie in *Appalachian Song*? For Songbird? For Walker? For Reese? Do their definitions change? What does your family look like?

About the Author

MICHELLE SHOCKLEE is the author of several historical novels, including *Count the Nights by Stars*, a *Christianity Today* fiction book award winner, and *Under the Tulip Tree*, a Christy and Selah Awards finalist. Her work has been featured in numerous Chicken Soup for the Soul books, magazines, and blogs. Married to her college sweetheart and the mother of two grown sons, she makes her home in Tennessee, not far from the historical sites she writes about. Visit her online at michelleshocklee.com.

CONNECT WITH MICHELLE ONLINE AT

michelleshocklee.com

OR FOLLOW HER ON

CP1889

TYNDALE HOUSE PUBLISHERS IS CRAZY4FICTION!

Fiction that entertains and inspires

Get to know us! Become a member of the Crazy4Fiction community. Whether you read our blog, like us on Facebook, follow us on Twitter, or receive our e-newsletter, you're sure to get the latest news on the best in Christian fiction. You might even win something along the way!

JOIN IN THE FUN TODAY.

 crazy4fiction.com

f Crazy4Fiction

 crazy4fiction

 @Crazy4Fiction